REWIRED

REWIRED

SHELLI R. JOHANNES

To Lara Perkins, my agent (a.k.a. partner in crime)
at Andrea Brown Literary Agency,
for her ongoing commitment and never-ending support—no matter
what!

"Until they became conscious
they will never rebel,
and until after they have rebelled
they cannot become conscious."

— George Orwell, author of *1984*

</THE DARK ANGEL>

SOME SAY TECHNOLOGY KILLS. BUT THESE DAYS, A COMPUTER IS my only lifeline.

I move through the warehouse and flip on the space heater before checking the outside security cameras, but the streets are deserted as usual. This is my safe space. A place to hide. Here, there's no IP address to track. No connection to trace. Here, I can sneak on and off the grid without anyone knowing.

Undetected and untraceable.

Hacker Commandment #1: One can never be too paranoid.

I turn on the desk lamp and sweep my hand across the ugly DIY desk made of a few cracked two-by-fours and a slab of plywood. Yesterday's pizza box and empty Dr Pepper cans jump off the edge, clanging to the floor.

I unzip my messenger bag. A tattered copy of George Orwell's *1984* snuggles up to my cell phone, and my laptop peeks through the opposite mesh sleeve. Its permanent resting place. In case I need to bolt unexpectedly.

Punching the ON button, I boot up my computer. "Rise and shine, Zed. It's show time."

I sit back as the laptop runs through its morning routine

without any complaint. The perfect companion. Someone who never talks back. Follows my every command.

Once Zed is up and running, I blaze through my ritual. Perform a few carpal tunnel stretches. Secure both wrist braces. And crack all ten knuckles . . . twice. Then I slip in my earbuds and jack up some Daft Punk. The louder, the better. My legs bounce to the beat, and adrenaline buzzes through my veins like data on a live wire. My nerves hum with anticipation.

As soon as the desktop pops up, I sign on to the satellite network with an encrypted password and return to my latest target: SocialNet. My fingers skip across my keyboard, adding a clicking beat to the music drumming in my ears. After editing my script for the umpteenth time, I hit </RUN> and watch my creation. The program floats up my screen, disappearing into the cybersphere. Hopefully this will open the back door I need.

I started the SocialNet hack with another hacker a few months ago after suspecting the company was lying about their privacy terms. Rumor has it the company stores teen data and makes a ton of money selling it. This means a teen's personal pictures, posts, and confidential profile information are up for grabs. Without teens knowing. All for a buck.

I would die if my information got out, so I wanna see if it's true. And if it is, I need to shut it down. But after months of coding, I still can't crack the stupid system. SocialNet is well protected, guarded by steel firewalls and an army of Geeks-on-Call.

Busting into the largest teen networking site in the world with a little laptop is like busting into Fort Knox with a wet firecracker. Nearly impossible.

Waiting, I tap my fingers on the table, hoping this program can find something interesting to make my day exciting.

Zed beeps two dirty words every hacker hates to see:
</COMMAND UNSUCCESSFUL>

"Hmmm." I bite my lip. "We'll see about that."

An alarm sounds off in the warehouse.

I race over to check the cameras.

A security guard strolls by camera three and stops in front of my door.

I freeze and hold my breath, waiting for his next move.

Last thing I need is to get busted hacking.

</THE CHALLENGE>

THE GUARD SHINES HIS LIGHT ALONG THE FRAME AND PRESSES one ear against the steel door.

Unless he's Superman, he won't hear a thing. Eventually, the guard gives up and walks away.

I exhale and go back to Zed.

A reminder message pops up on the screen.

"It's Orwellian time," I tell Zed.

I save my code and clear the screen. No matter how much I want to perfect my SocialNet code, I can't miss the weekly meeting. Challenging some of the best hackers in the world is important to my social life. Offline, jocks and spirit leaders are cool.

But online, the hip crowd is a bunch of techy misfits—just like me.

And right now, they're the only friends I have.

Hacker Commandment #2: Check and recheck systems. Leave no trace.

Before signing into the chat room, I reroute my IP address through several servers to make sure I can't be traced, tracked, or monitored. Casper, Blackbird, and QTip are already messaging with Taz, the Orwellian leader. As far as I know, Simone was the first female ever invited to join the secret hacking club. Then there was me. Of course, I guess one of these other avatars could be a girl too. Shrouded under a male profile.

Online, you can be whoever you want to be. Taz could be a dirty old man in tighty-whities who hacks from his basement while stuffing his face with stale Twinkies—instead of his spiced up profile of a young Polynesian linebacker addicted to Colombian coffee.

No one is honest in cyberspace. Everyone hides something.

Including me.

Offline, I'm Ada Lovelace. "Biggest Longshot to Hit the Principal's List" and senator's daughter. Average teenage girl who never dates average boys . . . outside of Sims. I'll never be voted "Most Likely to Run for Homecoming Queen" or be able to articulate to my ELA teacher whether Hamlet was faking it or just batshit crazy.

But online, I'm a fake single mom who homeschools twin girls. Computer genius well known in cyber circles as a white hat hacker and social media butterfly. My mother tongue is Java, though I'm fluent in computerese, able to speak any programming language. Totally multilingual.

As the Dark Angel, I'm more than just a regular girl—I'm somebody.

I pop into the chat room.

> DA: Hey guys. Sorry I'm late.
> Blackbird: Hey DA!
> Taz: DA, we were just getting updates. How's the SocialNet hack going? Any progress?
> DA: I'm getting closer.
> QTip: Close doesn't count.
> DA: Don't worry. I'll get in soon.

> Taz: Guys meet Casper. A new kickass hacker that's joining the group.

After we all say "hi," Casper asks a question. When I see the topic of conversation, that familiar tightness clogs my chest.

> Casper: Isn't the Red Devil part of this group?
> QTip: She was, but she hasn't been here in months.
> Casper: Going MIA is never a good sign. Did she give you guys any reason why she would quit?
> Blackbird: DA was Red Devil's girl. She tell you anything?
> DA: Nope. I'm clueless.
> Casper: So you hacked with the Red Devil? Then maybe you shouldn't be here anymore either.
> Taz: DA's proven herself. The Feds are starting to troll the net after our Walmart hack, maybe Red Devil got busted.
> Casper: Either that or she's dead.

My stomach drops. This new guy is harsh.

I shoot Casper's ninja ghost avatar an evil eye. Typical cocky hacker. Definitely male, probably mid-twenties. Always talking smack to feed his massive virtual ego. Dude probably loves to go rogue and attack random companies by hiding behind the Orwellian name.

Hacker Commandment #3: Stay clear of cocky jackholes.

A deadly feeling—the real heavy one that drags me into downward spirals so quickly—swallows my wavering confidence. I gotta make sure these guys trust me without the Red Devil around. This group is all I have left.

After all, the Red Devil is gone. She was around before me and introduced me to the Orwellians. Taught me everything I know. We spent many "geekends" hacking. No matter what we did—pranking crooked politicians or targeting insecure networks to expose weaknesses—every hack aligned with the

Orwellian mission of "defending the privacy rights of every person on the planet."

Nothing could shake our girl power. At least, that's what we thought.

> Casper: Let's get started. What's the challenge?
> Taz: Maybe we should help DA hack SocialNet. I bet one of us can get in.
> DA: Nope. No way. That's my hack. Red Devil and I were already working on a back door.
> Blackbird: So what else can we do?
> Casper: I say we hack the White House.

Hacking the White House? This idiot is insane! Anyone who gets busted on this challenge gets a one-way ticket to Club Fed. Guaranteed.

> Blackbird: Camfecting the White House? Isn't that a little risky?
> Casper: Sure. But we need to show them that they're not as secure as they think they are. Before the Russians do. This will put us on the cyber map.
> DA: The Orwellians are already on the map, Casper.
> Taz: Maybe he's right. What if we hack the first son's computer at the White House *AND* snap a photo through his web cam? First person in wins bragging rights.
> QTip: Yeah, but why target the kid?
> Casper: It's the weakest point. Plus, it's the only way to influence a parent—take out the kid first. So I'm in. What about you chickens?

As everyone pledges their commitment, I sit back and exhale.

"Holy crap," I whisper.

Casper must be jacked up on cyber-crack. The more

hacking he does, the more he needs. This is one of those rogue black-hat hackers. The one who does stupid hacks just because he can.

I wring my hands and rub them together. A swarm of butterflies somersaults through my insides. This challenge is super dangerous for me. Messing with the government is way too close to home. Not to mention illegal.

Then something dawns on me.

Since the Orwellians don't know my *real* name, they have no clue I've shared filet mignon with the first son himself, or that John's a good guy and doesn't deserve humiliation. One wrong photo or one leaked email could ruin him socially. And hurt the President politically.

I should know. I'm a senator's daughter. Keeping my privacy is hard enough.

So whether I like it or not, I have to play along on this challenge. I need to be the one to hack into John's computer before anyone else can. I will protect John from these hackers. And win some respect with the Orwellians. Once and for all.

> Casper: DA is pretty quiet. She in or out?

I watch the cursor blink, thinking about the question. This is it. Do or die. In or out.

There's still time to walk away. Unscathed. Intact.

The Red Devil's voice plays out in my head: *Never ever give up on a challenge. If you control cyberspace, you control the world.* Before second-guessing my decision, I type my answer.

> DA: I'm in!

</A HACKTIVIST>

Rubbing my hands along my jeans, I try to calm the butterflies slamming against the lining of my stomach. This is my chance to prove myself.

I can do this.

First, I tuck my short blonde hair into a small bun. Then crack each knuckle again before opening my little black book of factoids. The place where I record any and all of the juicy details I learn about people. Their habits, likes, dislikes, obsessions, fears, phobias, and secrets. No detail is too small. Never know what nugget of information could crack a password, decode a username, or answer a secret question.

Hacker Commandment #4: Always encrypt your messages.

The first thing I have to do is punch through the White House firewall. Undetected. Then I have to gain access to John's computer. This won't be easy. But it is doable. I just have to find a way.

I flip through my notes for clues.

John Callahan Jr., a.k.a. the first son. Age seventeen. Popular with the ladies. Gets a cheap buzz cut the first week of every month at a barbershop and orders a Red Eye from Starbucks every morning at approximately 8 a.m. Participates in every church mission trip 'under the Bible.' And despite being a political celebrity, insists on continuing weekly basketball games with his public school buddies at a public park.

I zero in on the "mission" angle. Churches are the easiest institutions to crack. They trust people to a fault, have minimal tech security, and most of the morning volunteers are from the BC era (Before Computers). Not to mention, these Godly-honest people would never suspect that anyone might want computer information they deem insignificant.

My online search displays a tabloid picture of John at a Sunday service. If I can get John to open a mission email from his minister, he will give me open access to his computer.

I browse his church's website and read about the upcoming mission trip to Haiti. Then I punch in the church's phone number and hold my breath. One ring, two rings, three rings.

My heart races and my breath quickens, hoping they pick up. I even throw in a quick prayer and amen for luck.

Finally, a church lady answers. "Seattle City Church. May I help you?"

I perform my best English accent. No one ever thinks a Brit will lie. They're too polite, too proper. I trace my finger down the Contact page. "Why yes, hello. Is this . . . um . . . Betty Langdon?"

"Yes it is. May I ask who's calling?"

"This is Heather over at SysArc, your computer service provider. I have to verify some information for your pending system upgrade. Do you have your computer model numbers and user IDs available so I can reset the passwords? I don't want to accidentally boot anyone off the system."

"Yes, of course. Hold on." The phone thumps when she sets it on the table. In the background, heels tap against a wood floor, papers rustle, and then a file drawer slams. A few more seconds go by before Betty returns. "Okay, Heather. I think I have the file right here. Tell me exactly what you need. I don't know much about this techy stuff."

And with that, I'm in. I almost want to cheer, but remain in character. SysArcs are way too serious for any funny business.

Betty blurts out the information as if she's in a confessional on Judgment Day: serial numbers, usernames, and system passwords. No hesitations. No questions. In the cyberworld, that's a major sin. By the end of the call, the sweet lady has also given me the serial numbers for two new PCs.

She has no idea the present she's given me: unlimited access to everything in her system.

Duly noted and mega-appreciated.

Before I move forward with my foolproof plan, I pause and fight with myself. This is dangerous. But in order to protect John's privacy, I have to invade it first. Seems unfair. But it's the only way. If any of the Orwellians hack into this guy's computer first, there's no telling what they might find. And worse, what they could leak to the media.

Moving forward, I push aside any doubts and draft a "Haiti Mission" email from the youth minister to John Callahan. Before hitting </SEND>, I press a button on my angel necklace. A hidden flash drive pops out. Instead of attaching an information sheet, I send an executable file disguised as "Mission.pdf" and request a confirmation of receipt.

Based on how many times John checked his phone at dinner, it shouldn't be long before he clicks on the fake mission file that will secretly give me remote access.

Smiling, I sit back and wait for the email receipt.

Waiting is the hard part for me. Waiting for information. Waiting for things to happen. Waiting for that rush of satisfaction I get when my plan falls perfectly into place.

> Taz: Thirty-two minutes left.

Other than Taz's pointless minute-by-minute countdown and Casper's overactive ego, the rest of the hive is silent. But I know that a bunch of hacker bees are buzzing around John's server, hunting for a way in.

I pick at flakes of my midnight-blue nail polish until a confirmation pops up.

The RAT has entered the building.

"Yes!" I clap once and get back to work.

Within seconds, I gain total control of John's computer. First, I disable the security function so there's no recording of my commands. Next, I plug in a bunch of random passwords and trigger his secret question.

Like most unsuspecting users, he chose an easy one: "What's the name of your first pet?"

This should be a cinch. Even though I only captured his mother's maiden name, street name, and favorite teacher, I vaguely remember John mentioning his hot blog over a helping of crème brûlée. I find the URL address and search for "pets." Johnny boy has had three furry companions: Hobbit, a three-legged guinea pig; Curse, a black cat; and the first puppy, Rascal.

Curse and Rascal don't work. But when I test Hobbit, the computer flings open its doors and welcomes me inside. I shake my head at his carelessness. Even with all the news about computer security, people still use personal facts as passwords and post private stuff on the web. Any personal details logged online—whether it's in a blog, email, news article, or on a social networking site—can be accessed and used. Good hackers can find anything. It's just a matter of someone like me taking the time to search for these nuggets of information. They can never be erased from Cyberland. And, therefore, they are always accessible.

> Taz: Ten minutes.

> Casper: We know how to tell time.

> Blackbird: Casper's dead serious :)

> QTip: Aww Casper, where's your *spirit*? *LOL.*

I laugh to myself as all the hackers bicker online.

Hacker Commandment #5: Never get distracted.

I chew the inside of my cheek. It's critical that I do everything right. One wrong move could ruin everything. My name. My future. My life.

I remind myself to breathe and shake out the tension in my wrists and hands.

When I'm ready, I dive in. First, I double-click my way into John's computer settings and flip on his webcam to take a picture of his empty room. Next, I upload firewall software to protect John from any future hacks. Finally, I go through Zed and erase anything that might link me—the Dark Angel—to this challenge.

For now, John is safe. His personal details are protected from the black-hat hackers who love to troll under the guise of good.

Once I'm done, I sit back in my chair and take a swig of Dr Pepper, letting the weight roll off my shoulders. I inhale slowly. I did it. Now, it's just a matter of time.

A message pops up, and I can't help but smile.

> Taz: Time's up! Dark Angel wins!

</CLOSE THE LOOP>

THE CHAT ROOM LIGHTS UP AS THE ORWELLIANS FINALLY CATCH on to my cyber brilliance.

Not only at getting in, but at keeping them out. Messages trail up my screen.

> Taz: Good job, DA! Did U get a pic?
> Casper: Of course she didn't. She doesn't have the balls.
> Blackbird: Most girls don't :)
> QTip: Give her a chance.
> Casper: She doesn't win without it.

My finger hovers over the mouse as I question whether or not to post the photo. Maybe I understand Hamlet more than I think: To post or not to post? I mean, what harm can the picture do? John's not even in the room. To be sure, I check for anything in the background that might be revealing or damaging—it's surprising what you can find when you zoom in on a digital photo. After waffling, I finally upload the picture.

> Casper: Show us UR code. Or R U afraid we'll find out U

cheated?

> DA: I have no problem showing you exactly how I beat you. But keep it on the DL.

> Casper: No one will know. We're untraceable. Like ghosts.

I scrub any traceable information in my script and upload the source code for everyone to critique.

> Blackbird: Brilliant! :) She kicked UR A$$ Casper!

> Casper: Anyone can make a few calls. This was a hacking challenge.

> QTip: A hack's a hack. Doesn't matter how U get it done.

> Taz: DA won with a genius strategy. Not only did she hack in, but she blocked U cyber clowns out.

At this point, it doesn't matter what anyone says. I won. Satisfaction pours through me. I'm good, with or without Red Devil. And now these guys know it too.

> Taz: DA, did U reroute UR IP address?

I chew on a gristle of frustration. Even after all this, he still doubts me! The hacking world is so sexist. If this was anyone else, they wouldn't be questioned.

> DA: Of course. Replaced it w/a proxy server address & disabled audit logs.

> Casper: DA, you should claim the hack. The White House needs to know the network is penetrable.

My fingers hover over the keys, waiting for my next command. I already feel guilty for hacking John's email and computer. Using his private information and our conversations to crack his code. By releasing the hack publicly, I'm rubbing this whole stunt in his face. John may never know what I did to protect him, but maybe my hack will encourage the White House to improve network security. Before someone else finds a back door. Someone who matters.

However, I'm not stupid.

Instead of signing Dark Angel, I give credit to the group by posting our motto: *Power to the Proles. We are Orwellians!*

George Orwell would be proud.

As soon as I hit enter, a </CONNECTION ERROR> message pops up on my screen. Zed's cursor freezes. My heart double-times with the music still thumping in my ear.

The Spinning Rainbow Wheel taunts me.

I freak out and pound on the ESC key, over and over and over. But Zed is stuck in cyber limbo. Without pausing, I immediately shut him down, severing all connections. I slump back and gawk at the black screen. This cannot be happening. I replay every stroke and decision point in my mind.

I did everything right. Covered every path. Hid every track. I'm always super careful.

Aren't I?

My head pounds. I press my hands against my temples and massage. No use logging back into the chat. If Taz gets the slightest hint something went wrong, he'll kick me out of the Orwellians. For good. Loyalty between hackers only runs screen deep.

Besides, I need to stay calm. Computer connections crash all the time. This could have been a bad cell or maybe even a satellite issue. Seattle's weather is famous for blocking out even the strongest signal. There's absolutely no reason to worry.

So then, why do I feel so sick?

I throw my bag over one shoulder and weave through the computer graveyard. A sparse collection of technology relics sits abandoned on wobbly tables: laptops, desktops, hard drives. Pausing in front of the ancient Apple III, I spot the flickering green light. Old Ben still has a pulse. I want to shut it down and put the poor thing out of its misery but can't seem to pull the plug.

Hacker Commandment #6: Thou shalt not touch another hacker's hardware.

A box of flash drives sits on top of the old IBM PC. Leaving drives out in the open is a major DON'T in the Hacker Handbook. I tuck them away in the fake keyboard we built together, except for one marked *Ghost Hunters*. Red Devil loved this show almost as much as she loved crappy PCs. I don't have the heart to throw it out. Maybe I'll want to watch it later. I scoop up the *Ghost Hunters* drive and toss it into my bag.

Sliding back the steel door, I step into the cold. The brittle Seattle air slices through my body, chilling me to the bone. I shiver and zip up my black leather jacket. The smell of dead fish drifts up from the wharf.

As I walk through the warehouses, drifts of steam creep out of the street grates, like ghosts crawling out their graves. Shadows rear up from long-forgotten crates, and the sounds of skittering rodents gnaw at my nerves.

I speed up and rush back to my real life.

Superman uses Clark Kent to hide his special powers.

I show up as Ada Lovelace to protect mine.

</SCHOOL ISN'T ALL IT'S CRACKED UP TO BE>

I sprint through the doors of Roosevelt High with seconds to spare.

The minute I see locker 17, I stop in my tracks. My guard crumbles. Stupid locker gets me every time.

When I'm online, I almost don't miss Red Devil too much. But at school, Simone's gap is much wider. The Great Divide in my world.

I trace the faded glittery stickers with trembling fingers. Nothing left, except the faint outline of something that was once beautiful and sparkly. Just like Simone.

Closing my eyes, I tug at the angel necklace. Touching it grounds me. It's the last thing Simone gave me before she died. At the time, I couldn't understand why she'd give me her beloved flash-drive necklace. Wonder Woman never handed over her Lasso of Truth.

But in hindsight, I can only assume Simone knew she wouldn't need it any more. She knew she was going to die. A strange piece in a twisted puzzle.

Someone clears his throat. "Excuse me."

I move aside as Logan—a skinny ninth grader who now

occupies Simone's old locker—fiddles with the locker combination.

According to my online research, Logan Scott is from Minneapolis. He lives with his mother and younger sister because his dad died of a massive heart attack, which shouldn't have been surprising since heart disease was listed in his dad's medical history. Logan suffers from a high anxiety disorder, which causes him to grind his teeth at night and gnaw his cuticles until they bleed. And according to his insurance claims, dental records, and CVS prescription history, both are being medically treated.

Logan wrestles with locker 17's stubborn latch. A duel that ends in defeat.

I lean over and pound my fist on the upper left corner. Like Simone did.

The door pops open.

Logan flashes me a silver smile decorated with an orthodontic zipper. "Gee, thanks." His eyes drop, and he quickly stores his heavy backpack. He wants to talk to me as much as I want to sing out loud in the hallway.

Once he heads off to class, I grab my physics book and cram it down in my bag. No matter what storage options are available, I never leave my laptop behind. Unattended. Too risky. Too dangerous.

My whole life is stored on that 2x2 hard drive.

In the wrong hands, that life would be over.

I walk to class and keep my eyes down, focusing on the scuffed tips of my black boots. The excitement of my morning hack is long gone. This school has become my personal kryptonite.

Here, I'm weak. Unprotected. Vulnerable.

Deep in thought, I turn the corner and slam into my school counselor. Folders and papers launch into the air and scatter across the floor.

"Oh! I'm sorry." I bend over and start collecting the mess.

Mrs. Crawford kneels and scrambles to grab the pages before they slide under the lockers. She stammers, "It's okay. I'll get it."

I hold up a piece of paper. Before she can snatch it, a few words grab my attention.

Ada Lovelace. Detached. Depressed. Withdrawn.

I stand there, silent. Arm outstretched. Paper in hand. Mouth open. Frozen in time. Like one of the White Witch's stone prisoners stuck in Narnia.

Mrs. Crawford takes the paper, her cheeks blazing a bright red. "Oh *dear* . . . Ada, I'm so sorry you saw that."

"It's okay," I utter. My knees tremble, I can barely stand. I want so much to run away. Hide. Instead, I stare down at one ant struggling to cross the hall without getting squashed. I know how he feels. Small. Alone. Desperately searching for a safe place to stop and take a breath. I force my chin up. "I'm fine . . . really."

But I'm not fine. And I'm not sure I'll ever be *fine* again.

My counseling sessions flash across my mind. All the things I've told Mrs. Crawford about Simone over our many sessions. The tears I've shed over my best friend's unexpected death. And now, somehow, all those raw feelings and confused thoughts have been summarized in a few clinical adjectives: **Detached. Depressed. Withdrawn.**

Mrs. Crawford touches my shoulder. "Maybe we should discuss this in my office."

God, not her office again. I clutch the straps of my backpack with both hands as if it's a flotation device. The only thing keeping my head above water. To keep me from drowning. "I have to get to class."

Without saying anything else, I rush down the hall, cutting a few sharp corners at high speeds. The whole time praying Mrs. Crawford isn't in hot pursuit. She's been known to run after students in need. And right now, I'm a target.

I race into the computer lab and lock the door behind me.

The room is empty and dark. With no purpose.

I fit in well.

I slide down the wall until I'm sitting on the floor and bury my head in my knees. My jaw locks and my eyes sting.

Mrs. Crawford thinks I'm a total mess. I pound my leg in frustration. I only went to her because Dad asked me to talk to someone, and I thought—maybe—I could find a way to understand why my best friend committed suicide. Suddenly. Without any explanation.

Without any goodbye.

I hit my head against the wall and pinch back tears. I've been on this trip before. Next stop: Meltdown City. I focus on the quiet room. All the sleeping desktops illuminate a soft blue glow, and the hard drives hum a lullaby in unison. Both are soothing and pull me out of the hole. I inhale a few deep breaths and think about Mrs. Crawford's files. I wonder if Simone talked to Mrs. Crawford before she died. She'd only been out of rehab a week, but maybe she came here and said something that will help me understand.

My heart races as a thought comes to me.

The pages I saw were not handwritten. They were typed, which can only mean one thing. Mrs. Crawford takes notes in our counseling sessions, and then stores them in online files. Hackable files hovering out in Cyberland, itching to be discovered. Any of that information could be disastrous if discovered by anyone: a college, a company, even my parents. And if the media gets wind of it, the political press will hound my dad, Senator Lovelace, about his mentally unstable and fragile daughter.

The room grows stuffy. I unzip my jacket to cool off. There's only one thing that will help me breathe again.

I gotta erase those files before it's too late.

This new mission helps me refocus and prevents me from having a complete meltdown.

I unzip my bag and wake up Zed. It shouldn't take me long to crack Mrs. Crawford's files. This isn't my first time in the school's system.

About a year ago, Simone and I hacked the network and rewrote the executable boot files so Michael Jackson's "Beat It" video played any time someone logged in. Over and over. Annoying but funny. Drove the sys admin mad. The second time was after we witnessed jock Craig Lovett bullying poor Logan in the hallway. Again. Simone and I hacked the security system and anonymously emailed the camera footage to Craig's football coach. The evidence awarded Craig anti-bullying classes and detention for life. But more importantly, we freed Logan from daily torture.

No one ever linked us to the hacks.

For a third time, I hack into the network and log in as Mrs. Crawford. This way nothing can be traced back to Zed or me. To crack the password, I pull out my notebook and skim the juicy deets I've collected on my counselor.

Mrs. Lucy Crawford's maiden name is Thatcher and she's 52.75 years old. Her daughter, Elizabeth (a.k.a. Lizzie), is currently on a full scholarship to Seattle University and recently joined Kappa Kappa Gamma due to her mom's active alumni status and grandfather's plushy trust fund. Mrs. Crawford recently divorced her yoga-teaching husband (who—according to local gossip—had an affair with a lady pretzel at The Yoga Studio), and she currently resides in a studio rental for $500 a month. She also has four active accounts at Wells Fargo, which reveal two bounced checks and several overdrafts in the last year.

If I can hack the White House network in an hour, cracking this woman's password is child's play. I crack my knuckles and test the most common ones first: 12345678, QWERTY, and the mysterious favorite, MONKEY.

Every attempt fails.

Time for Plan B. I eject the flash drive from my necklace and upload a password decryption software. Once it executes, Mrs. Crawford's secret code reveals itself.

SexyMama.

I cup my hand over my mouth, not sure whether to laugh or throw up. I'll never be able to look that woman in the eyes again. That is the creepy thing about hacking people. You learn about things you didn't want to know. And then when you uncover them, you wish you hadn't.

I skim the directory until I spot a folder: COUNSELOR RECORDS. After double-clicking on the icon, I open the file labeled: ADA LOVELACE.

Detached. Depressed. Isolated. Withdrawn.
Obsessed with death.
Needs formal counseling.
Medications unknown.
Possible suicidal tendencies!!!!!!!!!!!!

As if the words alone aren't bad enough, they're followed by an army of exclamation points. Judgements being yelled out for the cyberworld to hear.

I shake my head at the screen. This. Has. To. Go.

No one can ever read these things about me. If the media gets hold of it, they will drill Dad about his fragile daughter. Forever.

I right-click on my file and hit </DELETE>.

A message pops up: </ARE YOU SURE YOU WANT TO DELETE ADA LOVELACE?>

I pause. My hand shakes as the cursor hovers over the two answers. Don't know what good this will even do. Nothing online can be permanently deleted. Erasing information only makes it harder to find. Kinda like looking for a missing sock, coin, or key.

It's there somewhere . . . it's just a matter of someone caring enough to dig for it.

I click </YES> and delete myself.

Along with everything Mrs. Crawford thinks I am.

And everything I pray I am not.

</TIME TO DMP>

The bell rings, warning me of the next period.

I peek out and watch kids loiter in the hallway, enjoying every second of freedom until they are caged in boredom for another fifty minutes.

Simone was my LAN line to people. My hardwired connection to the real world.

After she died, I unplugged from the real world and dove into my online world. I stuffed all my free time with Orwellian chats, unleashed anger in WoW battles, and constructed a brand-new world in Second Life.

Being online helped me forget about the lonely, drag-out days at school. I couldn't wait to get home and plug in. Escape to a place where I could cry behind a screen without anyone knowing.

Offline, I was Ada, the sad girl who lost her best friend.

Online, I became the Dark Angel, kick-ass hacker extraordinaire.

I simply rewired my life.

Closing my eyes, I try to picture Simone's face. But the details are fuzzy as the dull ache of forgetting sharpens.

There's only one thing that makes me feel better when the small details peel away. Hearing her voice.

I call Simone's old phone, praying it's still in service.

As soon as her sweet voice answers, a knot forms in my throat. I don't breathe for the entire message.

Roses are red, violets are blue, sugar is sweet, and so are you.

The roses have wilted, the violets are dead, the sugar bowl's empty, and so is your head.

The roses stink, sorta like sheep, (Simone giggles) *now leave your message after the beep.*

The roses are molding, the violets are rotten, I might call you back, unless I've forgotten.

Her snorty laugh fills my ear, and I hang up the phone. Some people may think it's hard listening to a dead person's voice, but not me. It's just a brief resurrection of the past.

I click out to SocialNet and skim through the new comments that have been posted on Simone's board. Since yesterday.

Thinking of you.

I miss you.

Can't believe it's been three months today.

Three months? Simone has been dead one quarter of one whole year? Sometimes it seems forever ago. Other times it feels like yesterday. Either way, I can't believe she's gone. I'd give anything to see her show up at my door with a bucket of ice cream and some chocolate.

"Nothing better than a friend, unless it's a friend with choco-late," she'd say with a bright smile. So cheesy. But so Simone.

Next, I click out to my SocialNet page. A message pops up in the bottom right corner.

The Dark Angel will fall.

The words jolt me upright as if an electrical pulse has just raced up my spine. I swallow once, feeling choked and read the next line.

Just like the Red Devil.

I cover my mouth with one hand, in case I throw up. Someone knows about the Dark Angel and Red Devil! And by posting it here, they know it was Simone and me.

I click on the generic avatar responsible for sending the messages, but the profile is empty. No friends. No photos. No favorites. Nothing to track. I delete the comment, block the anon user, and change my password. Fast.

I sit back, still confused and scared when a private invite pops up on the bottom of my screen. The Orwellians have called an emergency meeting. This is a first. I immediately log in.

> DA: Hey, I'm here. What's up?
> Casper: Newsflash, QTip got busted today.
> Taz: I heard, but he hasn't been linked to us. Yet.
> Casper posts a link: Check this out.

I click on the article.

A few months ago, an alleged member of the hacking group, the Orwellians, broke into a secure FBI conference call with Scotland Yard. Today, FBI Cyber Crimes Director Paul Mitnick nabbed another hacker who goes by the handle of QTip. He's also believed to be part of the Orwellians. Anonymous sources wonder if he was involved in a recent hack on SocialNet. But Mitnick wouldn't give any more details on the case.

"Crap," I say.

> DA: What will happen to him?
> Casper: He'll go to rehab or jail. Maybe get a cell next to the Red Devil.

> Blackbird: We don't know she was busted.

> Casper: Only thing that makes sense if she isn't logging in anymore.

> Taz: Mitnick is a freakin' pit bull. Once he gets stuck on something, he clamps down. B sure to scrub hard tonight. Get rid of all the dirt. Power to the proles!

Part of me wants to ask more questions, but I don't want to raise any flags.

My fingers hover over my keyboard, trembling so much that I forget to repeat the Orwellian mantra until it's too late.

I slam Zed shut and jump to my feet. If QTip got busted and Mitnick is out for blood, Zed's weekly bath can't wait until tonight. I have to get home and scrub him…now.

Just in case.

With my head down, I bolt outside to beat the lunch stampede. Kids scoot by me, tripping over my feet. Bumping into my bag. It's like I'm not even here.

I race to the student lot and stop in front of Simone's pink Vespa. Her dad gifted me the retro moped right after she died. When Simone first showed me the bike, it was a hunk of junk . . . minus the hunk. The thing barely ran and was covered in puke green paint with two flat tires. Simone always loved the underdogs. First the locker, then this wheeled ugly duckling. I touched the cracked seat and straddle the bike. Simone's name is still airbrushed along the gas tank.

"Isn't she a beaut?" Simone said.

"THIS is the ride you're so excited about?" I asked.

Simone pretended to cover the scooter's ears. "Don't be dissin' the scooter, or I swear she'll go all Christine on you. Besides, I needed some wheels."

"Two flat ones?"

"Hey! Beggars can't be choosers."

"Pretty sure a beggar isn't choosin' this." I stifled a laugh.

"It's not about what it is." She patted the seat. *"It's about what it can be."*

In the end, I helped her (and her dad) hammer the bike back into shape. I voted for sky blue, but she painted it bright pink, yet insisted on keeping the ragged seat. Maybe as a small reminder that nothing is ever perfect. No matter what you do.

In everything ugly, Simone found something beautiful.

My eyes burn with tears as the school bell rings behind me, jerking me out of my thoughts. I tug on the pink helmet and race home, zipping past rows of large mansions and topiary landscapes.

At my brick mailbox, I urge the moped up the steep hill to the circular driveway and park. I race up the marble steps and into the house without stopping. Then I bolt up the two flights of stairs to my bedroom and punch in the code on my bedroom alarm. Without this security, I'd have about as much privacy as a goldfish in a glass bowl.

I shut the door behind me and take a deep breath. There's no place like home . . . especially if it has a secret war room equipped with extra laptops, spare hard drives, two monitors, multiple operating systems, and a personal router.

My phone dings. Before Simone died, I got hundreds of texts a day. Mostly from her. Now, I know it's just one of my hovering parents. I dig the phone out of my bag.

Hope school was fun. Leftovers in fridge, working late. XOXO

Mom hasn't told me anything I don't already know. Dad works at the office all hours, making calls and lobbying for his new technology privacy bill, while Mom attends her business dinners as a bank SVP. Meanwhile, I have a running date with Mrs. Stouffer.

I text back to prove I'm okay. If Mom doesn't hear from me in record seconds, she's sure to get Nancy Grace on the case.

Now it's time to work. I unscrew the back of Zed to switch out the old hard drive for a new backup drive that's already loaded with everything I need. While it's configuring, I run a scrub program on all my other hardware to erase anything that might incriminate the Dark Angel. Then I throw a few used CDs in my mini-microwave to toast the data and rub a magnet over a few tapes.

Outside, car tires scrape over my pebbled driveway. Someone is coming.

I jump up and peer through the sheer curtains.

When I see the car, I know exactly who it is.

The FBI.

</BUSTED>

The black sedan rolls to a stop.

The standard-issue car sticks out: black wheels, fancy hubcaps, and tinted windows. A young guy emerges from the driver's side dressed in the FBI uniform: dark blue pants and a white button-down rolled at the sleeves. A shiny badge is clipped to his boring black belt. This dude sticks out like a red rose growing in a field of white daisies.

No question. It's definitely the Feds.

I mutter a few cuss words in my room as the guy casually strolls up the steps, scanning my front lawn like he's already looking for clues.

Then he glances up at my window.

I duck under the sill and crawl across my room, scuttling over mounds of shoes, dirty clothes, and computer parts.

As Zed's install counts down to completion, I open my closet doors. I pull back a little rug and pry up the loose board where I hide any possible evidence under the floor. Then I stuff all the extra flash drives inside a hollowed-out copy of *War and Peace*. Once I'm done, I stand in the middle of the room and scan its contents to make sure I didn't leave anything incriminating out in the open.

If the FBI connects me or my stuff to any of the Dark Angel's hacks, a first offense might be labeled a lapse in judgment. Probation likely. But if they connect me to the White House hack, I'm toast. Game over. I'd be slapped with conspiracy charges and domestic terrorism, leading to mandatory jail time and a felony record. Not to mention, Dad's Senate career and his credibility on the Technology Security and Privacy Committee would be forever tainted.

Cradling Zed, I watch the program countdown to completion.

20%, 30%, 50%, 75%.

I rub my hands together so hard they could spark a fire.

87%.

The agent knocks on my front door.

I pound on Zed's keyboard. "Come on! Come on!" As if assaulting my laptop makes the countdown go any faster.

93%

Another knock. This time it's much louder and followed by the official stern announcement, "FBI!"

I shove Zed under the floorboards and pull back the rug. If I can stall this guy, any evidence will disappear before his posse can dig through my closet.

I lock the bedroom door and skid down the stairs on my socks, landing at the bottom with a loud thud.

Slowing down my breath, I settle down. Time to stay calm. From now on, everything I do or say—every look I give—is critical.

Just as the doorbell chimes, I fling open the door and try not to sound panicked. "Sorry I was…napping. Can I help you?" My welcoming phrase sounds a bit stiff and rehearsed like a fast-food drive-thru attendant who hates her job. Maybe the painted-on smile will mask any rattling nerves.

The FBI agent pulls off his sunglasses—obviously Ray-Bans, standard issue. The guy's cute and semi-young. Definitely not thirty, though super tired-looking. Curved lines around his mouth resemble parentheses or large commas, probably depends on his mood.

"Agent Mitnick, FBI Cyber Crimes Unit."

I lace my hands together and squeeze. "Pit Bull" Mitnick is at my house! No doubt for me.

Hacker Commandment #7: Stay calm and carry on.

"Sorry. My dad's not here. You might want to try his office." I attempt to shut the door, but Mitnick stops it with his hand.

"Actually, I'm not here for the senator. I have a search warrant for you." Before I can answer, he reads off a piece of paper. "Miss Ada Rose Lovelace at 545 Shadowy Lane. Is that you?"

If Mitnick knows my full legal name, this is definitely more than a house call. My knees start to quiver. Any moment, I might perform a full-fledge face-plant. On the inside, I want to shrink away—disappear. But on the outside, I work hard to remain completely stoic. Not a twitch. Instead, I straighten up and work hard to keep my face void of any expression. Simone showed me how to look blank.

I hope.

"Yes. That's me." I smile but can't decide where my hands should go so I hook them into my belt loops like a pro square dancer.

"Great," Mitnick grins back. "Can you come with me, please?"

"Am I in trouble?" I ask with wide eyes. Playing dumb or surprised can't hurt.

Mitnick puts his glasses back on his face. "Miss Lovelace, I think it's best if we discuss this at my office so my colleagues can search the premises."

On cue, a black van rolls up the driveway. A female agent gets out and heads inside, carrying a brown cardboard box.

"Um, sure." I mentally catalog any vulnerable items that could be exposed. Time to stall. "Let me grab my backpack."

Mitnick blocks me from reentering the house. "That won't be necessary. I wouldn't want you to *misplace* a few things. *Accidentally,* of course."

I appear shocked. "Wouldn't that be an obstruction of justice?"

"Yes, yes, it would." The guy smiles as if he's just been voted in as the president of his frat house.

"Maybe I should call my dad. *Senator* Lovelace," I say. Name-dropping never hurts.

"Good idea." Mitnick nods. "But your dad's already been called. He's meeting us downtown."

"Oh." All the air seeps from my lungs, deflating my body. Along with any shred of hope. If my dad's been called, this situation is worse than I expected. No one calls a senator about a case, unless it's a big one. I can only imagine what Dad is thinking. My legs weaken, and I pray I don't pass out because fainting has to be in the Top Five Signs of Overwhelming Guilt.

Mitnick waves the search warrant around like it's a hundred-dollar bill up for grabs. "Did I mention I have papers?"

I nod. "Yes, you did."

"Oh good! Wouldn't want to leave you out of the loop." He looks down and points at my bare feet. "Maybe you want to throw on some shoes."

I slide into my UGGs. Pretty sure these won't win me any street cred at the jailhouse.

He motions for me to lead the walk of shame. "After you, Miss Lovelace."

My shoulders sag as a cloak of guilt weighs me down. I barely make it down the steps without collapsing. With each step, the reality of my situation sets in.

My online life is over. And my offline life is gonna suck... even more.

I stop at the black sedan. When Mitnick opens the door, I

crawl into the back seat like a naughty dog. He slides into the driver's side and lets the car roll down the driveway in neutral. Crushing any pebble of hope that might be lingering.

As we head down the hill, little snow flurries smack against the tinted window. I watch as they melt and trickle down the glass, leaving tracks of tears.

At the bottom of the hill, I glance back.

My huge house fades into the landscaped horizon. A dim light shines out of my bedroom window.

The FBI invasion has begun.

I hope Zed had enough time to erase my tracks.

</THE STANDOFF>

Downtown at the FBI Cyber Crime office, Agent Mitnick bites into a chocolate chip cookie.

"Hungry?" he asks.

As if a sugar rush will get me to spill my guts.

"I'm trying to quit," I mumble. My stomach grumbles. Then again, why not binge? This could be my last meal. Plus, some people who refuse to eat or drink anything during an interrogation look ultra-guilty. I'm pretty sure I saw that on *CSI*.

I snatch a cookie, forcing down a dry bite while scanning the compact room. Nothing but a table, two hard chairs, and a cheap coffee bar.

When I look back at Mitnick, he shuts the box of treats.

If I want seconds, I'll have to fess up.

"Can I call you Ada, or do you go by Rose?" he asks.

When I glare, he smirks. The dude is taunting me, similar to how a lion stalks a baby lamb just before devouring it. I wait a long time before answering him. "*Ada* is fine."

He wipes the cookie crumbs off his mouth with a napkin. "Good."

I crack each knuckle, summoning the Dark Angel to fly in

and save me in real life. The same way she keeps me safe online. "I'm sorry, but what are we waiting for exactly?"

In perfect timing, the door opens and my father walks in.

Dad looks put together and in control, wearing the standard politician's costume: pressed gray suit and super shiny shoes that would make the sun squint, adding the perfect touch of authority—all topped off with perfectly- styled peppery hair. But beyond Dad's perfect appearance, his strained smile lets me know that he's secretly frazzled.

I sit up straighter, relieved for reinforcements. "Hey, Dad."

"Ada," he says flatly, displaying enough of a frown to let me know he's unhappy, but not one that would reveal any sign of weakness or worry.

My posture sags like a limp balloon.

Agent Mitnick stands, showing his respect, and shakes Dad's hand over the table. "Senator Lovelace. Thank you for coming so quickly."

"Paul." Dad gives a tough shake. "I appreciate you calling me before contacting Channel 11." He chooses my side of the battlefield and sits in the chair next to me. To show his support, he reaches over and squeezes my hand under the table.

I keep my head down, unable to look him in the eye. What have I done?

"What are the charges?" Dad's voice is stern. "And this better be good enough to provoke an impromptu search of a senator's private residence as well as the abrupt and unsupervised detainment of my underage daughter."

Hearing his confidence makes me feel more in control too. I rub the angel necklace like it's a genie bottle. If I'm lucky, maybe I'll get one wish.

"Sir, we believe your daughter hacked into SocialNet and attempted to download admin files."

Even though I'm shocked, I keep my eyes down. If eyes are the windows to the soul, I better hide mine or this guy will see everything. I try not to look too relieved. I thought this was about the White House hack. This is bad, but that would be much worse.

Unreactive, Dad responds calmly. "What proof do you have that this hacker was Ada?" His voice reveals no emotion. No fear. No judgment.

Mitnick brings over a folder. "This morning we got an anonymous tip that's someone was in SocialNet's system. SocialNet sent us the logs and I'm afraid we tracked the IP address to your daughter's laptop, proving she was in the system more than once. And this morning. My guys are confirming that as we speak, but I assure you we have enough proof to make an official arrest."

Dad drops his guard for a split second. "Jesus, Ada." A muscle in his jaw ticks as he wipes his sweaty brow with a handkerchief.

I shake my head, mainly to myself. This is impossible. There's no way SocialNet saw me sneaking in their system. Not to mention that Mitnick tracked my IP address. It was rerouted through several servers.

This guy has to be bluffing. Or someone ratted me out.

Mitnick continues after a long deliberate pause that he obviously learned in his training. "As you know, hacking is a felony."

"A felony?" I repeat. Even I know that a first offense is usually labelled a misdemeanor. "But I— "

Dad stops me by holding up his hand. "Ada, don't say anything else. Let me handle this." He faces Mitnick. "Does SocialNet know Ada's identity?"

Mitnick leans back in his chair. "Senator, I can assure you this is confidential. For now." He stands and strolls over to a long table where he pours coffee into a tiny Styrofoam cup. Mitnick hands the steaming liquid to my dad, who accepts the offering.

"There's more." Mitnick sits on the end of the table closest to me. "We think Ada may have worked with a hacking gang called the Orwellians."

My stomach drops. But I plaster on a straight face.

Being linked to the Orwellians forces me into a bad category. The "gang" is known for many hacks. And even though I'm one of the good hackers, there have been a few rogue Caspers of the cyberworld that have tainted our name. And our purpose.

"I've heard of them on the news." Dad faces me. His face is pinched into a scowl. "Ada…is this true?"

Mitnick waits for my answer like it's the million-dollar question. If I get it wrong, he wins.

Hacker Commandment #8: Never give up more information than you have to.

I crack a few more knuckles, preparing to be strong. Say little, admit nothing. I try not to shift in my chair. Can't give this guy any signs that I'm freaking out. If he connects me to Orwellians, he will connect me to the Dark Angel in just a matter of time.

"No," I say flatly.

No way I'm ever confessing until I know what evidence they really have.

</PHREAKED OUT>

THE CORNERS OF MITNICK'S MOUTH TURN UP SLIGHTLY. HE'S having fun with this whole thing.

He picks up another file and holds it up like a sign. "Okay. Do you know someone called . . . the Taz Man?"

I maintain my composure by staring at a spot on the table. I swallow an undercurrent of nausea and speak one word with total conviction. "No."

Mitnick drums his fingers on the table. "I hear he's the leader."

I shrug. "I wouldn't know."

Mitnick smirks as if he's winning the title of Most Likely to Win a Staring Contest and holds up two different files. "What about the Dark Angel? Or the Red Devil?"

I stare at the folder. "DA" is scribbled on one of them. A shot of adrenaline zips through me. My mouth turns dry. My mind goes blank as I stare at the letters. I can't think of anything to say.

When I don't answer, Mitnick presses me again. "Does the name Dark Angel ring a bell?"

"Sounds like a superhero to me." I mumble. But I don't even hear what I say until it's too late.

"Ada Rose!" Dad says. "This is serious business. Answer the question."

Part of me almost caves. But then I realize something. If Mitnick is asking me this question again and again, I'll bet money he hasn't made a connection. Yet. He's just phishing for information. Information I won't give him.

My confidence meter goes back up a little. At least out of the red zone. This time I make sure my voice doesn't waver. "Nope."

He doesn't stop chipping away at me. "Because we have information that the Taz and the Dark Angel are linked to much more serious hacks."

I shrug. "I don't know what you're talking about."

Agent Mitnick drops the folders on the table, making me flinch. "Did you know that the penalty for a felony in computer fraud—hacking into any system that you shouldn't be in—comes with a jail sentence and a hefty fine, especially if it hurts a company's reputation or harms their data in any way."

"Now, wait a minute. I don't like where this is going." Dad stands eye level with Mitnick and speaks loudly. "Paul, are you saying we need a lawyer?"

Mitnick gives up on me and appeals to my dad. "Sir, no offense to you or your daughter, but Ada's not the one I want. Why would I be hungry for frozen meatballs when I can score a filet mignon? I want her to give me intel on the bigger fish to fry."

I frown. My hacking skills are being compared to freezer-burned meat? Obviously this guy doesn't know how good I am. For instance, my WoW hack is infamous. Over 100,000 characters suffered in a virtual apocalypse all because of my code. Cyber friends dropped dead in the cities of Stormwind and Orgrimmar. I logged the most pretend deaths in any game's history.

"She's told you what she knows."

Mitnick cups his palms behind his head, all relaxed, like he's sunning on a beach somewhere. "She hasn't told me anything. And if she doesn't cooperate, I will have to arrest her."

Dad removes his jacket, revealing wet spots underneath his armpits. It's the first time I've seen him sweat under pressure. He slips his hands into his pants pockets and paces the room. "What other options do we have here, Paul? As you know we passed a portion of the technology bill, which gives hackers—especially first offenders—a chance at rehab."

"True. After her arrest, a judge would decide how she's charged." Mitnick rubs the Brillo pad of stubble on his chin. "ReBoot might help clear her record . . . IF I recommend it."

Dad isn't intimidated. "I'll be honest with you, Paul. Whether she gives you information or not, ReBoot is an option and you know it. Ada is a good teen with no prior record. My concern is not helping you nail a rogue group of hackers. My concern is finding the best place for my daughter. As you probably know, her best friend died this year, and I think maybe she's just gotten off track."

"Dad," I whisper.

But they ignore me and continue negotiating as if I'm not in the room.

My head spins. Faster and faster until I get dizzy. The guilt over Simone's death resurfaces. At the time, cracking into the local TV station network and leaking news about a zombie invasion was funny. Unfortunately, I made a mistake when we launched our attack. The FCC called in the Feds, and since we were on her computer, they showed up at Simone's door instead of mine. Luckily, they didn't connect her to the Red Devil, but she took the fall for me and made me promise not to confess my part. Next thing I know she was shipped off to ReBoot.

Simone was dead shortly after. ReBoot didn't help Simone. So why would it help me?

I clear my throat and speak again. "Dad, I can't go to ReBoot. That's where—"

Dad shakes his head as a warning for me to be quiet and offers a deal to Mitnick. "Paul, if Ada agrees to the thirty-day program, would you consider dropping the charges and clearing her record. Of course I would want this all to be confidential."

"Yes," Mitnick slowly nods. "As you know, it's not our policy to release the names of minors."

My body slumps in the chair. Considering what's going on, I'm wondering if ReBoot is even worse than jail.

"Good." Dad nods, smiling. "Because SocialNet is not a huge supporter of my bill. Since no harm was done, I wouldn't want them getting wind of Ada's . . . mistake . . . if it can be prevented. I would hate for them to drag Ada through the mud with the hopes of killing an important bill before it's even hit the Senate floor."

"I understand." Mitnick glances at me. "But may I speak with Ada alone first? You have my word it is off the record."

"I know your dad, Paul, so I hope I can trust you." Dad stands and touches my shoulder. "Ada, I'll be right outside."

As soon as Dad closes the door, Mitnick scrapes a chair across the floor and sits on it backward, facing me. "Listen, Ada, I get it. You love poking around networks, leaving your mark. It's how I started on computers." His face remains stern, but a hint of sympathy hides in his eyes. "But let's not play games. I think you're in deep with this hacking group, and they're bad news. I just want some names."

I don't flinch. "I don't have any information."

Mitnick rolls up each sleeve again. "Look, I busted you on this hack. It's only a matter of time before the Orwellians go down too. I've already busted a few of them.

"Then you should have all the information you need," I say.

"Do you want to sink with them?" he asks.

I have to warn Taz he's got some heat in the kitchen. Maybe QTip is leaking 411 to the Feds. "You're welcome to check my computer."

"Oh believe me, we are." He speaks sternly, but a smile hovers behind his eyes. "Obviously you're good—to pull off the SocialNet hack. So I assume you've covered your bases. But I know you're in deeper somehow. Eventually I'll uncover something big. I know hackers as good as you don't stop at one hack."

I meet his eyes. "You don't know me."

"Really?" Agent Mitnick leans in close and clicks his pen a few times. "Ada Rose Lovelace, sixteen and seven eighths. Volunteers at the local animal shelter. Loves computers and excels at Farmville. Has accumulated five hundred and six pals on an old SocialNet account, yet not many in real life. Best friends with the late Simone Watson, who checked into ReBoot for a short stint. Devastated by your best friend's suicide, you quit cheerleading and let your 4.0 GPA drop. Two years ago, you volunteered on your dad's Senate re-election campaign. You have two fish, two hermit crabs, and one old mutt named Charley."

I maintain my composure, yet a flood of adrenaline tumbles through my system. This guy has done his research. And I can only assume this is the CliffsNotes version, because if he's anything like me, there's way more than he's mentioning.

The hum of the air conditioner fills the room. I could just tell him about Taz and Casper to avoid ReBoot all together. But Simone didn't rat me out so I need to pay that forward. For her.

I speak softly. "Better check your sources."

He looks interested in what I'm going to say. "And why's that?"

I clear my throat. "I only have *one* fish now. Bubbles died last week."

He nods slowly. "I see. My sincerest condolences. I'll make a note of it in your new file . . . while there's still room."

His comment sends my heart spiraling all over again. I wish I could get a look at that file and find out exactly what he knows.

Mitnick may notice a weakness because he swoops in for the final kill. "If the media gets wind of this, they won't go easy on you. Or your dad. No one wants a senator who preaches privacy when his daughter's a hacker. His career will die and so will his bill."

I clasp my hands in my lap. "Only he has nothing to do with any of this."

Mitnick shrugs. "Doesn't matter in politics. Guilt by association is enough, especially if it's a kid getting trouble. What does that say about him as a leader? Now, surely you don't want to open yourself up to risk of public scrutiny. And I know you don't want to spend thirty days in a rehab facility, especially since Simone was there too. So what's it gonna to be, are you going to give me a name?"

I sit still and stare at my hands.

"Fine. Have it your way." Mitnick opens the door to let my dad back into the room. He waits a few minutes and then sighs, "Ada Rose Lovelace, you are under arrest for computer fraud."

</THE "HARD DRIVE" TO NOWHERE>

THE ROAD TO HELL TAKES AN ETERNITY.

As we wind along the mountainous route toward ReBoot, I stare out the tinted window at the snow-capped mountains shaped like jagged teeth, threatening to chew me up and swallow me whole. This place is more remote than I expected. The Cascade Mountains are a little over an hour outside Seattle, yet it might as well be in another country, because I haven't seen a cell tower in miles.

Mom and Dad have been oddly quiet since our fight about ReBoot.

Dad thinks it will look good for the judge when I go to court in thirty days. And Mom thinks Dad's right.

The closer we get to ReBoot, the more Simone fills my thoughts.

When she first left for the rehab center, I assumed everything would be okay. That she would do her time and come back as the same person. She called me the night before she left. At the time, I remember her laughing like she was grounded from shopping or something. No big deal. She seemed more concerned about her spot in the Orwellians than her place in life. Simone promised to call as soon as she got out, but I never heard from her again. She didn't return any of my calls, emails, or texts. She shut me out, and I let her be. After all, I deserved the silent treatment. It was a huge mistake letting her take the fall for something I did too. At the time, I hoped it would all blow over.

But I'll never forget the look on Dad's face when he showed up at school to tell me Simone was gone. No note. No goodbye.

To this day, I can't imagine why she'd swallow a bunch of pills. I never found out what pushed her over the edge. Or why she didn't reach out to me for help. I can't help but think if I'd reached out first—done something to help her. Or, if I would have stepped up and owned my part, she'd still be here now.

It's my fault Simone is dead.

Tears blur my view. Every day I wish I could go back and do things differently. Unfortunately, there aren't many do-overs at sixteen.

Mom studies me with sad eyes. She clutches my hand. "Everything will be okay. You'll be back by Christmas."

I keep my face toward the window. "I don't know why we're doing this. Mitnick said it wouldn't matter."

"Well, let's hope he's wrong and that Judge Barron takes into account the fact that you volunteered for ReBoot's Tech Addiction program into consideration. For your sake . . . and mine." Dad cracks the window, letting cold air into the stuffy space. I sense him staring at the back of my head. "Ada-pie, I know this year has been hard on you, but you can't lash out because Simone is . . ." His voice trails off.

Mom jumps on the positive bandwagon. "—Maybe this can be a fresh start for you. All we want is for you to be happy."

Simone was happy. Full of life one day. Suddenly, she was dead after binging on antidepressants. Pills I didn't even know she took.

I watch the trees pass by as Dad accepts an incoming call. The sound of his voice buzzes in the background while Mom checks email on her iPhone.

Yet, I'm the one addicted to technology.

My breath fogs the window, blurring the world around me. Eventually, the paved road morphs into a narrow dirt lane, and the edge of the forest inches closer. I breathe deep, feeling caged. Online, there aren't any boundaries. No limits to where I can go. No dead ends. No roadblocks. Here, everywhere I go feels like a dead end.

Dad sighs. "Well, that was the office. SocialNet is taking the hack public. I have to give a statement."

Mom pats my hand. "Today?"

"Considering that my bill advocates technology privacy, I have to say something. Paul has assured me that Ada's name will remain confidential because she's under eighteen. SocialNet just wants some publicity."

The anguish in his voice snaps me out of my mood. I face my parents. "Sorry, Dad."

"I know, sweetie." He pats my hand a few times. "Let's just fix it."

I nod. Because Mitnick's right. A conviction would affect more than me. Because no matter what risks there are, Dad will always come to my defense, which will tear down his credibility and undermine the bill's success.

I pick up the ReBoot brochure lying next to me on the seat. Considering what Dad has to deal with, the least I can do is stop fighting him, whether I want to or not. The program agenda includes live action role-playing, team-building ropes courses, and caving exercises.

Sounds more like an extreme sports camp than a rehab.

I deserved ReBoot three months ago, and I deserve to go now. Pay my dues. My life is about to be reprogrammed. Maybe ReBoot has the answers I desperately need to move on.

Without Simone.

I brace myself as the driver slams on his brakes to creep across a rickety bridge. Below us, the angry river sloshes and roars in protest of the disturbance. Above us, thick, webbed branches hang down and claw at the top of the car. No matter where I look, I'm trapped.

After a few more turns, the suffocating vines and crowding bushes pull back to reveal a massive estate. Old cracked statues and frozen fountains decorate the dead lawn. Dead trees wave crooked fingers at guests as they come up the circular driveway. This place lacks serious curb appeal.

An HGTV nightmare.

Dad whistles. "ReBoot is bigger than I expected."

"And much more…*antique*," Mom adds.

No…antique is an old, beautiful chair scratched with memories. This place is straight-up creepy. Not the image on the brochure. Gotta love Photoshop.

The car circles around the U-shaped driveway and stops in front of the dingy peach mansion. The massive building is crowned with Victorian turrets, giving it a castle-looking appearance. I notice the empty windows. Maybe one was Simone's. A chill threads down my spine. I wonder if anyone here remembers her. Or, if they knows she's gone.

As soon as we stop, a regal-looking lady with short gray curls walks down the front steps, mimicking the Queen of England. Same stoic face. Same stiff posture. She's dressed in a long gray skirt from the 1800s that's wet at the bottom from sweeping the snow-covered ground. Her choking, high-buttoned blouse resembles one of Nana's tattered doilies. Don't know which is more "antique," the house or the boots this lady stole from the Wicked Witch of the West. I mean, who is this lady?

Unfortunately, my last-minute research on the rehab director didn't give me tons of information.

Ms. Irene Gay Matthews, age fifty-five going on sixty-five,

earned a master's degree in education from a local college and worked as a history teacher. She was married and divorced—twice. Once to her college sweetheart and then to a local businessman. Her second marriage produced a son, Phillip, who mysteriously died at the young age of sixteen. When her mother died, Irene inherited the entire estate. Last year, a large donation by an anonymous angel investor helped her kick-start the rehab center. Obviously some bajillionaire looking to clear his conscience before entering the Pearly Gates. Either that or a hefty tax write-off.

The spinster-looking lady approaches the car and smiles; yet behind her dark eyes, there's a strange coldness to her smile. As if any shred of joy only rests on top of the wrinkled surface. "I'm Ms. Matthews." She holds out her hand.

"Hi," I mumble and fiddle with my angel necklace. When Dad nudges me, I reach out and shake her Arctic-cold hand that could make a penguin shiver.

Ms. Matthews turns on one heel. "Follow me."

I take my first step into hell.

</TIME TO REBOOT>

I follow the Grim Reaper to my doom.

My parents and I walk up the stone steps and across the porch. The weakening boards creak under my feet like a horror movie cliché. Pretty sure someone will cue the spooky mist any moment.

I rub the necklace again, hoping it will somehow help me grow a new backbone.

Ms. Matthews spurts out a few boring facts about the estate. "This mansion was built in the late 1800s. It was my great-great-great-great-aunt's home and has been in my family for years."

She lost me at the second "great."

Ms. Matthews clasps her hands behind her back. "Her husband was a gunmaker. When he died, she got a large inheritance." Ms. Matthews clasps her hands in front. "A local psychic told her that all the people who were killed by her husband's guns were haunting her. So the owner started building this home, a place where the spirits could live. Construction continued for forty years until her death."

Sounds like a wacko to me.

"Why did you open ReBoot out here?" Mom asks, plastering on a politician's wife's smile. "It's an odd location."

Ms. Matthews keeps up the history lesson. "At ReBoot, our goal is to remove all outside distractions and transport kids to a simpler time. Without technology. Give them an idea of what it was like to live in the past, in a different era."

And she would know.

No wonder Simone was depressed after being here. She went crazy after thirty days. I've been here two minutes and am already pushing nutzo on the insanity meter.

I stop at the railing and stare at the pine trees guarding the perimeter of the property. Even though the sun still has a few hours, the sky seems darker today. There's something odd about this place. Something cold and . . . dead. I'm struck by the eerie silence. Not one bird chirps. Not one animal skitters. The only sound is a soft moan whispering a warning.

I rub the necklace again, thinking of her in this dark place. Maybe Simone sensed the same impending doom. Walked along the same cold path.

When we reach the front entrance, Ms. Matthews barricades the door with her stout body. "This is where you must say your goodbyes. We want to protect the identities of our children and minimize the number of adults in the building. For security purposes. I'm sure you understand."

Even though Mom appears uneasy, my parents quickly hug me and say all the things perfect parents say when they leave kids behind. "Be good," "Take care," and "Be safe." Before they duck into the car, Mom flashes me her "everything is fine" smile. Only I know it's not.

I'm not sure anything will ever be *fine* again.

I watch them drive away until the car disappears. Along with any hope I have of leaving this creepy place. Warped Sleepy Hollow trees wave their crooked fingers at me. The wind howls as it whips through the mountainside. This remote rehab is isolated in the wilderness of the Cascade Mountains during a nasty Washington winter.

If Bigfoot exists, he hangs out here. For sure.

Ms. Matthews drops her chilled smile. "We must go. We're already way off schedule."

The woman is even colder than her grip.

I follow her through two huge silver and bronze inlaid doors. Both slam shut behind me, echoing like the steel door of a jail cell. I grip both straps on my backpack and trudge behind her. The deeper we venture into the house, the colder it gets.

By the time we hit the second floor, I can no longer feel my toes. "Is it always this cold?"

"We don't have central air and heat," Ms. Matthews answers.

Neither do igloos, but they gotta be warmer than this tomb.

As we walk through the dark house, the elaborate security setup catches my attention. An alarm trilogy lock protects the entranceway. Small cameras guard every nook and cranny. Even the doors have technology panels on the outside, most likely connected to a computer network. We pass a security desk surrounded by rows of small screens, each one keeping an eye on every spot inside and outside. A man in uniform stands close by with a walkie-talkie clipped to his belt and a gun on his right hip.

"Why all the security?" I ask.

"Standard protection."

Yeah. Right. This stuff is definitely not standard. Bill Gates has less security than ReBoot.

A camera follows me when I pass. Someone's watching me already. Can't imagine how Simone felt walking these same halls. Oddly, I feel closer to her than I have in a long time, as if I could turn around and spot her standing there. Warning me. Telling me to run.

As we continue, I note the "antique" details, adding extra creep to the already super creepy. A huge gold chandelier hangs over my head. In addition to twelve white candles, a thirteenth one has been weirdly welded on one side. The wooden floor's busy mosaic patterns make me dizzy if I look for too long. In one dim corner, a picture of an old woman hangs on the wall. At second glance, the lady closely resembles Ms. Matthews. The eyes look disturbingly real. I half expect them to watch me, like every other *Scooby-Doo* episode.

The more we walk, the more I question the real story behind this place. A strange half-built, half-deserted mansion locked down in high-end security that keeps tech addicts locked in the past; something doesn't feel right.

However, the real Ghost Hunters would feel right at home.

Trailing a few feet behind Ms. Matthews, I shuffle by some doors. Each one is secured with a technology panel with an upgraded communication system that connects to a phone or computer network. Yet, each room we visit is crammed with uncomfortable parlor furniture, complete with stiff backs and sunken velvet cushions, and furniture that had been well-worn over the years. This is what the brochure meant by "a rich, antique setting" and "an interesting history."

A haunted house built in the 1800s by a wealthy old biddy who created it for apparitions that threatened their eternal revenge.

Ms. Matthews picks up the conversation where she left off. "Ada, do you know that in a recent study, teens who stayed plugged in for long periods showed signs of serious depression?"

Every cell in my body stiffens. "I'm not depressed."

"Depressed people don't know they're depressed, dear." Ms. Matthews eyes my wrist braces and points. "This is our physical therapy center to rehabilitate the physical symptoms caused by technology abuse. For example, carpal tunnel."

I force my eyes not to roll. In this place, technology is somehow physically debilitating and a small "byte" has become deadly.

Ms. Matthews leads me to her office where she swipes a security card.

I step even farther back in time.

In one corner, a piano self-plays old music in the corner. A roll of paper spins as the keys bounce up and down to the notes—a true ghost concerto. A horror movie set couldn't decorate this place any better. Maybe this wacko is maxing out the Creepy Factor to scare us into submission. On the other side of the room, a scratched-up desk holds a black rotary phone, a stubby melted candlestick, and plume pen and ink set. Old family portraits trapped by tacky gold frames decorate the ugly green and white walls.

Bookshelves line the room, each decorated with bundles of antique knowledge and a layer of dust. I note the book subjects: child psychology, the harms of technology, and historical biographies. When I slide out a thick leather edition of *The History of American Mansions,* a flashing light in the wall catches my eye. The signs of a modem.

I hide my smile. I'm not as far from "home" as I thought.

After returning the book to its nook, I point to the over-stuffed wooden filing cabinets. "Wouldn't it be easier if you stored information on a computer? Gives you more space."

Ms. Matthews grins as if she's privy to my master plan. "We don't keep computers on site. Too tempting for our *guests.*"

I nod. "Good point."

And her first lie.

</THE CENTRAL PROCESSING UNIT (CPU)>

In my experience, one lie is the first in a string of many.

I crack a few fingers to ease my anticipation and excitement. That little beacon of light gives me important information. This lady's hiding hardware in here, somewhere.

And like a hound dog, I will sniff it out.

"Time to detox." Ms. Matthews pulls out a cardboard box for my possessions. She crosses out a previous name and writes mine on the front in permanent black marker. As if I'll be here forever.

"What do you mean?" I ask.

"To be admitted, you have to give up all your technology." She points to earbuds hanging around my neck. "Let's start with those."

I clutch the thin cords. "And if I don't?"

"Then I notify the judge, and your probation is revoked. You go to jail." Ms. Matthews raises her thin eyebrows. "What's it going to be?"

"Fine," I mumble because there's no other choice. I wrap the earphones up into a ball and drop them into the box. "What's the replacement for World of Warcraft? A dangerous game of Battleship?"

She ignores my snarky comment and holds out her hand, waiting for me to surrender my security blanket. "You'll need to give me your bag."

My heart drops. I knew this place confiscated technology, but I didn't know the extent. I death grip the straps, my knuckles white. "Why?"

Ms. Matthews flashes a crazed look, eyes wild. "I'm required to make sure you have no items of a technical nature on your person." She tugs on my backpack. Hard.

Busted. I knew I couldn't have technology here, but I wasn't about to leave Zed at home, unattended. Not with Mitnick circling like a vulture. Zed is safer here with Ms. Matthews than at home.

For a minute, I consider playing a useless game of tug of war, hoping to keep a shred of my privacy and online access. Instead, I surrender and let go.

Ms. Matthews opens the bag and slides out my laptop. Her eyes bulge as if she's uncovered a murder weapon. "I'm surprised you have the nerve to bring this here." Then she disrespectfully drops Zed into my box along with my calculator, extra flash drives, and digital camera. She also tosses in a mechanical pencil hiding in the bottom along with some old gum and change.

"Are we allowed pencil sharpeners, or do I gnaw the end until it's sharp again?"

"Very funny." She scoffs and points to my wrist. "Your watch."

I unclasp the strap and hand it to her, wondering if she noticed the Bluetooth capability.

As Ms. Matthews is closing the box, I tuck my angel wing necklace inside my shirt. My sanity hinges on keeping possession of this one little drive. I need this necklace like I need water.

Hopefully, she doesn't resort to a full-on strip search.

She picks up a piece of paper. "In case you have something else, here's a list of the items we forbid."

No iPods or MP3 players, digital cameras or video recorders, computers, game consoles, Bluetooth devices, eReaders, or iBangles. Access to limited TV and limited music. Absolutely no cell phones!!!

Out of habit, I pat my back pocket where my phone is stored.

Ms. Matthews holds out her hand and wiggles her fingers like little worms.

All of Simone's messages are saved on this phone. And I've never gone a day without listening to one of them. My heart drums in my chest. Then I remind myself why I'm here. I slide out my phone and drop it on the table.

"You can call your family on Sunday nights." Ms. Matthews points to a huge bulky phone that holds the caller hostage with a stationary mouthpiece.

I stare at the phone's mangled cord, twisted and curled from all the talkers fighting for freedom. An imaginary noose squeezes my throat. The room spins and my body teeters as if I'm standing on a high ledge and the height is messing with my brain.

Coming here, I expected to lose all of this stuff, but I wasn't prepared for how sickened I'd feel. Every link to my world is severed. Hacked in two. No connection. I'm cut off from everything—and everyone—I know.

And for the first time, I'm off the grid.

"I don't feel good." I grip the back of a chair with both hands and breathe deep. Each exhale skitters out unevenly while my vision blurs.

"It will pass." Ms. Matthews waves me off.

If Simone couldn't handle this place, how the hell am I going to?

My neck feels hot. "I don't belong here."

"Ada, you must have a problem if your parents doled out the hefty tuition." She flips through my file as if she's speed-reading a boring novel. "According to their questionnaire, you spend ten hours a day on your computer, your grades have declined, and you have no friends."

I shrug. "I have friends."

"SocialNet and Second Life do not count." Then she sneers as if she knows a secret. "Unfortunately, your only friend, Simone, died due to her addiction because she left ReBoot too early. Do you want to end up like her?"

"Excuse me?" I eye her, stunned by her insensitive comment.

Or is it a threat?

"I told her she wasn't ready to leave, but she was only required to do thirty days. It obviously got to her. She didn't stay clean for more than a day."

I shake my head. "That doesn't make any sense."

Ms. Matthews slaps the folder shut. "Denial is a common symptom of an addiction. You're here because you have a problem. And it is my job to get you through the program successfully or you might be sentenced to something far worse."

To avoid a lecture, I cave. "Yes, ma'am."

"Good, then let's get you settled. Come with me." I follow Ms. Matthews out of the office. "Wait here while I grab your schedule."

I stand in the empty hall, with the sudden urge to sleep. Then I hear muffled voices down the hall. I follow the sound into a room with stiff chairs facing an old TV.

The CEO of SocialNet, Mr. Gary Host, perches at a table with a moderator and my dad, discussing technology. Gary's dressed down in a navy hoodie and jeans. If he didn't shave his head, he'd look much younger than twenty-eight. The newscaster and my dad are both primped and sporting full three-piece suits.

The moderator jumps into the topic of internet privacy for teens.

Gary smiles a boyish grin. "Within five years, SocialNet has become the fastest growing technology company in the nation with the goal of expanding internationally. We are a teen-only site and have millions of teen users from the United States—all under the age of eighteen. We provide a safe place where teens can meet online and socialize. A place where they can let their guard down and get personal without worrying about adults barging in. We are their locked virtual basement, and parents are not allowed."

The crowd laughs.

Dad leans in. "Yes, but how do you ensure and protect the privacy of your teen users? How do you ensure that adults stay off the site? Can't anyone open an account and lie?"

"No, actually." Gary leans back casually. "Our security protocol during registration requires a Social Security number so we check to make sure each user is a legit teen. This keeps away adults as well as dummy or duplicate accounts. We are still working through the process of using international identifiers when we expand to continue the safety measures we already have in place."

Dad's eyes grow wide. He clasps his hands on the table. "So you have millions of Social Security numbers in your system? That's critical data, isn't it?"

Gary shrugs off the comment. "Yes, but we only use it for security measures to ensure a teen-only site. This is what gives our youth a safe and secure platform where they can be more open and vulnerable—a place where they can let down their guard, make more connections. Without having to worry about who is watching."

Dad maintains his composure. "And what do you do with all the data you collect online?"

"At this time, we do not use the data for any other purpose."

The crowd claps.

"At this time?" Dad says, "Isn't it only a matter of time before you collect more data and sell it to companies?"

"That is not in our plan," Gary replies, looking confident and calm. "We've recently added new privacy settings so if teens want, they can choose to keep their account information private. But it's their choice. As you know, we certainly can't force teens to do something they don't want to do."

The audience laughs again.

Dad pinches his lips together. "Maybe you can address the rumor that SocialNet's privacy settings are not that upfront. The default is that the personal information is open to anyone, no matter what the settings are. Kinda creepy."

Gary shifts in his seat, appearing frazzled. "That is exactly as you said—a rumor."

This time Dad shrugs. "Well, it won't matter soon. My Teen Technology Privacy Bill—the TTPV Bill—will write into law that companies may not access, collect, or sell a minor's information without parental consent. All teen accounts in any company would be automatically protected, and that includes social sites like yours. The bill would also have a retroactive clause, which means—if passed—companies would be required to purge any and all personal data they have already collected. We would also put punishments in place for those who abuse the new law." Dad smiles at Gary. "It's not personal, of course."

"It'll never happen." Gary shakes his head. "And, instead of worrying about protecting teens, shouldn't we be more worried about protecting companies against teens? Did you know that in Great Britain, the average age of a hacker is only seventeen? They start at thirteen with their game consoles. For example, the Orwellians are rumored to be a group of teen hackers who recently tried to hack SocialNet's network. So, why are we trying to protect teens when they don't respect privacy—for themselves or others?"

"Well, Gary, hacking is a whole other topic." Dad pats the

newscaster on the back. Poor guy hasn't been able to get a word in for several minutes. "And, a whole other show. Right, Tim?"

Tim nods with a weak grin, obviously overwhelmed with the heated conversation.

"Right." Gary says. "So are you saying your teen daughter's privacy—her name's Ada, right?—is more important than a company's protection against teen hackers?"

I freeze and study Gary's face, wondering why he mentioned me. Does he know I was the SocialNet hacker?

"That's ridiculous." Dad's jaw flexes. I can tell he's angry at the mention of my name. I wait for him to crack, but to his credit, he remains poised, except for a lone bead of sweat rolling along his hairline. "Of course I don't approve of hackers—at any age. But this show is about teen privacy on the internet. And I'm working to protect those rights— including my daughter's. So why don't we stay on the real issue?"

Gary Host doesn't say any more as they break for commercial. The noose tightens around my neck. I'm worried it's just a matter of time until someone discovers where I am and questions why. My only chance at redemption and anonymity is to finish this program and clear my record. Fast.

"Sometimes we hurt the ones we love." Ms. Matthews startles me.

I wonder how much she knows.

She hands me a schedule. "This is your daily routine. Make sure you follow it."

I study the list that includes morning inspections, chores, communication classes, group meetings, and daily exercise. "Is this boot camp or rehab?" I mutter.

Ms. Matthews straightens the pens on her desk until they line up in a perfect row. "Miss Lovelace, if you continue with the attitude, there will be consequences. Understood?"

A masked threat or just a suggestion? I'm not sure.

I nod. "Yes, ma'am"

"Good. The next step is to get you more socialized."

"What does that mean?" I ask.

She holds up a ring of keys larger than a prison warden could dream of and heads out into the musty-smelling hall. "It means you have a roommate."

I skip next to her to keep up. "I was under the impression I'd have a private room."

"You were wrong," Ms. Matthews grunts.

I slump along after her down the dimly lit hallway. An indecisive bulb blinks on and off, giving off the strange illusion that we're really in an insane asylum.

Ms. Matthews stops in front of a pine-colored door. The number 66 hangs at an angle.

I stare at my personal gateway to hell and prepare to share my personal space with a complete stranger.

Probably the Devil himself.

</TO FRIEND OR UNFRIEND>

Roommates are like family.

You have to live with them, and they're usually crazy.

"After you." Ms. Matthews opens the door. The room is tiny with two single beds. An old shaggy gray rug, which must be a health code violation, covers the scratched floor. Crooked pictures of proper old ladies and hunting dogs hang on the wall, sure to eye me while I sleep.

When I walk in, a redheaded girl tosses a grocery bag under her bed. She looks all wide-eyed and presses one finger to her lips, pleading for my silence. Her bubblegum-pink sweat suit stands out against the drab furnishings.

Ms. Matthews remains in the hall, refusing to cross the threshold. Maybe she's a vampire, which would explain a lot. She dresses like an old lady spinster from the past and is out for blood. "Ada Lovelace, meet Becca Stevens. She's been with us a while, so she can get you acclimated." She spouts off my itinerary for the day.

Before I can ask questions, she closes the door.

I walk over to my bed and bounce on the edge, testing the mattress. Hard and stiff. Not comfortable unless you were . . . let's say . . . *a vampire*. No doubt the mattress has been here since the beginning of time.

Gross.

Becca drags the hidden bag out from under her bed and empties it on her lacy bedspread. Chocolate and assorted candies bounce across the flowered cover. She unwraps a treat and pops it into her mouth. "Please don't tell Ms. Matthews about my sugar stash. She controls our addictions by insisting on a caffeine-free, sugar-free, and nicotine-free environment. Total drag."

Becca opens a huge jar filled with tiny foil balls. She balls up the empty chocolate wrapper and drops it into the sea of colored pellets.

I study her stash. "Then how did you get all this?"

"Sorry. Can't reveal my source." Becca fiddles with another wrapper, twisting it into a circle. She slips on the foil ring and holds her hand up to the light so the ring sparkles. "But I'm happy to get you something."

Some rehab. "I'm good for now. Thanks though." I slip off the wrist braces and toss them on the bed.

"You say that now. But after a few days offline, you'll be begging me for a *kiss*." Becca pops a Hershey's Kiss in her mouth. She immediately unwraps a different chocolate and says, "Your beauty is not skin deep."

Totally confused, I ask, "What do you mean?"

"Oh, I was just reading the message inside." She holds up the shiny wrapper. "Chocolate plus inspiration. Total bonus."

I can only stare, speechless. Becca's a cacao addict, same as Simone. It's as if my best friend has stepped into the room with me. I'm worried if I blink, she'll be gone again.

"Here. Have this," Simone said. "Chocolate makes everything better."

"Sweets can't help me pass a test." I took the chocolate and ate it. "It's just gonna makes me fat."

Simone ate her third piece in five minutes. "Chocolate has zero calories."

I laughed. "In your imaginary world. But in the real world, I'm trying to quit."

"Well, I'm never giving up chocolate because I'm no quitter." Simone said. *"Not now, not ever…"*

Only Simone did quit…on life.

My lungs clog up again. I head to the window for some fresh air. When I pull back the lace drapes, iron bars cover the window. The stupid thing doesn't open. I stand in front of the window etched in webbed glass. A battalion of trees line up along the edge of the field, like little soldiers guarding a prison. I shake out my hands. Wish I could jump into Cyberland. Escape from this strange place.

I pace in a small circle before sitting down. My legs bounce. For being such a big mansion, this room grows smaller by the minute. There's no room to move. No room to breathe. After a few seconds, the panic builds again. I jump back up to my feet and lap the room a few more times before glancing at the clock.

Only two minutes have passed since I last looked.

"Withdrawal sucks, doesn't it?" Becca reads another wrapper. "Sometimes you gotta jump and fall…instead of standing still. Well, who am I to ignore good advice?"

Becca stands on her bed and motions for me to move.

I barely clear her airspace before she flips off the bed. When she nails the landing, her arms shoot up in the air, as if she's waiting to be scored. Then she grins big. "I was a cheerleader."

"I see." No surprise there, especially since "SPIRIT" is embroidered in large white letters across her caboose. Not the best place for a message of any kind.

My rehab roomie is a peppy cheerleader with a sweet tooth who takes advice from inspirational quotes and tames OCD tendencies by folding foil.

"Last year, I made the SLCS cheerleading team. We have over three thousand members now. Makes for a tough practice."

This girl thinks her online cheer squad in Second Life is real.

Before I can ask any questions, she bounces on to the next topic like a flea at a kennel club. While she chatters in the background, my head starts to pound. Too much information, too fast. This girl has said more in five minutes than I think in five days.

I try and tune her out. Simone chattered incessantly too, filling in conversation gaps. Silence made her antsy. The more Becca talks, the more she reminds me of Simone. Forty percent perky, forty percent dark with twenty percent mystery. I can't help but soften a little. This girl somehow brightens this dreary place with her peppy chats and her Pepto-Bismol-pink threads.

I want to ask her about Simone, see if she knew her. But first, I need to relax and attempt to fit in. "So, why are you here?"

Becca flops on her stomach, propping her chin on her hands. "I spent waaaay too much time on social media, especially SocialNet. But who can blame me, right? That Host guy is the youngest sextillionaire in the world. A hottie in a hoodie."

Or a jerk. "A sextillionaire?"

"Twenty-one zeros, but the *sex* part is funny." Becca giggles and flips onto her back. "Did you know SocialNet has millions of teens? It's a huge prom party and everyone is invited, twenty-four seven."

"Impressive." Talking about SocialNet makes me itchy.

I know even more than she does. SocialNet has twenty million teen users, 50 percent of all teens in the US. They also utilize thousands of servers across ten server farms, manage over one hundred terabytes a day, host billions of photos each hour, and hide thousands of admin files in protected databases.

I chew on my necklace, not knowing how to respond. "How long are you here?"

"I'm almost done." She eats another piece of candy and hides her bag again. "How about you? What's your poison?"

I stiffen. Computers will be obsolete before I hand over any 411. Careful not to give any clues, I throw out the shortest answer I can without being rude. Becca will appreciate my Twitter version. "Hacking."

"I think Fisher's in here for that. Raven too." Before I can ask their screen names to see if I know them online, Becca jumps to her feet. "Time for dinner. You coming?"

"If you don't mind, I'm going to turn in early. It's been a long day."

She grabs a sweater. "Oh sure. I'll make sure you're up in the morning."

Once she leaves, I relish the quiet. I'm so tired, but my eyelids feel as if they've been Super Glued open. My mind is wired, and my body is still buzzing on adrenaline.

I hardly sleep that night.

I miss my bed, I miss my parents, I miss Simone.

But mostly because Becca snores.

</A STRANGE "SOCIAL NETWORK">

The next morning, I wake to a loud voice. "Inspection!"

I jolt upright in bed, still half asleep. I throw back the warm covers and jump up. My feet touch the cold floor. Shivering, I hop in place to prevent frostbite from attacking my toes.

Ms. Matthews stands in the center of the room, tapping the clipboard with her pen. "Miss Lovelace. Did you forget the schedule?"

"Sorry." I rub my eyes and focus on Becca, who's standing at the foot of her bed in a purple track suit. She's obviously been up for some time because she's already showered, styled, and shellacked in makeup.

Ms. Matthews rattles off my violations. "Your clothes are on the floor and bed is unmade. Extra thirty minutes on dish duty, Miss Lovelace."

As soon as she leaves, I snatch my jeans and hop from one foot to the other, yanking them on. Then I wrestle with my sheets to find the missing socks that slid off during the night.

"You're obviously a morning person," I mumble as I bang around the room.

Becca pouts her shiny lips. "Sorry. I'm not used to having a roomie."

After slipping on a black long-sleeve T-shirt and jeans, I head to breakfast. Kids scurry down the stairs like rats through a sewer, practically clambering over each other. By the time Becca and I enter the small kitchen, the line for fake eggs and burnt toast is too long. I beeline for the sugary cereal bar and load up on a bowl of cinnamon and brown sugar topped with a dash of oatmeal.

The checkout woman wearing a hair net swipes a card through the register, no doubt logging every item on my plate.

I eat in silence, but Becca talks the whole time. Then she squeals, "Jinkies, we gotta go!"

I shoot to my feet, still half asleep. "Where to?"

She points to the old cuckoo clock. "We have ten minutes 'til Group or Ms. Matthews will go nuts."

I study my schedule. "It's not listed on mine."

"Maybe Ms. Matthews expected you to come with me. But hurry up. If we're late, we have to sing something from Mr. Anthony's approved-song list. Trust me, you don't want that. His favorite singer is Barry Manilow."

"Okay," I can't help but smile. "Do I need to bring anything?"

"A thick skin wouldn't hurt." Becca zips up her hoodie and grabs her journal covered in candy pictures. A braided foil bookmark hangs out of the worn pages. "Oh yeah, and your *feeling* words. Mr. Anthony always tells us to bring those."

Becca grabs my hand and drags me through the crowd. She greets everyone like she's a party host. I keep my head down to avoid any conversation and follow her lead. If I look anyone in the eyes, it'll be an open door to talk. Or worse, share.

Downstairs, we get out of the bustle and into a private

room. A man and small group of kids sit in a circle. Calming instrumental music plays overhead and a few candles burn on a table. In this place, it's probably Loco for Cocoa.

Becca skips into the room and plops down in a chair. "Hey, Mr. Anthony."

"Hello, Becca." A young Richard Gere flips a wave. His distressed Diesel jeans and edgy boots make him look much hipper than the other counselors dressed in boring khakis and deck loafers. My new counselor balances his chair on two legs. "You must be Ada Lovelace. Please have a seat."

I grab the empty spot next to him. This reminds me of kindergarten—the dreaded circle time. Seems a little strange, but this is my life for the next thirty days. I take note of each kid in the room. Besides the peppy girl, we also have a punk chick, a goth boy, and some shy little boy who can't be much older than ten.

Mr. Anthony lowers his chair. "Guys, say hello to our new group buddy...Ada."

Becca sings her words like we did in preschool. "Hiii, Adaaa."

A strange girl with spiky pink-and-black hair studies me. The other kids avoid looking directly at me, which actually makes me relax. Thank God for normal computer geeks with antisocial behaviors.

Now I feel right at home.

"Come on, guys." Mr. Anthony crosses his arms. "Let's all introduce ourselves properly."

I pray I don't go first. My idea of "friendly" is being the first avatar to IM in a private chat room.

Becca's hand blasts into the air. "I'll go first! I'm Becca Adler and I'm addicted to social networking. I'm here because I did not follow SocialNet's posting terms and conditions. I love cheering and Jackie Chan movies. Oh yeah, and, of course, anything chocolate." She winks at me. "Oh, and Ada is my new roomie."

I can't help but smile. I bet this girl sweats glitter.

The grunge boy mutters and clinks something around in his pocket. "Who cares?"

"Great, who's next?" Mr. Anthony stares at the others, waiting for a volunteer. He stops at the pink-haired girl. "Raven?"

The punk girl rolls her doll-blue eyes rimmed in thick black eyeliner. She mumbles when she talks. "I'm Raven. I'm here because I got busted for hacking into a hotel."

The goth boy in the peanut gallery scoffs again. "Raven didn't just hack a hotel. She gained access to all the key cards. They caught her roaming through Harry Stile's penthouse suite."

Holy crap. I bet one hundred bucks Raven is Tweety Bird.

"Shut up!" Raven barks abruptly, practically spitting fire.

I draw back at the outburst and try not to make eye contact. Every hacker knows the infamous Hyatt hack. After the source code was posted publicly, the Hyatt had no choice but to reprogram the chain's entire security system, affecting more than four million rooms. Tweety Bird fell off the grid after that hack made the papers.

Now I know where she landed.

Anticipation pumps through me. This girl cannot make the connection between the Dark Angel and me. She probably knows DA's work. Because I know hers.

Raven fiddles with a long, multicolored string and eyes me. "You got a problem?"

I glance around to confirm I'm the target for her dagger eyes. "Who? Me?"

She squints. "Yeah. You're staring."

Before I can answer, Becca blurts out, "I'm in the mood for a sandwich."

Raven re-aims her loaded gaze and fires. "We don't need a minute-by-minute status. It only reminds us of how boring you are." Then she holds up the string design. "Done. Two dinosaurs in sixteen seconds."

Becca shrugs. "Like *that's* more exciting."

Raven lets the pattern fall. "Watch it, Becky."

"For the umpteenth time, it's Bec-CA!"

Oh boy. This is going to be a looong month.

"Enough guys. This is not a productive way to spend our time." Mr. Anthony points to the small skinny kid with a notepad resting in his lap. "Crash. Your turn."

The little boy looks like he shopped at a Big and Tall store. His oversized cargo pants and T-shirt swallow his bony frame. If I didn't know this place was solely for teens, I'd swear he was twelve.

He tears off a piece of paper and writes a note with one of those small bowling pencils.

The strange guy who outed Raven's history grumbles, "This is so stupid."

While we're all waiting, I can't help but discreetly eye the goth guy. He's removed from the circle and appears ready for battle, decked out in a leather trench cloak, black combat boots, and dark sunglasses. His jet-black hair parts straight down the middle and skims his shoulders.

If Judd Nelson and Keanu Reeves had a baby, this would be their firstborn.

Instead of paying attention, the guy stares at the ceiling, chewing on a toothpick, with his left foot propped up on his right knee. His hand is in his pocket clinking around with something, probably coins.

While Crash struggles to imitate a preteen, this guy must be hurtling twenty.

Crash hands his paper to Mr. Anthony.

Mr. Anthony reads the note and appears disappointed. "Crash, it's been a year since you spoke, so I want your mom to see progress on Family Day."

Shut the firewall! Crash hasn't spoken in a year? And if

he's been here that long, he must have known Simone. Unfortunately, he's not talking anytime soon.

When he passes the paper to me, I study the note, written in a standard email format.

From: Crash
To: Mr. Anthony
Subject: Introduction

My name's Crash and I'm a programmer. My mom sent me here because I was on my computer too much. Making and testing video games.

The frail boy creates circles along the dusty floor with the toe of his tennis shoe.

Becca crushes Crash with her hug like he's her long-lost teddy bear. He either doesn't pull away or can't. "Crash isn't *just* a programmer. He's an *amazing* programmer. He can code anything in any language."

Crash cracks a thread of a smile. This kid is probably the typical programmer—quiet, withdrawn, isolated. I bet he could program a *Star Wars* text adventure on a TI-84 calculator. Count to one hundred in binary numbers. The kind of programmer who teaches hackers everything they know.

"Who cares," Keanu's twin mumbles again, obviously annoyed with Becca's constant commentary.

Mr. Anthony shifts his attention. "Andrew? Can you join the group please instead of heckling from the sidelines?"

The guy rips off his sunglasses, revealing Siberian husky eyes. I assumed his eyes were as black as his soul appears. "It's. Not. Andrew. It's. *Varian.* King of the Alliance. And I'm wrongfully stuck in this hellhole for an *alleged* addiction to virtual gaming." He makes quote marks with his fingers when he says both A words.

I nod to acknowledge the introduction. Definitely don't want to ignore this guy, he seems unstable.

Mr. Anthony displays lines of frustration across his forehead. "Do you remember our healthy debate about World of Warcraft? Or WoW as you call it. King Varian is a *character*."

Varian shakes his head violently. Almost makes me dizzy watching. "Wrong. I had my name legally changed before I got thrown into this crappy joint."

I may hide behind the hacker persona of Dark Angel, but this guy believes he's King Varian, leader of the Alliance, and a gamer unplugged from reality.

Mr. Anthony nods once. "Fine. I'll call you *Varian*, but you have to join the circle, deal?"

"Affirmative." Varian loudly scrapes his chair across the room until he's almost in the circle.

WoW is right.

Before anyone can mutter more crazy talk, a cute guy rushes through the door and slides into the last empty seat. He's super tall and lean with purposely messy blond hair. He looks put together in a low-maintenance way in a vintage tee and tan Adidas. Probably just escaped from an Abercrombie & Fitch ad.

His look is topped off with an overtly coy expression and a three-day stubble. The only accessory out of place is the tortoise-shell glasses.

A hot techie geek. A rare breed, practically extinct.

"Fisher, nice of you to join us." Mr. Anthony smiles and holds up a piece of paper. "You know the drill, buddy. Hope you've been practicing in the shower."

Fisher messes with his bedhead and groans. "Aw come on, Mr. A. Cut me some slack." Then he notices me and raises his eyebrows. "Well, hello."

"Stop stalling, Romeo." Mr. Anthony slaps the song list into Fisher's hand. "Choose wisely."

I pinch back a smile. Can't wait to see how this works out.

Fisher checks out the titles. "No offense but these tunes blow."

Varian rolls his eyes. "Your *singing* blows even more."

"Yeah? And what's your talent...*Andrew*?" Fisher snaps back.

"It's King Varian! My talent is that I'm the only member of the Alliance who's reached level ninety with no kills."

I admit that is impressive.

Fisher circles one finger next to his head. "Your talent...is playing with marbles. Though you've already lost a few." He points to Varian's pocket, explaining the clinking noise.

I hold back a smirk for fear that King Varian will have his imaginary warriors hunt down my WoW character out of revenge.

Mr. Anthony interjects before the gamer's fuse explodes. "Varian, chill out. And Fisher, stop egging him on. Let's get on with it; we don't have all day."

"Yes, sir." Fisher salutes and starts rapping.

> *"Load it, check it, quick—rewrite it.*
> *Plug it, play it, burn it, rip it,*
> *Drag and drop it, zip—unzip it."*

I can't believe what I'm hearing. It's a bad episode of *GLEE*. Only Varian's right; Fisher sucks. And he couldn't care less. When he slaps his leg in a hoedown dance, I cover my face, embarrassed for him.

Becca squeals and claps along. Even Crash taps one foot to the off-beat.

The attention fuels Fisher's performance. He beatboxes badly for a few bars and keeps singing,

> *"View it, code it, jam—unlock it.*
> *Surf it, scroll it, pause it, click it,*
> *Cross it, crack it, switch—update it."*

Mr. Anthony raises his voice. "That's enough!"

Fisher freezes with his hand on his crotch in a Michael Jackson pose. "What's wrong?"

The counselor places his hands on his hips. "As much as I love Daft Punk, 'Technologic' is not an approved song. And inappropriate, considering the words."

"Really?" Fisher studies the paper. "Because I swear I saw it."

Mr. Anthony snatches the list out of Fisher's hands. "Follow the rules or Ms. Matthews will kick you out faster than you can spell Daft Punk."

Fisher sits down and Mr. Anthony faces me. "Ada, why don't you tell us why you chose ReBoot?"

Tears threaten to spring forward, and I frown at the counselor.

Let's see. Where should I start? That I hate being a senator's daughter? Or should I talk about getting in trouble because I hacked SocialNet and obviously made some stupid mistake? Or maybe I say I didn't *choose* to be here. I *have* to be here. Stuck in the same horrible place where my best friend spent the last month of her life before she killed herself.

When I glance up, the whole group is gawking at me.

Then I realize I just said all that...out loud.

Becca grabs my hand. "You're so honest."

"Or stupid," Varian mutters.

"You hacked SocialNet?" Raven asked.

"Badass!" Fisher says.

I'm not sure what to say or what happened. I didn't want the group to know any of that stuff. I'm usually more careful than that. Already losing my mojo.

Mr. Anthony appears stunned. "Well...thank you for sharing...so much, Ada. I must admit, all of that information was not in your file."

Before he can go on, a loud alarm echoes through the building.

Mr. Anthony claps loudly. "All right, you know the drill. Let's go."

I jump up, wondering what's going on, and follow the group. We head back to the main house where other rehabbers are already gathering. I study all the misfit kids. Some have blank expressions while others cover their ears. Several whisper to each other, but I can't hear anything they're saying over the 100-decibel alarm.

I move next to Becca and nudge her. "Did something happen?"

Varian overhears me and barks, "Well, it's not the freakin' dinner bell."

With tears in her eyes, Becca clutches Crash's hand and whispers, "This means someone else is dead."

</PEER TO PEER (PTP) CHAT>

Ms. Death saunters into the room.

The chill factor plummets with her.

"We've had another technology victim." Ms. Matthews clasps both hands behind her back and circles the room. Each time she turns, the long skirt curls around her feet. She makes eye contact with Mr. Anthony, who nods his approval.

She clears her throat. "What we do here is very serious. Technology is not a game that can be played without severe consequences. Let's repeat the mantra together and remember why we're here…and why we mustn't leave too soon."

All the kids chant in unison:

> *"I use technology.*
> *Technology does not use me.*
> *Without boundaries, I can lose control.*
> *A life that can lead to death."*

I scan the room, confused about what the hell is going on.

Ms. Matthews continues, "Mr. Sabitini was a smart kid. But sometimes even the brightest ones don't make it."

"Oh God," Becca interrupts. "It's William."

Ms. Matthews scowls at Becca's outburst. "I told William he wasn't ready, but a false sense of control is common in addicts. Gaining control of your life is critical to re-entering society. And if you leave before I say you are ready . . ." She stops moving and her eyes land on me. ". . . You will fail."

I avoid her gaze, but her sharp words stab me in the gut. Maybe I'm already a lost cause.

After Ms. Matthews leaves, the buzz grows louder in the room. Mr. Anthony pulls us aside. "I'll go see if I can get more details." He cups Becca's shoulder. "I know this is very upsetting."

We stand in a silent clump like a herd of sleeping sheep.

Becca whimpers softly. Everyone else stares at the ground.

"Can someone tell me what's going on?" I look at each person in the circle, waiting for an answer.

Raven speaks first. "This isn't the first time someone has died after they left ReBoot."

"Suspicious if you ask me," Varian says.

"How many?" I ask.

"Four." Fisher leans against the wall and props his foot up like a flamingo.

"But they were all because of technology," Becca explains. "First, there was Johnny. They said he was buying computer parts on the black market."

"No, he was *shot*," Varian clarifies. "Doesn't anyone think that's a little strange?"

"He was in some crack house," Fisher barks back. "What do you expect?"

Varian scowls. "Yeah, then what about Chelsea?"

Becca sniffs and pulls out a hanky. "She ran her car into a tree going one hundred miles per hour. Ms. Matthews said she was texting."

Varian flips his hair. "I've texted tons of times and you don't see me kissing a tree trunk."

Becca snaps back, her eyes moist. "Why do you have to be so insensitive?"

"Look. Don't get in my grill." Varian puffs up. "Death is death. Part of life."

"Gee, that's profound. Thanks." Fisher drops his head back, exasperated. "Watching 1,000 elves die in a WoW battle is pretend. We're talking real kids here. You know there's a difference, right?"

"I know about death. Trust me!" Varian shouts at the top of his lungs. Everyone in the room turns and stares.

I retreat two steps to clear his explosion zone. "Why does Ms. Matthews sound an alarm?"

"To warn us," Becca answers. "Ms. Matthews wants us to know who crashes, especially if they leave the program."

"Ah, man, you believe that bullshit?" Varian laughs crazily. "Unbelievable."

"Leave her alone, Andrew." Fisher says. This time, Varian doesn't yell back. Instead, he balls up both fists. The gamer obviously battles on the front lines of insanity.

Becca wipes her tears. "Poor William. Ms. Matthews says our addiction controls us. If we leave before we are rehabilitated, we freak out, triggering depression, anxiety, and anger. Makes us do careless things. Or bad things to ourselves."

"Jesus Christ." Varian pretends to hit his head against the wall. "Kill me now."

"You said there were four. Who's the fourth one?" I ask.

"You should know." Raven answers quickly. "You are... were Simone's friend, right?"

Her words catch me off guard. "What'd you say?" If my thoughts were daggers, she'd be sliced to shreds by now.

Raven shrugs. "But I recognize your name—Ada Lovelace. Simone's friend."

All the kids study me with renewed interest.

I swallow. "You knew her? How was she in here?"

Varian whistles. "The girl was too mouthy in my opinion. But she was hot. Wasn't she, Fish Boy?"

Fisher shifts uncomfortably. "Shut up, Andrew."

I analyze his mood shift, wondering if he and Simone hooked up. "Did you guys hear what happened?"

"We hear about all of them," Raven says. "Ms. Matthews makes sure of that."

Becca touches my arm. "I'm so sorry, Ada. I thought she was nice."

I shake off her pity and set her straight. "Thanks. Anyway, Simone's death was different than these other ones. It wasn't an accident. And we don't know why she . . . did it to herself."

"We heard she hacked into ReBoot after she left and got busted again." Raven says all this crap with a flippant tone. Like it's nothing.

"The girl had guts, I'll give her that," Fisher adds.

"Guts but no brains. Who does that when they leave rehab?" Varian says. "At least wait a week for the heat to cool."

I want to punch Varian in the face for his jackass comment but hold back. If this is true, I need to find out more. I've never heard any story of Simone hacking ReBoot. "How do you know that?"

"Ms. Matthews said she reported Simone to the Feds." Raven plays with her string. "She said Simone couldn't handle the consequences of her actions."

Becca flashes me a sad look. "Evidently, Simone killed herself before they could arrest her."

"No. She wouldn't do that." I wrap my arms around my waist, holding myself together. My parents haven't seen me cry in months, so I can't lose it here after a couple hours.

"Ada, I'm sorry." Becca touches my shoulder. "We were all upset about Simone when we heard."

"Thanks." But I stiffen under the sympathetic gesture as

my confusion morphs into anger. I've wanted to know more about Simone but I wasn't expecting this. For months, I've thought she just had a weak moment. Every teenage girl has them. That moment where they want to end all the hurt—the bullying, the pressure, the erratic moods—and disappear.

Unplug from life.

I scream in my head, angry at my best friend. Simone knew better than to hack in and risk everything. Unless.

"Did they say why she would do that?" I ask.

"Nope." Raven says while everyone else shakes their head.

Simone must have been looking for something. And I have a feeling someone in this place knows what it was.

I study each person in my group of misfits. Crash sits alone, not saying a word. Becca continues gabbing about nothing and everything. Fisher appears to strike different model poses as he obsessively tussles with his hair. Raven creates stupid string animals, showing no emotion. And Varian moves back into the corner's shadow. My hope fades, and I grow a bit disheartened. Getting my answers depends on a group of messed-up electronic junkies.

Ms. Matthews' voice blares over the intercom. "Everyone. We will also be offering grief-counseling sessions for those who need it. But remember the best thing you can do is return to your normal schedules."

Normal. Nothing ever returns to normal after something like this happens.

I think about the last time I saw Simone.

"You sure you're okay?" I asked.

Simone hugged me. "Yup. I'll finally catch up on some light reading. War and Peace has been calling to me. Maybe I'll even start knitting."

I gave her a look but smiled. "Come on. It's me. You can't sew on a button let alone knit a whole hat."

"These are lethal weapons." She held up her fingers. "They can do anything."

"How will you go without a computer?"

She grabbed both of my shoulders. "How will I go without you and your twenty questions?"

"I should say something. Then I can go with you."

"There's no reason for both of us to suffer." Simone held both my hands. "Ada, promise me you won't say a word. Please?"

I swallowed my guilt and nodded. "I promise."

Simone hugged me tight. "Don't feel sorry for me. I'll live. It's only thirty days. Then everything will be back to normal."

Of course, nothing has been normal since. Not without Simone.

And now, I can't stop wondering, why would she risk everything to hack ReBoot after she left?

What was she looking for?

Maybe this group of odd kids has the answer I need to feel normal again.

The Breakfast Club of the Cybersphere.

</A TIGHT DEADLOCK>

TEAM BUILDING IS NOT MY THING, ESPECIALLY WHEN IT'S outdoors.

My first activity is by the barn. So once it stops snowing, I leave the cold inside and venture into an even colder outside.

As I walk down the hill, I spot Becca and Varian behind the bushes. They appear to be in an intense conversation so they don't see me sneak in closer.

Varian hands her a wad of money, and Becca gives him a handheld Game Boy. Another "pass off." Only instead of drugs, chocolate and gadgets are the popular contraband of choice.

He slips the Game Boy into his jacket pocket and pats her shoulder. "So you are good for something."

When Becca walks off, Varian spins around and faces me.

I duck and sneak back down the hill, hoping he didn't see me. I don't need a Varian close encounter today.

Seconds later, he appears next to me like some kind of cloaked phantom. "I suppose you're going to rat us out to Ms. Matthews."

When in doubt, play dumb. "For what?"

"Don't play games." He grabs my arm to stop me. "I know you saw us back there."

I peel his fingers off my bicep. "Look, I have enough problems, so I'm not looking for any more battles to fight."

"Guess we'll find out." He points up.

My eyes follow his finger to a sign on top of the shack that reads "LARP." My shoulders sag. Just what I need. Live action role-playing with a guy who doesn't know the meaning of the word *pretend*.

"Don't worry. If you're lucky, I'll make it a quick death." Varian slaps me on the back, forcing me to swallow my gum.

Seven years of bad luck choke me in one gulp. Great.

I study the LARP sign and remember the last time Simone and I played laser tag. We were at an arcade where Craig Lovett, the school bully, was targeting poor Logan in a game.

"Let's join in?" Simone said when she saw Craig suiting up. "We can teach the bully a lesson."

I looked at Craig dressed in black, gearing up for laser tag. "Are you crazy? He'll slaughter us with no mercy."

"I can take him." Simone grabbed a laser gun and smiled. "Karma may have his mailing address, but I own the stamp."

That day, I watched Simone annihilate Craig with one kill shot. When her dad wasn't teaching her all about computer programming, he had been perfecting her target practice.

Maybe it's my turn to teach someone a lesson.

I catch a whiff of Becca's flowery perfume before she announces her approach—not such a smart move in a tracking battle. Varian will smell her coming a mile away.

Her head pops up between us, and she hollers, "It's LARP day!" Then she pats Varian on the shoulder. "What's your strategy this time?"

He frowns. "I plan to kill the annoying people first . . . so get ready."

"You're mean," Becca fires back. "Why don't you go shoot up a bank so we don't have to deal with you anymore?"

Varian throws off his glasses and vomits out his defense. "How many times do I have to tell you that I am innocent? But did the cops or the teller listen? Noooo, instead they assumed the worst and threw me in the slammer." He spits when he talks, making us lean away from the random fire. "Meanwhile, a pretty little cheerleader wins a Get Out of Jail Free card for cyberbullying some chick."

I look over at Becca. Cyberbullying? News to me. Seems like everyone in here is hiding something.

Varian kicks the ground. "For some reason, this world's got a double standard against guys like me."

"Dude, the black trench and anger issues don't help," Fisher mumbles from the back.

Varian holds up his fist and hollers. "Bring it on, pretty boy!"

"Guys, calm down," Becca says softly.

"Shut up!" Varian screams in her face. She recoils in fear.

"Gentlemen don't attack ladies." Fisher drapes an arm over Becca's shoulder, shielding her from another spray of Varian's words. "Didn't your military daddy teach you any manners?"

Varian grabs Fisher by his shirt. "Talk about my dad again and we'll see how tough you really are."

Mr. Anthony walks up with Raven and Crash trailing. "Save it for the field, boys."

"Just the way I like it," Varian murmurs under his breath.

Mr. Anthony holds up a black gun with a thick, round barrel. "Today's challenge is paintball."

"Yes!" Varian does a few fist pumps.

Becca picks up a fake gun and lets it dangle by two fingers like it's a dead roach. "Can't we use the foam swords again? They seem safer."

Raven sits in the back, playing with string.

Fisher raises his hand. "Should a bunch of *rehab* kids use guns against each other?"

Becca nods, "I agree. It's not a positive message, especially for those of us who may be unstable." She points to Varian behind his back.

Mr. Anthony throws gear onto the grass. "Studies prove that LARP is a great way to give techies the same adrenaline rush you seek online. Only this game encourages human interaction."

Varian looks confused. "Well, I don't know about you. But I'm not looking for that. I just want to win with a kill shot."

Becca shakes her head. "See, it's already promoting *violence*."

Mr. Anthony launches into a pep talk. "Actually, if we show you fun and *safe* ways to capture the online rush while encouraging personal connections, then it's a good thing."

"Pretend killing is therapeutic?" I whisper to Becca.

While we all arm ourselves for a battle, Varian suits up for World War Three. He straps a couple of guns to his legs and a rifle onto his back. Within thirty seconds, he's fully armed with five weapons.

Fisher points to Varian. "Hey! *She's* getting all the good ones." Crash appears more petrified than a baby duck at a chicken fight. He makes a face as he picks up the smaller pistol. Raven gears up next to him.

"There are plenty of weapons to go around." Mr. Anthony grabs a few more pistols and rifles out of the shed. "It's only a game."

"Not to me." Varian says, grabbing a couple bags of blue pellets.

"Here are your paintballs. Choose wisely." He hands Fisher green and then doles out the other colors. Becca snatches pink; Crash takes orange; and Raven chooses black. I grab the only color left—purple.

"Raven, hand these out." Mr. Anthony checks a few guns for hidden pellets. "Make sure the safety is on and always check to see if it's loaded first."

Raven gives everyone a weapon. Becca's accidently goes off, sending a stray paintball at an unharmed squirrel. She cringes. "Oops. Sorry."

Varian spreads mud on his face, chuckling. "Oh good, Becca will just shoot herself." Then he stretches by doing a few lunges.

"You will fight in teams until you hear my whistle. Then everyone will duke it out on the field solo until one person wins." Mr. Anthony teams Crash with Raven and Becca with Fisher. Then he points to Varian and me. "You two are a pair."

Even though I'm paired with Captain Crazy, I'm smart enough to know I'm on the winning team. Though I'm pretty sure no one is totally safe.

Mr. Anthony points to an area bordered in yellow tape. "The LARP course is marked. If you get hit in the chest or back, it's a fatal blow and you're out. Legs and arms are a flesh wound, so you can continue playing. Simple as that." Then he hands out safety goggles and vests. "Make sure you wear your gear. You too, Varian. You're not a hero if you lose an eye."

Varian jumps in place and rolls his head around, a boxer waiting for the final bell. "No *real* hero gets hurt or dies. They live to tell about it."

I roll my eyes and crack a few fingers. I'm not a gamer, but I want to take these guys down. Online, if a cyber fool questions my skill, I simply dox them by collecting a bunch of personal data and dumping it on the net. Just to shut them up. Out here, it's going to take more brains than brawn to beat these testosterone tanks at their own game.

Mr. Anthony sets his watch and comes around to double-check our safety gear. "You have thirty minutes as a team. Then we'll break up to get a winner. You have one hour. *Man* with the most points wins."

"Or *woman*," Becca mumbles under her breath.

When Mr. Anthony yells "go," everyone dashes off in

pairs, except for Varian and me. He takes off, leaving me behind.

As usual, Varian's got his own back.

When the group is out of sight, I slip behind a tree and formulate a plan.

My strategy? Camp out and let them all eliminate each other.

Then I can pick off the last lone sucker.

</LIVE ACTION ROLE PLAYING (LARP)>

GOOD THINGS COME TO THOSE WHO WAIT.

I peek out around the tree. The dim forest has very little light. Every tree looks like a person. Someone sneaks up behind me and taps my shoulder.

My heart slams against my rib cage. "Jeez!"

"Find your teammate, Ada," Mr. Anthony says, lifting the yellow tape. "You can't win a battle unless you're on the field."

"Right. Sorry." I leave my safe spot and venture deeper into the war zone. Alert and ready.

The world around me dims from the umbrella of trees blocking the light. The mossy ground is slick from the recent rain, and the air is filled with the smell of a fresh-cut log.

A few strides in, a noise sounds off to my left. I swing my gun around and fire a couple rounds. A chipmunk gets lucky. My pellets miss him but decorate his home with purple splotches.

Every time I breathe in the ice-cold air, my mask fogs. I wipe off the condensation collecting inside and move slowly. Simulation or not, being blind in the woods at dusk with a fake gun, knowing I'm being hunted by a bunch of pissed-off addicts, is not my idea of fun.

A few pops sound off in the distance followed by a scream.

"Becca's out!" Varian hollers.

Varian: 1. Everyone else: 0. Surprise, surprise.

Seconds later, Becca bounds out of the woods like a bunny in spring. A sunburst of blue paint decorates her black chest pad. Varian delivered a fatal blow. Without a care in the world, Little Pink Riding Hood skips off to Grandma's. Little does the Wolf know, she's packing heat.

As she clears the yellow line, someone fires at the letters on her butt. She stops and frowns at the forest. "Hey! I'm out! No reason to hit me again!"

I swallow a rising laugh and duck behind a bush. Becca is no longer skipping. Instead, she stomps out of the woods, a black blob decorates her left butt cheek.

Raven took a cheap shot.

I sneak deeper into the woods and weave between the trees. When something scuffles off to my left, I blindly shoot in an arc, hoping to hit someone. In mid-attack, my gun jams. "Shoot."

As I'm reloading, Crash ambles onto the path.

I tense up, anticipating a direct hit to my armor.

Instead, Crash grabs my gun. He unjams it, and then shoots himself in the chest pad.

"Why'd you do that?"

He points toward the deep woods and acts out a mini-gun fight. Then he flashes a thumbs up before walking out of the course.

Crash wants me to win. One for the underdogs.

A few seconds later, Mr. Anthony yells, "Crash is out. Varian: 1; Ada: 1."

Varian's voice booms from deep in the woods. "Bring it on, Lovelace. I don't care if you're the noob here."

Fisher's mouth fires off too. "Girl against girl. How cute."

I scowl at the overconfidence of these two clowns. Guys underestimate girls in sports and computers. Time for me to show them how wrong they are.

I charge in the direction Crash recommended, searching for Varian. The forest has grown much darker since we started. I scan the trees and hide behind a clump of low-hanging branches. The loud bass of my drumming heart fills my ears, blocking out any other sound.

Something creaks behind me, forcing me to stop in my tracks. The hair on my neck waves.

Someone is close by. Watching me.

I spin around and fire. Purple dots splash across Raven's vest.

She narrows her eyes as Fisher barks, "Ha! Raven's out!"

"Varian 1, Ada 2," Mr. Anthony tallies.

I smile and wave to Raven as she leaves the woods.

Then a shadow moves off to my left. I press my back against the tree and slowly reverse around the trunk.

A hand shoots out and covers my mouth.

Startled, I drop my gun.

Varian spins me around to face him. Without hesitating, I punch him in the chest. "What the hell? You scared the crap out of me!"

"You were in my line of fire." He moves his sunglasses up on top of his head and pulls a green bandana up over his mouth and nose. Mud streaks along his forehead and cheeks like he's part of some elite fighting force.

"Why didn't you just kill me?" I hiss.

"You're on my team. I can't shoot you until the thirty minutes is up." Varian lies down on his belly and props his paint rifle up on a log as if he's hiding inside a military barrier. "And I don't play dirty."

"I doubt that."

"It's true." Varian pans his rifle, waiting for Fisher to

appear in his sight. "Besides, I owe you one. You didn't rat me out about you-know-what to you-know-who. And I always pay back my debts so consider us even."

We sit in the grass, waiting for Fisher to show his face.

I pluck a blade of grass and watch this strange guy as he scans the woods for his enemy. What's his story? "You take this war thing pretty seriously, huh?"

"Yeah, so?" His eyes fixate on the woods with his pointer finger lingering over the trigger. "It's not smart to talk while we're in enemy territory."

I lie on my stomach next to him. "Why do you like to fight?"

"Why does there have to be a reason?" He shrugs. "Maybe I just enjoy it."

"Do you prefer battling online or in person better?"

"Both," he says stiffly.

I recheck my gun, making sure it's ready to fire. Maybe I can get Fisher out first. At the very least, I'll put a cap in his smart-ass. "When did you start playing?"

Varian doesn't answer me right away. It's the quietest he's been since I got here. "This isn't share time. It's war."

I nod. "Well, I could always tell Ms. Matthews about your Game Boy if it doesn't matter."

He snaps his head in my direction and the corners of his mouth climb into a grin. "You're blackmailing me? Nice." He takes some time before muttering, "I started playing after my dad died."

My body sinks at the pitiful look on his face. Before my eyes, the tough guy exterior crumbles. "Oh Varian, what happened?"

He keeps his voice low. So low I lean in closer so I don't miss a word. "Last summer he was stationed in Afghanistan. A week before coming home, his crew got ambushed with a roadside bomb. Dad fell on the IED." His voice cracks during the last sentence. "Saved all the men in his platoon."

"I'm so sorry," I say.

Then the two of us sit in silence. Maybe Varian isn't that different from me after all. He hid in games after his dad died the same as I hid in hacking after Simone. It's shocking to think we may have something in common.

Varian faces me. "You know that I never heard from any of his soldiers after the funeral. My dad left Mom and me to save their lives. Yet we didn't even get a flippin' card. Sometimes you're better off on your own, not responsible for anyone else."

I stare at his face and watch the sadness struggle to fight off the anger.

Part of me wants to reach out and touch his shoulder. But I play it safe. When you touch a wild animal, expect to be attacked.

Instead, I repeat myself for lack of anything else to say. "Sorry."

"Don't be." Varian pulls back the edge of his cloak, revealing a shiny elite medal pinned on the lining. "Dad got a Purple Heart. He died a hero."

I touch the shiny brass heart with the tip of my finger. "No wonder you're so good."

He smiles. "No kills in WoW, so I can't complain."

And in that moment, Varian slides away, giving me a tiny glimpse of Andrew.

The real kid with real pain.

I remain quiet, not sure what to say after that. It's weird how once you learn something about people, you see them in a totally different light. Or just more clearly. Maybe this is why Varian fights so much. Maybe fighting with people—whether online or in real life—is the only way he feels connected to his dad. Maybe it's the only way he can deal with his anger.

What Varian shared—the pain and anger—is not something I could ever look up online. Sure, I could have found the article about his dad, but not the deep emotions linked to it. The real story only comes out if someone decides to share it.

I can't help but wonder what kind of pain Simone was in that last day. And I realize I may never know because she's not here to tell me.

"What about you?" Varian sweeps his eyes over the battle-field once again, scanning for movement.

Before I can reply, Fisher leaps out of a bush and aims at Varian.

Without thinking, I stand and fire a round, giving Fisher a flesh wound.

He smiles in the dim light and shoots in my direction.

I dive into the grass for cover. Green dots splotch across both of my thighs. I'm still in the game. Lying on the ground, I wait a few seconds before the stinging wears off.

When I roll over, Fisher stands with his gun pointed at me. "Any last words?"

I tense up, preparing for the more paintballs and pain.

Instead, Varian leaps out of the underbrush. "Oh yeah, eat this!" He takes a clean shot, hitting Fisher square in the chest.

"Damn!" Fisher throws down his gun in defeat. "That sucks!"

"Fisher's out!" Varian pumps his fist a few times. "Ya big sissy."

I keep my eye on Varian's back and draw my gun. Can't help but wonder if the moment we shared will make any difference when it comes down to winning or losing.

As if sensing me, he spins around and fires with a sneer on his face.

I roll out of the way. Guess I know the answer. When it's one on one, Varian will always put himself first. No matter who he connects with.

I pop off one pellet, splashing purple across his heart. "Gotcha."

Fisher laughs and hollers, "Andrew's out! Ada wins!"

Varian freezes. He touches the wet paint spot on his chest and rubs his fingers together. You'd think he was examining real blood. An angry look spreads across his face. "You shot me."

"You fired first. It was self-defense." I almost feel bad.

Fisher jumps around like a kid. "How does it feel to have *one* kill on your perfect record now, *King* Varian?"

Without another word, Varian spins around and stomps off the course like a four-year-old boy.

"Come on, Varian! Don't be mad. It's only a game." I chase after him. My victory easily bleeds into guilt. Just when we connect, I have to go and ruin it. Act all tough. Even though I was just playing the game, I should've known he'd be upset. Varian needs to win. Just like I need to hack.

And now I know why it's so important to him.

Fisher chants, "Ada beat Andrew. Ada beat Andrew."

I ignore him and catch up to Varian. "Fisher would have won if I hadn't saved you in the first place."

Fisher is right on my heels. "She's right, dude. I had you until she jumped up and distracted me with her beauty."

Varian ignores Fisher and throws his gear down on the dirt. "Doesn't matter, you shot me. I could have shot you, but I didn't. You were on my team."

"Team? In case you *conveniently* forgot, you fired first. I wasn't going to shoot until you did." I bite my lip. "You looked out for yourself. As usual."

"And now you see why." Varian appears sad for a moment while he unloads his equipment. "Can't depend on anyone. How would you feel if your team turned on you?" He picks up another gun and takes quick aim, firing off one last shot.

I duck just as something swishes by my head and slams into the tree behind me.

Instead of splashing blue paint, a large chunk of bark flies off.

"Doesn't feel good, does it Lovelace?" Varian says and storms off.

Fisher studies the tree and gives me an odd look. "Dude! Uncool," Fisher barks.

Becca runs up and high-fives me. "Ada! That was awesome!"

Crash pats my back and gives me another thumbs up.

I take off my gear and dump it on the ground. "No, Varian's right. He won. Crash surrendered, and Varian could have gotten me out anytime. He chose not to."

"Doesn't matter," Becca says. "You won three to two. Fair and square."

"Though not the kind of guy you want as an enemy." Fisher nudges me. "Insane G.I. Joe."

We all watch as Varian huffs toward the building and kicks a trash can.

Becca whistles. "Man, he's mad. Serves him right; he shouldn't be such a jerk bag."

Raven leaves the field and Becca and Crash follow close behind.

Fisher hangs back. "Hey Ada, come here."

"What's wrong?" I ask, walking over to the tree where he's standing.

"That wasn't a pellet Varian fired." He points to a huge chuck in the tree trunk. "Don't touch it. I'll be right back."

As Fisher runs off, I study the hole in the tree and stick my finger inside. It's empty.

A few seconds later, Mr. Anthony walks up with Fisher. "This better be good, Fisher, or you're on bathroom duty." Fisher shows Mr. Anthony the tree, and he inspects the hole too.

"A pellet wouldn't cause that, right?" Fisher says. "I think

Varian tried to shoot something at Ada on purpose. The guy's a nut job."

"I'm sure Varian isn't stupid enough to try anything." Mr. Anthony faces me. "But I'll talk to him and find out what he was thinking."

I nod, wondering what Varian shot at me. Whatever hit that tree was no paintball. It was heavier and much harder.

As Fisher and Mr. Anthony head up the path, I lag behind and scan the ground until I spot something laying in the grass. I bend over and pick it up.

It's a marble.

I glance up at the building and watch Varian pouting.

When he sees me watching, he points two fingers at his eyes and then at me.

I get the message.

He's after me. And it's only the first day.

I better keep a close eye on him too.

</TIME TO TROLL>

SIMONE NEVER DID ANYTHING WITHOUT A REASON.

There's only way to find out what that was. I need to get on a computer. And I know just where to find one. In Ms. Matthews office.

When Ms. Matthews pops in for room check, I pretend to be deathly ill. Getting this lady to believe me isn't as hard. My fake gagging sounds cleared the room really fast.

After everyone heads to their first activity, I sneak down to the lunchroom and snag the lunch lady's security card from her register. After some time observing, I know the center uses a standard swipe system, so hopefully this card will gain me access.

I inch down the back hall and stop a few doors down from Ms. Matthews' office. As soon as the security camera swings away, I run to the door and swipe the card. When the panel beeps, I push open the door and close it behind me. I lean back and breathe. So far, so good. I roll the interior blinds shut so no one can see in and eye the bookshelves.

That modem light told me there was a computer in here somewhere.

I just have to find out where Ms. Matthews hides it.

Trolling around the cramped space, I'm careful not to shift anything out of place. Some paranoid people set traps. A moved garbage can, a misplaced pen, or a wrinkled cushion can all shows signs of an intruder. I'd bet all my typing fingers that Ms. Matthews keeps this office extra dusty, hoping to snag a fingerprint or two.

I nose around her desk, looking for a clue, and tug on the top drawer. It's locked but easily crackable. Using a letter opener, I jimmy the latch until it opens, careful not to leave a scratch. I sift through a few ancient photos of Ms. Matthews and a boy who I assume is her son Patrick, an old pack of hairy gum, and a letter from the bank about some missed payments. I also come across a book of deposit slips. The carbon copies recorded huge amounts. Wow, this place brings in some serious dough. Seattle has way too many computer addicts. I jot down the bank routing number and the account number in my notebook before replacing the slips.

Sitting in her chair, I twirl, taking in the view from every angle. When I spot the paneled wall, I stand and knock. Sounds hollow. The perfect place to hide a computer.

Or a body.

There's no door handle, but there is a keypad. The kind that usually has an open button for convenience or in case of forgotten codes. I go back to the desk and slide my hand around the drawer past broken pencils, dust bunnies, and lonely paper clips. In the very back, my finger grazes a small lever. The paneled wall slides back, revealing a hidden room.

Open Sesame!

I pull on the light cord and step into the damp space reeking of mothballs and mold. I squint in the dim light. Filing cabinets and stacks of cardboard boxes labeled with black marker crowd the tiny room. Jim. Sandi. Michelle. No names I recognize.

Unfortunately, there appears to be no order to this lady's stacking madness. I rummage through some old files until one folder catches my eye: CONSTRUCTION PLANS. There, I discover archives of the mansion's floor plans, including past building additions and blueprints. The schematics show me the enormity of this old place.

I shove a few in my back pocket. In case they come in handy later.

Something hums a familiar song, grabbing my attention. I spin around and spot an old school desk in the corner. Sitting on top is the prettiest sight I've seen since checking out of reality and into CrazyLand.

A computer.

And not just any machine. A state-of-the-art HP PC injected with a speedy processor. Matthews may pretend to live in the 1800s, but she's more tech-savvy than she lets on. Not to mention, a total hypocrite.

"Hello, beautiful," I whisper. The stress of the last few days dissipates.

The Dark Angel is back.

I sit at the desk and tap the space bar. A screen saver pops up. This should be easy to hack. I swivel on the stool and crack each knuckle before resting my hands on the keyboard. The second my fingertips kiss the keys, a jolt of electricity shoots back into my body, resurrecting me.

Since this HP is a newer model and linked to a network, it's got to be loaded with Windows XP. It will take too long to hack the internal network, but I can still gain access to the internet and local files.

I reboot the machine. As the computer cranks up, I press F8 repeatedly until the safe mode option appears. First, I pop over to SocialNet and pull up Simone's board. Her silly smile fills my screen and knocks the wind out of me. I sit back and study her face. I don't know who Simone was in here, but I know the real Simone. And I'm going to find out what happened to her in here.

Before I log out of SocialNet, a private message pops up at the bottom.

It's time to ReBoot.

I suck in a breath. Another cryptic message. I stare at the letters. This isn't spam or a pesky bot. Someone outside of Dad, Mitnick, and Mrs. Crawford knows where I am. Must be a teen since SocialNet is sooo secure. This time, I delete my account and close all my internet windows. Hopefully, the person will just go away.

Now, I search for a trace of Simone, any sign that she was on this computer. I scan through user logs, but Simone was obviously careful. If she was in here, she made sure she didn't leave one crumb behind. However, it's not a total bust because I find out this place has two networks set up.

So if this one doesn't pan out, maybe the other one will.

Next, I dig through the computer's hard drive. Nothing. I search the TRASH folder. Most people dump unwanted files and forget to purge the bin, leaving others access to everything they thought was garbage.

One file stands out: </DECEASED>.

Besides some personal data—Social Security numbers, birthdates, and addresses—there are a few details on the ReBoot kids who've died over the last six months.

Johnny King, 15: Fatal gunshot when buying computer parts on the black market (Released 6/12; DOD 6/15)

Chelsea Talbot, 14: Died in car accident while texting on her cell phone. (Released 7/19; DOD 07/23)

Simone Jordan, 16: Suicide after hacking into ReBoot, prescription Zoloft OD. (Released 8/16; DOD 8/19)

William Sabitini, 16: Died, diabetic seizure after being online for hours and forgetting his insulin. (Released 10/29; DOD 11/03)

My stomach ripples. Somehow, Simone's gone from being a girl who loved life to a name on a list of dead kids. I note the release dates of each person—each one died a week after checking out. The timing is too much of a coincidence.

I jot down all the information in case I need to reference it later.

Before I log out, I do what every hacker does to dig up personal information on someone.

Google.

First up, my roomie: Becca Adler. When I look into her case, there's way more to her story than she admitted. According to new articles, Becca not only broke SocialNet's terms of service, she cyberbullied some poor girl by creating a fake profile of some hot dude. When Becca's fake alter-ego ended the relationship, the girl tried to OD on 5,000 milligrams of aspirin, ten times the normal dose. The family hired a private investigator and discovered their daughter's online heartthrob wasn't Buckley. It was Becca. They pressed charges and settled on a deal that sentenced Becca to one hundred and twenty hours of community service, three years of probation, and six months in a tech rehab facility. These are some major charges. No wonder she's been in ReBoot so long.

She almost harassed a girl to death.

In addition to reading all the articles about her cyberbullying case, I also discover that Becca's mother is a famous chocolatier. Explains the sugar addiction. Becca has stellar academics and is a total overachiever in extracurricular activities—karate, fencing, dance, cheering, gymnastics, yoga, and jazzercise. She's also super active on practically every social network known to teen kind. According to her last post, she's afraid of the dark, which explain the 24/7 nightlight.

Varian's story on his dad checks out. I also find out that his mom works full-time, so he primarily lives with his grandmother. Varian's arrest was more than mistaken identity or a misunderstanding. He tried to rob a bank with a paintball gun. Explains his skill in LARP. He told police he was dressed up for a WoW party and was only withdrawing money from his account. But they charged him anyway. No one knows the truth.

Crash's story is horrible. He lives with a single mom and his baby sister drowned in the pool while he was babysitting.

Fisher. Surprisingly, there's not much online about him at all. It's not often that I can't dig up information on someone. So I still don't know why he's here. Something more to uncover.

Before I get a chance to research Raven, the office's security alarm beeps twice as someone swipes a card.

A few cuss words filter through my lips.

Ms. Matthews is back.

No doubt I am dead!

I freeze for a moment, paralyzed. Not sure of my next move. My brain quickly reboots and jumps into action. Reaching over, I quietly slide the secret room's door shut, leaving a sliver of space. My hands jitter as I control the mouse, shutting any open windows and erasing the history in case I get busted.

Ms. Matthews' shoes click against the hardwood floor. Moving closer and closer to the secret room.

I squat down and peek through the crack, steadying my convulsing breaths.

She slides open a filing drawer and retrieves a manila folder before sitting in her desk chair.

My hands feel sticky, and my legs burn from the awkward position. If the director looks my way, she'll notice the cracked door.

I spy on her as she reads paperwork and scribbles some notes, dipping her pen into a small jar of ink. Even pens are off limits here.

A few seconds later, she reaches into her top drawer.

The door to my panic room begins to slide open again.

My heart seizes, spiking unevenly. Pressing my back against the wall, my eyes dart around, searching for a place to hide.

But I'm trapped.

I suck in a final breath. There's nothing to do now, but pray. B&E combined with hacking equals a troubled repeat offender whose behavior is escalating. No way Mitnick will toss out my arrest record after that.

Just as Ms. Matthews' foot appears in the doorway, someone knocks on her office door.

"Come in!" she says and pulls the door almost shut. When the office door opens, she grunts her displeasure. "Fisher?"

I exhale, thankful for the distraction, yet annoyed at the delay. What is he doing here?

"Fisher. We've. Talked. Enough." Ms. Matthews speaks sharply, every word clipped short. "Your frequent visits will encourage others to assume I have an open-door policy, 24/7. Is there a problem?"

"It's not for me," his deep voice answers sharply. "Mr. Anthony wants to see you."

"Why didn't he come himself?" She takes a step forward.

"Who knows? I do what I'm told." Fisher's voice remains flat, unbothered and unintimidated.

She scoffs, reminding me of a dog that has a bad case of kennel cough. "That'd be a first."

"Do you want me to wait for you?" Fisher asks.

"Tsst. Don't be silly. Tell him I'm coming and it better be good to warrant the interruption."

After the door shuts, Ms. Matthews turns off the light and leaves, muttering under her breath, "I'm surrounded by a bunch of idiots." Luckily she forgets to close the panel.

Sliding back the door, I breathe in deep, welcoming the musty air. Without dawdling, I return everything to its place and erase any evidence of my visit. I sneak out and slip down the back staircase. Once I'm clear, I stop and press my back against the wall, exhaling a long sigh of relief.

That was close. Too close. I can't get careless. Simone got obsessed with this place and made mistakes. Look where it got her.

If I'm not careful, I could follow in her footsteps.

</A NEW SOURCE>

I BARELY MAKE IT TO GROUP ON TIME.

Ms. Matthews eyes me when I dash through the door. "Thought you were sick."

If I look half as broken as I feel, maybe she thinks I have the plague.

"Didn't want to miss anything in my recovery process." I flash her a wide, innocent smile.

She studies me for a minute, looking suspicious, but Mr. Anthony winks his approval.

Fisher scrapes his chair across the room until he's parallel parked next to mine. "So . . . you've been sick . . . in your room . . . all morning?"

"Yyyup." I keep my eyes down, chin tucked close to my chest. No way I'm looking up in case the word GUILT is written on my forehead.

He huffs, keeping his voice lower than usual. "Huh. That's odd because I went by your room. To check on you. But you didn't answer."

I shrug off his concern. "Maybe I was asleep or had left already . . . or something."

"I'm gonna lock in on answer C—*or something.*" Fisher

offers me a bemused smile. "But no worries, you can thank me later."

I stare at my hands, flipping them over. As if my manicure is messed up or something. "I don't understand."

"Sure you do."

Either Fisher's curious about the status of my health or he knows exactly where I was. And if that's true, he must have interrupted Ms. Matthews on purpose . . . for me. But why? Maybe he's threatening me with exposure. Or maybe he's toying with me and knows absolutely nothing.

Either way, I blow it off.

For the next hour, Mr. Anthony explains board game basics and the value of gaming offline. By the end of the lecture, I'm almost more excited about playing Yahtzee than Halo.

As Mr. Anthony pulls Raven and Becca outside for their teaming activity, Ms. Matthews passes out old board games from the '70s.

Varian and I reluctantly play a game of Battleship. I spend the next thirty minutes listening to him rant on about how his brain benefits from learning online gaming strategies.

After he expends all this hot air, I catch him peeking over the board.

"So your big strategy is to cheat?" I ask. "How does that grow your brain exactly?"

He leans back and radiates a superior expression. "Games are my specialty. I don't need to cheat because I always win."

"Only sometimes you don't." I raise my eyebrows and grin.

Varian catches my drift. "You didn't win on the field. I *let* you win."

"You mean, you let me *live*," I throw back.

He jerks his head back, looking confused. "What's that supposed to mean?"

I reach in my pocket and hold up a marble. "Missing something?"

"Hey, that's my Dark Star. Do you know how rare that marble is?" He snatches the glass ball out of my hand. "Where'd you get it?"

"Sadly, not in my body, which is where you tried to hide it." I eye him. "After you *shot* it at me."

Varian's eyes widen then he laughs. "Oh! So that's why Mr. Anthony was drilling me about LARP." He leans back and puts his big boots on the table, practically in my face. "So let me get this straight. You think I shot a marble at you? How dumb do you think I am? That's like leaving my business card at a crime scene."

"Where'd you get that?" Ms. Matthews pops up out of nowhere and holds out her hand. "Varian, I took that from you the other morning and hid it in my office. Did you break into my office?"

Varian points at me. "Hell now. Ada had it."

"I found it outside!" Last thing I need is for her to think I broke in. Even though I did.

Fisher comes to my defense. "Ada's right. I was there. We found that on the LARP field during paintball. Varian shot it at Ada."

"You wish. You're trying to protect your girlfriend," Varian yells. "Throw me under the bus."

Fisher puffs out his chest. "We should all be so lucky!"

"Enough!" Ms. Matthews screams. Everyone in the room stops and stares. "The three of you are on shaky ground." Then she eyes Varian. "I will keep this for now. If any of you steal it again, you're out.

I grab Fisher's arm after she leaves. "I don't need you sticking up for me. I can handle myself."

Varian laughs. "How does it feel to be rejected, Fish Boy?"

I push Varian's feet off the corner of the table. His boots slam on the ground. "And you, I don't care if you lose your marbles to Ms. Matthews and steal them back. But you could have hurt me with that thing. I thought we were friends."

"I already told you, I didn't do it. I wouldn't waste my marble." The look in his eyes tells me that he's not lying. So if he didn't shoot it, who did?

"Okay, I'm sorry."

"I don't care what you are." Varian fires off again. "And secondly, any chance of any alliance went bye-bye when you shot me on the field and now accuse me of attempted murder. Get that? We're not friends!"

Tears sting my eyes. I've never been great at fighting.

"Oh boohoo." Varian's nostrils flare. "You know, Simone used to whine about being her friend too. She and Becca would sulk together, probably spent hours crying about how bad their rich lives were and what gala they would go to when they left here."

"Whatever," I mutter. "Becca and Simone weren't *that* good of friends."

Varian mumbles, "No, they were roommates." Then he storms off, unaware of the aftermath he's left behind.

I stare at my feet. Simone was Becca's roommate? If that's true, Simone slept in the same room as me. In the same bed. Yet, Becca has never said a word. Not even a hint. Looks like she has a bad habit of leaving out very important details.

She has too many secrets, which means she's hiding something.

While everyone heads to the cafeteria, I race back to my room.

I stand in the doorway and study my room through a different lens. Simone was here. The room feels different now. Even in death, we share everything. All I can think is that Simone slept here. Simone sat there. And now she's gone.

I glance at Becca's side of the room. It's totally uncool for me to search her stuff, but the girl's been hiding so many things—she was Simone's roomie, her cyberbully charges, and she's ReBoot's contraband supplier— maybe something here can tell me more.

What else is this girl hiding?

The curiosity wins over my internal warning. I root through her nightstand. Nothing but a couple of chocolate wrappers, a pink pen with a fuzzy top, and some paperbacks: *The Essential Jackie Chan* and *The Art of War*.

I flip through the well-used copy, noting all the dog-eared pages on the strategy of fighting.

This girl gets stranger by the minute. The more I find out, the less I know her.

I return everything to its place and drop on all fours to look under her bed. A pink box hides behind bags of candy and colored foil. It's filled with pictures. Pictures of Becca cheering. Pictures of her family. And a picture of her with SocialNet's CEO Gary Host at a technology conference.

But one photo stands out.

I pick up the picture of my group. Simone stands in the middle, next to Becca, flashing a peace sign. Her signature pose. It's weird seeing her in this photo.

Everything in the photo looks exactly the same, except now, I'm the one sitting in Simone's place. I flip through a few more pictures of Becca and Simone.

A pang of jealousy stabs my heart. They appear closer than I ever expected in such a short time.

I stare at Simone's face. She looks happy. No sign of crazy or sadness.

I hear a click behind me.

"What are you doing?" Becca asks.

</GATHERING DATA>

Becca wants to kick my ass.

And if she's learned anything from Jackie Chan, I'm in trouble.

She stands in the doorway with her hands on her hips. Though behind her tough exterior, there's something else. Fear. Maybe uncertainty. Definitely disappointment.

I slam the lid shut and struggle to answer.

Becca snatches the pictures from my hand. "Why are you going through my stuff behind my back?"

My anger emerges. "Why have you been lying?"

"I don't know what you're talking about," Becca scoffs.

I stand. "Oh please. I know all about you and your cyberbullying. I also know that Simone was your roommate."

"Oh." She softens a bit, her eyebrows lower and her jaws unclench. A few seconds go by and she plops down on her bed. "I'm sorry. I should have said something, but I didn't want to upset you. Thought it might be too weird."

"So you *hide it*?" I study her face, searching for a sign of guilt.

"I was going to…eventually." She picks up a picture and smiles. "I liked Simone a lot. She was such a sweetheart.

Anyway, I'm surprised she didn't tell you we were rooming. I thought you guys were close. Then again, I guess best friends can grow apart."

"We were . . . close. I just didn't talk to her much when she was here." I pause, not sure if I'm trying to convince Becca or myself. "And we didn't grow apart."

"If you say so." She shrugs as if what I say doesn't matter.

Becca's cavalier attitude ignites my resolve. I want so much to prove her wrong. List out all the ways I know Simone better than she did. But that isn't going to bring Simone back. And I need to put all that aside. Focus on what I know and what I still need to investigate more.

Hacker Commandment #9: Getting the information is more important than feeding the ego.

"Becca." I swallow a helping of humility, which feels thick and sticky in my throat. "Did Simone ever ask you for anything?"

She tilts her head to one side. "Not sure what you mean."

"Look, don't play dumb. I know you get special stuff for people."

"Who told you?" Her eyes dart around nervously, and her chin quivers. "It was Varian, wasn't it? I'm going to kill him."

"No. I saw you hand him a Game Boy. You should be more careful."

Becca grabs a piece of chocolate from her stash and pops it in her mouth. Probably just to avoid talking.

I sit on my bed. "I won't tell anyone. But I need to know if Simone asked you for anything while she was here."

A long pause hangs in the air until Becca swallows her treat. Her body sags a little as if the chocolate released a little sedative. "Flash drives."

"Flash drives? Why those?" I ask. "What did she need them for?"

"I don't know, but a lot of kids go through withdrawals here," Becca says weakly. "Sometimes, having something we want is enough. Even if we don't use it. It helps to know it's there."

"Did she get anything else?" I crack a few knuckles against my thigh. Finally a new clue. Taking a step forward helps me refocus on why I am here.

Becca shakes her head. "No."

I study her face. I'm still not sure this girl can be trusted. But I can tell she's being honest. I rub my necklace and ask the question that's been haunting me. "Do you think something happened here—at ReBoot—to make Simone *hurt* herself?"

Her eyes dart around like she's tracking a fly. "Besides getting busted for hacking when she left? Not that I know of."

I stand there, waiting for her to say more. "There must be something. Anything."

Her shoulders sag. "I'm sorry. I can imagine how hard this has been for you."

I rub my forehead, thinking of any other question to ask.

Becca appears sad. "Look, Ada. I'm sorry you're going through this. Simone was your best friend. But obsessing over why she isn't here won't bring her back. Maybe you need a little something to relax you. Get you out of your head."

Shutting off my brain sounds nice. Even if it's only for a few minutes. "Maybe."

"I think I have something that might help." She pulls out another box from under her bed and holds up an MP3 player. "How about this? It's fully loaded with all the new stuff."

My heart dances in my chest at a chance of hearing music besides scratched Elvis records. I turn my head, looking away. It takes all my willpower not to snatch it from her hand.

She moves closer, drawing me in like a bug to light. "You can use it. I won't charge you."

"Really?"

Then the real reason reveals itself. "But you have to promise not to tell anyone about me."

My body stiffens, frozen with indecision about whether to accept the gesture. Can't help but wonder if Becca's trying to throw me off her track or if she's being genuine. I stare at the red iPod hanging from her hand. I have to admit I'd love to listen to music. Escape. Let the beats drown out my thoughts.

"Are you sure?" She nods and hands it over. Then she holds up some earbuds. "These too?"

"Uh, sure." I clutch the cords in a death grip and hold everything close to my chest in case she wants it back. "Thanks, Becca."

We both sit in the room quietly, letting the awkward silence dangle between us.

She speaks first. "You know, now that I think about it, Simone did say something strange right before she left. But maybe it's nothing."

I look up and face her. "What? Tell me."

"I said something about her being excited to start over fresh after she left here." Becca shrugs. "Then she said something about being afraid to leave."

I lean forward, hanging on every word. All I need is one small clue to keep me going. "Afraid of what?"

"Ghosts."

"That's weird," I mutter. Simone was never afraid of the paranormal. She'd seen every episode of *Ghost Hunters* and *Paranormal Witness*. More than once. "Do you know what she meant?"

Becca shakes her head. "No. It's probably nothing."

Or it could be something.

If Simone had flash drives, she had to use them somewhere. I scan my notes and spot the second network that popped up on Ms. Matthews' computer.

Time to find out where.

</ALTERNATE REALITY>

Snooping around the grounds is dangerous, but it's a risk I have to take.

I wait until Becca is asleep before sneaking down to the cafeteria. After rigging the alarm sensors, I slip out the window. The frigid air slams into me, forcing me to stop. I allow my lungs a few seconds to adjust before walking around the back of the house.

According to the mansion blueprints, there seems to be an opening somewhere along the forty-foot wall. I run my hands along the side of the building and scan the ground for anything worth investigating. My toe clips something hard so I shine my flashlight at the spot. Something long and black sticks out from under my boot. I jump back, assuming it's some sort of man-eating reptile. After a closer look, I recognize the thick cable winding along the building.

I pinch my lips to contain a squeal.

Since Ms. Matthews doesn't seem to be the HBO type, I follow the LAN connection until it disappears under the house. Using my flashlight, I search for an entrance. The light reflects off something in the leaves. Excitement and curiosity buzz inside me.

I clear away the debris and find a rusted door handle poking out of the ground. Clutching the flashlight with my teeth, I dig my fingers along the edges and tug on the latch until it releases. I lift the small door and lean into the hole. A rickety ladder descends into a pitch-black hole. Claustrophobia grips my chest, but there's no way I'm turning back now.

I lower myself down until my feet touch a rung. My legs shake as I step down carefully. At the end of the ladder, I close my eyes and drop into the darkness. After several feet, I hit the ground and fall, landing on my shoulder. I grit through the pain and retrieve the runaway flashlight that's spinning across the dusty floor. This is the perfect backdrop to a haunted house. Complete with cobwebs, construction materials, and broken furniture. Simone would have paid five dollars to enter this place on Halloween.

My light flickers a few times. I hit the handle against my leg to jolt the battery back to life. "Come on."

Instead, it goes out.

Pitch black engulfs me. In my slasher movie experience, nothing good happens in the dark. I slam the handle against my hand. When the light finally flickers back on, the beam illuminates a stark-white face.

I scream and jerk back, tripping over a paint can that clatters across the floor. Shining the light around, I stare at a mound of half-naked mannequins and holler at the dummies, "What the hell!"

Trying to reboot my skittering heart, I wait a few seconds before checking out the space. A sheath of dust covers the cement floor and reveals a footprint. Someone's been here. And I'd bet it was Ms. Matthews. Following the map, I head up the rickety stairs until my head slams into a low-hanging ceiling.

"Great. Steps to nowhere." I rub the bump and back down the steps until I spot a doorknob in the center of the wall.

When my hand touches the handle, a panel opens, revealing a hidden room. I crawl through the opening and pop out the other side.

The six-foot ceiling hovers just above my head so I am forced to hunch over. The walls are so narrow; my shoulders rub against both sides. Nothing in here—the doorknob, the windows, not even the doors—was built for a normal person.

With each step, the wooden floors creak, warning me of a possible cave-in. On the far side, I push through a heavy wooden door. The small room is decorated with gas lamps and uncomfortable-looking furniture that could be straight out of Queen Elizabeth's castle. I draw back the tattered lace curtain with one finger and peer out. Somehow I've already climbed a few floors.

I scan the uneven rooftop sprayed with moonlight and locate my position on the map. This place is a maze. If "freak house" is in the dictionary, a picture of this place would be next to it.

An odd place for a technology rehab center.

I shine my light along the passage painted an ugly brown and pea green with white trim. Moving down the skinny, twisted hallway, I check each door. Many are either locked or open into empty rooms. The corridor ends at a set of double doors painted an "Expired Mustard." When I jerk on both handles, the doors reveal nothing but a brick wall.

Another dead end. Reminds me of the time Simone and I got lost in the Halloween corn maze, trapped in a series of loops and false paths.

Minus the fake chainsaw-wielding psycho.

At the next opening, I move into another unfinished room. The open frame exposes the wall's guts as tattered sheets of cloudy plastic attempt to cover up the decorating crime. Two-by-fours and rusted tools scatter throughout the space, resting where they were dropped.

I step over the large holes in the floor. Carefully. If I drop into the mouth of this house, pretty sure I'll be swallowed forever. Down the hall, I see a blue light. I creep closer, sliding my back along the ice-cold wall. Moaning and clicking sounds echo from inside the room.

I reach the door and stop. No telling what's behind this door. But I muster up the nerve to peek through the crack, half-expecting something to peer back.

The freshly painted room is a welcomed sight, contrasting the dismal grays and browns. The space is stuffed with tons of cool technology placed along clean white desks. Large glass monitors display beautiful lines of translucent green and blue code on the wall.

Iron Man would be impressed.

And I bet Zed's RAM life that Simone found this place too.

On the far wall, a cursor skips across a 3D screen. Someone is coding.

I lean in farther, hoping to get a look at the lucky devil.

Raven sits at a desk, typing in total concentration. Bright green cords hang from her ears. She stares at the screen as her fingers tap-dance across the keys. The rhythmic clicking noises hypnotize my nerves. Almost forgot how much I miss the buzzes and hums of computers as they process commands.

A stab of jealously jolts through me. It's not fair that Raven is awarded computer lab time while the rest of us suffer from withdrawals. Then a bigger concern takes over. Why does Ms. Matthews house a secret computer lab inside a technology rehab center? Yet, she won't allow a mechanical pencil in to the lobby.

Part of me wants to bust Raven and question her. Who, why, and what? But if I go barging in now, there's no telling what she'll do. Rat me out to Ms. Matthews. Get me expelled.

A loud beeping noise echoes through the hall.

Raven launches out of her seat, propelling the chair across

the floor, and jumps feet first through a small window on the far side. Her odd exit tells me one thing—this isn't her first time.

I race after her and watch her drop through a hole in the floor. She's either running from me or chasing the white rabbit. There's no telling how many secret spaces and nasty nooks there are in this strange place. Let alone, what's hiding in them.

Or who.

I listen for footsteps to see if I can follow her. Nothing. Raven's long gone and tracking her down in this rat's maze would be virtually impossible.

I return to the lab and browse the space like it's a new computer store. Inspecting monitors and analyzing hard drives. Can't help but lightly sweep my hand over every piece of the badass equipment only seen in movies.

A hacker's heaven on Earth.

On the wall, a red dot blinks. Raven must have been warned I was in the hall. I sit down in front of her computer and tap the keyboard. A 3D picture floats in the air and spins 360 degrees.

I smile. Raven, Little Miss Hacker Queen, was careless and didn't log off. She'll kick herself for this one. After studying the computerized pattern made of symbols, letters, and numbers—I finally make out the picture of a beautiful woman. Raven soothes her soul by creating computer art. Who is this girl?

Time to find out. I crack a few fingers and roll my neck in a circle before researching Raven Crenshaw. Her parents died when she was a baby, cursing her to a damaged life in the foster care system. A self-proclaimed goth girl, Raven was handed off more times than a football. At ten, Seattle's Children's Shelter labeled her a chronic runaway. Soon after, she created a state juvenile record due to multiple shoplifting incidents. According to records, an anonymous angel investor donated money to put her through school. Maybe she used the cash for ReBoot instead.

I sit back and think about what to do next. I knew there was more to this place. Though I had no clue it'd be this awesome. And I'm pretty sure Simone found this place too. If she was here, I'll be able to follow her cyber steps, and hopefully get some idea of why she got those drives and why she was so interested in ReBoot after she was released.

Before I can scan the network, there's a creak in the hallway.

A red dot flashes on the wall.

Someone's here.

I bolt toward the back of the room, jumping over a chair, and hide in a narrow closet.

The lab door slams and footsteps echo across the old wooden planks.

The footsteps grow louder.

I cup both hands over my mouth so I don't make a noise.

A large shadow stops in front of the door. The handle turns and the door creaks open.

A light shines in my face, blinding me.

Then a deep voice startles me. "Ada Lovelace, what are you doing here?"

</CLOSE A DOOR. OPEN A CHAT WINDOW>

Now I know how a deer feels.

Mr. Anthony lowers the light. "Ada, we need to talk."

At first, I remain paralyzed. Only I could be found in a 25,000-square-foot house. Then again, I was never good at hide-and-seek. Online, the Dark Angel can sneak anywhere without being found.

In real life, I'm not so savvy.

Mr. Anthony leads me through the labyrinth of rooms and halls until we end up back in the lab. Somehow what took me hours to discover takes Mr. Anthony less than ten minutes to find.

He holds open the door for me. "Have a seat."

I grab a seat at one of the computers. The urge to jump online digs at my left brain. Until detoxing, I didn't know how much I depended on surfing the web or the rush of hacking. Or how much I needed the Dark Angel.

Mr. Anthony drags a chair over. "Well . . . I must admit . . . this is an interesting development. One I did not expect."

I crack under the pressure. "Mr. Anthony, I'm sorry. I found the door outside and got curious. Please don't kick me out. I . . . need to be here." Maybe for me as much as for Simone. To leave ReBoot now—before I get any answers—would be terrible.

He scratches his stubble. "Do you expect me to believe you *stumbled* upon this lab? Did someone tell you about it?"

I assume he's implying Raven. "No one. I got lucky."

"Maybe not so lucky."

I try not to look defeated.

He shakes his head. "I'll give it to you straight, Ada. You're smart. Maybe too smart."

"I'm sorry." I rub my necklace, summoning the Dark Angel's cyber-confidence that I lack in the real world.

"You are talented. If you put your computer skills to good use, I bet you could do amazing things." He taps his fingers on the table. "I can only assume you dive into systems where hackers wouldn't dream of dipping their big toe."

"Thanks, I think." I mumble, wondering if it's a compliment.

He pats me on the shoulder. "Look, I can help you focus those skills in a more productive way. If you're up for it."

"You're not kicking me out?"

"Not today. One of the reasons I work here is to help kids like you." He motions to all the technology nuzzling around us. "I —unlike Ms. Matthews—believe everyone in this place has different needs. Not all problems are the same. Many of the kids here have technology addictions that prevent them from living a normal life. They spend hours online and skip school. From what I can tell, your problem is hacking."

I nod but don't say anything. No need to give details.

"Problem is when residents don't think they belong here, they hang back. Refuse to participate. And I believe this program can help, if done right. Do I think you're addicted? Not really. Do I suspect you use computers to escape, get some control in your life? Absolutely. So, maybe I can help you."

I don't buy what he's selling. "What do you mean?"

"Your skills are gifts. And, they will serve you right someday." Mr. Anthony stands and walks a few paces. "But you need help finding the right balance, maybe discover how to use your computer skills in a more constructive way."

My fear ebbs and my hope flows. "Go on."

"I will let you have some time in here—give you a few hacking challenges to play with...but you have to take this program seriously. *Actively* participate. Give me a hundred and ten percent, one hundred and fifty percent of the time. You may not be addicted, but you're definitely disconnected."

I speak slowly to make sure I'm getting this right. "Are you saying you will let me come in here and get on the computer?"

"Yes."

I eye him, wondering if this is a trap. A test. "But ReBoot is supposed to get kids off computers. Why would you give me access? Isn't that kind of like housing a chocoholic in Willy Wonka's factory?"

He smiles warmly, seemingly amused. "Well, if I can motivate you to open up, maybe when you leave ReBoot, you can start over. Put Simone behind you. Her death was a tragedy. Such a waste; she had so much promise. I think if I had done something a little different with her, she'd still be here."

I glance around the lab, studying the set up. Blue and green displays twinkle in the room, exuding a warm light. Being off the computer for a few days has shrunk my world. No Orwellians, no communication with my family, and no Simone. But more importantly, no Dark Angel.

This offer could change everything. I could get online. Connect to Simone. Find out the truth about her death. And figure out what she was hunting for. I have a chance to plug in.

"What do you say?" Mr. Anthony leans against the wall and holds out his hand. "Deal?"

I reach out and shake his hand. "Deal."

"Good." Mr. Anthony nods once. "Let's walk out together and I'll show you a shortcut."

I half laugh. "*That* is not possible."

We leave the lab and move through another unfinished wing of the house, stepping over large holes in the floor, teetering across rotted floorboards, and climbing through secret passages.

"Ada, I trust you will keep this place and our conversation private. The lab isn't for everyone. The temptation could jeopardize someone else's rehabilitation."

"What about Ms. Matthews?" I ask.

He shrugs. "Ms. Matthews may not agree with my methods, but she knows about the lab. Though she's not one hundred percent behind it, so you're better off keeping it on the down-low."

"Sure, no problem." I certainly don't want Ms. Matthews interfering with my online time. He hasn't mentioned Raven, so I don't either.

Eventually, he opens a door, revealing the dark sky outside. "Remember, Ada. Work hard and follow the rules. If you get kicked out of here, I'm afraid you could end up like Simone."

His comment hits me hard. Fear and doubt clog my thoughts as I walk back to the main building. I can't help but wonder if Mr. Anthony is right.

What if Simone's fate is mine?

</FAULTY TECHNOLOGY>

The next morning, I look for Raven at breakfast.

I need to find out more about the lab and what she does in there.

When I don't see her, I head down to the field, hoping to catch her before the day gets started.

Fisher runs up. "Hey you."

"Hey," I mutter, walking at a brisk pace.

He walks backward in front of me. "You don't like me much, do you?"

"Don't know you." I trip on a small rock and stumble a couple steps. My legs have worked fine for sixteen years. One cute guy shows up, and they turn into noodles. "But I don't like being questioned all the time."

"To be fair. You don't have great answers. Makes me curious." He widens his strides, matching my quickened pace. "Aren't you the least bit curious about my backstory?"

"Nope," I lie.

Fisher stops. "Simone was."

I stop. How dare he mention Simone. He hardly knew her. Thirty days can't compete with ten years x 365 days. I spin around and poke him in the chest with my finger on each word for extra emphasis. "*Don't*. Talk. About. My. Friend."

He retreats with both hands up. His dark brown glasses frame his sincere eyes. "I'm just saying we were friends. She told me a lot about you."

"Funny, she didn't mention *anything* about you." Without missing a beat, I zigzag around him.

He won't let up. "She said you were a great hacker. Better than her."

I keep my eyes down, shaking my head. "Simone wouldn't say that."

"If you say so." He strides off.

My feet trudge along the dusty path until I reach my group gathering at the edge of the forest. No clue what we're doing, but pretty sure it's not going to be in my wheelhouse.

"You ready for this, Lovelace?" Varian whispers. "A senator's daughter probably isn't used to getting her hands dirty."

This guy's about as warm as an ice cube.

"Actually, we're splitting up for team building today." Mr. Anthony is wrapped in a black peacoat and floppy beanie that makes him look half his age.

Varian raises his hand as Raven walks up. I try to catch her eye, but she avoids me. "It's not really team building if we're separated, right, Mr. A?"

Mr. Anthony ignores the semi smart-ass remark. "Ada, Becca, and Crash, you three head down to the ropes course. I'll be there shortly. Varian, Fisher, and Raven are on barn duty today."

Fisher's mouth drops. "Hey, no fair. Why do they get all the fun?"

Varian groans. "Yeah, Becca needs to do some hard labor. Work off all that chocolate."

"I would call you a *jerk*..." Becca flashes him a look sharp enough to dice his ego into tiny pieces. Then she grins at Mr.

Anthony. "Instead, I'm going to use my feeling words and say, that made me *sad*."

Varian scrunches up his face in disgust. "Great, then I'll use my words to say I don't give a rat's ass about your feeling words."

Becca gasps and narrows her eyes, like she's going to take Varian out by beating him with one of her fluffy pink mittens.

"Chill out, Varian." Mr. Anthony hands him a shovel. "You better go get started."

"Aw, man," Varian mumbles. "I don't want to shovel shit today."

"Why? You're obviously full of it anyway." Fisher smiles, obviously proud of his timely joke.

Varian grabs his crotch. "I'm full of something."

Crash covers his ears with both hands. And I don't blame him. These kids are locked onto each other's throats constantly. Worse than a pack of wild dogs at a cat show. The fighting alone could have made Simone snap. I just got here, and this place is already grating on my fragile nerves.

Raven rolls her eyes and plays with one of the harnesses. "Obviously your inflated egos are overcompensating for a certain male deficiency."

Fisher laughs at the innuendo while Varian turns red, either from anger or embarrassment.

"All of you, put a lid on it. I'm not in the mood." Mr. Anthony points to Varian's crew. "You three, go now. Before I add in some *human* bathroom duty."

"Barn's good with me!" Fisher races off.

"I ain't cleaning commodes," Varian says. Only he and Raven head down the hill with less urgency.

Mr. Anthony faces my team. "You three give me any trouble, you'll get much worse. Now follow me."

"Yes, sir!" Becca salutes.

Mr. Anthony leads my trio into the woods. The ground is hard, and the ice-cold air slices my face.

I zip up my leather jacket and whisper to Becca, "How does this help us tackle our technology addictions again?"

"The chores are for discipline." Becca unwraps a chocolate as she talks. "The ropes course teaches us how to depend on others when we need help. It's supposed to help us form bonds."

I glance up at the highway of ropes strung across the trees. Reminds me of Raven's string designs. "But we just met."

"I did this on my first day." She pops the candy into her mouth. "Scared me to death!"

"Thanks for the reassurance."

"Sorry." She reads the foiled message. *"Friendship never leaves you hangin'."*

I keep my eyes on the course and notice how it disappears into the trees tops. "Let's hope not."

I trudge behind the group. All I want to do is jump online and find out why Simone was hacking this place. Instead, I'm wasting time hiking in the freezing cold just to dangle above the cold ground with strangers.

We stop at the base of a thick pine tree—so tall I can't see the top without backing up a few yards.

Mr. Anthony holds up a harness. "Ada, new people go first. It's tradition."

"Um, I'm kinda scared of heights." I attempt to keep my knees from shaking. "Maybe Becca should go."

"Everyone's nervous the first time." Mr. Anthony holds out the contraption. "Go ahead and suit up. The longer you wait, the worse it gets."

"I doubt that." I grab the harness and step into the leg loops.

"Don't worry, it's fun. No one's ever fallen." Becca helps me fasten the buckles. "And even if you do, the harness will stop you from hitting the ground."

"You'd think that would make me feel better."

Crash and Becca also suit up while Mr. Anthony reviews

the course rules. "If you get stuck, your team will help you across. No person left behind. Okay?" He motions me up the pole. "Ada? Whenever you are ready."

That would be *never*.

I grip the wooden pole and inch up. The higher I get, the more my legs tremble. When I finally reach the platform, I hug it and wait for Crash and Becca to climb up.

"You ready?" When I nod, Becca unhooks my clip and then hooks it to another rope. "Don't look down. It only makes it worse."

Of course I glance down and my world spins. I squat until the feeling subsides. This is too hard. My life depends on a girl who never sees the bad side and a boy who won't talk out of fear.

"You can do this, Ada. Go on." Becca pushes my shoulder, which freaks me out. Only I'm too petrified to yell for fear of losing my balance.

Standing at the platform's edge, I grip the top rope with both hands, and slide my foot onto the bottom rope. The rope swings from left to right, making me teeter.

Becca calls out instructions. "Ada, go slow."

I make my way out to the middle of the rope, which is now swaying wildly in the wind. Seems pretty stupid to be on a ropes course in winter, not to mention dangerous. The freezing cold must make the ropes more brittle. So what if they snap?

"Keep going." Becca calls out behind me. "Don't stop."

My foot slips.

Becca yells, "Ada!"

Before I know what's happening, I scream and lose my footing.

I'm going to die.

</SWITCHING GEARS>

The rope catches me and jerks me back up.

I bounce up and down, hanging in midair. I scream with my eyes squeezed shut. Then it dawns on me that I'm not falling anymore. I'm dangling thirty-five feet above the hard ground. Upside down. My breaths come in quick, sharp gasps. My first week in rehab and I'm going to die on a freakin' ropes course.

"I'm going to fall."

Mr. Anthony calls up. "Ada, you're okay. The safety line caught you, so try not to panic. Try and climb back up the rope."

"I-I can't." I shake my head violently.

Mr. Anthony's voice is calm but stern. "Yes, you can. How many times have you said that in hacking?"

"Never!" I scream down at the stupid analogy. "But I wasn't hanging upside down!"

"Ada! Grab this rope," Becca calls out. "Use it to climb back up."

"Good thinking, Becca," Mr. Anthony cheers from below. How can he be so calm?

Crash unclips a rope and swings it over.

When I reach over to grab the loop, my rope creaks.

"Please," I close my eyes as my rope spins in a circle. No doubt Simone loved this part of rehab. She loved adventure stuff. I —on the other hand—was always the more cautious one.

"I'm going to fall," I said.

She laughed. "Falling is another way of flying. It just depends on how you look at it."

I screamed at her, "Then I'm going to fly into the freezing rapid creek."

She didn't give in. "If you fall, I get to laugh. But all you get is wet. So keep going already; you can do this!"

And she was right. I made it without falling.

On the next swing, I catch the rope, and force my foot into the loop. I push up into a standing position.

Mr. Anthony yells instructions. "Focus, Ada. It's like any other hack. One line at a time."

My arms and legs strain to keep my body balanced. I shake out each arm and reach up toward the tightrope until my fingers touch it. On three, I force myself to let go and grab the line. I sigh once I feel the solid rope in my hand.

"Now get yourself to the other platform," Becca says.

My hands walk over each other until my toe almost hits the platform. Then a loud snap. The clip on my harness pops off the safety rope, and my foot slides off the edge. Now, I'm suspended without a safety net.

"Help!" I scream.

Mr. Anthony yells, "Hold on!" I can't see his face, but detect a hint of panic in his voice.

My hands burn from gripping the rope and start to slide. I swing my foot over to the side, but am still inches platform.

"I'm slipping." I glance over my shoulder at Becca and Crash standing on the far platform. "Becca, help me!"

Instead of moving toward me, she takes a step back, making it clear she's not coming to my rescue.

My hands are cold and numb. "Crash, help!"

He immediately jumps into action. First, he clips his harness to the safety line and then inches out onto the rope. Each step makes me bounce.

"Crash, wait!!" Mr. Anthony calls out from below, but his voice sounds closer. "The line won't hold both of you."

But Crash doesn't listen to the warning; he moves closer. He doesn't look down, and he doesn't hesitate.

The rope digs into my hands. I clutch tighter as the rope sways from his shifting weight. My fingers slip a little more, and I drop another inch. My hands burn, but I refuse to let go.

Crash moves closer and closer. I'm thankful he's even putting his life on the line to try. Heroes come in small sizes; and sometimes, you don't see them until they reveal themselves.

I stare up at the sky and concentrate on my grip. It seems to take forever until Crash reaches me. He carefully sits down and balances his body on the rope. Once he's settled, he grabs hold of my wrist and clips the extra safety line onto my harness.

I look up and he winks as if to say, *Don't worry, I gotcha.*

A few seconds go by before Mr. Anthony speaks from underneath me. "I'm almost there, Ada. Hang tight just a few more seconds." He moves up the pole and onto the wooden platform closest to my legs. He clutches the tree with one arm and reaches out to grab my legs. "Let go. I'll catch you."

Crash releases his grip on my wrists, but my hands refuse to unclamp.

"It's okay, Ada. Trust me."

I allow my fingers to release. As promised, Mr. Anthony catches my weight and yanks me onto his platform. I clutch him and wrap my arms around his neck, my whole body trembling.

"If you choke me, I can't save you." He pats my back once and pries my arms off his neck.

I laugh out loud and release my vice grip. My legs give out, and I sink down on the platform, weak and speechless.

Mr. Anthony and Crash help me down. No one says a word until my feet touch the ground. I collapse onto the dirt. The whole horrible experience catches up to me, and I whisper, "Jesus." This whole thing is crazy, and I don't want to be here anymore.

Mr. Anthony kneels beside me while Crash touches my shoulder. "Ada, you did great up there. I'm proud of you." He pulls my chin until I'm facing him. "You okay?"

I nod slowly. "I think so."

He checks my hands. They are seared red, raw with rope burns. "Do you need to see the nurse?"

I clear my throat. "I'm good . . . I'm okay."

Mr. Anthony and Crash help me to my feet.

"I can't imagine what happened up there." Mr. Anthony tugs at the hook of my harness. "Let me see this thing."

I step out of the straps so he can inspect the contraption. "Hmm. That's strange." He holds up the buckle covered in scratches along the metal. The rope is frayed. "I can see why it snapped. Looks like it's been cut by something."

Or someone.

"Maybe something sharp in the tree. Because I checked the harnesses this morning and everything looked fine." Mr. Anthony frowns. "Ada, I'm so sorry. You could have been seriously hurt."

"It's not your fault." I glance over my shoulder and catch Becca slinking down the path. Not stopping to check on me. She was the one who insisted I go first. She may have even been the one that hooked me in.

Mr. Anthony grabs the rest of the stuff. "I'll have maintenance check all the harnesses before anyone goes up again. I don't want anyone else in danger. Until then, the ropes course is off limits."

Thank God.

"You did great today. I can see you are trying." He stops and faces me. "You want some reward time in the lab tonight?"

"Does a coder code?" I grin and my spirits lift a little. After the ropes course, I need to blow off steam. I also need to see if Simone was in there.

"Great." He smiles and studies his watch. "Eight o'clock."

We separate and go our own ways. I run to catch up with Crash and grab his hand. "Thank you for helping me. You saved my life."

Crash shrugs and looks embarrassed.

I hook my arm through his and walk with him. "You know. Mr. Anthony says once you talk, you can leave this place. Bonus, if you ask me. I bet one small word counts." I raise my eyebrows, hoping to draw him out. Like that time Simone used a hot dog to trap a one-eyed Chihuahua living on the streets. She ended up keeping the little stray outcast, naming him Wink.

Crash stops and opens his mouth, as if he's about to talk. Until his eyes scan upward and his body goes rigid. Then he lowers his head and runs off.

"Crash, wait," I call after him, but he's already halfway up the hill.

I wonder what spooked him. When I look up, a shadow stands in a high window. Ms. Matthews is watching me. I speed walk until I'm out of sight and stop. No wonder Crash left so quickly. The lady gives me the total creeps too.

When I pass by a bush, two voices whisper.

A girl's voice says, "Where's my pocketknife?"

"Thanks for letting me use it," a chipper voice answers. "Remember, don't tell anyone. Ms. Matthews wouldn't want me using a knife, even if it's only for whittling wood. Oh, and this is for you." A bag rustles. "It's on the house this time, but next time you have to pay me. This candy's hard to get."

"Thanks Becca." The girl pops her head out of the bush to

make sure no one is watching and then walks past my hiding place. A few seconds later, Becca follows her inside.

I remain hidden, shocked.

Is Becca picking up wood whittling? Or did she use the knife to sabotage my harness? Then again, why would she want to hurt me—unless she's still mad about me snooping?

Maybe she feels threatened because I know more about her than she wants. Side business and all.

</THE MOTHERBOARD>

By the time I get back to my room, I have a renewed sense of urgency.

I need to get back in that lab and see if Simone's been online. If I'm right, maybe I can trace her steps on the system. Figure out what she was doing last.

But that means I have to get in there before Mr. Anthony.

I wait until Lights Out before sneaking out of the building. Luckily, no one has found my rigged alarm sensor so I can come and go as I please. Outside, I fish through the music Becca gave me. Got to give it to her, she has good taste. "Addicted" by Morgan Page seems appropriate. The second the music kicks in, my head clears. Amazing how a few tunes can shift a mood.

I trudge up the hill to the beat and enter the back building the same way Mr. Anthony let me out. When I step inside, the wind slams the door behind me; the sound echoes through the space.

Halfway down the hall, the lights flicker. Not sure if I'll ever get used to coming down here. The lights flutter again and then go out. In the pitch dark, dizziness washes over me. I press my hand against the wall for support.

Thumping noises sound off close by. Sounds like someone is running. Then a shadow moves across the far window and disappears.

Someone—or something—is here with me.

On guard, I head down the stairwell where the shadow disappeared. Simone loved spending the night at spooky places. So why would she tell Becca that she was afraid of ghosts? Unless there is one here, now.

The stairs end at a thin door. I stand on my tiptoes and peer into the small window at the top.

On one side of the room, Ms. Matthews sits on a thin cushion, holding a burning candle. Her free hand waves at the smoke, sending it floating off in different directions. In front of her is a photo of a young boy. Her eyes roll in the back of her head, and her lips move as she sits alone. I have no idea what she's saying. Maybe she's asking for guidance, patience, and hopefully some freakin' sanity.

Unable to look away, I stay and watch.

Ms. Matthews comes here to summon the dead. And evidently ghosts have a lot to say because she sits there for a while. I assumed she was off her rocker.

But now I know just how crazy she is.

Eventually Ms. Matthews blows out all the candles and exits through the far door. I want to follow, let the freak show continue, but I only have thirty minutes until Mr. Anthony meets me.

Eager to find the lab, I move down the hallway. Once I see the blue light illuminating under the door, I speed up, welcoming the state-of-the-art room over the crazy-lady room any day.

After peeking inside to be sure it's safe, I beeline to Raven's station and bring up the desktop.

Back to civilization.

The first thing I do is jump on SocialNet to check Simone's board.

Happy Holidays, Simone. We miss you! Hope you're eating some pumpkin pie in Heaven.

The notes remind me of the dreaded Christmas I'm in store for this year. One without her.

I quickly surf the Net to see if anything else about my hack has leaked to the press. Today the big story is about the NSA spying on US citizens. Maybe the privacy controversy has moved from teens to Americans losing their privacy to a suspicious government. Then one article headline grabs my attention.

SocialNet Invaded by Teen Hackers

SocialNet has confirmed they were hacked earlier this month by more than one hacker. They have learned that one identity is that of the late Simone Jordan, a teen hacker who was already arrested for hacking into Channel 7 and falsely reporting a zombie invasion. Unfortunately, Jordan committed suicide shortly after leaving a technology rehab facility in Washington, reportedly after being caught on her third offense.

My stomach sinks. The article flashes some pictures of Simone. One is of her in a mask that makes her look super psycho. Another is of her holding a gun, which I happen to know is from our game of laser tag last summer. This photo has been doctored because she never posted it publicly. Instead of laser tag, the photo is paired with a quote of hers that says, "Someday Corporate America will die." So misleading! That quote was originally posted with another picture of Simone reading her favorite book, *Pippi Longstocking*, and said, *"Someday, Corporate America will die. . . but books live forever."*

Next, the article mentions Simone's strange purchases and prescription for antidepressants.

A clip of Mr. Gary Host streams at the top. "Miss Jordan was into a dark side of the internet. Sadly, she's no longer here with us. But her death won't stop us from identifying the other teens responsible for hacking our site. Outside of the opinion of some, we do respect the privacy of our users and will not allow teens to invade our customer accounts or profiles."

Respect? SocialNet believes in privacy about as much as a peeping Tom.

I sit back and stare at the freakish portrayal of my best friend. It's scary how a couple pictures and posts can be misconstrued in the media and create a different picture of someone. Because this person is not the Simone I know.

My heart sinks. Not to mention, she's taking the heat again for me, and she's not here to defend herself.

After seeing that article, I want to stay focused and uncover what Simone was doing in here with those flash drives. I log in to the network using Raven's ID so my keystrokes won't link to me. After searching a bunch of directories, I stumble on a short list of anonymous computer IDs. All I need are the names tied to each ID. Then I can track down what each person did.

And I know who to ask for help.

After rerouting my IP address and adding a few other safe diversions, I log into the Orwellians private chat room. As I suspect, Taz is online.

> DA: Hey. I need your help.
> Taz: Hey stranger? Where U been?
> DA: White house hack in media freaked me out. Laying low.
> Taz: Was worried u got nabbed on the SocialNet hack.

I pause with my fingers shaking over the keys. Taz will cut

me off if he thinks I've been busted or am chatting with the Feds. I exhale and type:

> DA: Wasn't me! I'm just laying low after QTip. How are the Orwellians?
> Taz: We're not meeting right now. What do you need?
> DA: Any idea on how to find out who's attached to a User ID? I need something quick and dirty.
> Taz: Fireforce will grab packets of data & look for usernames. U should B able 2 track down the history with Wireshark too.
> DA: But then how do I ID the person?
> Taz: The packets will show every command for each ID, including visited sites and stored cookies. Hopefully, the users checked email or something personal. Then it's easy to decode. Here's the EXE file.
> DA: Thanks!

I download Taz's software and command the program to pull specific data packets. As the code runs in the back-ground, I also upload a keylogger software on Raven's desktop.

Now I will know every move she makes online.

A red light blinks on the monitor.

I quickly log off and stand as Mr. Anthony appears with Raven trailing close behind.

Busted again.

</WHO'S THE WEBMASTER?>

I wonder if I look as guilty as I feel.

Mr. Anthony squints and surveys the lab. "Ada? You're early."

"Sorry," I stammer, hoping I left nothing out of place. "I…I couldn't wait."

He appears amused. "That doesn't surprise me."

Raven glares at me from behind. Still not sure why this girl hates me.

I flash her a fake grin while I appease him. "Sorry about today. I was a little freaked out."

Mr. Anthony waves me off. "Don't worry about it. At least *you* tried the exercise. That's enough for me, and you earned some time in here, so win-win." He flips on the light, blinding me. "But from now on I want to know when you're coming in here. This lab is not a free-for-all, and you need to be monitored. We don't want you to fall back into old habits now, do we?"

I don't think this is meant to be a real question. "It won't happen again."

"Good." Mr. Anthony walks in front of the screen, creating a looming shadow. He hands me a slip of paper with a username and password. "How about a fun hacking challenge to work on? See which one of you two can complete it first. Just for fun."

Though part of me is anxious about the interruption in my Simone investigation, the other part is ready to kick Raven's cyber ass. Plus I need to keep her focused on beating me so she doesn't notice my programs creeping in the background.

"Sounds good." I smile and spin around on my chair. I complete the Orwellian challenges every day, so this will be a cinch. Once I log in, my screen projects on the wall. I shut off the image and eye her. "In case you *accidentally* look."

"Trust me," she scoffs and takes off her display too, "I don't *need* to cheat."

"A little healthy competition never hurt anyone." Mr. Anthony seems a little too excited. "The first one to complete the challenge wins extra time in here."

"No problem." I shake out my wrists and crack a few knuckles. Adrenaline rolls through me, springing my nerves to attention. In here, I feel alive.

Goth Girl is going down.

"The challenge is capture the flag." Mr. Anthony retrieves a website. "I've created a custom application server for each of you to host. You have to keep it operational while trying to break into the other's server."

Raven huffs and drops her head back. "Ugh, this is way too easy."

"You only have an hour with no source code," he adds.

"I won't need an hour." Raven slaps the table and rubs her hands together like she's cold. "I've won the DefCon contest, and that was way harder."

Last year, the Orwellians discussed the biggest hacker contest in the country. Had no clue Raven was the one who beat them all. "That was you?"

"First girl to win . . . ever." Raven juts out her chin proudly. "Only took me fifty minutes to capture all the flags."

I have to give her credit. Raven succeeded in getting an unsuspecting executive to spill critical information: the type of PC he used, the make and version of his computer's operating system, along with the web browser and antivirus software. She also got him to link out to a fabricated internal site and create a log in, which she used to snatch data.

"Never underestimate your opponent." Mr. Anthony studies his watch and sets a time. "Here's a list of flags or information you need. The first one to capture three flags by uncovering three system weaknesses wins."

I shake my head. "They do this at DefCon in a day with a whole team of people. It's impossible to do alone."

"Speak for yourself," Raven mutters. "I'm sure you're used to things coming easy to you—being a rich senator's daughter and all—but this is *real* hacking."

"Good thing I know a lot about *real* hacking then." I roll my eyes at her arrogance. This girl can't be much better than me.

"I have faith in both your talents." Mr. Anthony waves on. "Go ahead and start."

As soon as he leaves, I plug in my earbuds and begin coding to the music. If Raven notices my contraband earbuds, she doesn't say anything.

My heart soars with excitement as my fingers glide across the keys. The only thing missing is Zed.

For the next hour, both of us code quietly. Every time I spot her sneaking in my back door, I toss out a cyber defense. With each one, she sneers and tries another.

While inputting a string of code, I distract her with chitchat. Part of being a hacker is knowing how to stay focused. "How long have you been part of this place?"

"Not long," she mumbles as she types.

"Who else is part of this?"

"Don't know. I'm usually in here alone," She says. "And I liked it that way."

After reviewing my script, I type again. "Was Simone ever here?"

She throws back her head and huffs in frustration. "I'm sooo tired of hearing about Simone. Simone *this*. Simone *that*. She's gone. End of story. Doesn't matter what she did or didn't do."

"How can you say that?" I stop typing, not sure how to react to such an insensitive comment. "What did she do to you?"

Overhead, a buzzer goes off, announcing that one of my flags has been captured.

Raven winks. "Gotcha, blondie."

I frown. "You said that about Simone on purpose. To throw me off."

"If it's that easy to make you crack under pressure, then you suck more than I thought you did." Raven grins. "Maybe you should code more and chat less."

It takes me a few minutes to squeeze through a hidden directory in her system and nab her. When the alarm sounds, I mimic her phrase and tone, "Gotcha."

"Not for long," Raven says. "I'm not worried. If you were dumb enough to get caught on the SocialNet hack, this won't be tough at all."

I patch a gap in my system and continue scanning Raven's code for holes. While hunting around, I come across a file. Looks like more of Raven's art, similar to the woman's picture. I click on a file and open a fairy with wings made from a detailed sequence of numbers, characters, and wingdings.

But at second glance, something doesn't look right.

I lean in to get a closer look when the buzzer sounds off again.

Raven captured another flag. "Only one more," she gloats.

I tear myself away from my art analysis and refocus by

sending an exploit that connects to a vulnerable process Raven hasn't yet closed.

She cusses under her breath as the alarm informs her she has lost a flag too.

I attempt to dump malware on her site to bog down her speed, but she skillfully blocks me.

This girl is good. Better than I anticipated.

We go back and forth defending and attacking each other's systems, trying to find that one unprotected crack for the win.

Then my last buzzer goes off, startling me.

"Done. I win." Raven shows no emotion about the victory, like she's not that surprised. She simply stands and stretches as if her yoga class just ended. Then she snatches her jacket and heads for the door as she gloats. "Not too bad for a politician's daughter."

After she leaves, my insides twist. I hate losing. More than I hate old versions of Windows. If I would've stayed focused, I could have won.

That stupid picture got me off my game.

When I'm sure she's gone, I project the fairy picture up on the wall. Squinting, I lean in for a closer look, and spot something odd. I smile. This picture isn't just art by numbers.

It's lines of complicated code.

</DOWN THE RABBIT HOLE>

THE WEEKENDS ARE BORING, LEAVING ME TO LIE AROUND AND think.

The most dangerous activity of all.

Thank goodness my parents came for New Family Day, but by the time they left, I felt worse. None of us talked much. Dad looked tired, and Mom cried the whole time. It was hard saying goodbye, knowing it'd be a couple weeks before they could visit again.

Week two, I stand around with my group and try to guess the "special activity" for the day. So far, bungee jumping, wilderness winter hiking, and mud wrestling are high on the list.

Mr. Anthony shows up and claps. "Today will be fun. We're the first group who gets to try the new activity. Caving."

Becca whispers in my ear, "Um, did he say *caving* or paving?"

"Yeah, Becca, we're gonna pave a road in the wilderness today," Varian scoffs. "What do you think?"

Fisher laughs at that. "Cool people call it spelunking."

Caving is the last thing I need. So far these "extracurricular" activities have brought me nothing but stray marbles and upside-down trapeze stunts.

"Let's load up." Mr. Anthony walks off before anyone can drill him on the whys, hows, and what-ifs. Not to mention the safety precautions. We all hop into the van and head up the mountain. The rickety transportation shakes along the uneven road, giving me motion sickness.

When the van finally stops, we all pile out. Mr. Anthony passes out helmets, kneepads, and harnesses. So far I haven't had great luck with harnesses. I inspect each one three times before choosing the most solid-looking one. Once we're suited up, our counselor leads us to a large opening in the ground. A nearby tree serves as an anchor point for a rope that dangles over the edge.

Becca gets one glimpse of the opening and backs up. "No freakin' way." Her hands tremble uncontrollably as she wrings them together. "I hate the dark."

I peer over the cliff. She's right. Complete darkness except for a few dots of light far below.

"There are many caves up in these mountains," Mr. Anthony says. "For months, we've been scouting out the safest route for this exercise."

Yeah. I've heard that before.

He pitches something that none of us are buying. "Spelunking is a great way to build rapport with someone."

Raven twiddles with her string art. "How does this place help us make connections?"

Varian nudges me with his elbow. "I can think of a few things we can do in the dark."

I sneer at him while Becca yells, "Gross!"

"Varian," Mr. Anthony frowns. "Be respectful." Then our counselor shrugs like caving into a deep dark hole is no big deal. "This challenge is designed to help you get over your deepest fears. To trust your partner. To trust yourself."

"Well, I trust myself, and *myself* is saying 'no way' am I doing this," Becca mutters.

I raise my hand like I'm twelve. "Is this safe to do in the winter? I mean, wouldn't spring be better? What if it's cold and slippery down there."

"Spelunking is a year-round sport," Mr. Anthony boasts. "So let's stop complaining and pick a partner."

Before I can move, Becca clutches onto Crash. Varian jumps next to Raven.

Fisher winks. "Guess it's me and you, Lovelace."

"Great." Just what I need. To get stuck on a journey to the center of the Earth with a guy who loves to play One Hundred Questions.

"You will work as a team to get the flag and hike your way out of the cave. We need a volunteer to go first." Mr. Anthony must sense the resistance. "First one in, first one out."

I sigh. Right now I need to push through this activity so I can get back in that lab. Tonight.

To prove how hard I'm trying, I raise my hand. "We'll go."

Fisher raises his eyebrows and lowers his voice. "One thing about teams you forgot—we should make *team* decisions."

"I did." I shrug his attempt to be a leader. "I'm the team leader."

"Okay, fine," he whispers. Then he speaks much louder so everyone can hear. "Ada wants to go first."

"Great! You won't be alone for long. I'll make sure of it." Mr. Anthony pats the top of my helmet. "You can do this, Ada. If you run into any trouble, follow the yellow rope out. It's for your safety."

I stare into the hole. I wonder what else is down there, keeping me company, until Fisher shows.

"Yeah," Varian starts heckling from the back. "And don't worry. Who needs caving experience anyway?"

I ignore the heckling and stare into the black abyss. Not sure how this is part of my healing process.

As they lower me into the hole, Fisher stands above me, watching. He calls down, "Don't worry, I'll be right behind you."

As I descend toward the cave floor, I talk to myself in the dark. "All I have to do is go down, wait for Fisher, and search for the flag. How hard can it be?" My rope drops me a few more feet. "I mean, these people wouldn't send teens down here if it was dangerous, would they?"

Then again, I almost met my untimely death on the ropes course.

As I descend, the temperature drops. The deeper I go, the faster my heart races. I flip on my helmet lamp, but the thin beam of light barely helps. My eyes attempt to focus in the dark.

When my feet hit the ground, I fumble with the cord until it releases. The harness floats back up to the top. The hole seems so far away, it almost could be a large star in the sky.

"You okay, Ada?" Mr. Anthony yells down. His voice echoes down the deep tunnel.

"Couldn't be better!" I shout out and then mumble to myself, "No place I'd rather be." I pull out my flashlight and study the tomb. The floor is covered with a soft dirt, intermingled with bits of broken rock.

A few tunnels lead off the main artery. One has a yellow rope leading out of it. My lifeline.

Focusing on my breath, I keep steady and calm. No use freaking out. Fisher will be down any minute. I just have to wait. I lean against the rock and feel my shirt go damp. The cave is wet with moisture.

Fisher hollers, "Heads up!" He zooms down the rope, dropping much faster. When his feet hit the ground, he salutes. "Bet you're glad to see me!"

I am secretly relieved but hide my relief. My goal is to

escape this place fast so I prefer to skip the small talk and not waste any time. "Let's get out of here."

Fisher points his head lamp ahead. "Maybe you'll realize that you love being in the dark with me and want to stay."

"I doubt it." I push him ahead of me. "Move."

The tunnel is narrower than I estimated. This section of cave reminds me of a mine. I can almost picture rusty mine cars on rail lines, and dust-covered miners with blistered hands, gripping dull picks. That awful feeling of being trapped—buried alive and unable to breathe—consumes me. I inhale a few deep breaths and clutch onto him. Don't want to lose my partner.

"Either you're breathing heavy because you're scared or because I get you excited."

I drop my hand from his belt. "Why do you do that?"

"Do what?" he asks.

I slow down, adding some space between us. "Be sarcastic. Make people feel uncomfortable."

"I overcompensate for my rock-bottom self-esteem." Fisher looks back at me. The light on his helmet burns my retinas. When I shield my eyes, he turns around and keeps talking. "Oh wait, maybe it's because I'm afraid of being vulnerable."

This time, I can't help but laugh. But more from nerves than his lousy joke. "Can you ever be serious?"

"I could try." Even though the air is cool, he pulls the vintage dragon T-shirt away from his body and takes in a few breaths as if he's about to stay under water for a record time. Then he gives me a serious look. "Here goes, you were amazing at LARP. You impressed me. A lot. And that's hard to do."

My face heats up, and I pray the color doesn't show in the dark. "Wooow, how did it feel?"

"It hurt a little." He presses one hand against his chest dramatically. Then he leans in, accelerating the pace of my breath even more. "I'm serious though. Getting a mute to help you win and an anger management dropout to team up with you is impressive. I also heard you cheated death on the ropes course. Deserves extra points in my book."

"And what book is that?" I pretend his close proximity isn't unnerving.

"My book of favorite people."

"Was Simone in that book?" I avoid eye contact and walk around the rocky room, peeking down each corridor.

Fisher sits on a boulder. "So you're ready to talk about Simone now?"

I inhale before asking my question, trying to be casual. "Were you guys . . . close?"

Even in the dim light, I can see that his expression changes. He rubs his hands down his thighs. "She was a *friend* of mine."

"You sure about that?"

Fisher looks wounded. "What? You don't believe me?"

"Should I?" I ask sharply.

"I think so." Fisher walks over and turns his headlamp up, leaving us face-to-face in a dimly lit room. We lock eyes and for a split second, I'm frozen. My dork factor rises, forcing my face to grow hot and tingly. Simone was the cool one around cute boys and always trying to get me a date.

"He's cute. How about him?" Simone said.

"Not interested."

"What's wrong with you?" Simone looked around the cafeteria. "You're only shopping to rent not to purchase."

I laughed. "I'll leave the dating pool testing to you."

Simone chewed on her straw and shrugged. "Boys are like purses. Cute, full of crap, replaceable. So why not have a few?"

Maybe I could use a new purse.

Fisher leans in as if he's about to kiss me. When we're only inches apart, his breath warms my cold cheeks. For a second, this kiss is all I want. To not feel alone for just one second.

But then his helmet bumps mine, knocking me back to reality.

I'm in a dark cave trapped with more than one weakness.

Jerking my hand away, I step back as if his touch will burn me if I stand too close. "We better go."

"Don't pull away." He moves closer. "Why were you in Ms. Matthews' office?"

"Oh my God, you're unbelievable." I try to get around him, but he blocks my path.

"If I wasn't trustworthy, I would have ratted on you. But I didn't." Fisher grabs my shoulders. "Where'd you sneak off to the other night?"

My mouth hangs open. "You are following me now? What a creeper! You don't want to know me, Fisher. You want to figure out what I'm doing and get some dirt on me so you can snitch to Ms. Matthews." I push past him and run down the dimly lit tunnel.

He storms after me. His light shines ahead of me, bouncing along the walls. "I'm not tattling. I think maybe I can help you. Why won't you talk to me?"

"I don't know you!"

He grabs my arm and swings me around. His eyes soften and he touches my face. "Come on, Ada. I thought we were connecting."

"Connection denied." I jerk away again and rush down one of the tunnels, searching for a quick exit to this stupid activity.

My body is fuming. He just had to ruin the moment with his questions. No matter what I want, this guy can't be trusted. No one at ReBoot can. Here, I get the sense that everyone is hiding something. And no matter how much I want to open up, let Fisher in, get someone on my side, I'm afraid he'll ruin everything.

And I can't let that happen.

The narrow passage winds deeper and deeper. Tears

stream down my face. I can't tell if Fisher's sincere, but he may be right. Maybe I need help. Maybe I should confide in him about the lab. About my suspicions about ReBoot. About how I suspect something bad is happening, but I won't stop until I figure it out.

About how much I miss my best friend.

So badly that my whole body aches. And the only way to stop the pain is to find out the answers to all my questions.

Maybe then I can let Simone go. Let Fisher in.

I slam into a dead end and scrape my elbow on the jagged wall.

I spin around and shine my light down the tunnel, waiting for Fisher.

It takes a few minutes for me to realize something.

Fisher didn't follow me. And now I'm stuck in this deep, dark cave—alone.

</CRASHING>

The silence messes with my head.

"Fisher?" I call out to the darkness.

No answer.

"Fisher!" I scream and then listen hard for a noise. Any sound. I can't believe he bailed.

I walk back down the passage, retracing my steps. If I find the yellow rope, the path out should be easy. But every time I reach a split in the tunnel, there's no yellow rope.

Several passages shoot off the side. Choosing the right one is key. One leads to life, the others lead to death. And I have no idea which way to go.

Soon, everything starts to look the same.

After a few circles, reality settles in. I'm alone. Lost in a dark cave. Deep underground.

I sweep my flashlight back and forth, searching for some sign of an exit. Eventually I spot a footprint and pray it belongs to someone who knows the way out. I follow the tracks. The hall seems to shrink, getting narrower and shorter. Then the tunnel dead-ends into a space that is only two feet high.

I drop down on my hands and knees, and shine a light

into the opening. At the far end, there's a sliver of sunlight peeking in from the outside. If I can crawl through this fifty-foot stretch, I can make it out.

I hook my flashlight to my belt and lay on my stomach to avoid smacking my head on the low ceiling. Dragging my body over layers of pebbles and dirt, I inchworm through the shallow space. Sharp rocks slice my palms and knees, but I don't stop for fear of getting stuck. With each movement, my helmet scrapes against the rocky ceiling, sending dust into my eyes. Something scurries ahead of me, but I ignore it and keep moving.

After a few minutes of crawling, I check my progress. I'm hovering somewhere between halfway in and halfway out.

"Come on, Ada. You can do this," I say to myself. Even though the crack tightens, I urge myself forward.

A faint rumbling sounds off in the distance. I stop to listen. The faint noise is followed by the hiss of crumbling rock. I drop to my stomach and cover my head just as bits of debris fall around me. A rock hits my helmet and knocks out the light, throwing me into pitch-black darkness. Again.

A wail slides up my throat. I've never known darkness like this before. My hand remains invisible until it's practically touching my nose. I keep still until the mini-avalanche stops. Dust billows around me forcing me to cough. For a few seconds, I freeze, waiting for things to settle. Don't want to set off any more trembling.

Once it seems safe, I attempt to squirm forward.

But my body won't budge.

My foot is stuck under a stubborn rock big enough to hold me back. I kick, hoping to release its grip, but there's not enough room. Panic creeps in.

I'm going to be stuck down here. In the dark. Forever.

I lose my cool and scream. "Help! Someone!" After a few minutes of yelling, my voice grows hoarse. I better save my voice. Tired, I rest my forehead on my arm. What am I going to do? And why does this always happen to me? My eyes close and I think I fall asleep.

Until a bright beam of light shines in my face. "Ada! You there?"

Relief spreads over me. "Becca! I'm stuck."

"Don't worry. We'll get you out." I hear her talking to someone.

I rest my forehead on the dirt and sigh a breath of relief. I'm so thankful someone is here to help.

Becca's head pops up at the end of the tunnel. "Ada, you're going to be okay. Crash is going to stay here with you while I go and get Mr. Anthony."

"Wait! Don't leave!" I don't want to be left in silence again.

"Ada, I'll be right back. I promise," she calls back and disappears.

I take in a deep breath. If Becca can go off into the tunnel alone when she's scared of the dark, then I can wait in a tiny space.

A light shines on my face. When I look up, Crash's head appears at the opening.

I mumble, "Hi, Crash."

He gives a weak smile.

"Don't suppose I can bribe you into talking today? I could use a distraction about now." I cough and bury my face. Even though he doesn't talk, it's better having him here.

In the distance, rumbling noises start up again.

"Crash, be careful!" I cry out. "The tunnel's gonna collapse again!"

But this time it's much shorter. Soon after protecting my head, the noises stop and the tunnel goes silent again.

"Crash? You there?" He flashes the beam of his light three times in Morse code to answer, so I keep talking. Just to stay sane. "I'm sorry about your sister. I know how it feels to lose someone. Someone special."

Silence.

I keep chatting, probably from the nerves. "I also know what it's like to feel guilty. Even now, I still feel like it's my fault Simone died."

When I look up, Crash's eyes lock onto mine. Even from far away, I can tell they're watering. Don't know if it's from the dust or if it's tears. But I can tell that he's hurting.

What would Simone do right now? She definitely wouldn't give up on Crash. Because she never gave up on me. Even when I had the smallest of problems.

Simone hugged me. "I know something's wrong."

I mumbled, "I failed another test. I suck."

"Was it in Positivity 101?"

I tried not to smile. "Very funny."

Simone shrugged. "Oh well. Can't win them all."

I rolled my eyes. "Thanks for the inspirational quote."

"Anytime. I'm always here for you." Simone squeezed me hard. "Kinda like an awesome new bra that hugs you, supports you, and will never, ever leave you hanging."

I remember laughing after that. Even though I felt so crummy.

No matter what was going on. She could always make me laugh. Sometimes humor overrides sadness. I try this approach with Crash. "You know, if you don't talk, I won't have anyone to debate with…which means I will always win. You don't want that, do you?"

Silence.

I sigh and whisper, "Don't worry, I won't give up on you that easily."

For a second, I'm not sure who I'm talking about.

Simone, Crash…or myself.

I ramble on, hoping to break through his emotional wall, but also to prevent me from freaking out about the real walls that are slowly closing in around me.

"For a long time, I couldn't accept that Simone would leave me behind. With no explanation. No goodbye. Just gone. After she died, I shut down. Bottled it all up inside. Not because I didn't care. But because I didn't want to hurt anymore. Maybe if you share what's bothering you, get it off your chest, you'll feel better. I think it hurts more to keep it inside. Trust me, I know. Maybe pushing the pain down doesn't make us feel any better, maybe it makes us feel…more alone."

Still nothing.

I stop talking and bury my face in frustration. What's the point? If my best friend of a lifetime wouldn't talk to me, what makes me think Crash would open up in just a couple of weeks?

Soft words crack the silence, barely audible.

"I loved my sister." Crash's voice is scratchy, much deeper than I expected.

I snap my head up but don't respond. Instead, I give him space to talk and sit in the uncomfortable silence.

"I killed her," he says quickly. As if the words were so heavy he had to toss them out before they could weigh him down any more.

My heart pounds in my chest, but I keep still. Deep down, I'm afraid he's like a baby bunny and the slightest flinch will send him scampering off.

Crash's bottom lip trembles. "I was supposed to babysit her that day when Mom was out. I only planned on checking email. My sister was watching cartoons, so I thought it'd be fine. Five minutes tops. Didn't realize how much time went by. Too much time."

Words flow out of him like water through a hairline crack. First it's a little, then as the flow speeds up, the hole expands, growing bigger and bigger, tearing down the walls of his emotional dam.

"Somehow she got the screen door open and went outside. She loved to swim. *I don't swim like a fish, I swim like a turtle*, she would say. I had no clue anything was wrong until I heard my mom scream. She found my sister floating in the pool. I did CPR for thirty minutes but nothing worked."

He pauses and his face pinches as if he's in pain. "Oh God."

"I'm so sorry," I whisper across the empty space between us. If I was closer, I'd hug him tight. Sometimes that's all someone can do.

He clears his throat. "You know the worst part?"

I shake my head but don't say a word. Sometimes I wish I had someone who could listen to me talk. Not talk or judge or give advice. Just someone to listen.

"The worst part is that I don't remember what I was doing while my sister was drowning in that pool only ten feet away. Isn't that horrible?" His voice projects louder than before. "It was my fault Suzie died. She was only four, and my mom will never forgive me."

"You're going to be okay," I say. "I promise."

"We both will," Crash whispers and dries his eyes with his sleeve, looking like a small boy who's lost everything. And I know exactly how he feels.

Then I hear Becca squeal. "Crash, you talked!"

Crash disappears and Mr. Anthony's appears in his place. "Hello, Ada. Strange seeing you here. You ready to come out?"

I force a smile, thankful this nightmare is almost over. "I think so."

He tosses me a rope. "Grab this and I'll pull you out."

I grip the lifeline and hold tight as they all tug together. My shirt rolls up underneath me, exposing my skin, but I don't care. I want out.

The light at the end of the tunnel grows bigger and brighter. When I finally reach the opening, Mr. Anthony and Becca each grab one hand and pull me out to safety.

I jump on Mr. Anthony and hug him tight. Again. "Thank you! For coming back."

"You're welcome," Mr. Anthony says. But instead of smiling, he's frowning. "And always remember, when you're lost, stay where you are. Trying to crawl out of that cave using an unmarked path was dangerous. You could've gotten stuck down there."

"Sorry. When I couldn't find the yellow rope, I panicked."

Becca walks up with the first-aid kit. She touches the scrapes and scratches along my arms. "Ada, you're hurt." She tends to my wounds as Mr. Anthony gathers the gear. He hands me a large men's T-shirt. "You can use this until you get home.

It's only then I notice that my shirt is ripped up, exposing my stomach and ribs. Most of the cloth is stained in a thin layer of blood and dirt. After pulling on the T-shirt, we all walk out together. Becca holds my hand and Crash walks next to me, pointing out rocks so I don't trip and fall.

"Where's Fisher?"

Becca throws a blanket over my shoulders. "He surfaced a while ago. Said you took off into the caves alone. What were you thinking, Ada? You could've have been lost forever. I was afraid we wouldn't find you in time."

I hug her. "You saved me."

She hugs me back. "I owed you one for the ropes course. I'm sorry I was mad at you."

"It's okay, I deserved it. I shouldn't have snooped through your stuff. That was uncool." I squeeze her hand. "Let's call it even."

When we step out of the cave and into the fresh air, the sun warms my face. I've never appreciated how much I miss inhaling air and expanding my lungs. I'll never take the process of breathing for granted again.

Crash helps me over the rocks.

I lean over and kiss his cheek. "You're the real hero, Crash. Thanks for getting me through that."

Crash smiles. "Don't ever say I talk too much."

"It speaks," Varian barks.

Becca snaps. "Oh shut up, Andrew!"

Varian storms toward me, looking annoyed. "Thanks for the drama, Lovelace. Now they won't let anyone go caving in there again. You're such a drag."

Raven ignores that I'm out. She couldn't care less if I'm safe.

"He's not worth a response," Becca says and leads me to the van.

Fisher leans against the door, biting his nails. When he sees me, he looks relieves and races over. "Ada! Thank God, you're all right. You scared me." He reaches out as if he's going to hug me.

"Don't." I hold out my hand to stop him. "You left me. I have nothing to say to you."

"Excuse me?" He frowns and takes a step back, obviously wounded at the rejection. "As I recall, *you're* the one who bolted. I wasn't sure which way you went."

I lean against the van and rub my ankle. It's not broken, but it sure is sore. "Yeah, right."

"Wait, you think I did this on purpose? Is that what you think of me?"

"Fisher, I don't think anything. In fact, I won't *think* about you at all."

Becca opens the van door. "Fisher, back off. This is not the time."

No one talks the whole way home. I stare at the back of Fisher's head. Once my adrenaline subsides and I'm able to relax, I can't help but feel bad for blaming him. He's right; I was the one who walked off.

But I won't apologize. Because maybe now he'll stop questioning me and leave me alone.

</LAB RATS>

When I sneak off to the lab, I can't help but feel like a dirty rat.

The kind that slinks along the halls silently without anyone knowing.

Walking in the lab, I see Raven is already at her computer, pounding away. Damn, I want to get on her station so I can grab that program.

Mr. Anthony greets me happily. "Ada! Good to see you. Ready for some cyber therapy?"

"Yes, sir." I sit down at my desk and log in. Even though I'm excited, part of me is crushed. I was hoping to get to those keyloggers, but it'll have to wait. If they are working in the lab today, I can't risk him seeing me pull data. Last thing I need is to lose computer privileges or his trust.

He rubs his hands together. "I have a really exciting exercise for you today."

I glance over at Raven, who is already deep in her work. I'd love another chance to battle her today. If I can hack into the White House and kick Casper's cyber butt, I can beat this girl. But I guess that will have to wait.

"So what's the challenge?" I ask.

Mr. Anthony leans over my shoulder. "Today, I want you to mess around in our simulation environment to see how good you really are."

I sit up straighter. "Really? That sounds interesting."

"It's more than that. This activity will give you a serious challenge."

My body quivers with excitement. Not sure how this challenge could beat my White House win, but I'm up for anything that will get my adrenaline pumping again. Even if it's just for a short time.

Mr. Anthony walks over to my terminal. "May I?"

When I scoot aside, he pulls up a server on my desktop and then steps back. "Ada, I've set up a fairly intricate testing environment here where different hacks can be tested without doing permanent damage. Thanks to former ReBoot kids who have played around in here—just like you—the simulation server has accumulated hundreds of detailed websites to play with. For fun. This is a real-life-looking hacking simulator in which you are given a virtual operating system to build code and run scripts. You will wonder whether you are in a real environment or a virtual one."

My hopes sink. I click around on the computer. "You want me to code a website?" Boring!

Mr. Anthony chuckles. "Oh no. This is much more than that. You will be given a scenario to complete. Similar to your challenge with Raven but way more complicated and exciting. The purpose of this is to give you a cool goal and a safe environment to practice your coding skills."

This is awesome. "Good, because I'm feeling more and more like a noob every day I'm off a computer."

"You can't be this good at hacking and ever be a noob, but I understand," Mr. Anthony says. "And it is important that you keep your skills sharp. There are information security jobs out there where they actually hire hackers and computer wizards to test out technology environments."

"Great." I shake out my hands. Finally some challenging stuff. Hacking with Raven is okay, but it's not exciting. "So what's my challenge?"

"Here's your scenario. The FBI director is worried that an unauthorized person has access to the national Shared Arrest System or SAS. It's a shared database for all law enforcement to access any arrest records and other sensitive data. This could be used to find information on active shooters, gang members, drug dealers, and even domestic terrorists."

I'm familiar with a similar system. My dad has mentioned it before. "Sounds like the Joint Arrest Records System, JARS?"

"Exactly." Mr. Anthony nods. "This is our simulated version. Cool, right?"

"Very," I say. Eager to get started, I rush him a little. "So, what am I supposed to do?"

"Good question." Mr. Anthony hands me a sheet with the scenario on it. "The director thinks a hacker has found a vulnerability and breached the system, downloading data and selling it for a profit. As you can imagine, in the wrong hands, this information could be dangerous. They need to stop him, but they don't know how the hacker's getting in and out. The director wants you to test SAS and locate any vulnerabilities that could be used as a back door. Then they can have information security close it. I also want you to run a query to prove your access is legit."

I'm feeling confident. "Doesn't sound too hard."

"The system has multiple levels of security you will have to disengage. And you have to do all this without being detected. Or you can get locked out of the simulation."

"What is the query?" I ask.

Mr. Anthony shrugs. "I don't know. Maybe query all cybercrimes for teenagers between thirteen and eighteen and run a full report. When you're done, I want to see your source code. The director will want to pass it off to security. Think you can handle it?"

I salute. "No problem." I crack my knuckles and roll my head before working my magic. First I use programs to surpass all the levels of security protecting the system. Then I search for vulnerable entry points that might let me gain access to the private portal. I sniff around for passwords, search for unsecured wireless networks, and look for an open-source operating system.

After about an hour, I find a back door into SAS.

I run a report on teenagers who were arrested for any cybercrimes. The system generates a list of arrestees for ones that include unauthorized access, damaging of a computer, trespassing, and intent to defraud. The charges look much worse on paper than they sound. Makes me sick. I don't want to have an arrest record hanging out there on me. That's for sure.

"Done!" I sit back in my chair, feeling exhilarated. "That was amazing."

"Wow, that was quick." Mr. Anthony walks over. "How did it feel? Challenging enough?"

I shrug. "Maybe for a beginner." Then I study the list of fake criminals generated.

My heart drops when I spot Simone Jordan's name. I click her file and read through the charges. There are more than I expected. They even noted her butterfly tattoo and chicken pox scars. At the bottom, Mitnick is listed as the arresting officer. Seeing a formal file makes her arrest so official. So real.

I swallow. "Mr. Anthony?"

"What is it?"

I can't stop staring at Simone's name. "I thought this simulation wasn't real."

He nods. "Yeah, it's not. But it looks real, doesn't it? The things we can do with simulations now are scary."

"Then why is Simone's name on this list?" I ask.

"What?" He leans in and studies my screen. "Oh! We prefilled the SAS data from our registration files. So it looks real. It's a private system and stored on our private network, so it's secure of course."

I sigh and sit back. "Makes sense." So why does it bother me so much?

He sits on the edge of my desk. "I'm sorry, Ada. I didn't even think about Simone's name being in there. Are you upset?"

"No, I'm okay," I say. "It just freaked me out. For a second, I thought I made a mistake and hacked the real system."

He pats my shoulder. "Goodness, I can see why! That would suck. I'd have some serious explaining to do, huh?"

"You and me both."

He points to my screen. "Don't forget to save your source code for me to review. I'll let you know if there's anything you could have done better."

"Okay." I grin. "But there isn't."

He laughs. "Don't get too confident."

I make a file of the source code but stop before saving it. An icky feeling surfs around in my stomach. I know it's a simulation, but after seeing Simone's name, I can't help but feel bad exposing her. Even if it is fake. After some thought, I delete the list of cyber offenders and run a query on DUI offenses instead. Following instructions, I upload the newly-compiled list to the system. Before saving the source code, I edit a few key code lines. Mr. Anthony says the system's secure, but I can't take any chances. Not after the SocialNet hack getting out. Besides, he knows I hacked in, and it's not like any of this is real anyway. The query and code might be different, but Mr. Anthony won't care. I still completed the exercise. Successfully, I might add.

When I turn to leave, Ms. Matthews is standing in the doorway. The blue light from the computers reflects off her face.

I almost scream.

"What is going on in here?" she yells.

Mr. Anthony shoots to his feet. "Irene. What are you doing here?"

She crosses her arms. "I should be asking you the same question." She eyes Raven and me. "And more importantly, what are *they* doing here? Computers are off limits to program residents. You know that."

The woman's face turns beet red. She looks like she's going to implode. Right here, right now.

I grab the headphones off my neck and shove them in my pocket. Bass beats blare from my left hip.

"Oh, don't even bother trying to hide them." She holds out her hand.

I yank the MP3 player out of my pocket, still blaring, and drop it in her palm. "I'm sorry," I mumble and hang my head, knowing I'm in deep now. "Ms. Matthews, it's only music."

Forbidden music. Hidden flash drives. And some extra coding in a secret computer lab.

"I don't care what it is," she says, scowling. "It's against the rules."

"Irene," Mr. Anthony says. "Don't be mad at the girls. It's my fault. I can explain."

"And you will." She folds her hands. "But first I'd like to see Raven and Ada in my office. Now!"

</BUSTED>

IF LOOKS COULD KILL, THIS LADY WOULD BE A SURE-FIRE murderer.

Raven and I follow Ms. Matthews to her office. She opens the door and motions to Raven. "You first." Then she looks at me. "Sit tight. And don't move."

Raven stomps into the room, and Ms. Matthews slams the door behind them. The director yells a few times, but I can only make out a few select words: *Disappointment. Probation. Disrespect.* And a few others that are much more inappropriate. I never hear Raven's voice.

When the door finally opens, Raven storms past me without making eye contact. She mutters a few expletives of her own as she races down the hallway. At the very end, she screams at the top of her lungs, "I'm tired of this shit!"

Ms. Matthews breathes heavy. Her face is flushed in anger and sweat. "You're next."

My voice quivers. "Yes, ma'am."

I follow her inside and sit in a stiff chair, bracing myself for a raging storm.

"What do you have to say for yourself?" she asks.

I don't want to throw Mr. Anthony under the bus, so I speak my words very carefully. "Mr. Anthony caught me in the lab after I accidently found it. He didn't tell me about it. But he said if I worked harder in the program, he'd let me play a little to blow off some steam."

"And that's what you need to do in order to work hard?" Ms. Matthews spouts back. "A computer fix."

I didn't think much about it. But it sounds way worse when she says it like that. "I guess."

"Don't you find that completely pathetic?" Ms. Matthews asks. Her voice is sharp and tight with each word.

I wanna say 'not really', but agree by nodding.

"The infraction on the lab is bad enough, and I will deal with Mr. Anthony on his lack of judgment." She holds up the MP3 player like it's a dead rat. "Did he give this to you too?"

I shake my head. "No, ma'am." I find being super polite can help diffuse a situation.

Ms. Matthews slams down one hand on her desk, forcing me to jerk in my seat. She gets in my face and speaks sharply through gritted teeth. "Then *who* gave this to you?"

I'm confused. She busts me on the computer in a hidden lab at her rehab facility, but she's angry about a music player?

My eyes dart around the room until they land on an empty box. "It's mine. I hid it the first day." It's a total lie, but it's all I have in the moment.

She squints her eyes as if the sun is unbearably bright. "Liar! You think I don't know about the illegal contraband in this place? I've seen it. Found it. I've just never been able to tie it to anyone." She holds up the MP3 player. "I want to know who gave this to you. Now!"

I chew my bottom lip so hard the taste of iron tells me I've cracked the surface.

"Oh, you're not talking?" Ms. Matthews grabs the old phone on her desk and begins to dial. Each number takes forever as the rotary rolls back to home position. "Maybe your parents can jog your memory before I kick you out of the program."

An obvious threat. If I fail this program, it'll look terrible in court. I'll go to jail. Dad's career will be over, and I will never find out what happened to Simone.

The Dark Angel will be dead.

"Wait!" I yell as she sticks her finger in number nine's hole. Even though I promised Becca I wouldn't tell, I promised Simone—and myself—even more.

Ms. Matthews slams down the phone and leans in. Her breath reeks of burned coffee. "It was Raven. Wasn't it?"

Raven has nothing to do with this, but for some reason, I don't dispute the accusation. Maybe for fear of ratting out Becca.

The woman sits back and rocks in her chair. "Tell me it's Raven and you can stay. I've been eyeing her for months, and she's up to something."

I look away, afraid to answer. If I say yes, I falsely accuse Raven. And although I don't like her much, it's not fair to throw her under the bus for something she didn't do. On the other hand, if I point a finger at Becca, not only will she get kicked out, but I will never find out what's going on because right now, Becca is my only link to Simone and those flash drives.

Before I can answer, Ms. Matthews clears her throat. "I'll take your silence as a yes."

I want to protest but don't. Deep down, I feel horrible for not speaking up. Dad always says, *not saying something is as bad as lying.*

Ms. Matthews stands. "Pack your things; you are leaving ReBoot in the morning."

I snap my head up and shoot to my feet. "Wait, what?"

She sneers. "I might be able to look past the lab because it was Mr. Anthony who allowed it, right or wrong. But defying me and my rules while refusing to be honest is a whole other story. If anyone finds out I let you off the hook when you cheated the system, I will have a mass rebellion. Total chaos. Technology will creep in everywhere. And I need to maintain control in this facility." Her voice has escalated to a full-on yell by the end of the sentence.

She's losing it. Big time.

"Please, Ms. Matthews. Give me one more chance." I pinch back tears and shake my head in denial. Because if I leave this place now, I'll hurt the people I love. Plus, I'll never get what I need. I'll never move on. I'll always be haunted by what really happened to my friend. And I'm too close to let this go now. "Please."

Before she can dismiss me, someone knocks on the door.

"Go away!" Ms. Matthews yells.

Mr. Anthony opens the door. "Irene, we need to talk."

"I told you that lab would lead to trouble." She holds up the MP3 player. "I caught your group member with this. Raven gave it to her."

I cringe when I hear her blame Raven again. If I can get Mr. Anthony alone, maybe I can tell him the truth. Maybe he'll be understanding of Becca's involvement.

"Now, wait a minute." Mr. Anthony steps into the room with both hands up like he's under arrest. "Let's not overre-act. It's music, not a computer. If you're upset about the lab. That was my fault, so be mad at me."

I glance back and forth between them. A drop of renewed hope sits on the distant horizon. Maybe Mr. Anthony can turn this thing around for me. If anyone can, it's him. He's her partner after all.

Ms. Matthews shakes her head so hard, I feel like her head is about to roll off. "No. It doesn't matter. Ada makes her own decisions."

"Isn't this her first offense?" Mr. Anthony asks. "You gave

Raven another chance. Why not Ada? As I recall, you and I agreed the official policy was one warning."

"I can do what I want. No matter what you and . . . well . . . *they* think. I run this place. It's *mine*." Ms. Matthews emphasizes the last word.

Mr. Anthony narrows his eyes. It's the first time I've seen an ounce of anger spew from him. "Can we discuss this in private?"

Ms. Matthews' face turns a blood red and she faces me. "Ada, we are done for now. You can wait outside."

I beeline for the door, practically running, eager to escape her wrath. Out in the hall, I listen to the directors go at it. Their voices are garbled, but from what I can tell, Mr. Anthony talks and Ms. Matthews freaks out. Yelling and slamming stuff around. At one point, she shrieks out a few cuss words.

A couple minutes later, Mr. Anthony jerks open the office door, but then quietly shuts it behind him. His hair is ruffled and his clothes are wrinkled. If I hadn't been standing here listening the whole time, I'd swear they sparred to see who won the showdown.

"I'm sorry about this, Ada. It's my fault. I should've been more frank with her about the lab and how I was using it. It's not on you, so you won't be punished for that." He stands in front of me with his hands on his hips. "But regarding the music Raven gave you, that was careless. Consider this your official warning."

Before he walks off, I have to clear Raven's name. "Mr. Anthony I have to tell you something."

He holds up his hand. "Please, Ada, not now. You need to learn when to stop talking."

But I don't. "It's about Raven. She isn't the one who gave me the music player."

He faces me. "What?"

"Becca did," I admit.

His face drops, but his curiosity shoots up even higher. "She's the one giving kids all that stuff?"

The knot in my throat chokes my words. "Yes. I didn't want to rat her out, but I don't want Raven to get kicked out because of something she didn't do."

He frowns. "Please don't mention this to Ms. Matthews. I'll deal with Raven *and* Becca on my own." He pats my shoulder. "Thank you for being honest. You need to lie low for a while or you'll be out too." After the warning, he spins around on his heel and charges down the hall.

My stomach drops. I just threw Becca to the virtual wolves.

I want to chase after Mr. Anthony and apologize for having the music and letting him down. Not to mention for allowing Ms. Matthews to believe Raven was leading the whole contraband thing. But I need to give him a little time or I'll push him over the edge too.

Feeling guilty, I reluctantly let him walk away.

Ms. Matthews stands in her office, glaring at me through the window. Her eyes flash anger as she closes the interior blinds.

After I duck away to avoid a counterattack, I exhale. That was close. My days here are numbered, I can feel it. From this point forward, I have to be careful. Ms. Matthews is suspicious, and Mr. Anthony is on guard. My life teeters on the edge. I'm walking along a tight rope and could fall either way. Brings back memories of the dreaded ropes course.

I race back to my room to warn Becca, but she's already asleep. I'll have to clear this mess up first thing in the morning. And it's not going to be fun.

I'm a rat. Worse than the RAT I put into John's computer at the White House that helped me sneak into his computer.

The worst rat there is.

I crawl into bed quietly and stare out the dirty window. Thick fog moves in and blankets the trees, protecting them from the ominous clouds that smother the skies along with any lingering stars.

I pull the covers over my head, hiding from the world. Today was bad.

And I have a feeling tomorrow isn't going to be much better.

</PHISHING FOR ANSWERS>

Becca avoids me all morning.

Her eyes are swollen and red, like she's been crying. I can only assume Mr. Anthony has already spoken to her.

I suck.

As we head for Group, I run up behind her and grab her arm. "Becca, can we talk—?"

She yanks her arm away and glares with sad eyes. "No, you've talked enough. Too much really."

I lean in and whisper. "I'm so sorry. I couldn't throw Raven under the bus, and I would have been kicked out."

"Good, I'm glad you saved yourself." She shrugs. "Anyway, it's my fault. I trusted you because Simone trusted you. I was wrong. Maybe she was too."

I stop, unable to speak, and watch her enter the room. I swallow a lump of regret. Maybe I should have let Raven take the fall. The girl's obviously used to getting in trouble. Not to mention, she'd never save me from anything. Ever.

By the time I gather myself, my group is already paired and doing a communication exercise. Becca and Crash face each other while Varian sits in front of Mr. Anthony, looking pissed. Fisher relaxes across from an empty seat. Obviously meant for me.

Raven's MIA. She's obviously late too.

Mr. Anthony either ignores me or doesn't notice I'm in the room because he continues his lecture. "Communication with people is important. When we stay online too much, we lose the exchange of valuable hormones that comes with social-izing face to face. Today we'll practice communicating with each other."

I claim the lone chair in front of Fisher. "What are we doing?"

"Exchanging hormones, weren't you listening?" Fisher grins his one-sided smirk.

Mr. Anthony notices me. "Ada. Nice of you to join us. One more time and you're on singing duty for 'Copacabana.'" Thanks to Fisher's rap stunt, Mr. Anthony chooses our musical punishment now, and he doesn't pick anything recorded after 1980. The way he looks at me makes me drop my head in shame.

I glance at the door. "Where's Raven?"

"Haven't seen her." Fisher smiles. "But who cares. Thanks to her, Varian got stuck 'communicating' with Mr. A. Hilarious."

Varian glares at us over his sunglasses.

Mr. Anthony cups both of Fisher's shoulders. "Why don't you focus on Ada and leave Andrew to me?"

"No problem. I've got her covered." Fisher hops his chair closer until our knees touch. "I'll teach her everything I know."

"That's what I'm afraid of." Mr. Anthony rubs his three-day-old scruff while studying me. He motions for me to engage Fisher. "Go ahead. Remember, eye contact is impor-tant in the real world. You guys should try it."

My mouth dries out. The thought of looking into anybody's eyes for a long period of time—let alone a staring contest with Fisher's navy blues—makes me nervous. Uneasy. As if he can see everything hiding deep inside me.

But now is not the time to object. Today, it's time to suck it up and do whatever Mr. Anthony asks.

I owe him.

After grabbing the bottled water from under my chair, I twist off the top to take a sip. "What do we do?"

"You have to gaze into my dreamy eyes." He bats the long eyelashes hiding beneath his dark frames. We stare at each other a long minute. Fisher's eyes are dark navy blue with specks of white, reminding me of Zed's Milky Way screen-saver. Looking at him makes me feel as if I'm floating off into space. Sucked into a black hole. "Think you can handle it?"

I laugh midsip. Water shoots out of my mouth and drenches Fisher's face.

Fisher laughs. "Say it, don't spray it. I want the news, not the weather." He wipes his chin with the hem of his T-shirt, revealing a chiseled stomach.

"Oh geez, I'm so sorry." I fumble with my drink and try to screw the lid back on. Instead, the bottle squirts out of my hands, dumping liquid in Fisher's lap.

He jumps to his feet and squeals like a girl. "Whoa! That is some cold water."

Varian cackles. "He'll never get a date now. Shrinkage is not sexy."

I close my eyes and cringe. Murphy's Law loves the crotch shot. Couldn't hit that kind of bullseye if I was offered a million megabytes. My face grows warmer by the minute, overheating like a failed hard drive. "Fisher, I am so sorry. I'll help you clean up." I snatch a paper towel off the table and dab his soaked pant leg.

Fisher pushes his wet blond hair away from his face. "Now, *that's* more like it."

The comment only eggs on Varian. "Ada, you can paper towel me down there any day."

I throw the balled up paper towel at Fisher's face, hitting him square between the eyes. "Jerk."

Mr. Anthony's voice saves me from drowning Fisher with my bare hands. "Mr. Parker. This is about communication. Not getting a laugh…or a date."

Fisher leans back and lifts one eyebrow. "We were only practicing eye contact, sir."

Mr. Anthony taps my shoulder. "Ada, switch with Becca so Fisher can *cool* down."

"Oh don't worry." Fisher wipes his damp pants. "Ada's cooled me down plenty."

I stick out my tongue, because I'm mature like that.

Then that same loud alarm goes off.

Everyone in the room glances around in complete horror.

Becca covers her mouth with both hands and mumbles, "Oh no. Not another one."

Crash hunches over, burying his face while Mr. Anthony corrals us. "Come on guys, you know the drill."

We all mull out into the main room and stand around in silence. It's so quiet, we could hear a ghost sneeze.

Ms. Matthews strolls in through the door. "I'm afraid I have more bad news." She swings her head in my direction and makes eye contact with me before looking away. "Raven is gone."

There's an audible gasp in the room.

"Unfortunately, she violated a rule and was being transferred out of ReBoot today," Ms. Matthews says robotically. "However, she took it upon herself to run away and we have no idea where she is. They found some of her things in a dumpster nearby, but she is nowhere to be found."

I press a hand against my chest, struggling to breathe.

I ratted out Becca. All for nothing.

Fisher touches my shoulder. "Are you okay?"

I cringe under his touch. The dude can't stop drilling me.

"I can't deal with your twenty-one questions right now Fisher. So leave me alone."

Fisher looks wounded, but I don't care. The guy's been following me and hammering me about stuff he knows nothing about. And I don't care what he says, I don't think he *accidently* left me alone in that cave. He did it out of spite, to prove I needed his help. But I could have died if Becca didn't find me. I shudder thinking about the small dark space. That feeling of suffocation consumes me again.

I breathe in deep…because I can.

Ms. Matthews stops in the doorway and throws out a bit more detail before she leaves. "I wanted you to know about Raven, but try not to worry too much. As many of you know, she has a long-standing issue with authority and is a professional runaway. She always takes off when things don't go her way, so this isn't a surprise. I suspect she'll pop up eventually."

When the speech is over, kids remain standing.

No matter what Ms. Matthews says, we're all thinking one thing.

There's a good chance Raven is dead. Just like Simone.

Just like the others.

Mr. Anthony makes us return to Group. He tries to refocus our attention, but I can't concentrate. All I can think about is Raven and Simone. When I scan the room, I realize I'm not the only one looking lost. Crash curls up in the corner by himself. Becca is no longer her spirity self. And Varian and Fisher have obviously called a truce in their Battle of the Egos because they are ignoring each other. Which is a miracle.

Maybe if I reach out, someone will reach back.

"Hey, you." I slide next to Crash and touch his shoulder. When he doesn't answer, I nudge him with my elbow. "You okay?"

Crash scribbles a note and slides it in front of me.

Without reading it, I push his hand away and sit facing

him. "Crash, you talked in the cave. You can talk now. What's wrong? Is it Raven?"

Crash doesn't move. Instead he keeps his head down, disconnected.

Tears claw at my eyes. I'm worn down. Tired of fighting. Tired of hurting. "Please, Crash. Don't shut me out."

He scoots his chair a few inches away. Like he's slowly drifting off.

Simone did the same thing. Only I didn't notice her drifting away until she was gone.

Crash tries to hand me his note again.

"No! You talk to me if you have something to say." I snatch the piece of paper and shove it in my pocket. Then I wait for him to say something. Anything. Just one word to show he cares. One word to give me hope. Hope that we can all screw up, but still come out okay in the end.

Hope that life can go on after ReBoot.

After Simone.

Crash stares at me with flashbulb eyes. He opens his mouth but then lowers his head, shifting his eyes back down to the floor.

"I have to go," I mutter. I can't—won't—let anyone see me cry.

I storm out of the room and sprint down the hall. My feet slug along, like I'm on a treadmill. Running, yet going nowhere. My hands slam into the double doors, and I burst outside, gulping in the night air. Glancing around, I take off down the field and race into the arms of the somber woods. The cold air freezes my lungs, and the frozen snow crunches under my feet. Sounds like the Earth is cracking and will soon collapse underneath me. Forcing me to fall into complete darkness. With no way out.

Eventually, I stop running so my heart doesn't explode. I lean against the tree and catch my breath before sliding to the ground. It's only been two weeks, yet it seems like I've been here for ages. Only somehow, I'm still in the same place. No information on Simone. Varian and Fisher laugh at me. Crash isn't talking. And Becca and I are strangers again.

I hug my knees to keep warm and shiver from the icy wind searing my skin. The cold shows no mercy and forces its way into my pores and bites on my bones. Maybe I'll sit here and freeze to death quietly. Slip away without a single sound. Nothing left behind but a frozen heart no longer able to beat. No longer able to feel.

When the tears finally release, the chilled air freezes them to my cheeks. Sitting in a ball, I cry. For me. For my parents. For the way I've unplugged from my entire life. I cry for Becca; I cry for Crash; I even cry for Raven.

But mostly, I cry for Simone.

Because I miss and need my best friend—now more than ever. And no matter what I do, who I meet, or what I find out, she's never coming back.

Simone is gone. Forever.

And I still don't know why.

</K.I.S.S.—KEEP IT SIMPLE, STUPID>

A VOICE CUTS THROUGH THE BITING WIND.

"I would ask if you're okay, but I've quit the Inquisition."

Not bothering to wipe away tears or fix my makeup or hide the pain, I glance up through clouded eyes. "Fisher, I'm fine."

"Fine, huh?" But Fisher's smirk droops when he notices my face. He removes his jacket and wraps it around my trembling shoulders. Then he squats down in front of me and balances on his toes. "Fine, huh? Ada Lovelace, I hate to break it to you, but your dream of being an actress is over because you will never win any Oscars with that weak performance. Needs more conviction."

"Stop," I grumble, too exhausted to banter. "I'm not in the mood for jokes."

"You're right. I'm a jackass." He sits on a patch of frozen grass and drapes his arm over my shoulders.

I tense.

"Don't worry, I don't bite." Fisher pulls me close and then whispers, "At least not until the second date."

I surrender to his warmth and bury my head in his shirt that smells of pine and sandalwood. I relax. Wrapping myself in Fisher's coat is almost as good as being wrapped up in his arms.

Only the jacket's much safer.

"At the risk of sounding repetitive, are you okay, Ada?" Fisher's rough voice soothes me, and the sweet way he says my name melts the walls freezing around my heart.

"You know what? I'm not okay. And I haven't been for a long time." When I glance up at the treetops, tears stream down my face. I'm not sure how to stop them.

Fisher uses his thumb to wipe a clinging tear. "Aww, man, please don't cry. I'm not very good with crying."

I half laugh and half sob. "Me neither. Until now, I guess."

"Seriously, it's like I'm scared of it," he says. "I have a real fear of crying."

I nudge him with my elbow. "Pretty sure that's not a disease recognized by WebMD."

He hands me a light blue and green handkerchief. "Then I have no choice but to give you the hanky off my back."

I flip over the cotton square and stare at the three embroidered initials: FPM. "Wait, you carry a *handkerchief*. Isn't that a little *old*?"

"It was my grandfather's hankie. He carried it everywhere. Said it helped woo the sad ladies. Thought I'd try it out . . . after I washed it of course." Fisher grins.

I wipe my face with the soft cloth that smells a little like lavender mixed with guy's deodorant and eye him. For once, he appears serious. "Looks like you're quite the crying pro. The handkerchief. The coat. Great listening skills. Empathetic phrases. What else could I ask for?"

"What do you need?" Fisher stares at my lips.

My defenses jump to attention. I'm not sure I can trust Fisher. Or anyone else here. Not Becca. Not Crash. Not even myself. And one cry doesn't outweigh all my questions and suspicions.

"I gotta go." I stand and Fisher practically rolls off me.

I drop the jacket in his lap and speak fast. "Thanks for . . . talking." Then I speed-walk up the hill toward safety.

Fisher catches up and grabs my hand, swinging me around. "Wait. That's it? I lend you my hanky and you ditch me?"

"What else is there?"

He clutches my frozen hands. "I think you know."

Luckily, I don't feel his grip; and therefore, his touch doesn't affect me as much as it could…or should.

"Fisher, don't." I pull my arms away, but he grips them tight like he's not letting go. For anything.

"Please, Ada. Trust me. I won't hurt you." Fisher stands there pleading with his eyes. He studies my lips and gives me that silly lopsided smirk of his. "Don't push me away."

In fact, that's the last thing I want right now. No matter what my head says, my heart craves a connection. With someone. With Fisher.

My eyes focus on his chest. *Do not look into his eyes.* The warning repeats in my head. Do. Not. Look. Into. His. Eyes.

Living on the edge, I glance up and stare look into Fisher's dark eyes. They make me feel free and light.

Without analyzing it or questioning why, I clutch his shirt and pull him close. I rise up on my toes, pressing my lips to his. For a second, neither one of us moves. I hold on to him tight, not wanting to let go. Like every chance I have to be okay is wrapped up in this one kiss.

A small flame ignites in my belly and burns softly, thawing me from the inside out.

When I finally pull away, he smiles that smile I love so much. "Miss Ada Lovelace, connection accepted."

I cover my face, totally embarrassed I threw myself at some guy while everything around me crumbles. "Oh God! I'm so sorry."

"Wait. Stop. No thinking. Stay with me," he says and holds my face with one hand.

Our eyes lock and he smiles before pressing his lips against mine again. At first our teeth clink awkwardly, but we find a groove. The last few months peel away like a crumbling building under demolition.

Fisher's kiss is more than just a kiss. It's the first time I've let go of everything—all the hurt, all the confusion—in a long time. It's the spark of hope. Hope that I can be okay again.

Hope that I can let someone in and be me again.

He pulls back gently, and it seems to take forever until our lips part, leaving only an inch gap between us.

I open my eyes and suck in air, unsure of what to say first: *Wow, how dare you, more please.* Instead I say, "What was that?"

He kisses the tip of my nose. "That's what I call team building."

I playfully smack him, trying to act all cool about the kiss. "You're taking advantage of my vulnerability."

"Guilty as charged." He shrugs. "Hey, I'm not ashamed of kissing a beautiful and unbelievably smart girl, especially if it makes her feel better."

Before I can slither away, he traps me against the tree with one hand above my head and pecks me on the cheek with his velvety lips. If my back presses into the tree any more, I'll melt into the bark.

My body shivers and my teeth chatter. "Um, it's getting cold. We shouldn't stay out here much longer."

He lightly kisses my chin. "You're right. It's way too dangerous . . . or I could keep you warm."

I place both hands on his chest and push softly. "Fisher, we should head back inside. It's almost time for dinner."

"Your wish is my command."

We don't say a word as we walk up the hill. I already feel tons better than I did only a few short minutes ago. It's amazing what a great kiss can do to set off endorphins that lift your spirits . . . and your core body temperature. Maybe that's the excuse I'll go with. I kissed Fisher to avoid hypothermia. Warmth by kissing.

Strange how a relationship between two people can change in an instant. One minute you are distant friends. And the next, you're awkward kissing buddies.

I wonder if we can be more than one kiss. After all, he went out of his way to find me, so he obviously cares. Maybe I should confide in him. Let him in. Maybe he can help me figure this thing out.

"Fisher, can I tell you something?" I ask.

"Sure. But if it's real juicy, I have to warn you, I might sell it to the tabloids. A senator's daughter can mean a big payoff."

"That's bad."

"I was kidding. Obviously." He faces me. The moonlight light sprays through the trees and streaks his face. "What do you want to tell me?"

He waits for my answer. But I'm not sure what to dive into first.

Why I'm in here. How I almost got kicked out. How I sneak off to a computer lab at night. How Mr. Anthony makes me code for him. Or should I start with my secret online identity as the Dark Angel?

Then again, maybe I shouldn't kiss and dump.

"Ada? What did you want to tell me?"

Doubt seeps in again. "You know what, we can talk later," I say. "It's not important."

"You sure?"

I nod. "Positive. Let's not ruin the mood."

He studies me for a second and then nods. "Fair enough, but that means you have to join me for a recycled meatloaf dinner tomorrow night."

"Only if you're buying," I answer.

"Deal."

At the door, I give Fisher a quick kiss goodbye and head to my room. At the corner, I look back and watch him walk the opposite way, praying he doesn't turn around and bust me. He pulls up his jacket collar and shoves his hands into his pockets. I like how slow and smooth he moves. Gliding from moment to moment. Never in a hurry.

I can't help but smile, still feeling his kiss on my lips.

Simone was all for kissing. I can hear her now. *"One good kiss is worth a thousand more."*

After Fisher disappears, I walk by Ms. Matthews' office and speed up until the voices catch my attention.

"I want that lab shut down," Ms. Matthews hisses.

Mr. Anthony's voice is softer. "Irene, you know as well as I do we can't shut it down. We made a deal and we need the money."

A few questions stick in my head: What money is he talking about? And who are "we"?

"I don't care what we lose or who doesn't like it. The lab comes down tomorrow or I'll burn it down myself."

The silence lingers for a few minutes until Ms. Matthews speaks again. This time much softer. "And you're fired."

Mr. Anthony's voice changes. "You're kidding. Because of this?"

"Because I can't trust you anymore. So get your stuff and leave. Tonight."

My heart sinks. I can't help but feel guilty and somewhat responsible for this too.

The door opens, and I step back into the shadows as Mr. Anthony bolts out of her office.

One thing's for sure. With Mr. Anthony leaving and Ms. Matthews' threat, I have to get back in that lab tonight, or I'll never get the program data on those user IDs. My last clue to Simone.

I can also check out the keylogger I loaded on Raven's

computer. See what she was doing the last time she was in there.

Maybe it will give me a clue where she is now.

</A LOOPHOLE>

It's now or never.

Unfortunately, ReBoot is on lockdown so I haven't been able to get back in that lab. Ms. Matthews upgraded the first floor security system to make sure no one leaves. Ever.

I lie low a couple days until I can take a chance again. Because of the weather, Ms. Matthews gave us a build-your-own-schedule day. To avoid everyone in my group, I pick anything I know the others wouldn't choose: feeding the animals, shoveling muddy snow, and square dancing. I don't want to see Crash, can't take Varian's stupid outbursts, and Becca hates me.

But if I'm really honest, my main goal is to avoid Fisher. After the other night, I'm not sure how to act or what to say. The days after a kiss is so awkward. Now, I don't know if it meant something or nothing.

Tonight, I skip dinner and pretend to be asleep when Becca comes back.

Once she's in full-on snore mode, I tiptoe out of our room and sneak down the stairwell. A security guard sits at his desk guarding the front door. His back is facing me, and his feet are propped up on the corner of his desk while he watches an episode of *Family Feud*.

"No one would say that!" The guard takes a bite of his sandwich and yells with his mouth full. "Ask real people these questions. Not your fake audience."

When he yells obscenities at the survey answers, I creep past him, praying he doesn't turn around. At the bottom, I slip into the broom closet across from his station. *Family Feud* is now at the Fast Money Round. Seeing as he's temporarily distracted, I have less than ten minutes to shut off the system and lure this guy away long enough for me to sneak out the front door.

I squat behind the computer and pull up the center's intranet. First, I scan for the security program and then double-click the file </SECURITY SYSTEMS>. I turn off the alarm on the front door and reprogram it to appear engaged. I also flip off the outside cameras outside along the north perimeter. I don't need any recorded proof of my illegal movements.

Once the alarm disengages, I drum up a distraction to pull this guy away from his desk. I click through the system and trigger a window alarm at the far end of the house.

Seconds later, the alarm blares in the distance.

I hide in the closet and wait.

Ms. Matthews' voice blares over the guard's walkie-talkie. "Barry! I hear an alarm in the cafeteria. Get over there! Now! If someone sneaks out again, I'm firing you this time."

The guard radios back, "10-4." Then he whispers a couple of swear words, proving he hates Ms. Matthews as much as anyone. He grabs his flashlight and runs off.

The minute he's out of sight, I slip out the front door unnoticed.

The icy wind blasts me hard in the face, so I'm forced to take a step back. My leather jacket is perfect for sneaking around in the dark, but it's not warm enough for arctic conditions.

No time for comfort.

I wait for the cameras to pivot before bolting across the yard. Hiding behind the hedged border, I check both ways before slipping into the trees and circling around the main building. My body shivers, a mixture of fear and the below-freezing temperatures seeping into my skin. The only sound is the wind calling out to the trees with a bellowing howl.

Behind me, a stick cracks, warning me someone is close by.

Then two hands clutch onto my shoulders. "Ada?"

Startled, I jump. "Jesus, Fisher! What the hell are *you* doing here?"

The look on his face tells me I scared him too. "I'm following *you*. Very easily, I might add. Your hacking skills may be top notch, but you need to work on your slinking skills. Where have you been the last couple days? Talk about kiss and run."

I shrug and blow in my hands so he can't see my face turning bright red. "I've been around."

"Why are you sneaking out?" he asks.

"I'm not." I step back, keeping him at a safe distance. Because all I really want is to collapse in his arms and explain everything. "I was out getting some fresh air."

"Little cold for that." He crosses his arms. "Try me again."

One thing I do know, Fisher is stubborn. Bickering with him is not going to get me in that lab any faster. Not to mention, I don't really want to do this alone anymore. So maybe I should cut Fisher some slack and give him a chance.

He reaches out and moves a piece of hair from my face. "Come on, Ada."

I melt and explain everything. About Simone's mysterious flash drives. About the strange code on Raven's computer. About my ID program tracing every person who has been in that lab. I also tell him that Ms. Matthews found the lab and that I have to retrieve the user ID list before I lose the last clue I have to finding out why Simone hacked ReBoot after she left. And why she had to die.

Fisher listens until I finish. Then he whistles. "Sounds heavy."

I must admit I feel lighter knowing someone else gets what's going on.

"So we need a plan." He points up. "If we sneak in through the roof, we can save tons of time."

"We?" I ask.

"I'm not letting you go without me. Someone has to protect you."

"Right," I mutter. Then I follow his gaze up the old trellis leaning against the side of the house. Shaking my head, I back away. "I'm afraid of heights."

"You set off the alarm in the back. It's probably swarming with Matthews' minions by now. Would you rather face her or accept a vertical challenge?" Before I can answer, he tugs on the wooden slats to test that the structure is securely fastened. Then Fisher jumps on and creeps up the wall like Spiderman, taking one step at a time. When he's at the top, he motions for me to follow.

I do a quick sign of the cross before gripping the trellis and scaling up the structure built for vines. Each time I grip a slat, it bends slightly, warning me that it could snap any minute. When I only have a few feet left, I glance down at the ground. A wave of dizziness overcomes me and I teeter, struggling to balance.

"Don't look down," Fisher hisses above me.

I mumble, "Too late."

"Keep your eyes on me."

Though I'm pretty sure, that will make me even dizzier.

On my next step, the old wood cracks under my weight and my foot slips, leaving me hanging twenty feet above the frozen ground. I regain my footing and breathe a few times. My hands and legs quiver from a cocktail of fear, adrenaline, and strain.

A beam of light sweeps across the wall. The security guard comes around the corner, swinging his flashlight back and forth.

Fisher holds his hand up, motioning for me to freeze.

I hold my breath and pull my body close to the trellis. My arms shake from the strain as the guard stops under me. He'll either look up and bust me for climbing the wall, or I'll lose my grip and fall on his dome. Either way, I'm dead.

I glance at Fisher and grimace, eyes wide. He motions for me to stay calm. Easy for him to say. He's not the one suspended over a life sentence. The wooden slats crack. My legs shake underneath me, and my biceps tremble in agony. Then my fingers go numb, loosening my grip.

I can't hold on much longer. I'm going to fall. Nightmares of the ropes course come back to me.

I open my eyes wide, silently begging Fisher to *do something*.

He tosses a stick off the far side of the roof. The branch clatters through the tree and lands on the frozen ground with a thud.

The security guard jerks his head in the direction of the noise and scampers off like a dog fetching a ball.

This diversion gives Fisher enough time to yank me up onto the roof. "Man, I thought you were a goner."

"Me too." I rub my stiff hands along my jeans until feeling returns in my fingers.

He massages my throbbing palms with his thumbs. The sweet gesture makes me think this guy's a keeper. The revelation warms me as we slink along the rooftop, hopping over cupolas, careful not to slip on the stucco tiles. We discover a skylight leading into the top floor of a wing under construction.

Fisher opens the glass and motions me inside. "Ladies first."

I roll my eyes. "You're full of it, you know that?"

"You ain't seen nothing yet," he teases.

I sit on the edge and drop a few feet into the building. As soon as I land, a cloud of dust billows up around me. I wave my hand in front of my face and cough a couple of times.

Fisher drops next to me and buries his mouth in the crook of his elbow. "You know where you are?"

I nod. "Yeah, the lab should be directly beneath us, a couple levels down."

Each room we pass has plastic hanging over the doorways and stacks of rotting wood lining the walls. I cringe from the cobwebs and step through the layers of dust decorating every room. The other way to the lab wasn't pretty, but it wasn't dangerous.

Fisher moves ahead of me and disappears in a dust cloud.

Behind him, I stay mindful and take a deliberate step, testing the floorboard before shifting my weight.

A piece of rotted wood cracks in anger and the floor swallows me whole.

</WEDGED BETWEEN A CRACK AND A HARD DRIVE>

No one likes a rough landing.

I plummet through a jagged opening and land on the level below, wrenching my knee. Losing balance, I fall back on my tailbone.

Fisher yells through the ceiling gap. "You alright?"

"I think so." I sit up and cough, gulping in mouthfuls of dust and air.

"Don't move. I'm coming down." He hangs through the hole and drops next to me. His hands trail over my shoulders, down my waist, and along my legs.

My body shivers under his soft touch. Hopefully he doesn't notice.

"Doesn't look like anything's broken," he says. "But that was quite the fall."

"By the way, watch your step," I say, rubbing my butt.

"Funny, I was thinking I'd better watch *yours*. Can you stand?" I nod and Fisher pulls me into an upright position.

As soon as I put pressure on my foot, a bolt of pain zips up my calf and sprays into my hamstring.

"Ow." I wince and collapse in pain. He holds me, his face

hovering a few inches from mine. For a split second I want to kiss him.

He steadies me with his hands. "You okay to walk?"

"Yup." I shouldn't move, but I'm not going to complain.

"Good." Fisher points to a thin stairwell. "That should take us to the lab."

I limp behind him, trying not to drag my bad foot like a hunchback. We venture past grimy windows bordered by scratched frames and shredded walls. Looks as if someone tried to claw a path to freedom.

When we finally reach the lab, I appreciate the clear air.

"You get what you need in here, and I'll keep a lookout." He kisses my forehead and holds my chair for me. "Do your thang."

Sitting at the computer, I retrieve the Wireshark data from the hidden directory. I open the packets for each user ID the program located. Maybe there's something in the data that will help identify who is assigned to each ID. The log time-stamps give me my first clue.

There are nine IDs. Four active and five inactive that haven't been accessed in months. One ID stands out because the last recorded login was on 051613. I double-check my deceased residents notes and place my finger on Simone's checkout date: 051613.

This ID must belong to her.

After filtering the data, I clinks the links until one leads me to Simone's SocialNet page.

I sit back and smile. This ID is proof that Simone was connected to this lab. I continue skimming everything she worked on until my eye is drawn to a file: </DARK ANGEL>.

A gasp sticks in my throat like a piece of gristle. Is this for me? I open it and read the note: *Email Walt Disney in Hotlanta but beware of ghosts.*

I know exactly what it means. But why is Simone asking

me to hack into her email? I open Hotmail and attempt to log in Simone's account by testing passwords she's used in the past. Unfortunately, we both religiously change our email accounts and access codes every month. So it's like finding a broken bit in a megabyte.

When they all fail, I massage my scalp. Think. Think. What would she use? Simone and I always had fun coming up with crazy passwords. We were never worried about each other knowing because we had a hack pact and promised never to violate each other's privacy. No matter what.

The last password I used was: *thisgirlisa#1badasshacker*. I figured it might stop any lone hacker from opening a can of cyber whoop ass.

I decide to go ahead and trigger her customized question.

What is eight characters long and includes one capital?

I think for a second and then grin while typing the answer Simone created after spending spring break with my family at Walt Disney World.

MickeyMinniePlutoHueyLouieDeweyDonaldGoofySEATTLE

When I press </ENTER>, Simone's inbox opens. She created a back door, just for me. She knew the clue would help me crack her account.

Then my heart sinks. If Simone went thought all this trouble to give me access, that can only mean one thing. She knew she wouldn't be around to tell me herself.

I scan her inbox. Mostly spam until I spot one email at the bottom, received the day before she died.

Even though it's encrypted, I decode it pretty quickly.

After all you've been through, it's time for the Red Devil to join me. – Casper.

Casper? The same Casper from the Orwellians?

Surely there aren't two egotistical ghosts floating around cyberspace.

The pit of my stomach burns. Simone wanted me to know about Casper. I've been so focused on finding answers that I didn't suspect a mole in the Orwellians. Sitting back, I finally put some pieces of this crazy puzzle in place. This email proves that Casper made the link between Simone and the Red Devil. Which also suggests he knows about the Dark Angel and me, because we hacked together. I bet he's the one who turned in QTip and me to the Feds. And I bet he's the one who's been hacking my account and leaving threatening messages.

I quickly ping Taz.

> DA: The mole is Casper. Go 2 a safe house.

I clamp my jaw, getting a grip on my anger. My jaw grinds. Casper has been stalking his fellow Orwellians. And he has major ammo. He knows about the White House hack, so why hasn't he used it yet? That hack would take all of us down. It's all Mitnick would need to nail me.

I have to find out who Casper is and what he's up to before he suspects I'm onto him and leaks everything to the Feds.

In the email, I click "message header" and scan the full script for the IP address that I then input into a locator website. *Seattle, WA.* That's the problem with IP address locators; they can home in on a general area, but an actual location is hard to nail down.

I jot down the IP address in my notebook and close Simone's email. I'll track Casper later. Right now, I need to figure out who is connected to the other user IDs. I compare the deceased residents list with the ID logs. All of the last sign-in dates match the release days of all the other dead kids: Johnny King, William Sabitini, and Chelsea Talbot.

Fisher pops his head in. "How is it going, Watson?"

"Pretty sure I'm Sherlock and you're the sidekick." I tell him what I think he needs to know and no more. "I'm tracking the IDs to people. Four of the five inactive IDs match the dead kids, including Simone." I don't mention Casper or the email because it opens up a whole topic I'm not ready to discuss.

Fisher rolls over a chair. "So…every one of those kids worked in this lab before they died?"

"Yup, the last log dates are the date they checked out," I say.

He glances over my shoulder. "You said four out of five. Who belongs to the fifth inactive one?"

"I'm still trying to find out." I study the last remaining inactive ID. After reviewing the links, I pop out to a SocialNet account. "Patrick Matthews?"

I recognize the name from researching Ms. Matthews the night before coming to ReBoot. Seems like her son died young, but I can't remember if I ever found out why.

"Mean anything to you?" Fisher asks.

"I think it was Ms. Matthews son." I Google the name and find more information than I had before. "Interesting. Patrick Matthews died a few days after checking out of ReBoot too. Wonder why he's not on the deceased list?"

I stare at the photo in the article. Ms. Matthews is barely recognizable. The picture shows a vibrant woman, well dressed, and…happy. Then I pull up the picture of Ms. Matthews at the funeral dressed in a black dress and veil. The smile from the first family photo has been erased from her face and replaced with a scowl, masking pain and sadness. The same expression she has today.

"No wonder she's so miserable," Fisher says.

"I feel sorry for her." Because I know that feeling of total despair when you lose someone you love. "But if he was in ReBoot and died, why isn't he listed in the file with the others? Why is she hiding it?"

"Maybe she's trying to forget," Fisher guesses. "If her son's death is related to this place, that means the deaths started way before we imagined. And it might have caused some red flags in keeping this place open. Ms. Matthews' son must have been the first victim in this whole messed-up thing."

I shake my head, "So how the hell hasn't anyone noticed?"

"Five deaths, five IDs. Weird coincidence. Don't you think?"

"I don't believe in accidents." My thoughts run wild with the information. "Maybe someone hurt these kids because of something they've done in here."

"You've been in here. What have you done?" Fisher asks. "Anything worth killing someone over?"

I shrug. "Not really. A couple of hacking challenges and some fake test scripts."

Fisher sits back with his hands clasped behind his head. "Do you know who else has been in here lately? Anyone besides you and Raven?"

Out of the four active IDs, one is mine and one is Raven's. I pull up the third ID and scour through the history of links until I find one that shocks me.

Computers can kill; Brother lets sister die while playing on computer; Kid binges online and crashes; Sister left to die.

I slump back in my chair and exhale. "Holy crap."

"What is it?" Fisher studies the screen.

"It's…it's Crash. This ID belongs to Crash," I stammer. "I can't believe he's been working in here too. This whole time. I never saw him, not once. And I never even suspected he was involved."

"We can talk with him later," Fisher says. "What about the last active ID?"

I hunt around for some links to help me identify the forth owner but nothing gives me any leads. "Nothing."

"Were all of you working on the same thing?"

"I doubt it." I skim all the IDs and search for any similarities. What do these people have in common? And is it anything that links to me? Something stands out. "Hey, look at this. Every ID has a coded art file that looks similar to the art Raven uploaded."

"Do you?"

"No I never did any art." Now, I'm confused. What am I missing?

Fisher leans in and studies the pictures. "Looks like a bunch of random codes. But it must mean something. How many pictures are there?"

"Nine. One for each ID. But I didn't do one. So I'm not sure who the extra one belongs to."

"Maybe Raven did more than one."

"Let's see." I retrieve her keylogger data and notice something strange. "Weird. Her last timestamp was this morning. She's been in here once since we got busted by Ms. Matthews."

"This morning? Ms. Matthews said she was gone by then. This means, Raven logged in *after* she went missing?" Fisher appears baffled too. "Can you tell what she was doing?"

I trace Raven's cyber steps and piece together her last entry. "She copied a bunch of files from the directory."

Fisher paces the room. "Raven knew she was leaving and wanted to take these files with her. Must be something very important."

"Then why didn't she delete them? Why leave them behind?" I stare at the code and study the picture, line by line. Character by character.

"Maybe she didn't want to raise any alarms." Fisher leans in, his face only inches from the screen. "But what do they mean?"

"Shouldn't be too hard to crack, given time . . ." I zoom in on the pictures and stare at the 0s and 1s. "And skill."

"Then we should download them too. Take them with us." He searches through a few desk drawers. "Seen any drives around here? We'll need a big one. This is a ton of data."

"Too much for a drive." I grab my necklace and pop out

the flash drive. "I can upload a sniffer to grab all the data from the IDs and dump them on an external drive."

Fisher eyes my necklace. "You're kind of turning me on right now."

I roll my eyes and keep working. "Not the time."

"Okay, but hurry up so we can get out of here. This place gives me the creeps." Fisher checks the hallway again while I capture the files from every ID, zip them up, and drop them onto the remote server. I can't help but wonder if this is exactly what Simone was trying to do. Only from the outside. Maybe this is why she was hacking in to ReBoot before she died.

I have to figure out what this code means.

Once the files load, I reach out to Taz. If anyone can figure these patterns out, it's him. Instead of an email that can be tracked, I encrypt a private message, explaining the art files and ask for his help in cracking the code.

> DA: Gorgeous art. Makes you want to read between the lines to see what the artists were thinking. What do you see???

When—or if—Taz sees this message, he'll know what I am asking.

Maybe he can decipher what these codes are really for. Help me crack this mystery open.

I catch a whiff of something in the air. "Fisher, what's that smell?"

</THE FIREWALL>

The lab smells like burned toast.

Fisher races back into the room. "Ada, I think this place is on fire. We gotta go." When I finish uploading the files, he grabs my hand and yanks me out of the room.

We race down the hall and push through a door that leads us to an empty stale room with nothing but a mahogany fireplace in one corner. The small space is already filling with thick, black smoke, and the heat is unbearable. When I glance back, the steel door starts to turn red from the intense temperatures.

This must be what hell feels like.

Fisher tugs on my sleeve. "This place is going to torch quickly. It's a freakin' tinderbox."

And he's right, the place is already blazing with fire. My eyes burn as I cover my mouth with my shirt, coughing. "Which way?"

"There." He points in the opposite direction.

As we weave through the labyrinth of suffocating rooms and tiny hallways, neither of us speaks. The air is heavy with soot, burning my throat. Thick gray spirals of smoke crawl out of the cracks in the walls, curling finger-like tendrils around my throat.

I try to control my smoke intake. "Now what?" I choke out.

"Breathe shallow, stay low, and keep moving." He hands me his handkerchief. "Keep this over your mouth."

We wind through the twisting hall until we reach a stairway. Flames nip at our heels like a pack of seething dogs. The searing air singes the tiny hairs on my face. I panic and gulp in dirty air, igniting a fit of hacking. The fire alarm remains silent, so I'm guessing help is out of the question. It's possible that no one at ReBoot is aware of the danger stewing behind the main house.

I holler into the rag, muffling the rising panic in my voice. "We're trapped!"

Fisher dashes around, frantically opening and slamming cupboards, searching for a hidden escape route. In this place, you never know. The fire prowls across the floor, roaring at anything in its path. The flames chase us, rolling in from all sides.

Fisher steps on a trapdoor in the floor. "Here!" He dusts off the opening with his shoes and jerks the round latch. The wood planks squeak open, revealing a kitchen on the floor below us. He drops through the hole and lands in a kneeling position on the rusted stove.

A beam in the ceiling splits and comes crashing down behind me. I scream and lower myself through the opening, hanging by my hands.

"Drop!" Fisher screams.

I release my grip and hit the counter.

This time, he breaks my fall by grabbing my waist, but pain sears through my sore leg. I crumple to the floor. Without missing a beat, Fisher scoops me up and races toward an exit, half carrying me.

Somewhere in the maze, a door slams. Clunky footsteps cross the floor moving closer and closer.

"Someone's chasing us," I hiss under my breath.

"It's gotta be the person who set the fire. Who else would be out here?" Fisher yanks me into a thin closet. He closes the door and presses against me. Our faces are only a few inches apart. I try not to move and hold my breath as his body rises and falls against mine. Eventually we breathe in rhythm, creating an unexpected intimacy by sharing the same air.

I whisper, "We can't stay here. The fire is moving too fast."

"Shhh."

Someone enters the room.

Fisher holds me tight; his breath singes my cheeks. His warmth is much cozier than the angry flames. Yet they both feel dangerous. The tiny space grows hotter. I can't tell if it's because of the fire or the sparks.

I glance up and spot fear hovering in Fisher's eyes. He looks down over his glasses and gives me a sad look, almost as if he's admitting defeat. He presses his lips to my mouth softly.

In the distance, massive explosions sound off as a few windows blow out. The smoke rolls in the stuffy room. We pull away from each other and cover our mouths, blocking out the fumes. The urge to cough tickles the back of my throat, forcing me to gag. Smoke burns my eyes, making them water. Both the fierce fire and a stranger are hunting us down. And one of them will win.

Someone stops on the other side of the door.

No matter how much I want to call out for help, we can't risk being caught. If this person started the fire, there's no telling what our fate would be. I shift to get some room and my butt presses against the back wall. The solid structure gives into my weight. Bending. It's hollow.

Someone rattles the closet's doorknob.

I run my hand over the wall until my fingers touch a small

nodule. A small door opens behind us, setting us free. Sweat pours off my bangs as the heat intensifies. If I don't die here, I'll surely melt.

Fisher points to the rickety elevator. "There! It's the only way out!"

I step into the unstable car and press into the corner. Another beam falls down, blocking the door.

"Fisher!" I yell. "Jump!"

He dives in at the same time a slab of sheetrock crashes down and lands where he was just standing. Sparks swirl around us like angry fireflies. Fisher removes his jacket and wraps both his hands before dragging the hot steel door closed. Then he slams the lever. The elevator jerks as it descends, inch by inch. The merciless fire leaps onto the ropes.

Within seconds, they eat through one of them until it snaps, throwing the elevator off balance.

"We're going to fall!" I scream over the roar and crackle of the surrounding inferno.

Not to mention, burn alive.

The steel creaks as the heat compromises its sturdiness. Without warning, the second rope surrenders to the heat, and the car drops down the shaft.

I scream, gripping onto the sides.

"Hang on!" Fisher pounds the emergency brake, and the car jerks to a stop. The elevator pauses halfway between two floors. We swing in midair a few stories above the bottom level. If Fisher takes his hand off the button, the elevator will plummet. If the fall doesn't kill us, the fire will be there to finish the job.

"What do we do?" I yell.

Sweat beads along Fisher's forehead. He points to an opening and keeps his voice calm. Though I can tell it's an act. "Ada, see if you can crawl out."

I inch over to the edge and touch the wire caging before

jerking back my hand. Red welts rise up angrily. "Ouch! It's too hot." I take off my jacket and wrap it around both hands for protection.

The elevator drops another inch.

Fisher keeps his hand on the brake. "Hurry! Climb out! It won't hold much longer."

I crawl to my feet and slide the door back. Gripping the floor above me, I manage to haul myself up and over the edge.

I lay on my stomach and reach down. "Fisher! Take my hand!"

Our eyes meet as he lunges for me. His fingers skim my palm when the last rope snaps, dropping the elevator into the red inferno below.

"Noooo!" I scream and watch the elevator disappear into the flames. Looking over the edge, I lay there for a second in shock. Searching for Fisher. Waiting for a sign that he's okay. After a few long seconds and no sighting, a primal scream creeps up my throat. "Fisher! Fisher!"

I wait for him to call out. He can't be gone. Not that fast. Not like that.

"Fisher!" I shriek again, my voice already hoarse from the smoke and strain.

Then a large explosion shakes the whole foundation. A wave of smoke and fire blast up the shaft, forcing me back. The reality slowly settles in. Fisher is gone.

"No, God, please! Don't do this to me." I sit up on my knees and stare down the smoking shaft. Waiting. Hoping. Praying for a miracle that he's still alive.

It takes another explosion somewhere in the house to jolt me out of my daze.

Fisher is dead. But my nightmare isn't over yet.

</THE BACK DOOR>

I don't want to die.

I force myself to stand and drag myself out of the room. I don't want to leave Fisher behind, but there's no way he survived that fall. And if he did, the fire and explosion would have been too much.

Crying, I race through the halls, tugging door after door. The ash and soot punch my lungs and poke my eyes. The guts of the building drop around me, but I hop around each piece of debris without thinking. Part of me wants to collapse and give up, let the fire burn away the misery, but something pushes me forward.

Someone keeps me going.

With each near miss, I'm convinced Simone's here, guiding me to safety. Protecting me like she always did.

By some miracle, the next door I push open dumps me outside onto the frozen grass. My lungs welcome the fresh, cold air. As shingles and gutters fall off the building, I cover my head and sprint across the lawn. Just as I leap over the hedge, the roof collapses, sending shards of debris my way.

My chest heaves as I roll onto my back. I can't believe I made it out alive. Once I catch my breath and clear my lungs,

I peer through the leaves and watch the old mansion burn. The starry sky fills with the rising smog. Little pieces of burning ash skitter across the air. Smoke jumps from the windows as red flames reach up and punch the stars.

I can't move. Instead, I sit and stare at the house. Praying for a miracle. Hoping to see Fisher burst out through the flames. But he never shows.

I lay down in the cold grass and cry, coughing and hacking at the same time. Tears streak down my face and splash on my soot-covered hands. All the energy seeps from me as I lay down on the frozen lawn like a dead plant, not caring if I ever get up again.

Fisher. Poor Fisher.

I can't believe he's gone. Before I got a chance to tell him how I feel. About him. About us.

A sound floats over the wind. I think I hear my name.

I jerk up and look around, searching for the voice. Wondering if it is all in my head. Maybe I'm hallucinating.

Then a huge ghostly figure appears in the mist. Maybe this is the spirit Ms. Matthews talks to at night. As it approaches, the blob slowly takes form, revealing not one but two people.

Fisher hobbles into the moonlight with his arm draped over Ms. Matthews' shoulders. She's holding him up as he limps toward me. Black soot paints his entire face, and a crack in her glasses divides one lens into two halves. The ash and dust have dyed his hair a chalky gray.

When he sees me, he flashes that unnerving smile. "Now, that was one *hot* first date." Ms. Matthews lets go and he drops to his knees.

I jump to my feet and leap onto him, crying. "Fisher! Oh my God, I thought you were dead."

He collapses in my arms. "Ada, thank God you're okay. I wasn't sure if you made it out." He buries his head in my shoulder.

I'm bawling and trying to talk at the same time. "I would

have never forgiven you if you died," I say, kissing his sooty cheeks.

He grins weakly. "Why doesn't that surprise me?"

I squeeze him tight to make sure he's really here with me and then pull back to look at him. "But I saw you fall."

He turns and stares at the blazing fire as the house crumbles to dust. "I thought I was a goner. The elevator dropped a couple floors and the door sprang open. I crawled out but all I could think about was getting to you. I tried to run up the stairs, but the elevator exploded behind me. A ceiling beam landed on my leg, pinning me. Luckily Ms. Matthews found me and pulled me out."

I face the director. Her hair is mangled, out of place. Her dress is ripped and covered in soot. I release my grip on Fisher and hug her stiff body. "Thank you so much for saving him." I study her burned hands. "Oh my gosh. You're hurt."

"Yes," she says weakly and then sits down on a log. "No thanks to you two. I told you that lab was dangerous and to stay away. You are both lucky to be alive."

Even in times of peril, the woman has to go there.

I rip off a piece of her skirt and wrap her hands. "Is that why you started the fire? To destroy the lab?"

She smooths out her tattered skirt and repins her hair in a bun. "Of course not. Do you think I'm crazy?"

I bite my tongue, assuming it was rhetorical, and she doesn't really want my answer. Instead, I push for hers. "So, how did you know we were in there? And how in the world did you find Fisher?"

"When the alarm went off, I checked it out myself," Ms. Matthews explained.

"I set that," I say.

Ms. Matthews nods. "I assumed. When I didn't find any reason for it, I assumed it was used to throw me off, and that maybe someone was sneaking back to the lab. By the time I got there, the building was already on fire. I thought I heard someone screaming. Fisher got lucky I found him. What I don't know is why were you going in there after I asked you not to?"

Before I can answer or explain, Fisher points, "Look. Over there."

A figure wearing some kind of jacket or hoodie slinks along the side of the building. Neither of us says anything until the mysterious stranger disappears out of sight.

"Who is that?" I ask, squinting.

Ms. Matthews stands and barks, "I don't know, but I'm sure as hell going to find out. You two stay here. I'll be right back."

"Maybe we should call someone," I say. "We have no idea who that is, and someone started that fire."

She shakes her head adamantly. "I refuse to let this person hurt any more of my kids. This ends tonight!" Without waiting for a response, she charges off into the night.

"Ms. Matthews!" I yell after her, but she disappears over the hill. "Maybe we should stop her."

Fisher tilts his head toward me. "She said 'hurt any more of my kids.' Who's she's talking about?"

I shrug. "Maybe she knows more than we think she does." And maybe she knows what really happened to Simone. I make a note to ask her.

"We should find out," Fisher says. "Let's go after her."

As we walk down the hill, the whole building crashes behind us. A large chunk of the roof folds in, kicking embers high in the air. The rest of the back building goes up in flames. Luckily, the main house appears to be spared.

Then Fisher says what I'm thinking. "Someone knew we were in there."

The words hit me hard. He's right. Someone set that fire on purpose.

And I can't help but wonder if it was to end the lab, or to kill me.

Seconds later, a scream echoes in the distance.

</BLUE-SCREENED>

Some people run away from danger, I race toward it.

Without blinking, I shoot off in the direction of the noise. My feet slide along the grass covered with a thin film of ice. A blanket of smoke hovers over the ground. Finally, the fire alarm in the main house blares, warning everyone of the danger growing behind them.

Behind me, Fisher's boots slap the ground unevenly due to his injury. "Ada. Wait!"

I ignore the throbbing pain in my leg and search for the source of the scream.

Down the hill by the barn, I spot a mound lying in the overgrown weeds. I fly down the slope toward the shape, but freeze a few feet from the twisted body. Rising up on my toes, I notice the wrapped hands. "Ms. Matthews? Are you okay?"

Fisher bolts past me and drops next to her body. His face drops and he flops back on his heels. "Jesus. She's dead."

"Oh God." I turn away and cup my mouth, holding back the urge to hurl. I bend over and stare at the grass. "Are you sure?"

"Looks like she broke her neck." He balances on his feet in a squat position. "Either she fell or . . ."

I keep my back turned. "Or she was killed."

Fisher kicks the ground. "Of course she was killed. Someone tried to fry us and then went after her."

"I'm think I'm going to be sick." I suck in a breath, composing myself, before facing Ms. Matthews' body. I gasp when I see her face. Her skin looks much paler in the moonlight. But it's her eyes that bother me most. They have a grayish tint now and are open wide, staring at the night sky. Vacant. Flat. Dead. Whether I liked Ms. Matthews or not, to see her life end is sad. No matter who she is or what she's done, in the end, she saved Fisher.

Tears spring to my eyes. "We have to warn Crash."

Fisher cups my face. "First, we need to call the police."

I nod as he ushers me away from Ms. Matthews' lifeless body. But I get her eyes out of my mind.

I skipped Simone's funeral. Didn't want to see her like that. The last image of someone stays with you. Burned in your memory. And I needed to keep Simone alive in my mind, the way I knew her. The pretty girl with a full-on smile that not only told you she was happy . . . but somehow made you happy too.

Now I realize, it was more than just avoiding a last look. I was avoiding the truth. Seeing death makes it so final. And I wasn't ready to see the end of Simone. I'm still not ready.

Something she said once sticks in my mind.

"I spent all night on Super Mario," Simone bragged. "Earned over ninety lives."

"How'd you do that?"

"I'd have to kill you if I told you," Simone said and paused. "Fine, I'll tell you my secrets. I hear that if you jump on top of the turtle on the third step, you could earn a max of ninety-nine lives."

"So, how many do you have left?" I asked

"One," Simone said casually.

"One?" I yelled in the phone. "How'd you lose so much so fast?"

"I guess I like to take risks."

"I'd say; you almost died."

Simone laughed. "Trust me, I'm not about to die. Unless I die winning."

The memory sends a chill down my spine.

I stumble behind Fisher, allowing him to drag me up the hill. Away from the burning building. Away from Ms. Matthews' dead body. As we move to the front yard, a crowd of fellow addicts stands along the circular driveway, watching their temporary home burn. By now, the flames have engulfed the back of the complex, and the fire department has arrived on scene, fighting to keep the stubborn flames from swallowing the main building.

Varian steps in front of us. "Hey, where you two been hiding?"

Fisher tackles the question with an obvious response. "The center's on fire."

"Thanks, Smokey the Bear." Varian stares up at the black smoke rising from the building. Then he eyes me and points to my face. "What happened to you? When you cook s'mores, you aren't supposed to jump in the fire." I can almost see his brain ticking to decode the real story.

I make up something fast. "We were in the barn when the fire started."

"Nice, Fish Boy." Varian drapes his arm over Fisher's shoulders. "I want deets."

Becca appears out of nowhere and hugs me tight. "Oh thank God. Ada, where have you been? I've been looking for you the last day or so. Every time I come back to the room, you are either out or asleep."

"She's been busy." Fisher adds. I give him a look.

Then she pinches her nose. "Eww, you guys smell like a bonfire."

"They've been team building in the barn," Varian says, using air quotes around "team building."

"Oh!" Becca gives me a look. "Is that why didn't you show up this morning?"

"Show up where?" I ask.

Her eyes get wide. "To see Crash."

I scan the crowd, hoping to find him. We have a lot to discuss. "Where is he?"

Her smile fades. "He left ReBoot yesterday."

Fisher and I say, "What?" at the same time.

"You didn't know?" Becca stammers. "He said he gave you a note."

Then I remember the bad session. How I walked out on Crash. And his note. I shove my hand in my jacket pocket and pull out a crumpled piece of paper.

From: Crash
To: Ada
Subject: Goodbye

Ms. Matthews is releasing me today. Thank for you helping me get out of here.

No matter what happens, just remember, us lab rats need to be very careful what food we take out of here.

Goodbye and watch your back. Here's my email so we can keep in touch crashandburn@gmail.com.

How could I miss this?

Becca rambles on, but I only catch a few broken sentences. "Because he finally talked, Mr. Anthony released him . . . Ms. Matthews didn't approve . . . said he wasn't ready . . . but Crash's mom picked him up."

Fisher touches my back. "Ada?"

I nod, thinking about my last interaction with Crash. "I never read it because I was mad. But I had no idea he was leaving." I skim the note again as if answers will appear. "What was the hurry?"

Varian scoffs. "Hurry? The kid's been here a year."

"You're the one who got him talking, after all." Becca says. "Everyone here has been trying for months. But you did it in a couple weeks. A miracle. You saved him."

Or sentenced him to death.

I yank Fisher to one side. "If Ms. Matthews is dead and someone killed her, then that means this thing isn't over yet. Someone else is involved."

Fisher lowers his tone to match mine, only his has more urgency in it. "It's got to be Mr. Anthony. Do you think he knows you've been snooping around? Because that means he knows you downloaded a bunch of information."

"No, he'd never do that. Plus, he's saved my butt too many times. If he wanted me dead, he could have let me fall or die in that cave. Doesn't make sense." I think for a second. "Maybe it's Raven. She had access, and the art is hers. Maybe she's doing something dirty and doesn't want to get caught. Maybe that's why she bolted.

Fisher shakes his head. "I don't know, seems far-fetched. She's not even eighteen."

"The other kids who worked in the lab died within days of leaving ReBoot. I'm worried Crash is in trouble." I cover my mouth. "We need to find him . . . and fast."

While Varian and Becca bicker, Fisher and I sneak away, inching through the thick crowd. I glance down at the barn and see Ms. Matthews' body, now covered in a white sheet. A few people stand around her.

"What's our plan?" Fisher asks.

"What plan?" Varian steps in front of us. "You're going after Crash, aren't you?"

Fisher and I steal a look at each other.

I sigh and give in. "Listen, guys, we don't want to drag you guys into something dangerous."

"Is *that* supposed to deter me?" Varian grins. "I love danger. Fess up."

"Yeah, what's going on with you two?" Becca asks, looking concerned.

There's no use wasting any more time. These are my friends and if they want to help, I should let them. Crash was important to them too. Even Varian. I quickly explain everything that's happened including the lab and how all the kids who were tied to the lab died when they left the facility.

Varian rubs his face. "I knew there was something fishy going on! I called it!"

I ignore him and keep explaining for fear that time is running out. "We downloaded some files. But before we could get out, someone set the building on fire. Ms. Matthews saved us, but now she is . . ."

Becca's eyes are huge as she awaits the last word. "She's what?"

I drop my voice low. "Gone."

Becca covers her mouth. "You mean *dead*?"

"Yes." I have to be careful or she could crumble like a stale cookie.

Varian glances toward the field. "What happened?"

"Looks like she broke her neck," Fisher says. "But I'm not sure. We didn't stick around to find out."

Varian frowns. "Well, did she fall and break it? Or did someone break it for her?"

"We saw someone leaving the fire and she went after them," I answer. "But we don't know for sure."

Fisher wraps it up. "What Ada is saying is that we think we're in danger. Not only is Ms. Matthews dead, but now Raven is missing and Crash has been released. And we know what happened to the other kids when they left."

Varian rubs his hands together. "What do you want me to do?"

"*Us*, Varian." Becca plants her hands on her hips like she's about to lead a cheer. "Not *you*. Us."

He frowns. "Right. How could I forget? We're a *team*." The way he says the T-word makes it sound dirty. Makes sense because Varian works best alone.

Fisher pulls us into a tight circle. "Varian, you and Becca cover for us here in case anyone comes looking. Ada and I will go find Crash."

"No way, Fish Boy," Varian punches his hand with his other fist. "I want some of the action."

"Me too." Becca nods eagerly. "I don't want to stay here alone. Plus, I know where Crash lives."

I hadn't thought of that. I study both of their faces. The angst and frustration is written in big, bold letters.

"Varian would be good to have around," Fisher says. "He's got tons of battle experience."

Becca steps forward. "Please, we can't just sit here or we'll go crazy."

Her words dig underneath my skin. I know how she feels. I would have done anything to help Simone if I'd known she was in danger. Being helpless is worse than taking a risk.

"Fine." I sigh. "I need something before we can leave. But it might be dangerous."

Varian claps once. "Exactly how I like it. What do I do?"

"Can you grab Zed and my bag from Ms. Matthews' office? Before the cops get in there. I can't do anything without it." I direct. "Fisher, Becca and I will find a way to get us all out of here."

Becca looks around. "Wait, who's Zed?"

"My laptop." I say it before realizing how weird it sounds.

"You *named* your laptop?" Varian raises his eyebrows. "And they say I'm crazy for taking characters seriously. This chick thinks her laptop is a person."

"Just go," Fisher pats Varian's shoulder. "We'll meet you at the back gate."

"Done." Then he points his finger in Fisher's face. "Don't ditch me, Fish, or I'll hunt you down."

Varian walks back into the building with his cloak whipping behind him.

Even though he's infuriating, I feel safer knowing he's helping us. Never hurts to have a superhero on your side fighting the forces of evil.

</OFF THE GRID>

Sneaking around in the pitch dark in freezing temperatures isn't fun.

But we have to move fast. We don't want to be here when the sun comes up.

Though the thick clouds predict a dark and wet morning.

While Varian sneaks in to grab my computer, Becca, Fisher, and I head down the property line toward the faculty parking lot. A veil of snowy clouds drapes over the moon, sifting light. The trees play tricks on me by casting moving shadows along the ground. The air bites my cheeks, and the snow chomps at my boots.

Fisher stops at the entrance and studies the gate keypad.

"Do you think anyone saw us?" Becca's eyes dart around.

I reassure her. "We're good. Trust me. Everyone is too busy with the fire."

I glance up at the heavy wrought iron gate looming in front of us. My Spidey skills are all tapped out from earlier. "There's no way we can climb this."

"We'll drive through it," Fisher says.

"*After* it opens, I hope," Becca mumbles. To stop from freezing, she hops in place to keep her blood flowing.

Varian runs up and bends over, winded. "That's the most exercise I've had since I killed Teemo in League of Legends."

"That was fast," I say.

Fisher scoffs. "Told you. He's a pro at B&E."

I cringe, waiting for Varian to explode, but instead he hands me my backpack with Zed tucked safely inside. "Don't say I never did anything for you."

I snatch my backpack and squeeze it close to my chest. My only link to the online world and a whole bunch of evidence is back in my arms. Safe and sound. I'm so happy to see Zed, I pounce on Varian and kiss his cheek. "You are the best!" Even in the moonlight, I see his cheeks flush.

Becca sings, "Aww, he's a big softy after all. Who knew?"

"We gonna yap all night or get on with it?" Varian wipes off my kiss and punches Fisher in the arm. "How are you gonna get us out of this prison, Fish? You have a plan?"

Fisher pulls a cell phone from his jacket pocket. "You guys aren't the only one with talents."

"Nice!" Varian points. "Where did you score that?"

"Shoved it down my pants on day one." Fisher flashes a mischievous look. "Took a chance that Ms. Matthews wouldn't frisk *every* bulge."

Varian laughs and gives Fisher a high five while Becca groans, "That's disgusting!"

I ignore the burst of testosterone and wrap my arms around my body to stay warm. "Can you hurry and work your magic before I get frostbite on my face?" The sharp cold air slices through my skin and wiggles into my bones.

Fisher punches in a few numbers on his phone. "Open Sesame."

Seconds later, the gate creaks as it scrapes along the ground.

Becca nods her approval. "How'd you do that?"

I study the gate's keypad. "He must have programmed his phone into the gate's receiver. But how?"

"That would have been smart." Fisher grins, obviously proud of his feat. "But I just befriended the maintenance man and got the codes. Amazing what you can get from people."

"Stick with Ada's version, it's cooler." Varian barrels through the gate. "Now, let's blow this joint!"

Fisher leads us to a side parking lot and stops in front of a white catering van.

"I was hoping for some faster wheels than this." Varian checks out the van's tires. "What's our disguise? An ice cream man? Or a creepy child snatcher?"

"Beggars can't be choosers. Watch and learn." Fisher sends an SMS on his phone and the car immediately unlocks. "I figured out the OnStar protocols. Took me two hours to intercept the wireless message between the car and the network. After that, it was easy to manipulate the security and control systems."

"Oh please," mutters Varian as he climbs in the back seat. "The guy does one thing and he gets a hard-on for himself."

"I'm so tired of penis talk." Becca huffs and climbs in.

Fisher opens my passenger door.

I climb inside. The van that isn't much warmer than the outside. "I must admit I am impressed."

"Yeah? That's not all I can do." He winks.

I try not to smile as I grip the handle and close the door. "Well, that's all I want to *see* . . . for now."

Fisher walks around and slips in the driver's side. He turns on the engine and cranks the heat.

A blast of cold air hits my face, chilling me. Thankfully, the warm air kicks in soon after, slowly thawing my body, inch by inch. Piece by piece.

He forces the car into neutral and glides down the hill until we're out of ReBoot's sight.

Once we turn on the main road, I relax and snuggle down into the seat, growing tired from heat. Feels good to be out of that place. It's like I've been sprung from prison after a lifetime behind bars.

Fisher keeps his eyes on the hood. "Butt warmers?"

"Thought you'd never ask," I reply. "You sure know how to keep a girl happy."

"Oh brother," Varian mumbles from the back seat. "Get a room."

Fisher laughs and snakes along the two-lane. "Becca, you got the address?"

Her head pops up in between us. "Turn right here."

Fisher takes the corner a little too fast, sending Becca sliding across the seat into Varian's lap.

"Take it easy on the corners." Varian grabs onto the headrest. "We're like loose cans back here."

Fisher laughs. "Just keeping you on your toes."

"You're puttin' me on my ass," Varian mumbles.

Becca sighs. "Do you think anyone noticed we left?"

Varian loosens his grip on my seat. "I wouldn't be surprised if every cop in town isn't after us with Mr. Daytona 500 behind the wheel."

Now it's sleeting again and so nasty that the sun refuses to wake up. Instead of looking forward to where we're going, I keep my eye on the rearview mirror, studying where we've been. The world slowly disappears behind me. It's hard not to focus on the past when the future doesn't look much brighter.

To pass the time, I pray over and over in my head. *Please let Crash be okay.*

Thirty minutes later, we pull down Crash's street. The neighborhood is quiet except for a dog barking in the distance and a wind howling through the alleyway.

Fisher stops in front of the address. "This is it."

The old, dilapidated house is dark, except for one window lit at the very top, making the house look like a monster with one eye open. An old beat-up car sits in the driveway and an above-ground pool covered in a tarp peeks through the broken fence.

Must be where Crash's sister died. What an awful reminder. No wonder he hid out at ReBoot for a year.

I focus on the front door. My breath fogs the glass. "Maybe I should go up alone."

No one argues with me. So I get out of the van and walk along the broken walkway. At the top of the stairs, I stop in front of the screen door hanging off one hinge and knock on the chipped-paint door. The cold, hard surface shoots needles into my arm, making me wince. Somehow even with the overhang, I'm soaked to the bone.

I wait a few minutes with no response.

Leaning over the railing, I peek inside the window. A dim light from a TV flickers. I knock again. When there's no answer, I lightly kick the door with my foot.

Several clicks echo from inside the house as someone unlocks a slew of bolts. The door opens until a rusted chain catches it.

A pale face appears in the crack. "What do you want?"

Even though my lips are frozen, I force out a smile. "Hi, I'm Ada. Are you Crash's mom?"

"You mean Nathan?" Her eyes twitch back and forth nervously. "Yes, I am. Why?"

I realize that Crash never told me his real name. "I'm a friend of his."

"Nathan doesn't have any friends." She starts to close the door.

I jam my shoe between the door and frame. "I'm from ReBoot."

Without saying anything else, the woman pushes against the door. I rescue my foot from being crushed, and the door slams in my face. Sighing in defeat, I turn to leave.

Behind me, the chain jingles as it's being removed and the door swings open.

A tiny lady—similar in stature to Crash—wears a dingy bathrobe and fuzzy socks. A nub of a cigarette dangles from her mouth like a toothpick. Orange embers highlight her puffy eyes. Her hair slicks back into a thin, dirty ponytail. She was probably very pretty once, but the years have distressed her face and dimmed the sparkle in her eyes, leaving nothing but a shell of a woman.

She takes out the cigarette and clears her throat. "You're from ReBoot? Little good that place did. I tried to tell Crash's daddy it was a waste of Ben Franks, but he insisted on dishing them out anyway. Guess he felt guilty for leaving us and shacking up with Beverly Hills Barbie."

Her anger is obvious, but I tiptoe around the pending rant. "I'm sorry it's late, but is Crash—I mean—Nathan here? I'd like to talk to him."

She takes a drag off her cigarette and her eyes water. "What's your name again?"

I inch forward and out of the sheet of rain pouring off the roofline. "Ada. Ada Lovelace."

The woman's face brightens for a second like a shooting star then quickly dims. "Nathan told me about you. You're the one who got him to talk again. Thank you for that. It was nice to hear his voice again before . . ." Her voice rides off on the wind.

"He helped me too." I nod, a little embarrassed. "That's why I'm here. I didn't get a chance to say goodbye."

She flicks her cigarette. The snowbank hisses in disgust but swallows the pieces of ash anyway. "My daddy always told me, *never leave things unsaid or you may not get to say them.*"

Her comment hits me hard. I picture Simone the last time I saw her. Before she left for ReBoot. There's so much I wish I'd said. Nothing life-changing really, just some sappy stuff that friends don't really take the time to say.

"If you don't mind, I'd love to see him."

"Me too." The woman slumps in the doorway, eyes on her feet. The frame provides support. "But Nathan isn't here, baby."

I shift from foot to foot as the icy breeze permeates my clothes. I wish I could speed this up, but I don't want to be rude. "Do you know where he is?"

The lighter shakes in her hand as she struggles to spark another cigarette. "Only the good Lord knows that now."

I lean in, wondering if I'm not hearing her right. "I'm sorry? I'm not sure I understand."

"Baby, he's *gone*." She looks up, her eyes bloodshot and dark. A single tear runs down her cheek, a trail of black mascara marks its path. "For good."

"What?" My voice sticks to my throat. I tilt off balance and stumble back a couple steps. My legs turn weak and wobbly. My mind goes blank, and I struggle to find the right words. "Where did he go? To his dad's? If you could give me the address, maybe I could go and—"

"He's *dead*, child. They found him in an internet café early this morning."

The woman's words echo in my head.

He's dead, child. He's dead, child. He's dead, child.

"He's dead?" I repeat it out loud as if it will make the words more real. Reaching out, I grip the rust-covered railing to steady myself. My hands burn from the frozen metal. This woman must be mistaken. I want to force the truth out of her. Demand she explain where my friend is so I can save him.

I shake my head. "No. He just left ReBoot yesterday. There must be some mistake."

"I wish." She wipes the tear sliding down her cheek. "Didn't even get a chance to cook him his favorite clam chowder."

I'm too late.

"What…what happened?" After I ask, I'm not sure I really want to know. Not sure I can take the answer. I attempt to focus as she explains, but her voice cuts in and out, like a bad cell phone connection. The words are fragmented in my head as I try to piece them together.

Binging on a video game. No food or water for over twenty hours. Heart murmur. Cardiac arrest.

"Heart attack?" I shake my head in disbelief.

"I didn't know about the murmur. But they say it was in his medical files. Maybe deep down he wanted to be with his baby sister. God rest his soul. He never did get over that." She sighs and her voice trails off. She removes an old crumpled tissue out of her pocket and blows her nose. "Neither did I."

I want to be mad at this woman for even saying that. She blamed Crash and practically forced him into silence. But now, watching her cry, I want to hug her. And crumble along with her.

"I'm so sorry." I reach out and touch her shoulder. The protruding collarbone tells me she's frailer than she looks in her terry-cloth armor. Like the life is draining out of her.

One kid at a time.

The woman dabs her tissue on both eyes. "Me too, baby. Me too." Her eyes moisten right back up. She reaches into her other pocket and retrieves a scrap piece of paper. "Crash only said a few words after he came home and then he went straight to that café. Said he was getting coffee. I didn't know it had computers. Should have known it was a lie. They dropped off his bag and things earlier this evening."

Something doesn't fit. Dying of a heart attack after a twenty-four-hour binge is rare.

"Did he say anything strange before he left?" I keep my emotions hidden. This lady's lost a son and daughter for a lifetime. I'm losing another friend after only two weeks.

"Not that I remember. As you know, he didn't say much," she answers. "But I found this note. It was for you. Wasn't sure what it meant. Sounds like crazy talk to me."

Ada, the ghost is everywhere!

She reaches into her robe pocket and places a wrinkled piece of paper in my palm.

"Mean anything to you?" she asks.

It's a clear warning.

"Not really." I lie. I know exactly what he's talking about. "Do you want this back?"

"No." She crosses her arms. "You keep it. Don't mean nothing to me no more."

I stand there, like my feet are cemented to the Earth. All the feelings I have about Simone —the panic, the sadness, the confusion, and the anger—return. I don't even feel cold or wet anymore. Just numb. Dead inside.

Tears fill my eyes. This woman has lost everything. I kind of know how she feels. Her two kids are gone, and the only two friends I've ever had are gone too.

I swallow, forcing out words. "I'm so sorry. About everything."

She takes another puff and exhales a long smoky breath. "Those damn computers took everything from me. Should have never let him go near them. Should have kept him home. With me. Where he belonged."

I squeak out a single question. "Can you tell me what café it was?"

"The DotCom Café. 53rd and 10th." With that she adds a period to her statement by slamming the door.

I stand there. Alone. Each time she bolts one of many locks, I flinch. My brain struggles to form any command. It's as if I'm frozen in place. In time. Unable to move. Unable to walk away. Unable to feel. Anything. My heart shreds. I'm too late. If I'd read Crash's note, I would have stopped him from leaving,

And he'd be here with me now.

I force myself to turn around and trudge back to the car, away from the hope of Crash being okay. Toward the realization that he's gone. It's a short walk, but it's the longest one

I'll ever make. With each step, my body drags, feeling heavier and heavier.

Crash's sweet face hovers in my mind. Even though I only knew him a short time, he touched me more than anyone at ReBoot. Watching him struggle was like watching myself drown. By talking again, he helped me believe I could have a second chance too. That no matter what has happened in the past, we all can fight for another shot at life. A real one. Crash made me feel like I could make a difference. Like what I said could matter. Now all I can think about is how I let him down. How I failed. Again.

I fall into the car, knowing I have to break three more hearts.

</DOTCOM CAFE>

My heaven doesn't have pearly gates.

It's stocked with eternal computers, internet access faster than the speed of light, and hellish coffee.

If there are any answers or clues to Crash's death, they'll be here.

When the four of us pull up outside, the café looks like something out of a Crate & Barrel catalog. A minimalistic setting with brown leather chairs and wooden desks. Splashes of red add bright color to the earthy space, while smudge-free computers and chrome trim keep it modern enough for the teen crowd. Little round lights hang from the ceiling like tiny UFOs. A few TVs hang in the corners showing different channels.

Becca hasn't said a word since I broke the news about Crash.

Before leaving the van, I hug her and whisper to Varian, "Can you stay with her? We won't be long."

He groans under his breath. "Why do I have to babysit?"

"Because we're a *team*…" I shoot him a dirty look and hiss back, "…And she doesn't need to be alone."

"Not sure I like teams anymore," he grumbles. "They spoil all the fun."

Fisher and I hop out of the car and walk inside. Soft acoustic music plays alongside the hum of the machines. It's so nice to be out of ReBoot and back in the real world. An updated world.

Unfortunately, the circumstances suck.

I glance back at the van in time to catch Varian wrap his arm around Becca. He pulls her close and she buries her head in his jacket. G.I. Joe has a heart after all.

And Becca just lost hers.

Fisher points to a girl behind the counter. "I know her. Maybe we can find out what terminal Crash was on."

The girl pushes up her bra and reapplies cherry lipstick. She perches high on a stool behind the counter, listening to music and smacking gum while she reads *Wired* magazine.

He whispers as we draw closer, "Let me handle this."

I stay by his side. No way I'm letting Fisher talk to the Katy Perry look-alike alone.

Without looking up, the girl removes one earbud and recites a canned welcome phrase from her training manual. "Welcome to DotCom Café, where we offer cache for free." Her monotone voice sounds unamused as she flips the magazine page. "Get it, *cache*?"

Fisher glances at me before speaking. "Hey, Stace."

"Hey Fish," A grin stretches across her red-hot lips. She tucks a short piece of black hair behind her long dangling earrings and leans over, flashing us her twin peaks wrapped in a tight black top. "Long time no see. Where yah been hangin'?"

I study him out of the corner of my eye, but he keeps his gaze forward. Avoiding mine.

"I've been around." He tries to appear relaxed. His voice drops an octave, changing from a tenor to a bass. Typical.

She winks at him with a flirty smile. The eat-shit-and-die look is for me. "You been wasting time, I see."

I want to fire back, shove all my frustration and anger and guilt down her skinny throat. But Fisher doesn't give me a chance. "Listen, Stace, I need a favor. A friend was in here recently, and I thought you could tell us what terminal he was working on."

Stace eyes Fisher and blows a large bubble that pops across her face. She dabs her gum along her lips to pick up the sticky pieces while still attempting to be sexy. As sexy as Gum Face Girl can be. "What will you give me in return?" she asks.

I roll my eyes and rock on my feet. I don't have time for silly games. I want answers. Now.

Fisher presses for information. "His name is . . . was Crash."

I step forward. "Actually, he may have gone by Nathan. He died here this morning."

Stace sits up straight on the stool. A serious expression fills her heart-shaped face. "Shiitake, that's the kid who blue-screened. How do you know him?"

"He is...*was* a friend," Fisher says. The change in tense stabs my heart.

I jump in and steer the conversation where it needs to go. "Do you remember him?"

She wrings her hands. "Sure, I worked the night shift yesterday. Didn't realize he'd been here the whole day. When I left early this morning, his head was down on the desk, I assumed he was asleep. Lots of kids do that. I had no idea he—"

I cut her off, growing more impatient by the second. "Which station?"

She glares at me for interrupting her dramatic monologue and points to the last row. "Number ten."

"Has anyone been on there since?" I ask.

"I don't really know. I left when the cops were here, so they could have shut it off." She shrugs nonchalantly. "I came back in to cover Buster's shift until he gets here. The asshat is running late. Again."

While she traps Fisher with her mundane conversation about the newest release in the never-ending *Fast and Furious* movies, I beeline to the desk and search around the computer for any clue that something's out of place. I rip off the "Out of Service" sign and flip on the hard drive, waiting for it to boot up. If the cops think Crash died of natural causes, they scoured his searches but may have left the drive alone.

I log in with DotCom's general ID and password. White I'm waiting, I stare up at the TV.

CNN cuts to breaking news. I can't hear the newscaster, but I read the story tagline scrolling along the bottom: WHITE HOUSE HACKED BY TEEN.

A picture pops up of John's room. The one I took. My heart drops. I climb on the table and reach up to turn up the volume.

Mitnick walks up to a podium, and I hold my breath. "As you know, we have had some recent hacks into a few different companies by a hacker group called the Orwellians. We have been tracking them for months now and have made some arrests that have given us information. A couple weeks ago, someone hacked into the first son's personal computer. Although this was at the White House, we have no reason to believe any secure systems or information of the nation have been compromised. It appears to be a stunt. Or a warning."

A reporter raises his hand. "Do you know who the hacker was?"

"Our investigation is ongoing. But we do have evidence that links a hacker known as the Dark Angel, but at this time, we have nothing to confirm."

Another reporter blurts out. "We heard that someone hacked into the JARS arrest system. Can you confirm?"

Mitnick appears frustrated. "Well obviously that's been leaked. I will say that we've also found evidence that a hacker tried to enter the JARS system through a back door. We don't know if they accessed any arrest records, but we will find out. We are looking into the possibility that the two may be connected. I—along with the entire FBI Cyber Crimes Unit—plan to get to the bottom of the hack. And I promise, we will prosecute to the fullest."

Hands shoot up into the air as reporters try to ask about the details of the case.

Mitnick holds up his hands to quiet them and gives a safe reply, "I cannot speak to any details in an ongoing investigation. That's all we know for now. Thank you." He turns and walks away from the mic stand as people continue yelling questions.

My body shakes as I stare at the TV. Hearing the Orwellians and the Dark Angel named in the media is bad. Mitnick knows way more than he should. But the news of the JARS breach hits me even harder. That sounded way too similar to the exercise Mr. Anthony made me do on his SAS simulation.

Did I break into the JARS system and not know it? And if so, who linked it to the Dark Angel?

"Why are you up there?" Fisher asks from below.

The channel cuts to Gary Host, who's making a statement on behalf of SocialNet.

"Shhhhh." I wave him off and turn the volume up more, staring.

Gary clears his throat. "As you know, the White House was hacked. It's also not a secret that SocialNet was hacked about a month ago. And although nothing was compromised due to our outstanding security, other companies are also reporting hackers attempting to access their data. We have to take this seriously and stop these hoodlums from hacking our systems, jeopardizing our businesses and invading the privacy of our customers. I hope they find the Dark Angel. Even if she's a teen, I believe she should be prosecuted to the fullest extent of the law."

Fisher calls out. "Man, that's crazy. Someone hacked the White House. How stupid can you be? They can track that in a heartbeat. The first son must be pissed that some hack-head trolled his computer. No telling what information they have on him now."

"Yeah." I climb down and sit at the desk where Crash worked.

Fisher rambles on about the announcement. "That dude will probably serve the next twenty years in prison. Hacking is one thing, but the White House is considered an act of terrorism."

I'm irritated that he assumes it's a guy. But my head spins from the blow. The White House hack is finally out. And someone is hacking into a bunch of companies and uploading viruses. And they know it's the Dark Angel. All they have to do is tie the job to me, and everything around me will crumble.

Dad will lose his privacy war and be forced to resign.

Mom will have to quit the bank. No one wants an executive who deals in money all day to have a hacker daughter. Too risky.

And the Dark Angel will die. Alongside the Red Devil.

I have to track down this Casper guy before he releases any information that connects me to these events.

Fisher leans over me, his breath hot on my neck. "We should hurry. Varian's already going nuts out there. I don't know who has it worse, him or Becca."

"She's upset." I give him a look. "He's a big boy."

"Correction. He's a big, *angry* boy who hates to wait."

"Noted." As soon as the desktop pops up, I comb through

the temp files and the directory, searching for the time stamp of Crash's binge. "The logged times are scattered; it's hard to pin down Crash's last keystrokes."

"Seems like a weird thing to do. Put a note in a bag," Fisher says. "I think I would have emailed instead. To make sure it wasn't lost."

"Good to know."

But his words jog my brain. I reach into my pocket and pull out the note Crash's mom gave me. A wave of clarity rolls in and washes away the fog clouding my brain.

"Oh my God. That's it." I hold up the paper and shake it in Fisher's face. "Crash didn't write this note. Someone else did. This note is proof someone else killed Crash."

"I lost you back at God."

I scan through the computer's log. "Someone else was here. According to the history, Crash was only online for a couple hours. It wasn't all night like his mom said. It wasn't a binge. It doesn't make sense he would write some strange note—that's *not* in email format—and then die a mysterious death from a minor ailment he's had his whole life that no one knew about?"

"It does sound weird." Fisher pulls up a chair. "But maybe he stopped formatting his notes like emails once he started talking."

"I don't think so." I shake my head and show him the warning note Crash gave me at ReBoot. "This was written in email format too. Why change now? I think someone else wrote this to scare me. Even the handwriting looks a little different."

Fisher compares the two pieces of paper. "Who would do that? A ghost?"

I think of Simone's clue, an email from Casper. Maybe Crash's email will tell me something too.

I pull up Zed and spend a few moments hacking into Crash's email. His inbox is empty so I check his deleted folder. Can't help but feel super dirty scrounging through personal messages, ones from his dad, his friends, and his therapist.

Then one email grabs my attention.

You can't hide. It's time to crash and burn. –Casper

I show Fisher. "Look at this. I found a similar message from this guy Casper on Simone's email. Plus they both mention ghosts. So I tracked it down to an IP address somewhere in Seattle."

"You think it's the same person?"

I don't say anything about the Orwellians or the ghostly hacker. "How many Caspers have you met?"

He smirks. "Only one, but he was friendly."

I hit him in the arm. "This is serious. Casper's behind all this. I just don't know who it is."

I rub my eyes. The mental exhaustion of the last few weeks is beginning to take its toll. I think through the strange deaths, including Simone's. "ReBoot is the only thing that links all these dead kids. Maybe Casper is the one killing them. But why?"

"It's either money or power," Fisher says.

Then I remember the fight I overhear between my counselor and the director. "You know, that night when Mr. Anthony and Ms. Matthews were fighting, she said something strange."

"What?" Fisher asks.

"When Ms. Matthews wanted to close the lab, Mr. Anthony was worried about losing a deal and money. But Ms. Matthews didn't care who else would be 'upset' by that."

"And you think it could be this Casper guy?"

I nod, remembering the account numbers I recorded in my notebook. "Maybe we can track the money."

Fisher pokes his temple. "Let's track down Casper first. Then we can trace the money."

I swallow. He's right. I could be next on the list. "Only clue we have is this IP address."

Stace walks up. "Hey, Fish, Buster's here so I gotta go. Listen, please don't tell anyone I let you snoop around. I don't want those men who came in earlier to find out I was dishing out 411. Okay?"

I snap my head up. "What men?"

</INVADING BOTS>

Two guys dressed in suits came in this morning and asked about Crash."

"Cops?" Fisher asks.

"No. Weird guys. One was an albino. All white and spooky like a ghost. They spent some time looking around and then left."

Fisher and I look at each other. "I bet Casper came to clean up his mess."

"Casper?" Stace asks. "Who's that?"

Fisher ignores her. "Did they take anything?"

"Not that I saw." She glares at me over his shoulder. "But then again, I wasn't *draped* all over them." She spins around and heads out the front door. As Stace passes by the window, she winks at Fisher and flashes a "call me" sign.

Once she's gone, Fisher jabs me in the side. "I think you're jealous."

"You wish, Romeo." I say. "As much as I'd love to talk about Stace, let's focus on tracking this Casper dude. I have a feeling it won't be easy."

Time to go ghost hunting. I don't want to create a trail here. So I jump on Zed and get to work on tracking this guy down. First, I post some inquiries on a few discussion boards. Someone knows who this guy is. Then I search for any other trace of Casper on the internet. If he's careless or ballsy enough to send a risky email, he must have left a trace somewhere. Every hacker makes a mistake. It's just a matter of someone finding it.

A hacker's ego—the thought that they are untouchable—is the thing that usually brings them down.

I track Casper down to a few sub-private IRC chat rooms and finally uncover a mistake. A few months ago, he posted a link that included his private server name. When I paste it into the browser, the same IP address comes up, but this time it has tracked it through several routers and to a more targeted location. "Know anything about Issaquah?"

"Yeah," Fisher says. "Not much there though."

"Looks like this guy is hiding somewhere around there," I say. "Unless he rerouted through a satellite server."

"Which is very likely." Fisher doesn't seem convinced.

Varian knocks on the window, making me flinch. When I look, he taps his watch and then slices his pointer finger across his throat before holding up five fingers.

Fisher interprets. "You have five minutes or he'll kill you."

"I got the message, thanks," I mumble. "Can you tell him I'm almost done?"

"Why do I always have to do the dirty work?" Fisher pinches my cheek. "But I'll do it for you."

"This won't take long, I promise. I'll sift through the data and see what I can find."

I hate asking Fisher to leave, but if any of my friends find out about the Dark Angel, things will get even more confusing. And there's only one person who can help me now.

As soon as he leaves, I jump in the Orwellians' private chat room to see if Taz has looked at the art and has any ideas.

> DA: Did you see my note about Casper?

> Taz: Yes. Thx 4 warning. You find out who it is?
> DA: Not yet. Did U get my package?
> Taz: Y. Just looking.
> DA: Any idea on what it is?
> Taz: Looks like it's some kind of morphing algorithm. Once it's uploaded, it's almost impossible for security systems to track b/c it changes. Where'd U get it?
> DA: Red Devil had it.
> Taz: WTF? I thought she was off grid.
> DA: I thought so too.

I don't like lying, but in this case it was necessary. No one in Cyberland knows the Red Devil is dead and for right now, I want to keep it that way.

> Taz: Whoever is using this is pretty damn good. Must be important. Do U know the main source? Looks like some chunks are missing.
> DA: No. But I tracked an IP address so I can hunt around more.
> Taz: If you can find the source, you'll be able to fill in the gaps pretty easily. It's like a puzzle. You can't see the full picture until all the pieces are there.
> DA: Thanks.
> Taz: And don't worry, I'll nail that Casper dude.

For now, I need to find the missing pieces to this code. Maybe it's all at Issaquah.

As I'm logging off, Fisher pops up from behind my screen. "Hey. We need to go."

I jump up and my chair falls over. "You scared me."

"Sorry. Some black car keeps circling the block, looking suspicious, so Varian moved the van."

I pack up Zed and erase any keystrokes from the DotCom computer.

The café door jingles and a gust of frigid air whips across the room. Two guys invade the café. Both stocky, both wearing jeans and button-downs. They scan the room.

Fisher and I spot them at the same time. I'm not exactly sure why—maybe the vibe, maybe the scowls on their face, maybe my paranoia—but we both instinctively drop behind the desk. For all we know, they could be patrons looking for a nice cup of java.

The two men stomp up to the counter and ask Stace's replacement a few questions. The kid points in our direction.

"Do you think they're looking for us?" I ask.

Fisher peeks over the desk. "I don't think they're here for coffee and an online game of chess. Let's get out of here."

We hunch over and run through the aisles until we push into the back of the store. The two men check out the computer Fisher and I had been investigating. Maybe these guys are here about Crash too.

"Think they saw us?" I stop and peer through the door's round window. One spots me spying. I jerk back. "If not, they just did."

"Let's not hang around to find out." Fisher grabs my hand. We push through the building's rear exit and into the narrow alleyway used for shipments, trash, and rat conventions. The wind scrapes my cheeks. The sleeting has stopped but now it's nothing but slush.

I groan. "Which way?"

"This way." Fisher yanks me down the steps and keeps a firm grip as we both bound through the alley.

My boots slap against the puddles of melting snow, moving as fast as they can with my legs throbbing in pain. I glance back in time to see the two men crash out of the building. When they spot us fleeing, they charge in our direction. "They're coming!" I yell.

"Run!" I'm certain Fisher is just as sore as I am with our leg injuries, so we move much slower than we want to. He still limps a little, but doesn't show an inkling of any pain on his face.

At the end of the alleyway, we turn right and hobble a few steps before realizing it's a dead end. Then we backtrack and zigzag through the city's hidden arteries. With each jarring step along the frozen ground, prickly pain shoots into my lame leg. My foot skitters out from under me when I hit a patch of iced-over goo. Fisher tightens his grip and saves me from a bad fall, all without slowing us down.

The two men gain on us, their steps growing louder and louder. For big guys, they move fast.

Fisher and I veer down another alley, venturing deeper into the urban maze. Each time we pass a nook or cranny, we check for a place to hide. A doorway, a deep indent in the wall, or even a dumpster. Any small space where we can hole up until our pursuers give up and go away.

"There." I whisper and yank Fisher's arm. We race down the dead end and squeeze through a gate.

I wrap the heavy chain around the latch, making it appear locked. Then we slide back into the shadows and squat down behind a stack of boxes and trash cans. The alley smells like a cocktail of frozen oil mixed with a splash of urine. I breathe through my mouth, trying not gag.

Feet smack the wet street as the men charge down the same path. They stop in front of the gate and jiggle the chain before heading off in the other direction.

We sit in silence for a while before sneaking out of the makeshift hiding place. At the main street, we peek out before briskly walking down the sidewalk, searching for the van.

"Where's Varian?" I hiss.

"Knowing him, he left." Fisher scowls and grips my hand. "Only takes care of himself."

"No. Becca wouldn't let him leave us." Would she? I can't help but wonder if Fisher's right.

In the distance, a few drunken people stagger along the

road, laughing and slurring. Totally oblivious to everything going on around them.

As we turn a corner, the black sedan skids up to the curb with squealing wheels, blocking our path. Before we can run, the car door opens.

Someone grabs my arm and yanks me inside.

</WEB OF LIES>

AGENT MITNICK SITS IN THE BACK OF THE SEDAN.

"What are *you* doing here?" I ask, holding my hands up to the heater, welcoming the warmth. "You gave me a heart attack."

Fisher climbs in next to me and sits in silence, staring at his hands in his lap.

Mitnick grins mischievously. "Impossible. Your medical records state you're a hundred percent healthy. Though your mental state is still in question." Then he reaches out and squeezes Fisher's shoulder. "Fish. You okay?"

Fish answers flatly. "Yes."

I look back and forth between them. "Wait, you guys know each other?"

Mitnick frowns. "You didn't tell her?"

"Tell her what?" Fisher circles his fingers against his temples. "That my older brother is a total traitor who busted me for hacking and shipped me off to rehab?"

"Your brother?" I half laugh. "Come on! Is this a joke?" It's only then that I notice the resemblance. Same chin. Same eyes. Same cheeky grin. My stomach sinks. "But your last name?"

Mitnick shrugs. "I checked him in under our mom's maiden name. Didn't want to cause any attention."

"Don't let him fool you. The name change was for him. He's embarrassed to have a criminal bloodline. It's not good for his job advancement plan," Fisher says. "Meanwhile, I've been busy protecting Ada and running for my life from some goons."

"Hardly." Mitnick rolls his eyes at Fisher's dramatic statement. "Those were my guys."

"Wait. Your men were chasing us?" I ask. "Why?"

Mitnick nods. "They were trying to get you to me. Not chase you. You were the ones who ran."

"Maybe some identification would have helped." Fisher scoffs.

"Wait, will someone please tell me what the hell is going on?" I stare at Fisher because he hasn't made eye contact since we got in the car.

"Ada, please don't be mad," he says quietly.

I slide away from him until my back presses against the door. Now there's enough space for the big bomb he's about to drop. I hope I'm wrong.

I swallow. "Why would I be mad?"

"Because Fish works for me," Mitnick says matter-of-factly. "And it sounds like he's been lying to you."

"Working? You arrested me and forced me into a death trap to do your dirty work." Fisher frowns and looks at me. "And I didn't lie."

Mitnick rolls his eyes. "You broke the law. Broke into a secure FBI conferencing line. And let's not exaggerate. ReBoot was better than jail. And, you should have told her about our connection. She deserves to know."

As the boys bicker, I study Fisher. Mitnick is his brother? No wonder he's been asking so many questions. Like brother, like brother. Do I even know him? "Look I hate to break up the sweet family reunion, but I deserve some answers here."

Fisher opens his mouth, but Mitnick holds up his hand to stop him from talking.

Mitnick explains instead. "Ada, for the last year, many kids have been released from ReBoot. However, as you know, a handful of them have either committed suicide or wound up dead due to unexplained accidents. After Chelsea Talbot died, we started looking into the deaths. I mean, *something* was sending these kids over the edge and the only common thread was ReBoot. At the time, it was only a suspicion. Without any proof, I couldn't dispatch any agents to investigate; plus, it's locked down as a teen facility. We got wind of large amounts of money coming in and out of the facility and focused on that until we had more."

I don't even know where to start with my questions. There are so many.

Mitnick nods to the agent in the front seat who merges out onto a deserted street. "When my brother got busted hacking, I offered him a deal. He could go into ReBoot and snoop around. Report any suspicious activity back to me. Not to mention, he needed the program. It was a win-win."

Fisher mumbles, "For you maybe."

That explains why I could not find information online. I bet Mitnick scrubbed it to protect his brother. I close my eyes and think about everything he's saying. "So, you sent your brother into a place where kids were mysteriously dying?"

"Exactly my point." Fisher throws up his hands. "See? Even she thinks it was crazy."

"It was the only way to get more information." Mitnick loosens his tie. "The deaths all took place off-site. At the time, I didn't think the facility posed any danger."

"No, but getting out of there does," I add. "You set me up."

Mitnick acts as if this mission is no big deal. "I thought it was the best place for you, considering everything. But I admit, I assumed you'd snoop around a little too, knowing

Simone was your friend. That's why I asked Fisher to keep an eye on you. To make sure you stayed safe."

"You had me under *surveillance*?" My chest tightens. And there it is. I knew it was too good to be true. That's all I am to Fisher, the subject of a secret stakeout.

Mitnick rubs his hands on his jeans like he's wiping them clean. Fisher does the same thing when he's nervous. "It wasn't surveillance; it was a favor. And like I said, there was no evidence of any danger at that time. It was a hunch. Obviously the minute I found out Ms. Matthews was dead, I decided to extract you two until we knew more."

"How'd you get here so fast?" I ask. "I just saw you on the news."

Mitnick crosses his arms. "That clip was from earlier. Looks like the Orwellians and the Dark Angel may have struck again. Any ideas?"

"Nope. I've been in ReBoot." I keep my head down. "Every hacker I know is there."

Or was.

"How did you know we'd be here?" I ask.

"I keep tabs on Fisher's phone and saw you were at the café." Mitnick's shoulders squarely face me. He doesn't look the least bit ashamed. "I'm sorry about your friend Crash. I heard about his accident right before we picked you up."

"It wasn't an accident," I blurt out.

Fisher interjects, "Ada may have proof that Crash was killed."

"Tell me everything you know." Mitnick leans forward and stops clicking. He pulls out a notebook and waits for me to say something he can write. "If there's a shred of evidence, I can open this case formally with the bureau."

I arch my back and extract both of Crash's messages from my pocket. "Crash always wrote his notes in email format. Like this one. But this one—from his mom—is written regular." I hold out the papers to Mitnick. They are no use to me anymore.

Mitnick appears disappointed. "I'm not sure that's enough evidence."

"I think someone else wrote that note," I say a little too loudly. "Someone else was there when Crash died."

Fisher chimes in, "Maybe you can pull prints."

"I can try. Though you all have touched it so I doubt it." Mitnick plucks a Ziploc out of the car's side pocket and holds it open. "Anything else?"

I drop the notes in the bag. "I hacked into Crash's email account. Some guy sent a threatening email to Crash and Simone before they died."

Fisher nods. "We think it was a dude named Casper."

We? I snarl at Fisher for stealing my thunder. Like he figured this out too.

"The ghost." Mitnick studies the car's ceiling. "Yeah, the name rings a bell."

I speak fast before even thinking about what I'm saying. "I think he's part of the Orwellians."

"I thought you didn't know them," Mitnick asks with squinted eyes.

"I . . . I don't. It's a hunch. You said on the news there have been tons of hacks. Maybe he's involved with those too." I avert my eyes. I slipped up, forgot who I was talking to. This man can put me away, especially if he links me to the Orwellians and the Dark Angel. "I tracked an IP address to . . . somewhere in…Seattle. Maybe you can narrow it down more."

Fisher glances in my direction. He knows I tracked the address to Issaquah.

Mitnick raises one eyebrow and clicks his pen once before jotting down notes. "Wow, Ada. Not even rehab can keep you off a computer."

Fear creeps in. I have to be careful. "I got the information, didn't I?"

"I admit you did a good job." Mitnick asks the driver to head back to the café. "Can you tell me more about the lab or Mr. Anthony? How do you think he's involved?"

"That's Fisher's theory." I picture my group leader. How positive and supportive Mr. Anthony really was. Surely he's not part of this.

Fisher explains, "Ada found a hidden computer lab where Mr. Anthony was letting kids do coding exercises in exchange for participating in the program. Ada was tracking the IDs to see who they belonged to when the fire started."

"What about Ms. Matthews? Was she involved?"

I jump in. "I thought so at first. But she seemed surprised when she found the lab. She ended up being the one who saved Fisher from the fire. He almost died." I watch Mitnick grab his brother's shoulder affectionately. My words pour out. But I'm thinking more out loud than sharing the information. "Once we were safe outside, someone in a dark hoodie ran out of the building. Ms. Matthews chased the person down. Told us to wait. Then we heard a scream and found her body. She was already—"

Fisher interrupts. "Dead."

Mitnick nods. "Yes I know. We have men on the scene now. I'm sorry you had to see that. When did you last see Mr. Anthony? Because we can't find him at ReBoot, which does seem suspicious."

Fisher shrugs. "Maybe he killed her and bolted."

"No, he wouldn't be there," I say. "The night they argued, Ms. Matthews fired him and he left ReBoot."

"You didn't tell me that," Fisher says, surprised.

"I guess I forgot." Unfortunately, I can't remember what I've told Fisher and what I've kept to myself. It's all starting to run together.

"That gives him motive but if he wasn't on site at the time,

Mr. Anthony couldn't have killed her. I'll check it out more and let you know if I find him." Mitnick scribbles his pen across a small notebook. "Anything else that might help us piece this together before we get you home?"

Home? That means he has no intention of letting me help.

I go on to explain the user IDs and the link to all the dead kids, including Ms. Matthews' son. I pull the printout of IDs from my backpack. "Here's a list of the user IDs and passwords. The last log-in date coincides with their check-out date. Maybe you will find something in there."

Mitnick frowns. "This gives me a new angle to check out. I'll look into the deaths again and see if this will help me find a link." Mitnick runs his finger down the short list. "Unfortunately, the computer lab was destroyed. Along with any evidence. Anything else?"

"Nope, that's it." I say. Of course, I omit everything about Raven's art and how we downloaded all the files to see if I can crack the code. I also leave out that I asked Taz for help.

Fisher studies me and I give him the eye, nonverbally asking him not to say anything more.

He obviously gets my cue because he changes the subject. "Any news on Raven?"

"I'm afraid not. But I'm hopeful she will turn up as a witness." Mitnick sighs, obviously frustrated. "So, I'll take it from here and run down these leads. Hopefully we'll catch a break in Matthews' murder."

I sit forward. "Maybe we can help."

"Thanks, Ada. But at this point, it's way too dangerous to send anyone back in. Not to mention, I need to keep you safe. You're tied to that lab now, and so far, the others there didn't end up so well. I don't want you to be next."

"There has to be something I can do." I nudge Fisher for backup.

He jumps in. "If anyone can find something helpful, it's Ada."

"I can't risk either of you getting hurt. Now that Matthews is dead, we have a whole new ball game on our hands. It makes it much easier for my guys to get inside ReBoot and investigate." Mitnick exhales and tucks away his pen before handing me his business card. "But if you remember anything else, Ada, call me. No matter how small it is, okay? Never know what could help us."

"Fine." I slump, feeling defeated.

Mitnick motions the driver to pull over. At the end of the deserted street, I spot the nose of our white catering van sticking out. I'm relieved Varian and Becca didn't ditch us.

The driver comes around the car and opens the back door.

Fisher and I climb out, and Mitnick leans forward. "Ada, are your parents in town?"

I shake my head, remembering what they told me at Parent Day. "I think they're are on a business trip until tomorrow."

"I want you to call them and tell them you have been released." Mitnick faces his brother. "Fish, I want you to get Ada home and stay with her until they get back. Call me if anything seems out of place. You hear me?"

Fisher nods.

Mitnick closes the door and opens the window. "You both should be proud of everything you've gotten so far. It's more than we ever had before. I'll be sure to give a recommendation of leniency to the judge so you another chance. Use it wisely."

Simone never got a second chance. Neither did Crash.

I mumble, "Yeah. Thanks." But it's not what I really want right now. I want to find out what's going on. Because it will help me figure out what happened to Simone. And Crash.

Mitnick rubs his chin. "And don't tell anyone about this, especially your dad. Until I figure this case out, I don't want to tip off anyone." The two men in jeans who chased us earlier stroll out of the café and climb into the car with

Mitnick. This time, I spot the FBI badges swinging from lanyards around their necks.

Somehow I missed that little clue. Would have saved me a lot of hassle.

Mitnick slaps the car door twice. "Fish, I'll see you at home. And stay out of trouble. Ada, I'll call you if I need you."

We stand on the sidewalk until he drives away.

"Sorry." Fisher mumbles. "My brother can be a total ass."

"Must run in the family," I snap back and march off toward the white van still parked in the side alley.

My brain is blank, and my body goes numb.

Fisher is a liar. Because of him and his brother, I did all this work and I still don't know what happened to Simone.

</RESCUE AND RETRIEVE>

WHEN I REACH THE VAN, VARIAN DOESN'T LOOK HAPPY.

"I'm tired of being in the getaway car. You guys are getting all the action while I'm playing stupid chauffeur. What happened?" He almost sounds worried.

"It's a long story." I climb in the car with Fisher on my heels.

He faces us. "Those guys looked like Feds."

"Yeah, Fisher wanted a playdate with his *friends*," I add.

Varian hits the gas as soon as Fisher hops in the front seat. "You're a rat for the pigs?"

"You can label me any animal you like." Fisher props his shoes up on the dashboard. "I can't choose my family."

"Shit, the Fed is your blood?" Varian says. "That sucks."

"You could have just been honest with us," I say.

"No, I couldn't, Ada," Fisher sounds irritated when I'm the one who should be mad. "And besides it's doesn't matter. It's over anyway."

My stomach drops, assuming he means him and me. No more us. No more we. I pinch back tears. Who cares anyway? This guy is a liar. There was never a real "we" anyway. I prop my head against the window. I knew something was up with Fisher. I never should have let my guard down.

"What's *over*?" Varian glances in the rearview mirror.

"Our investigation. My brother told us to back off," Fisher mumbles, watching the buildings blaze by.

I should feel better but I don't. Everything between us was lie.

"Yeah? Well, so did the Taliban, but that didn't stop my dad," Varian says.

"Well, we don't have a choice. Sometimes you just have to walk away." I say and then glance in the back of the van. "Hey, where's Becca?"

Varian spins around. "What do you mean? I thought she was with you."

"Nooo. She was with you when we saw the car," Fisher says. "I went back in for Ada, remember?"

"She followed you in there." Varian frowns. "You didn't see her?"

I press my face against the window, searching for a mane of red hair. "Let's circle back around the front of the café. Maybe she's waiting where the van was parked."

Varian shifts the van into drive and circles around the front. Becca is nowhere to be found.

"Where the hell did she go?" Fisher says, scanning the dark street.

"I am gonna kill this kid myself when I get my hands on her," Varian grumbles.

I point down the side street. "Wait. Look."

A black car rolls around the corner.

We all scoot down in the seats and watch, hoping not to warrant any attention.

A pale guy, whiter than the moon, gets out and stands by the car, smoking. Little puffs swirl around his head. His eyebrows and hair perfectly match his stark white suit. His frame is frail and his eyes are a strange pinkish-white. With his skin and the thin veil of mist, he looks like a ghost.

"Looks like the albino guy Stace mentioned," Fisher whispers.

A few seconds later, the beefy man storms out of the building with Becca. She's walking calmly, and I wonder why she isn't fighting. Then I notice the gun poking in her side.

The albino opens the back door, and the big guy shoves Becca into the back seat. Once she's inside, they all pile in the car and tear off. It happens so fast it almost seems like it didn't.

"Follow them! We can't let them take her!" I can't take my eyes off the car. If it gets out of sight, Becca could be gone. Just like Crash.

Varian punches the gas and speeds along the thin alleyways, whipping the van left and right. Determined to keep the car in his sights.

The car speeds straight down the alley before taking a right.

"There!" I point to the side street so Varian doesn't miss the turn, grabbing the seat as he swerves. I keep my eyes on the car, afraid to blink or the car might disappear. Along with Becca.

Fisher scowls and mutters what I've been thinking. "It's got to be Casper."

Varian makes a hard left. "Great, we're chasing ghosts now?"

As we tail the black sedan, I fill in him on the emails from Casper to Simone and Crash.

Varian responds with only one sentence. "This is turning into some heavy shit." He speeds down the street with oily water spraying off the road, splashing against the side windows.

Fisher cups his shoulder. "Dude, stop driving like the Road Runner or they'll see us following."

"I've watched the same episodes of *Cops* that you have." Varian grips the steering wheel, knuckles white.

"Only you probably starred in a few." Fisher mumbles.

"Guys, this isn't the time to fight." I say, annoyed. "We have to find Becca."

Thankfully the two listen and cork their mouths.

Varian backs off and trails the car through the city. Once we merge onto I-90, he hides behind a couple of large trucks until they exit onto the Issaquah ramp. We tail them for a few miles and then stop when they turn down the road leading to a large building towering in the distance.

Fisher points to another side road. "Turn there."

Varian obeys and slowly rolls down a dirt road parallel to the one Becca's traveling on. Gravel crunches under our tires like muffled firecrackers.

He pulls over and stops while Fisher tries to get a signal on his phone. "We should've called my brother sooner. It was stupid to wait. He was right there and could have helped us."

"Too late now. Besides, we didn't know it would lead to all this." I follow him out of the van's sliding door and look over the huge field. Past the remnants of an old airfield and the mess of a new construction site, a huge modern glass building stands erect in the distance. Scaffolding frames one side and a crane looms over the back.

Fisher squints and then his eyes light up. He frowns and jerks his head toward me. "Do you know where we are?"

"No."

Varian whistles. "We're at one of SocialNet's buildings. I recognize it from an article in *Wired*."

"This is their main server farm," Fisher says. "The Holy Grail of databases."

The building looks familiar. Ever since Simone and I started our hacking project on SocialNet, I've always wanted to take a field trip here. See it for myself. The mother lode.

Now I'm not so sure I wanna be here at all. "This is strange. How is SocialNet involved in this?"

"I guess we'll find out," Fisher says.

"We don't have much time, so we better do it fast." I grab my backpack. "If I can get close to that building, I might be able to tap into their network, find a way in."

Fisher searches the van and finds a huge flashlight. "Your wish is my command."

"Know what, guys?" Varian rubs the back of his head and doesn't budge. "I think I'll wait here."

I spin around and stare at him with my mouth open, shocked at his casual statement. "Wait, are you serious right now? Varian, they have Becca. We need your help. You've come all this way, and now you want to quit?" I walk over and grab his hand, tugging him after me.

"This is different. The Feds are involved now and I can't risk it." Varian shrugs. "Besides, I never play a game I can't win."

"How can you do this?" I try not to show too much disappointment but it oozes from me. "This is your chance to finally fight for something real and you bail?"

"Don't worry about him. We can do this on our own." Fisher eyes Varian up and down. "We don't need any AWOLs on board anyway."

I keep pressing. "Varian, do it for your dad."

He looks away, avoiding eye contact. "I'm not getting myself killed for someone else."

"I don't believe this," I croak out and throw my hands up. "Typical."

"Sorry, Ada. But I got your computer for you, and I helped you get you here," Varian says. "But this isn't my fight anymore."

"This is your chance to save someone like you pretend to do in your stupid games, but instead you turn your back? You run?" I shake off the urge to cry. I don't know why his actions surprise me. Varian has always been about himself. About winning. I guess I thought he'd changed. Really changed. But maybe people can only change so much. "Your dad would be so ashamed."

Varian drops his guard for a split second. Moisture forms in his icy blue eyes, but he catches himself in time to throw on his sunglasses, darkening the windows to his soul. "Maybe. But I'm alive and he isn't, so it doesn't matter. Does it?"

"At least make yourself useful." Fisher throws the keys to Varian and hands over a business card. "Get to a phone and call this number. Tell my brother what's going on and send him here."

Without saying another word or making another stupid excuse, Varian climbs in the van and drives away.

I stand in the middle of the dirt road, watching his taillights, hoping, praying he'll turn around and come back. But the lights disappear. Varian is gone.

Fisher touches my shoulder. "Come on Ada, who needs him?"

"I did." I jerk away from his grasp. Not sure why Fisher thinks he can lie to me and everything will be okay between us.

He shoves his hands in his pockets, looking defeated.

I soften a little on the inside but pretend not to notice his puppy eyes. Instead, I strap on my duffel bag and climb over the fence. Fighting back tears, I stomp through the thick weeds blanketing the open field. My throat burns with all the words I wish I'd said to Varian.

Please don't leave. We can't do this without you. I need you on my side.

I walk toward the SocialNet building, feeling a bit betrayed. Maybe I'm not an emotional recluse because people let me down. Maybe it's because I expect them to do too much. I expect them to be a certain way. And if they aren't exactly what I want or need, I assume they will change to fit me.

But they don't and I know Varian can't. He's just that way. It's who he is. It's who he wants to be.

I get lost in thought as I trample the tall grass. No matter how hard I try to boost my spirits, I can't help but feel somewhat doomed. The hope of ending this nightmare fizzles. With Varian and his blazing guns, I felt like we had a chance.

Without him, I'm afraid he's right. We can't win.

Which means Simone and Crash died for nothing. Maybe Raven too. Becca might not come out alive either. If that happens, I'll never be able to live with the guilt, especially since I let her come.

Fisher catches up. "Hey, forget about Varian. You can't trust crazy people."

My frustration bursts like a firecracker lit by anger. "You can't say anything about *trust*." There I go again, blaming Fisher for the one thing he's done wrong instead of judging him for everything he's done right. Then again, he did lie.

"Nice, Ada," Fisher says quietly and stops. "Why do you push away everyone who tries to help you?"

I hold up one hand, motioning for him to stop talking. "You lied to me. I knew something was off, but you tricked me into believing I could trust you."

He bangs his head on the chain link, shaking it. The way he's rattled me. "Look, Ada. I couldn't tell you anything. This was a chance to clear my record. To start over. I want to be more than a computer hacker. More than an FBI agent's brother."

I study his face. I want so much to hug him and kiss him again. To feel special. Besides the friendship I started with Crash, this pseudo-relationship with Fisher is the only real one I've had since Simone died.

"Fisher, I came here to start over too. My best friend is gone. Crash is dead. And I don't know why. I'm scared and confused; yet I *still* let my guard down and confided in you. But all this time, you held back."

He strokes my hair. "Ada, I meant everything I said and did."

My thoughts tangle inside, and I wring my hands. Is that true? My head begs me to walk away, but my heart pounds against its self-imposed prison. Begging me to find one reason to stay.

He flashes me sad eyes. "Can you honestly tell me that I know *everything* about you?"

I break eye contact. I'm still concealing my Dark Angel identity, yet still persecuting Fisher for holding back. This whole time, I'm only showing him half of who I really am.

"No." I shake my head, determined to keep my secret. Maybe I should cut him some slack since I'm guilty of the same thing. "I never said I was *perfect*."

Fisher touches his forehead to mine and I frown. "Well, you're perfect for me."

I can't help but smile inside. Here I am bashing him when he's the only one here with me. "Look. Let's not argue, okay? We need to focus on finding Becca."

"I agree," Fisher says and inches closer, giving me that look. "So let's work together."

"Deal." I nod and take one step back. "But for the record, you can't kiss me. I'm still mad."

"Maybe I don't want to kiss you." He reaches over and grabs my hand. His touch sends electric ripples through me, recharging my feelings for him. Then he holds out a deadish dandelion. "I'm sorry."

"You picked me a weed?" I smile in the darkness and bite my lip.

"You see a dead weed. I see a flower."

I can't help but smile. I'm a sucker for letting this guy get under my skin. I hate it and love it all at the same time.

I can only hope Fisher doesn't squish my heart under his shoe like a puny bug.

</ON THE DOWNLOAD>

Look away from the light.

I break our eye contact and regroup. Fisher has a way of sucking me into his world.

"Let's go." I reclaim my hand and walk across the field, keeping my back to him.

We stop at the chain-link fence surrounding the property. Keeping people out and secrets in. The black sedan is parked in front of the glass building. Empty. Yet, even at this time of night, men in construction gear move throughout the construction site with building materials. We squat and wait as another wave of men pass by us.

I bite my lip as the cold stings through my garments. If we don't make a move, I'm going to freeze right here, right now.

After they're gone, Fisher points to a side door. "We should move in before someone spots us." He grabs my hand and leads me around the side where we hide behind a large truck. As soon as the area is clear, we race to a row of bushes along the building and hide.

I peek over the top and study the exit. "Now what?"

Fisher picks up a thick stick.

"You're going to beat your way in?" I ask. "That's your plan?"

"I'll get us in quietly." He smiles in the dark as shadows cover half his face. "Trust me."

I mutter under my breath. "I've heard that before."

Fisher places a finger to his mouth as the building door opens. The albino pops out of the building for a quick smoke.

I almost want to jump him and beat him until he tells me where Becca is. Instead, I watch the albino smoke until his cigarette whittles down to a nub. He takes one last puff before smashing the butt into a cement ashtray. Then he coughs a couple times before sliding his swipe card and yanking the door open. The albino enters the building and lets the door slowly close behind him.

Fisher hisses, "Wait here." He jumps into action and races toward the door. Just as it's about to shut, he slides the stick into the gap. He turns and gives me a thumbs up.

I run after him, half hunched. "Good job. I can't believe that worked."

He shrugs it off. "That albino dude was smoking outside the café. I figured he'd come out to abuse his lungs sometime." Fisher clutches the handle and kicks the stick away, pulling the door open a crack. He checks inside and then bows, "After you, my queen."

"You're impossible."

He grins. "Impossibly charming."

Inside SocialNet, we walk down a long hallway, making me feel so exposed. If anyone popped out a door, they'd spot us. We sneak down the passageway until we spy a conference room with a swipe card keypad. From what the Orwellians taught me, conference rooms give employees and visitors open access to the building's wireless network. The problem is most companies don't secure them like they do regular offices.

I grab Fisher's hand. "In here."

He follows me inside and locks the door behind us. "That was easy."

"Maybe too easy." I twist the internal blinds shut. Can't help but picture poor Becca sitting in a room somewhere, crying. Defeated. Or worse, what if she's hurt? Or dead? I change my mind and charge the door. "Maybe we should find Becca first."

Fisher blocks my path. "Wait, this may be our only shot to get in and find what we need. Then we can rescue her."

I boot up Zed and access the wireless network. When a screen pops up, I sign in using the common ID and password of "Guest" and "Password." It's the number one generic login used in companies today.

I click through the directory and pull up an internal website. I smile when it works. Can't believe conference rooms are left this unsecure.

Fisher rolls a chair over. "What are you doing?"

"Hunting for that IP address." I search through the schematics and get an idea of the layout. After a couple searches, I trace it to a terminal on the top floor. Before moving forward, I confirm that it's the same address attached to the person who emailed Simone and Crash. "I've got it."

"Now all you have to do is hack in and see who it belongs to."

"Easy peasy." I attempt every trick I know to hack into that terminal. But every time I find a way in, I get booted out. No matter how hard I work, I can't seem to get in and stay in. My frustration mounts when nothing works. "Damn, I can't do it. Maybe it's because I'm in a conference room. It'll be much easier if I gain direct access."

Fisher throws his head back. "Why can't it be easy? For once."

"I'll head up to the office." I point to the number 2405 on the map. "You go find Becca."

Fisher scratches his head and frowns. "That's what they

always say in horror movies right before someone gets axed. Maybe we should stick together."

"This is our best option," I say. "We can't leave Becca up there much longer. There's no telling what they'll do to her."

Fisher rubs his chin. "Fine. See if you can trace the albino's swipe card and tell me what room he went into.

"I need to figure out his card number first." My fingers jump back on the keys as if they never left. I sift through the directory for security logs, but once again error messages keep popping up and slowing me down. "This system is messed up. I can't seem to get in anywhere."

Finally, I come across some building schematics and identify the door where we entered. I reenter the system another way and click on the last card number to enter the door. The card's whole route displays. My cursor follows Casper's path through the building, noting every door where he scanned his card. Bingo.

The system boots me out again.

I groan. "Well, I lost the connection. But the last time he used the card was on the tenth floor. Let's hope Becca is still there."

Fisher squeezes my shoulders. "Good job, *Sherlock*."

I grin and raise my eyebrows. "Here's the plan: you go after Becca, and I'll get to Casper's computer. Maybe I can find the rest of those codes and figure out this algorithm. If not, it'll be evidence Mitnick can use. I'll meet you outside by the van."

Fisher pushes my hair behind my shoulders. "Kiss for luck?" He leans down and pecks me lightly on the cheek. "Be careful."

"Always."

Fisher slinks out into the hall, leaving me in the dark room. My heart pounds. I hope he stays safe. I can't lose another person. Shaking off the fear, I leave my safe space and head straight for the stairwell. I stand on the landing and glance up the spiral tunnel toward the twenty-fourth floor.

Only twenty-three levels to go.

I begin the long climb, stopping at each floor to rest and listen for movement. By the time I reach the twenty-fourth floor, I'm winded. Not only from the exercise, but also from the adrenaline flooding my body. I crawl underneath the stairwell and press against the wall so no one sees me. Time to create a diversion and clear the floor.

Squatting, I open Zed. First, I connect to the wireless network and then launch the "Emergency Systems" application. Within seconds I'm kicked out again.

"Damn it!" I stare at the frozen cursor. "What the hell is going on?"

I attempt to gain access a different way. This time with no delays or blocks.

Pulling up the schematic, I let the cursor hover over an area. "Hmm, I think we need a fire. Right. About. Here."

I turn on the alarm and cover my ears as the blaring sound wails through the building. This location will force everyone to evacuate down the opposite stairwell. Voices and footsteps thunder down the hallway. Once everything is quiet, I sneak down the hall and stop outside office 2405.

I jump online and access the door remotely.

Once again, I'm blocked. After my third attempt, the green light flashes and the buzzer sounds, letting me in. I slip in and close the office door.

The office doesn't appear to be used much. It's empty, except for a shiny mahogany desk, a computer, and a filing cabinet that sits off to one side.

I slink around the desk and park my laptop next to the large LED monitor. "Let's see what we can find."

First, I go into Bank of America and search the account numbers I wrote down in Ms. Matthews' office. Doesn't take long to spot the huge wire transfers coming in from random banks in China and Russia. I pull out my notebook and match the account numbers on the deposit slips from Ms. Matthews' drawer.

Obviously, SocialNet was paying her to do something.

I can only guess it wasn't legal, considering how much has happened.

I hack into the local directory and peruse the temp files for any connection. Then I find a link to the unidentified user ID in ReBoot's lab. Just as I suspected, Casper is the missing user.

Somehow he obviously hacked into ReBoot's system too.

I pop in my flash drive to download the extra art file, but the system crashes.

"Shoot. What is wrong with me?" I don't know why I expected SocialNet's system to be easily crackable. After all, I've been trying to hack it for months. But even here, it's almost impossible to enter. It's as if someone is keeping me out. Maybe a ghost.

Refusing to give up, I try again. Once I'm in, I quickly merge all the art files from every ID into one. I add in Casper's secret file and Simone's picture of a ghost hunter. The code is almost complete, but there's still one small gap.

Maybe I have the missing piece.

I pop out my flash drive and upload my real code. The code I didn't give Mr. Anthony.

For a second, nothing makes sense.

And then it does.

This algorithm creates a back door into tons of systems. I search the server and find data downloads from tons of companies including the DMV and the DOT. I also see documents from medical companies, credit card companies, pharmacies, and banks.

That's it!

Each art file is a different code made for a different system. Mr. Anthony used ReBoot kids to code these algorithms. One file for each critical system they wanted to invade. The code was created to open a back door and sneak in—just to compile confidential data packs. Then the code exported the information to a hidden server, and uploaded a virus to cause havoc.

Havoc the Orwellians are being blamed for in the media.

Havoc that someone at SocialNet is causing. All to distract from the mutating algorithm, and giving it time to morph so it can't be traced. Just like Taz said.

Simone must have figured out what was going on early. Only, she didn't get the files before she was released. That's why she hacked back into ReBoot. To copy all the algorithms for proof. She must have been busted by the Feds after she copied the data. So why didn't she just wait and hand over this proof when they came that night to arrest her. No doubt, it would have gotten her off any charges. And I know Mitnick would have listened.

So why kill herself just to avoid jail when she had everything she needed to be free.

Then my mind races through a different scenario.

Unless...she didn't overdose. Maybe Casper got to her first and killed her for the files.

I drop my head and try to breath evenly. Is it possible Simone was killed?

The real question is why?

I spot a file labeled: JOHN CALLAHAN. A profile of the first son. Everything you ever wanted to know about him is in it. Every purchase, every prescription, every driving ticket. All compiled in one easy-to read file.

I hunt around and find another profile saved. SIMONE JORDAN. This profile is just like John's and includes everything that was anything in Simone's life. Prescription records. Driving records. Texts. Photos. Simone's whole life was packaged up in one small file. And any of the data could be manipulated as they saw fit.

Some if it is a duplicate of the information SocialNet leaked to the media when they identified her as one of the hackers. They were angry and wanted to make her pay for trying to bring them down.

Then I spot my own name: ADA LOVELACE. When I skim the pages of information gathered on me, there's not one thing from my life that is not recorded. This file has everything about me and my life along with my parents' lives. It has my medical history, my credit card purchases, and even my driving record. It's not just a profile of me. It's a profile of my life.

When I flip to the last page. Words jump off the paper: ***Ada Lovelace is the Dark Angel***.

I sit back and run my fingers through my hair. Air escapes my lungs and I cover my mouth.

Whoever compiled this information, knows that I am the Dark Angel!

"Oh my God." I glance at the door while chewing my bottom lip.

Instead of sitting on this information, I have to get these files and my theory to Mitnick. And fast. In case I'm not around to tell them. It won't take these guys long to figure out that I know what they've done.

Right now, I still have some time to turn this around.

My hands tremble as my fingers glide across the keyboard. Except for the dim glow of the monitor, the room remains dark. I zip up the art files with all other files that prove what Social Net did. After creating a folder on a hidden server, I encrypt the files so the contents are secure and upload it. Once I'm done, I pull out Mitnick's card and create an email, giving him instructions on how to find the hidden files and how to decrypt the folder.

I hit </SEND> and watch the progress bar creep across the screen. I delete the files from the directory, including my piece of art. Now no one—not even SocialNet—has access to the full algorithms except for me.

A message pops up: </CONNECTION DENIED.>

Someone cut me off. Again!

Before I resend, muffled voices sound off in the hall. Two shadowy figures stop in front of the office window. They peek in, searching for something. Or someone.

My heart punches against my rib cage. My throat constricts and dries like I've eaten a spoon full of peanut butter. I'm barely able to swallow air.

But if I can stay calm, everything will work out.

I hide under the desk as the door handle jiggles. Then I remember I left my flash drive in the USB port. If they come in now, they'll know exactly what I was doing. Every piece of evidence I have will be in their hands. And I won't be able to prove anything. No one will ever believe a teenager hacker who has a record over a wealthy company with credibility and a plan.

That information is all I have to clear my name. And it looks like someone is killing people for it.

The reality hits me.

This is not one of Varian's online games or one of Taz's hacking challenges.

If I get caught here, I will be 'unplugged.'

Just like the rest of them.

</WHAT A WORMHOLE>

The security panel beeps.

Then the door cracks opens and feet shuffle across the floor. Slowly. Quietly.

I scoot farther under the desk. Pulling my legs to my chest, I bury my head between my knees and muffle my fast-paced breathing. This time, I'm sure to be discovered, and the information on my drive will be confiscated. All the work I've done for the last couple of weeks will be for nothing.

The world pauses.

I listen to the office's natural environmental noises, trying to distinguish one from the other. The ventilation hums. The hard drive churns. The blinds on the office window crinkle together every time the heat shuts off. But one sound is out of place.

The desk creaks as someone adds weight to the top.

I stare at the opening, waiting to be discovered.

Then a face drops over the top.

I yell and throw out my fist, making contact with flesh and teeth.

"Ow!" Fisher yells and cups his mouth. His head disappears.

"Jesus, Fisher!" I scramble out from under the desk as he walks around the room groaning. "You scared the *crap* out of me. Thought you were one of them." I take in a deep breath and notice blood on his teeth and lips. "Whoa, did I do that?"

"Don't look so happy. Plus, I'll deny it if anyone asks, especially Varian." He checks his fingers for blood. "I have a rep to protect."

"You shouldn't have come up here. You were supposed to take Becca and meet me outside."

"I wasn't going to let him leave you in here alone." Becca says from the middle of the room. Several lines of concern are etched across her forehead.

"Becca!" I circle around the desk and pounce on her, giving her a big hug. "Oh my gosh. Are you okay? Did they hurt you?" I check her out for any scrapes or scratches.

Fisher smiles. "Pretty sure she hurt them way more than they hurt her."

Before I can ask for details, Fisher stares at me. "What'd you find out? Anything?"

I keep my voice low. "You won't believe this. The kids were creating an algorithm that gathered information from major critical companies and systems and compiled it into massive profiles. They hid the code in the art. Only I never packaged mine, so they didn't have the right code. Mine was the final piece. Simone must have found out, and Casper has been involved in this whole thing."

It takes him a second to digest the information.

Fisher shoves his hands in his pocket. "Why are they creating profiles on teens?"

"I don't know exactly." I scoff and sit down at the computer again. "But there was one on John Callahan, Simone and me."

Fisher rakes his hands through his hair. "Holy . . . still doesn't say why though."

"That's obvious." Becca shrugs like she's solving two plus

two. "John Callahan is the first son. Ada's a senator's daughter. Simone's dad is on the board of Google. Don't you get it? They're gathering information on you so they can use it against them."

Fisher and I stare at her and then glance at each other. "This girl's brilliant!"

I decipher what she's saying. "So they are compiling teens' information—everything on the internet from their SocialNet profiles and other companies they use. Then creating profiles to use against people they don't like?"

"Or . . . people they need to stop. For whatever reason." Becca shakes her head, appearing exasperated.

The alarm goes off.

While the email is still sending, I decrypt my computer with a passphrase before shutting it off. This will protect Zed against anyone who may get their hands on him.

This time the loud noise short-circuits my fragile nerves. Sounds like more of an intruder alert than a fire alarm.

"Can we go?" Becca yells. She wants to leave this place so bad she's yanking on my jacket sleeve.

I shove Zed back into my bag. "Hopefully the files sent."

"Let's make sure we stay together." Fisher crouches by the door and surveys the hall before waving us to follow. Becca and I walk close behind him. We all inch our way down the corridor with the alarm shrieking above us.

The sound is so loud, my head pounds with each wail. I even can't think without plugging my ears to muffle the irritating noise.

Up ahead, the elevator dings, warning us of a visitor.

Fisher signals for us to go back the way we came. Our heavy strides beat along the thick-carpeted floor. At the end of the hall, we push through the EXIT door and slam into something.

I fall backward, taking Becca and Fisher down with me.

The albino from the alley stares us down. "Gotcha."

The three of us scramble to our feet and take off the opposite way. My limbs flail this way and that, trying to decide which way to go. Where to move, when to turn, how to move.

The albino charges after me. I try to escape, but he gets a tight grip on my arm. "Looks like we got a nasty bug crawling through our systems."

I sneer and yank away from him. "Let go of me . . . Casper."

He stares at me out of the corner of his eye, like a one of those petrified white rabbits in the pet store. The creepy ones with red eyes. The ones that always look suspicious of you holding them.

He snarls when he speaks. "Why would I be named Casper? Because I'm an albino? Kind of a cliché, don't you think?"

"Never know. Maybe you're not that creative." I try to jerk free, but he's stronger than he looks. His white boney hand clamps down on my arm as he drags me after him, kicking and flailing.

I squeeze away and run, but the big guy pops out and wraps one arm around me, holding me back. "Fisher! Help!"

A flash of pink catches my eye.

Before I can focus, Becca flies out of nowhere and lands in front of the guy holding me. She smiles sweetly and says, "Hello" in a childlike voice. Without waiting for his greeting, she spins around once in a perfect roundhouse kick, snagging the guy right under his chin.

The man's head whips to one side. But instead of going down, he lunges at her with his free arm extended, trying to grab her throat.

Becca counters his attack by blocking his fist with her forearm and then lands a reciprocal punch to his solar plexus.

The big guy gasps and drops to his knees as if praying for her mercy. This gives Becca the perfect chance to jam her fist in his face. The guy falls back slowly and hits the ground.

Fisher and I stand there gawking. Mouths open.

Becca beams and nudges the guy with her toe. "Sleep tight, jerko." Then she notices us watching. "What?"

I glance down at the bulky man, who has to be at least three times her height and twice as wide, then eye Fisher, "Did you know about this?"

He smiles, looking equally impressed. "Not until tonight. She knife-handed the dude downstairs with one blow to the throat. If I'm totally honest, I didn't rescue her; *she* rescued *me*."

"I wouldn't admit that to anyone else." I spin and face Becca. "Explain yourself, you imposter."

She wipes her hands together as if she's cleaning them after dragging out the trash. "You saw me practice. Don't know why you're so surprised."

"I saw you do a kick or two." I point down to her victim. "I didn't know you were *that* good."

She shrugs. "I give full credit to Jackie Chan in the *Rush Hour* movies."

"Remind me to thank him. I'm a new fan," I say. "And I will never doubt your martial arts skills again."

Just proves that we never really know a person. We can only combine the bits and pieces we find out with the other stuff we accidentally uncover.

Without wasting any more time or energy, the three of us swerve around the body and race back toward the elevators. When I glance over my shoulder, the albino is bending over the beefy guy who still hasn't recovered from Becca's knuckle sandwich.

In front of us, a fat man pops out of the stairwell.

"We're trapped!" I yell.

"Not for long." Becca does a flying front kick, taking out Goon #3.

"Kick-Ass Barbie has gone cray cray," I say.

Fisher doesn't even laugh. Instead, he jerks me toward the elevators. "Come on, this way."

Two cars open at once. Becca and I jump in one, while Fisher runs to the opposite one. He pounds all the buttons before jumping back out and joining us.

Thundering footsteps shake the whole floor.

I frantically hit the "Close Door" button repeatedly. "Come on! Come on!"

Just as the albino pops into view, the doors close. Soft elevator music fills the small space encouraging me to slow down my breath.

Becca slides to the ground for a quick break. She huffs. "Let's hope no one else is waiting to go down or we'll never get to the first floor."

"I've got it covered." Fisher moves in front of the panel and presses "Close Door" at the same time he punches "2" for the second floor.

"What are you doing?" Becca asks.

He concentrates, with his tongue sticking out the side of his mouth. It's kind of adorable. "When you press the buttons together, it throws the elevator into 'express' mode. Skips all the floors." He leans against the stainless steel walls as the car descends. "They'll expect us to go all the way down. I mean, who in their right mind would go to a floor with no outside access? That would be suicide." Fisher keeps his fingers on the buttons.

I'm pretty sure I look as confused as Becca. "Why don't I feel good about this?" she says.

"Trust me." Fisher smiles.

"You say that...a lot."

Despite the danger or odds against us, Fisher seems to be enjoying how this is all playing out. And I must say, I'm impressed with his social engineering skills. He obviously has a unique ability to get in and out of places by watching people and figuring out how everything works. Fisher can sneak around buildings the way I sneak into systems. Maybe we're more alike than I thought.

The elevator jerks to a stop on the second floor.

"Time to go." Fisher stands in the middle of the car.

When the doors open, it takes me a second to process the person's face staring back at us.

I say the name out loud or I might not believe it. "Mr. Anthony?"

</THE MAIN INTERFACE>

"Hello, Ada," Mr. Anthony says. "We really have to stop meeting like this."

Mr. Anthony jerks me out of the car as Fisher lunges. "I knew it!" he yells.

The beefy guy comes out of nowhere, sporting a swollen eye, courtesy of Becca. And without warning, he clocks Fisher square in the jaw with the butt of his gun. Fisher drops to his knees like a rag doll.

Becca charges out of the elevator after us, but this time, the beefy guy is prepared. He points the weapon at her head before she can kick him 'down under'.

She freezes with both hands up. "Okay. Okay. Take it easy."

"Why? You didn't," he sneers.

Mr. Anthony squeezes my wrist. "Looks like you've all been snooping around where you shouldn't be. Why am I not surprised?"

"We're lost." I writhe under his grip. "It's a big building."

"I meant in the network." He snatches my backpack from me. "We tracked everything you did."

How is that possible? How long has he known I've been in here?

Then I get it. "You used me. You lured me here so I'd bring my code with me. It was the only one you didn't have."

"I had it until you changed it at the last minute." He says. "Now I want that code."

"No can do," I say.

"We'll see about that." He holds up my bag just as the albino and third goon from upstairs bust through the stairwell doors. They both glance around with dumb looks on their faces until they see us. One of them has tissue crammed up his nose from Becca's beating.

"Well, thank God for security!" Mr. Anthony screams. Then he tilts his head toward Fisher and Becca. "Bring both of them too." Then he shoves me down the hall as the other guys drag Becca and Fisher behind us.

"How can you be a part of all this?" I watch him as he forces me to walk, still in shock at his involvement. And I even stuck up for him. "You were supposed to be helping us. Helping me."

"Ada, I tried to warn you, but you wouldn't take any hints." He refuses to look at me.

"What hints?" I ask.

"I saw you snooping around on day one. I tried to help you, redirect your attention, but you wouldn't let anything go."

I think back to my time at ReBoot. I certainly don't recall any warnings. "You tried to kill me, didn't you? On all those activities. The marble at LARP, the broken harness, the rope in the cave. You tried to make sure I didn't find out anything."

A lump bulges in my throat. I can't say any more. For fear of crying. I can't believe this man, my counselor, is the nasty person in front of me. I thought he believed in me. In my friends.

Yet it was all fake. A big fat lie.

Mr. Anthony doesn't flinch. "I don't know what you're talking about. I never tried to kill you. I'm not a monster."

"Could have fooled me." Fisher yells from behind.

When we reach the end of the hall, Mr. Anthony opens an office door and forces me into a chair. Behind me, the other men drag in Becca and Fisher, who are both flailing like two wild cats. One dumps Becca into a chair on my right while Fisher gets tossed into the one on my left. A large gash splits his forehead into two, and blood trickles down into his eye.

Mr. Anthony yells at the albino. "I told you not to hurt anyone. Now leave me alone with them." When the three men leave the room, he faces us. "I must say, I am very sorry to see you all here."

Fisher growls. "Yeah, I bet you are." He rocks forward on the chair, acting like he's going to lunge again.

"Calm down, Fisher. Don't do anything stupid. Someone could get hurt," Mr. Anthony says as his phones rings. He picks it up and speaks softly, "Yes sir, I have them. See you soon."

"How could you do this?" Becca asks with tears in her eyes. "We trusted you."

Mr. Anthony kicks my bag under the table and paces the room. "I never wanted anyone to get hurt. I had no choice but to recruit hackers to help us out. We needed money for ReBoot. It wasn't supposed to go this far. Whether you think so or not, Ms. Matthews and I believe in ReBoot and its rehabilitation. But it's not cheap to run."

"SocialNet is paying you?" I think about the deposit slips and the money, assuming SocialNet bailed ReBoot out of some kind of financial problem. "And now, Ms. Matthews is dead. Because of you."

He looks down. "That wasn't supposed to happen. I tried to warn her. But it's out of my hands now. Just do as we say and this will all be over. I will do everything I can to make sure you all go home safely."

I scoff. "I bet you said that to Simone and Crash too. Didn't you?"

Mr. Anthony opens his mouth to talk, but he doesn't get a chance to say any more because the door opens.

Gary Host, the CEO of SocialNet, walks in.

I sigh in relief. At least someone is here to help.

Becca smiles wide. "Thank God. Mr. Host. You have to help us. This man is crazy."

Gary studies the three of us and frowns. "Tony, what the hell is going on here? Why are these kids being held against their will?"

"We caught them breaking into the building." Mr. Anthony appears more nervous than usual. I've seen the look before. It's what happens when you're busted and you need a way to save yourself. "Sir, may I speak with you outside?"

"Are you kids okay?" Gary smiles. The three of us nod in unison. "Then please excuse me. I'll be right back to make sure we work out this misunderstanding." Then he follows Mr. Anthony out into the hall.

As soon as the door shuts. Fisher's on his feet. I'm surprised the bruises and blood don't keep him down. "I told you Mr. Anthony was dirtier than a pig in mud."

Becca shakes her head and stares at her folded hands. "I still can't believe it."

Exactly what I was thinking. "Fisher was right the whole time. Mr. Anthony was using us to create some code. He even admitted it. All for money."

"Can you say that again?" Then he winces and holds his head. "Man this hurts. How does it look?"

"Like the other guy won." I lean over and inspect the wound, feeling slightly queasy. "You okay?"

Fisher looks at me with weepy eyes. "Actually. I could use a Band-Aid. One with those funny little characters on it."

"Stop it." I give him a look. "It's not a boo-boo. It's deep. You need stitches."

"I want to leave now," he says weakly, his face pale. He sits back down. "I'm not having fun anymore."

"We gotta get out of here. Any ideas?"

"Gary will help us." Becca says. "There's no way he'll let Mr. Anthony get away with this. He's an advocate for teens."

"Let's hope so." Because I am not so sure.

Becca scowls and hits her knee. "But if you wanna get me closer to Mr. Anthony, I will deliver a left hook to his chinny-chin-chin."

I'm amused by Becca's wholehearted belief in the young CEO . . . and her spunk. Can't believe I doubted this girl. "Um . . . who are you and what did you do with my chocolate-loving spirit leader?"

Becca does a head roll, speaking with total attitude. "Oh trust me, you'll be *cheering* when I take this guy down. Jerk."

"So?" Fisher looks pale. "What's the plan?"

"I assume that means you have no plan," I say.

He rubs his face with both hands and pinches his lips together. "Of course I do. I have two in fact. Plan A is to sic Becca on him and then run for our lives."

Becca and I exchange looks before I dare ask, "And Plan B?"

He closes his eyes and leans his head back, his face pinches in pain. "Plan B: Don't mess up Plan A."

"I knew you were going to say that," I mumble.

"I vote for Plan A." Becca shrugs and holds up a piece of chocolate and reads the quote, *"Sometimes doing nothing is all you need.* Well, that's crappy advice, isn't it?"

You know it's bad when chocolate can't even offer a smidgen of hope.

Before we can discuss any more bad plans, Gary walks back in the room. Mr. Anthony won't look me in the eye. Instead of coming in, he positions himself by the door while the other goons come in and stand behind us.

We're surrounded.

The young CEO struts over to a table against the wall. He pours hot water into a cup and drops in an herbal tea bag. He sits down and sifts flakes from the steaming water. "I hear you have something that belongs to us, Miss Lovelace."

Becca narrows her eyes. "Wait. You're in on this too?"

"How do you know my name?" I cross my arms, trying to hide my hands. They're shaking wildly, and I don't want to give this guy the satisfaction of knowing he's freaking me out.

He seems amused. "I know your father, so I've heard all about you. He's proud of you and I can see why; you're very smart. Maybe too smart."

"Great. Can I call him?" I stand, though my legs want to fold under my body. "We could use a ride home."

"I'm afraid that's not possible." Gary crosses his legs at the knee like a polite woman and sits back, unzipping his gray hoodie. His voice remains calm and steady. No waver of anger or fear. "This is not the best decision you've made. Coming here. You never seemed like the proactive type."

I practically growl. "You don't *know* me."

"Really? You'd be surprised." Gary slurps his tea as he holds his pinky out like a true lady. He carefully places the fragile teacup down as if it's about to shatter. "I know more than you think . . . or hoped. You're an average student, expert hacker. Devastated by her friend's death. And I'm sure Daddy Lovelace won't be happy to find out about this little breaking-and-entering escapade. Did you know you three are wanted as suspects in a murder case? Just gets worse and worse, doesn't it?"

"What?" I sink into my seat. Becca's exterior appears to be cracking, the trembling lip gives her away. Fisher, on the other hand, eyes the man like he wants to kick his ass. I shake my head. "No, you're lying. No one would believe we killed anyone."

Gary nods. "Well, you did flee a murder scene. Usually the guilty people flee after they steal a van." He dumps more sugar into his tea and keeps stirring, the spoon clinking against the cup.

I lick my parched lips, wishing for a glass of water. But this guy's waiting for me to crack. Show the slightest sign of weakness. I maintain my composure and flash the secret weapon. A politician's smile. "I happen to know they will think Mr. Anthony did it. He had motive. He hated Ms. Matthews."

Mr. Anthony doesn't react to my accusation. He keeps his head down and stays silent in the back.

Gary studies me. He zips his hoodie up and down. Over and over.

Then I shrug. "Unless you did it. You're the one we saw running away from ReBoot. The hoodie gave you away. Guess I'll have to tell the authorities all about that."

"Dead people don't talk," He says.

"You'll never get away with this." Fisher jumps up and slams his hands on the table. "There are witnesses."

"Maybe. But not for long." Gary doesn't flinch.

The albino kicks Fisher in the back of the legs for the outburst. Fisher crumples to the ground and yelps in pain.

I swallow a scream at the hard blow, but it takes every ounce of will power I have to remain seated and calm. If these people smell my fear, they'll attack even harder.

Gary takes another sip. "I believe you have important information I need."

I shake my head emphatically. "So does Wikipedia."

I sense Fisher and Becca staring at me like they think I'm crazy to confront this guy. And maybe I am. But there's nothing else to do in this moment except be strong, and do what I need to do to shut this guy down. I'm tired of hiding.

Gary leans in and smiles. His teeth are very white and very straight. All made from the same perfect veneer mold. "Trust me when I say that now is not the time for jokes. Tony tells me you have downloaded those codes and I want them back."

"I don't have anything." I put my hands up when he doesn't seem convinced. "You can frisk me if you like."

Gary nods to Mr. Anthony who approaches me, humming a Barry Manilow song.

Fisher pops to his feet and blocks them from getting too close. "Don't you dare touch her."

Gary laughs at this. Instead of showing anger or surprise, he breathes evenly and speaks slowly as if he has all the time in the world on his side. "Why don't you check her then? But let me warn you, if we find out you *accidentally* missed something, *she* will pay your price."

"Fine." Fisher stands in front of me. He runs his hands over my shirt like airport security checking for hidden items. The way he touches my waist sends a few chills down my spine.

I glance at the ceiling to avoid eye contact as he reaches into my jeans pocket and slides out a couple drives. He mouths, *sorry*, and then lays them on the table. Then he trails his hands down my legs, patting my jeans and ankles until he reaches my boots. However, he knows about the drive hidden in my necklace.

He fake-checks my boots and then comes up again. "That's it."

Mr. Anthony grabs the confiscated drives, filled with nothing but crap, and tosses them to the albino. "Go check these and see if it's what we need."

The three goons leave to sift through the drives.

"If you're looking for my file. It's not on there."

Gary's face turns hard, his eyebrows furrow. "You have no idea what's going on here, do you?"

I raise my eyebrows. "It's not hard to figure out. You paid Mr. Anthony to find good hackers in ReBoot who were naive enough to program separate pieces of an algorithm. Smart though. That way one didn't know what the other was doing. We only had a piece of the whole puzzle. You're using the algorithm to download personal information from major sites and creating profiles."

"Then you know too much."

"Bad news for you. Good news for the Feds." I accidentally glance down at my backpack.

Gary picks up on the mistake. "For God's sake. Did you go through the backpack?"

Mr. Anthony yanks the bag out from under my chair and rifles through my belongings, violating Zed's privacy. He slides my laptop out along with Simone's flash drive, some pens, and a few straggler M&Ms. "You better take a look at this."

</DECRYPT OR DIE>

Mr. Anthony places the hardware in front of Gary.

He eyes me. "She's encrypted her hard drive with a passphrase."

Gary shrugs. "Then just hack in. Find out what's on it."

"It would take a supercomputer to do that," Mr. Anthony says. "And knowing that it's Ada, add in about twenty million years."

Gary faces the laptop in front of me and leans in close. The smell of herbal tea rides his breath. "Unlock it. Now."

"I forgot the key."

"Maybe this will jog your memory." Gary draws a gun from his jacket and points it at Becca's temple. "How about now?"

Mr. Anthony steps forward. "Sir, I don't think we need to go to this extreme."

"Shut up, Tony! I'll handle this," Gary yells.

I sit there. Frozen. I want to jump this guy and scratch his eyes out. Hurt him the way he's hurt people I care about.

"Ada, you don't want to lose another friend, do you?" Gary sneers. "It's not like you have a large pool to pull from. It's already shallow enough."

The CEO's sharp words throw me off balance. I mutter, "Only because you killed them all."

Becca squeezes her eyes shut as if preparing for the final shot that will end her life. Her body shakes uncontrollably. She whispers with tears streaming down her cheeks, "Ada, please. I don't want to die."

"What are you doing?" Fisher hisses. "This isn't a game, Ada. Do it."

This time I may have to put my agenda aside and save her life. I can't lose another friend. I won't.

"Okay, give me five minutes," I say. My whole body trembles.

"You have three," Gary replies stiffly. "I want that code you developed. And I know it's on there."

I type in my passwords. At first, my fingers touch the wrong keys, giving me an error message. Then I input every password I've ever used and get error after error. I wasn't kidding before, in my haste, I forgot to log the passphrase in my book. Now I can't remember it, and my friend's life depends on it.

Gary says robotically. "You have two minutes."

I work hard to focus, but Fisher whispers in my ear, "Come on, Ada. What's the passphrase?"

"I told you, I can't remember!" I type in a sequence and repeat it in my head before entering it again. I could have sworn this was it. But that's the problem with passphrases and encryption keys, if you forget them, even you can't get in. And your data is inaccessible. Gone. Forever.

"One minute." Gary cocks the gun.

Mr. Anthony moves closer. "Come on, Ada. He's not kidding. This isn't a game."

"Everybody be quiet!" I scream. Then I carefully type in the entire sequence of words again. I punch every key extra hard as if that will make the commands sink in faster.

Gary counts down the last few seconds out loud.

Then Mr. Anthony calls out, "Ada, time's up."

"Done! I'm done!" I punch ENTER and flip the laptop around to face them.

Gary releases Becca and she collapses to the floor. "Tony. Check the computer."

Becca crawls over to Fisher and me. The three of us hug tighter than ever. An unbreakable bond.

"It looks like she tried to send an email to Paul Mitnick," Mr. Anthony says. "The email is encrypted, but it never sent. The connection was broken in time."

I slump down. This means Mitnick won't get any information. He probably doesn't even know we're here. The only good thing—that these guys don't know—is that I still have a hidden directory out there with the files encrypted. But since no one can see it or access the information, it won't help us one bit.

"Good." Gary smiles and tucks his gun away. "Now, Ada. You do one more thing and I'll let you guys go. Pull up all the files and run the algorithm again. With your piece in it. It'll capture more than corporation data. Now, it'll capture government systems too, arrest records and personal information, including your friends in the FBI."

That's what Mr. Anthony had me doing with Raven. The SAS system wasn't fake. It *was* JARS. That's why Simone's record was in there. They used me to find a backdoor into the national arrest database so they can get dirt on anyone they like. Anger surges in me. Mr. Anthony used me.

This time I make my own demands. "Let my friends go and I'll do exactly what you say."

He stares at me, as if contemplating my offer. "Tony, take them down the hall."

Mr. Anthony helps Fisher and Becca to their feet.

Fisher holds Becca and shakes off his helping hands. "Don't touch us."

As they walk to the door, Mr. Anthony turns around,

looking sincere and worried all at once. "Ada, do what he says. I'm sorry I got you into this. I had no idea it would go this far."

"Go, Tony. Before I kill you myself," Gary grunts. He waits until they are all gone before he walks behind me. All my senses are at full attention. "Run the program. Now."

"And if I don't?" I don't even know why I'm fighting anymore. Varian was right. This was a battle we couldn't win from the very beginning. Only I had to try.

"If you don't do it, I will tell everyone you are the Dark Angel."

I work hard not to show any emotion. As if his accusation doesn't throw me off balance.

He sits on the table. "I have proof you did the White House hack too. In fact, I watched you do it."

Instead of crying or screaming or bluffing, I burst out laughing. At first Gary appears shocked, then he frowns. "What's so funny?"

"*You're* Casper?" Everything starts to fall into place. "G. Host. Ghost? You're Casper." I crack up again. "That's the dumbest name I've ever heard."

"You can laugh all the way to prison. If I leak any of this White House information to the press, you are through. And your dad's career and his stupid bill are done too."

"Wait, this is all about his bill?" I ask. "That's why you have a profile on me. You think if you set me up, he'll give up on it?"

"His stupid teen bill is like a virus. It's eating away at my plans. Bit by Bit. If it was between protecting you or saving the bill, we both know which one he would pick. And with him out of the way, nothing will stop me from gathering data and using it how I see fit." Gary points to Zed. "The only way to save yourself and your father's career...is if you give me that damn code."

"Fine." I don't care so much about me anymore. Or the

Dark Angel. But I don't want my dad's career ruined, all because of me. But I can't let Gary win either.

Then I spot the flash drive sitting on the table. The one I took from Simone's warehouse, also labeled *Ghost Hunters*. Just like her art algorithm.

Then it hits me. I can't believe I missed it. I know exactly what Simone's drive is for. And I know exactly what to do with it. My idea is risky, but it's my only way out of this mess.

And if I'm right, I can take down SocialNet before Gary even knows what hit him.

I point to the drive. "Can you hand me the files?"

Gary picks up the drive and spins it in his hand. "So it was in front of us all along?"

I shrug casually but my whole body is tense. If Gary walks out with that drive, my plan is over.

He hands it to me. "No tricks. I want the codes."

First, I pull up his network and attempt to access his main servers, but they are all password protected.

"I need the passwords to your servers if you want to store the algorithms when they run automatically in a nightly batch." He pauses so I reassure him. "You can change them when I'm done to make sure they're safe."

Gary gives me the pass codes.

Minutes later, I am in SocialNet's system and have access to all the servers his company uses.

However, that's not his only mistake. He also chooses to sit across from me while I work, which means he isn't watching what I'm doing. And he should know better than to ever let a hacker have control of his systems when he's not breathing down their neck, proving he was never as good as the Red Devil or the Dark Angel.

I execute the algorithm and display a fake error message. I show him my screen. "I told Mr. Anthony I hadn't finished yet. Do you want me to edit the code? It's a quick fix."

"Do it. Fast."

I tweak the fake mistake in my already-working code. While the code compiles, I secretly open the file on Simone's drive. When I see what's inside, I force myself not to smile.

I was right. *Ghost Hunters* is not a compilation of her favorite show.

It's a customized computer virus.

And Simone made it just for Casper. She just never got the chance to use it.

I swallow hard at the thought of Simone trying to take these guys down—all on her own. She probably went through the same process I did and discovered everything I know. Only she tried to handle it by herself. If she would have reached out for help, maybe she'd still be alive today.

I wouldn't be here either if it weren't for Becca, Fisher, and Varian.

They are the reason I am still alive.

After disguising the deadly file, I upload it and display it as the executable algorithm. I turn my laptop to face Gary sitting on the other side. "It's fixed. Do you want the honors?"

Gary calls Tony back in the room to watch. He lets his cursor hover over the file as Mr. Anthony stands behind him and waits. "Your piece of this code was the hardest part. Now we have access to the FBI and entire arrest databases. We'll know who was arrested for what and we can use that information how we see fit. Blackmail is sweet. Ada Lovelace, you're much smarter than I give you credit for."

I smile. "Thanks." He has no idea how right he really is.

Gary clicks the file and laughs as data starts to run.

Mr. Anthony is the one who notices something is wrong first. "Gary, stop it. The program is corrupting all our data."

I sit still with no expression. Only my hands are sweating. This will not go well for me.

Gary's smile drops and he starts pounding the keys, trying to reverse the damage that's happening before his eyes.

"The virus is attacking all your data servers!" Mr. Anthony says. "All your users' profiles will be gone."

"What did you do?" Gary's teeth show as he talks, like he's snarling. He comes over and pokes the gun against my head. "Fix it."

I squeeze my eyes shut and lower my head. "Sorry, Gary. The virus is eating every single user profile you have. In about five minutes, you won't have anything left. Including a company."

Gary cocks the gun and screams.

I wince, waiting for the gunshot.

Mr. Anthony steps forward. "Sir, wait! You don't want to do this. Not here at SocialNet. Let me take care of her so you can keep your hands clean of this."

Gary focuses back on the screen and helplessly watches each file melt into the cybersphere, killing everything he has built, including the algorithm that promised him power and control over anyone he chose. "Take her! Now! I don't want to see her alive again. You hear me! Go!"

Mr. Anthony yanks me out of my chair and shoves me toward the door. "You will pay for this."

As soon as we leave the room and clear the corner, he pushes me away from him. "Go, Ada. Run before he kills you."

Instead, I stand still. Shocked. Confused. Scared. "Why are you doing this?"

"Because I never signed up to kill anyone." Mr. Anthony grabs his hair and pulls. "And I will never forgive myself if you die too."

I swear I see regret all over his face. "But what about Gary?"

"It's about time I stand up to him. I'll handle it." He points down the hall to a door and throws me the keys. "Becca and Fisher are waiting in there. "Go!"

I grab the keys and sprint to the locked door. Fiddling with the lock, I finally let Becca and Fisher out of the room.

A gunshot rings out behind me.

Startled, I turn around. Mr. Anthony has a surprised look on his face and mouths one word, *run*, before he slumps to the ground. A pool of blood fans out around him.

Fisher shields me with his body as Becca screams behind us.

I push past Fisher and race to Mr. Anthony's side. "Oh God." Mr. Anthony was part of all this and probably a big reason why Simone isn't here. But the man died in the end because he tried to save me.

He looks at me with regret and whispers, "I'm sorry." Then his head rolls to one side.

A tear trails down my chin and drops onto his face.

"Clearly Tony and I were not on the same page." Gary stands above me, holding a gun as his goons come running around the corner. His eyes are frozen on me in an icy stare. "Now get up."

The albino grabs Fisher and the big guy pins Becca in an arm hold that even she can't escape.

Gary forces me to my feet. "I'm taking Ada to the roof. This is getting too messy. Give me a few minutes and then bring her friends up to watch."

As he escorts me out the door, I reach for Becca and Fisher. The thought of being separated from them after all we've been through together is unimaginable. Scares me more than this maniac.

Fisher calls out to me as Becca sobs.

"I think we need a little fresh air." Gary forces me into the elevator and waits for it to shut. Cutting me off from my friends.

</INFORMATION DUMP>

My fear of heights just doubled.

We shoot up to the top floor so fast my stomach drops into my shoes.

As soon as the elevator stops, Gary pushes me up a small set of stairs and through the roof exit. When the door opens, icy cold air blasts my face. The wind almost knocks me off my feet. It's much stronger up here than on the ground. The sky is pitch dark, except for the glow of the Seattle skyline in the distance.

Gary drags me onto the roof. We move closer and closer to the edge. His vice grip is like a steel clamp. Hard and unbendable.

I claw at his jacket and dig my heels into the gravel. "What are you doing?"

He pulls harder. "You're going to die because of what you did tonight. And because I don't like you . . . or your father."

"And how will you cover this one up?" I ask, still fighting him.

"Your death is tragic really. You've been so distraught over your friend's death that you can't handle life anymore. You hated ReBoot and blamed Ms. Matthews for Simone's death.

When she busted you in the lab, she threatened to kick you out, which of course would send you to juvie. So you set the place on fire, killed her and fled with your co-conspirators."

My head pounds as he talks, every word hammers into my brain, smashing the truth. "What are you talking about?"

He rambles on like a crazy person. "You and your friends came here on behalf of the Orwellians to sabotage SocialNet for finding out your real identity as the Dark Angel, the one responsible for hacking the White House and the FBI."

I shake my head. "This is insane. You're insane."

"Insanely smart. I've even created an online trail that will prove your instability. By the time the police investigate, they will find notes from your therapist, confirming your mental instability. Unfortunately, it was too much . . . so you committed suicide by taking pills and throwing yourself off a building." He pulls a bottle out of his pocket and holds it up. "Look, your name is even on the prescription. And no one in your family knows how long you've been taking them, until now. The death of your friend was too much. Unfortunately, you took too many. I guess you'd rather die than go to prison and humiliate your family. Just like Simone."

My world tilts like I've been thrown in a spin cycle and tossed about. For a second, I don't know which way is up or down. Like I'm already falling.

"You hacked into my medical records and faked a prescription?"

"I didn't hack. Simone's algorithm let me in." He smiles wide. "Kind of ironic, right?"

"You killed her that night. How could you do that? She was only sixteen!" I thrash against him, trying to break free.

Gary's eyes glaze over. "At first, Simone was on board. But once she found out about the code, she double-crossed me. Unfortunately, she hacked back into ReBoot after she left and copied important files. Only, she didn't know we tracked her. That night I went to get the files she stole. I knew her dad was out of town because his airline ticket was on his credit card record."

I bit my lip to hold back a cry. I can't crack or this guy wins. That's why she didn't call. She knew it was only a matter of time before these guys would hunt her down. That's why she left me the encrypted messages and the virus on her flash drive. As backup.

And she knew I'd find it.

Simone believed in me and the closeness of our friendship that much. To protect me.

I speak slowly as each piece pops into place. "Simone didn't commit suicide. You changed her prescription so she would OD. Then the cops would label it an accident."

"If it makes you feel any better, I didn't *plan* on killing her until she refused to give the files to me. She was good. She was one of my favorites. She chose to die."

"No, she chose to fight you." This time, I can't stop myself from sobbing. Imagining Simone lying there, dying. "So none of those poor kids died accidently. You hacked into the systems to make it seem that way."

"Yes, well, Chelsea had tons of speeding tickets. That one was easy. For William it was just a matter withholding his insulin. For Johnny – a gangster will kill anybody for money. And Crash, well he didn't even fight back."

These kids were all killed. And no one knew.

"And Raven? What about her?" I keep talking. Stalling. "Why kill them at all?"

"Those kids knew too much. I couldn't risk some of them squealing." He eyes me. "But I actually wanted to keep you and Simone on my team. You both could have worked with me. You're that good."

The thought of them inspires me to fight back.

I scream and kick Gary in the shins, catching him off guard. All with a newfound vengeance.

But he wraps his arms around me, trapping me in a bear hug.

I grit my teeth. "So people died so you could data mine stupid information? What's the point?"

"Adults will do anything for their kids. If I can control what happens to their kids, I can control anyone and get anything I want." Gary's face distorts like he thinks I'm the crazy one. "In the technology age, information is power. But we only have that power if people give us the information freely. Teens share more than anyone. They put themselves at risk by posting everything online. Take all their personal data combined with all the records that companies keep, and I can know anything about anyone. What excites them. What hurts them. And I can add whatever information I need to their profiles. This wasn't really about teens; it was about using their information to get what I want." He drags me to the edge of the roof.

I wiggle in his tight grasp, trying to escape. "You won't get away with this."

His breath is hot on my neck. "I will because no one will be able to prove anything. Everything is untraceable."

"Not anymore." I force my knee up into his groin. When he doubles over I run back to the roof door, but it's locked. I pound on the door, yelling for help.

Gary walks up behind me. When I spin around to fight, he slaps me hard across the face.

I fall on the ground and try to kick him while I'm down. He grabs my hair and slams my head into the cement. Loose pebbles dig into my cheek, and my sore knee jams onto a big rock. My vision ripples.

Once I go limp, he yanks me back toward the edge and holds me there.

"What are you waiting for?" I ask, trying to keep my toes on the ledge.

"Your audience."

The roof door slams open as the two goons push Fisher and Becca out onto the roof.

"Ada!" Fisher yells. "Let her go."

"You sure that's what you want to say?" Gary asks.

Fisher spins around, catching the big guy off guard by punching him square in the face. As soon as he breaks free, Fisher races across the roof and lunges at Gary, tackling him to the ground.

The big man recovers quickly and slams a gun on Fisher's skull.

Fisher drops to the ground and doesn't move.

"Fisher!" But he's out cold.

This ignites Becca's rage. She stomps down hard on top of the albino's foot. Then she spins around and swipes his legs out from under him. When the albino crumbles to the ground, Becca faces the big dude hovering over Fisher's body in a classic karate stance, legs apart and fists up. She's already kicked this guy's ass once.

"You wanna go again?" she says.

Gary scrambles to his feet and brushes off his pants. He storms toward me and grabs my throat, ripping off my necklace. The angel emblem drops to the ground and the flash drive pops out.

We both see it at the same time and scramble for it.

Unfortunately, Gary gets there first and stomps on it with his shiny shoe.

"No!" I crumple to the ground. In one small step, my whole life is crushed. Everything I have or have ever used was on that little drive. Everything I am is gone.

Angry and inspired to fight, I charge him and jam the heel of my hand into his nose. It bursts like an overripe tomato.

Gary stumbles backward as blood trickles down his face. As soon as he notices the damage, he screams and lunges. Before I can move, he grips my throat again, this time with both hands, and squeezes. Hard. A slight growl escapes his throat as I sink to the ground.

My vision dims. I claw at his face and fight for air as Gary clenches tighter and tighter, almost crushing my windpipe. A few random images of my life fire off along with a few stray thoughts. If this guy kills me, no one at school will miss me. My counselor will think I gave up. And my parents will wonder why I jumped. They will never know how much I've changed or how much I love them.

I'm going to die. Only one thought makes me relax. *Maybe I'll see Simone again.*

Off to one side, the roof door slams open and a dark angel glides toward me.

Pressing my back hard on the ground, Gary bends over me. He grits his teeth and mumbles to himself, "No snotty teenage girl is going to take me down."

"How about a hero?" a voice says.

</COMMAND SUCCESSFUL>

VARIAN STANDS ON THE ROOF, HIS BLACK TRENCH COAT FLAPPING behind him in the wind.

His arm is extended and something black is in his hand. "Let. Her. Go."

I can't tell what he's holding, but I can imagine. I try to stop him but my voice isn't working.

"Dude, this is not a simulation." Varian yells with his arm out front. "This shit is for real."

Gary doesn't obey. Instead, his grip remains clamped down on my neck like an alligator's jaws.

A loud noise sounds off and a bolt of lightning zips across the midnight sky.

Gary spasms next to me, jerking around so hard he releases my throat.

I roll to my side, gasping for air and coughing uncontrollably. Life slowly returns to my body. Within a few seconds, I can feel my body again.

Gary groans but makes a quick recovery. He picks up his gun and points it at Varian. "Say goodbye." Then he shoots Varian at point blank range.

Varian slumps to the ground with his coat fanning out around him, the wings of a fallen angel.

I shove out a hoarse scream. "No!"

Gary kicks Varian in the ribs when he's down. "Not so tough now, are you?"

Anger swells through me. I'm in pain, but I force myself to my feet and kick the gun out of his hand. I scramble for the weapon. Just as my fingers graze the barrel, Gary stomps on my back, sending a fiery pain through my nerves. He grips my jacket and drags me toward the edge of the building. He pinches my mouth open and tries to force me into swallowing pills.

I knock the bottle from his hand.

"Have it your way." Gary pushes my feet over the side, but I grab on to the railing with both hands.

A primal scream escapes my lungs as I hang twenty-four stories above solid ground. Tears stream down my face. "Help!"

"Ada!" Becca crawls toward me and grabs my hand. We make eye contact. Determination fills her brown eyes. "I won't let go. I promise."

In this split second, it becomes clear how much I really need people in my life. My family. My friends. I can't believe how much time I've wasted by hiding from the real world. By spending time online in a false world with strangers who are never what they seem.

My arm throbs in its socket as my legs dangle under me.

Gary takes his attention off me and kicks Becca in the ribs. Over and over. With each kick, she yelps out in pain. But she never lets go of my hand. With one last kick, Becca slides toward the edge.

I drop an inch. "Let me go. Or you'll fall too."

She grits her teeth and squeezes my hand. "You go, I go."

I have to do something to help or we'll both fall off this

building. I don't want to be the cause of Becca's death. I don't want my parents to lose their only daughter. And I don't want to die.

Straining, I muster up all my strength to reach up with my free hand and grasp Gary's ankle.

He tries to shake me off his leg.

But I yank on his pant leg, forcing him off balance.

Gary teeters on the edge. He flails and flaps his arms for a couple seconds until he plummets over the side.

At the last minute, I think about saving him. Instead, I watch him fall and look away right before his body smacks into the ground. Tears fill my eyes. A man died. Because of me. And whether he deserved it or not, I took a life. I killed a living, breathing human.

Becca yells to get my attention. "Ada! Pull up, I can't hold on much longer."

I use every muscle I have to grip the railing with my free hand.

She presses her feet against the railing and yanks hard. "Push up!"

I dig my toes into the side of the brick building and launch my body over the edge, onto the roof.

To safety.

Becca and I clutch each other tight. We hug without saying a word. Both of our faces are buried into the other's shoulder as we cry together. I'm relieved she's okay. This girl who I doubted—the one who I thought I couldn't trust, the cheerleader who wears letters on her caboose—just kicked butt and saved mine.

"Thanks for not giving up on me." I mumble.

She grins. "Never. That's what friends are for."

Simone sounds off in my head. *Real friends never give up on someone they can't imagine living without.*

"Ada." Fisher calls out softly, but something in his voice

isn't calm. When I glance over, he's sitting next to Varian. Blood trickles down Fisher's face from a deep gash at his temple. He makes eye contact with me and shakes his head.

Varian is not going to make it.

I crawl across the roof and settle next to Varian. His face is pale, and his T-shirt is soaked in blood. Putting on a brave face, I grab his hand and squeeze. "Hey, you can't sleep here," I tease.

Varian cracks his eye lids. "You okay?"

"Yeah. Thanks to you." I kind of laugh and cry at the same time. "But right now we need to get you to a hospital." I clutch his hand, red with blood. I try to fight back tears but they fill my eyes anyway.

"Oh no," He frowns. "Don't you dare cry, Lovelace. It's a sign of weakness."

"It's a sign I care." I touch my forehead to his. "You came back."

"Don't get all soft on me." Varian stiffens at first, but then his bloody hand touches my face. "I'm sorry I bailed."

"I knew you'd come back." I manage a smile. "You're nothing but a big teddy bear."

He grins. "A teddy bear who saved the day."

"Your days in the Alliance definitely paid off." Then I notice the rectangular object resting at his side. I pick it up and laugh out loud. "Wait a minute. You *tased* the guy?"

Varian closes his eyes. "You didn't think I'd put a plug in him, did you? I'm not going to jail for some scumbag in a suit."

"Seriously? You, King Varian of the undefeated WoW Alliance," I say. "The tough guy who wields swords around and plays LARP as if it's on a real battlefield...and you *tased* him?"

"What can I say, I'm against gun violence." He smiles weakly.

Fisher pats Varian's shoulder. "Andrew, I promise you will never live this down."

My throat tightens because I'm not sure Varian will live at all. His breath becomes labored with each second that goes by. I can't help but focus on how much he did. How he put his life on the line. For me. How many people have done that today?

I whisper in his ear. "You're a hero. Just like your dad."

"I know." Then one tear rolls out of his left eye and slides toward his hairline. Then his eyes close and his breathing becomes jagged.

The roof doors burst open. "FBI!" someone yells. A team of men in dark jackets crashes onto the scene, wielding guns.

Mitnick steps forward out of the pack. "Where's Host?"

I point to the ledge.

A team of his people race over and scour the ground below, searching for Host's body.

Mitnick rushes over and drops next to Varian. He checks his pulse.

I grip Becca and Fisher's hand, awaiting the verdict.

It seems to take forever before Mitnick says, "He's alive. But barely."

"Thank God," I say. The three of us hug in relief.

Mitnick waves to a few of his guys checking out the rooftop and yells, "Hey! Get this guy to a hospital!"

The three of us back up as one man radios for a helicopter. A woman runs over with a First Aid kit and packs Varian's wound. A few guys pick up Varian and buckle him onto a stretcher.

Mitnick cups Fisher's face and studies the deep gash on his head. "You okay?" When Fisher nods, Mitnick pulls his brother him close and I hear him say, "Damn, I thought I lost you, Fish."

"You're not that lucky," Fisher mutters.

Minutes later, a helicopter appears overhead. The blades spin in rhythm to my heart, first fast and then slowing to a steady beat.

Mitnick pats Fisher's back. "Why don't you ride with Varian and get checked out too?" Mitnick motions to the helicopter landing on the roof.

"Okay." Fisher kisses my forehead. "I'll see you later?"

I nod and watch him follow Varian's stretcher onto the helicopter.

Once it takes off, Mitnick walks to the edge of the building and peers over the side. "Awful way to go. Falling to your death."

"I didn't mean to kill him." My voice shakes as I relive the moment. "He was trying to push me off the roof. I grabbed his leg and he fell."

Becca jumps to my defense. "Ada actually tried to save him. More than I would've done." Then we both alternate explaining the sequence of events.

Mitnick puts up his hands to calm us down. "Girls, listen, it's not your fault. Don't worry. I'll take care of everything. I'm just glad you're all okay. Becca, I want you to go downstairs and give your statement. Then we'll get an EMT to check you out."

Becca lets a lady FBI agent drape a blanket over her shoulders. She places a little chocolate in my hand before letting the agent lead her away.

As Mitnick calls out directions to his men securing the scene, I open the morsel. *There's nothing better than a friend, unless it's a friend with chocolate.*

I swear this girl makes up these sayings herself. They're just too perfect.

Mitnick tosses a blanket over my shoulders too. "I'm sorry I didn't get here in time," he says. "Varian called. I told him to wait for me, but he was so worried about you. It wasn't smart for any of you to come here in the first place. You should have called me."

I nod. "We weren't thinking straight."

Mitnick leads me to the elevator and we ride down to the lobby. "Don't suppose you have any evidence I can use? Something more than a couple dead guys?"

I pull the crushed flash drive out of my pocket and place it in his hand. "It's all right here."

He holds it up and studies the damage. "You think anything is recoverable?"

"Maybe." I sigh. "But part of me hopes not. Don't worry, you should be receiving some information very soon."

Mitnick narrows his eyes. "From the Dark Angel?"

I stop walking and face him. "What?"

He rolls his eyes. "Oh please, I've always known. Anyone else know?"

I shrug but maintain my composure. "Even if I was the Dark Angel, and I'm not saying I am, I'm pretty sure she's dead now anyway."

"That's too bad. Because I could use someone as good as her on my team."

"Who says she'd work for you anyway?" I smirk and watch the numbers light up as the elevator descends. "Are you going to arrest me?"

Mitnick holds up the mangled drive. "Something tells me I don't have enough evidence to do that." He shoves his hands in his pockets. "But it doesn't mean you're out of the woods yet."

I study his face. "What do you mean?"

"Ada, once this case breaks open, if the media or anyone else finds out about your part in this whole thing—or the Dark Angel for that matter—you and your family could be in serious trouble, especially if more people are involved."

This grabs my attention. "What do you mean *more people*? Ms. Matthews and Gary are dead. Mr. Anthony too."

"Actually, Mr. Anthony is alive."

"What? But I saw him die." I don't know if I'm relieved or bummed.

"He's pretty damn close, but I think he's going to be okay." Mitnick studies his shoes. "But since we're not sure if this is the end of it, do me a favor and lay low until I can wrap up this case. There are still a few loose ends and unanswered questions I need to chase down."

I must look petrified because he smiles reassuringly. "Ada, don't worry. No one will find out your role in this. Or your friends. I got your back until this thing blows over. Trust me."

"Thanks." I pause. "I'm sure if the Dark Angel were here, she would thank you too."

"Maybe someday she can tell me herself."

Outside, Mitnick sits me in the front seat of his car. "Stay here and I'll drive you to see your friends. I'm not letting you out of my sight until your parents come back. Or your dad will have my badge."

"I think you're going soft." I say. "I'm not sure 'Pitbull' Mitnick fits anymore."

Mitnick laughs as he walks off.

Something in my peripheral vision catches my eye. I press my face against the window and stare outside.

A small figure in a black hoodie walks out of the SocialNet building and past a group of people standing outside.

I roll down the window and yell, "Hey!"

The figure tears off through the field and disappears in the darkness. But not before I spot a flash of bright pink hair. Raven is still alive.

"There's someone out there!" I point to the field and an FBI agent charges off in Raven's direction.

My brain spins the new information. Raven was working with Mr. Anthony and Gary. Here. Tonight. She's the person who kept blocking me out of SocialNet's system. That means she's involved in this mess. Maybe she was the one trying to sabotage me at ReBoot.

I collapse into the seat and lay my head back. My whole body aches and my mind remains murky. Every detail of the night replays in my head. It sucks that a lot of people died for no reason.

A sick feeling churns in my stomach. Somehow, I know this thing isn't over yet.

</REBOOT...AGAIN>

A COUPLE WEEKS LATER . . .

Coffee always helps me plug in.

Without it, I crash.

Walking into the DotCom Café, I ignore the computers and beeline for the comfy chairs. After all, I came here to talk, not surf.

The café buzzes with the after-school crowd. Kids huddle together talking. Some are probably finishing their homework while others research past-due projects online. A couple loners hide in the back, surfing the Net.

I collapse into a leather armchair and sink into the cushion. The smell of vanilla and coffee wafts past my nose, encouraging the weight of the last few weeks to seep out my fingertips. Lying my head back, I relax for the first time in a long while.

Since Gary died, things have been super quiet and Raven is long gone, leading me to believe Mitnick is wrong. This thing is finally over.

To be safe, the Dark Angel hasn't logged into the Orwellians' chat room in weeks. There's been no contact with Taz. Even though I may never chat with him again, I hope he's okay. He helped me as much as he could, but now the only way I can repay him is to stay away. Though, I assume the Orwellians will disband since Casper doxxed them all.

It's too dangerous now.

Two hands cover my eyes, making me smile. "Hey, Fish."

"Hey, you." He jumps into the chair across from me, landing his butt in the cushion. He straightens his new black specs and moves closer, resting both hands on my knees.

I smile but stay in my relaxed position.

He frowns when I don't make a move. "What, no love?"

"Oh sorry." I push up and lean in for a kiss, tracing the scar on his head with my thumb.

Fisher pretends he's going to kiss me, but then turns away at the last minute to tease me. "Never mind. I don't like PDA. It's cheesy."

I smack his hand. "You'd leave a girl hanging?"

"Okay, fine. If you *insist*." He cups the back of my neck and pulls me forward. His lips brush lightly over mine, sending my heart skipping at a high speed. He presses his warm mouth against mine for a short time before slowly pulling away. My body goes limp.

Fisher gets to me in a way no one else can.

He kisses my cheeks and the tip of my nose before sitting back. "I knew you wanted me."

I smack his arm. "You're impossible. That will have to tide you over for now."

"Excuse me, but I'm not the kind of guy who needs physical attention." He puts his nose in the air and looks away.

I raise my eyebrows and stand, pretending to leave. "Then I am with the wrong guy."

Fisher grabs my hand and jerks me down into his lap. "Okay, fine, I'll be your slut. Lay it on me, baby."

"You asked for it." I wrap my arms around his neck. This time I press my lips against his and hold them there. Fisher tastes of peppermint spray. His mouth is warm and inviting. His lips soft. Always prepared. Since that horrible night at

SocialNet, the last few weeks with him have been amazingly easy. He's breathed life back into me. Of course, I don't tell him that. He says I saved the day, but really, he's the one who saved me.

Part of me can't help but wonder how long 'we' will last. *If* it will last. The constant fear of losing Fisher distracts me and I pull away.

"Uh-oh, I know that look." He cups my face and tries to get me to focus back on him. "Don't think. I'm not going anywhere. Where else can I get this kind of action?"

I pray I'm not turning bright red. "If you keep this up, you won't get any action."

"Whatever. You couldn't resist all this." He motions to his body and then kisses the top of my hand. "How about if I romance you? You want to have dinner?"

I smirk. He knows how to break down my walls and feed my lonely soul.

Food.

"Can't, I have a family dinner tonight."

"Again?" He feigns shock. "Man, it's like those old '50s shows."

"It's a new tradition. Every Sunday." I raise my eyebrows. "You can come if you like."

"It wouldn't be fair to Sharon and Ted. You wouldn't give them any attention with me around. Guess I'll have to suffer through another night without you." He glances up at the front counter. "But how about if I buy your love with a Red Devil cupcake?"

I can't help but smile, thinking of Simone. As far as I can tell, Fisher doesn't know about the Red Devil or the Dark Angel. He's never mentioned it, and I don't know if I'll ever tell him.

I tilt my head. "That's why I like you. Because you stuff me with an endless supply of sweets."

"If that's all it takes, I'm your man." I scoot off his lap so he can move. He stands and glances at the door. "Oh brother. Here comes King Trouble and the Ninja Warrioress."

"They sound like two additional dwarves." I jump back into my chair before I lose it.

Varian and Becca walk up, bickering about something.

She yanks off her pink knit beanie and shivers. "Man, it's cold out there." Then she makes a *brrrr* noise and rubs her hands together. The bruise on her cheek is almost gone.

"She's said that about fifty times just in the last block. Like she's surprised." Varian parks his butt on the arm of my chair and takes off his sunglasses. "I mean, it's Seattle, cold and rainy. Get over it."

Becca slides a piece of Dove chocolate out of her coat pocket and unwraps it. She pops it into her mouth and reads it but doesn't say anything as she hides the wrapper.

Varian holds out one gloved hand. "Must be good because you never miss a chance to prophesize."

"It's not a big deal." Becca's cheeks turn as pink as her beanie.

When he motions his fingers, she sighs and drops the foil ball in his open hand.

He reads it and chuckles. "*Enjoy the childhood joys of winter.* See? Even the chocolate wants you to stop your bitchin'."

I hold back a giggle as Becca flashes Varian an *I'm about to kick your ass* look. She holds up one pink fist. "Watch out. You're on shaky ground mister."

And I believe her.

Varian scoffs. "Jesus. She kicks one guy's ass and now she thinks she's freakin' Wonder Woman. I could take her out with one arm." He holds up his lame arm still resting in a sling.

I bust out laughing. "Or you could just tase her."

"Very funny." He reaches over and squeezes both my shoulders. "What's up, Lovelace? Long time, no speak."

"I texted you yesterday."

He frowns. "That's not funny. You know I don't text."

Becca looks up from her phone, fingers in mid-text. "Don't look at me, my social networking is down by fifty percent."

I laugh. "That is an improvement."

"Bad thing is, now her talking percentage has skyrocketed." Varian tries to squeeze in next to me.

"Hey," Fisher hits Varian in the arm and points to an empty chair. "Grab your own seat."

"Awww, you jealous, lover boy?" Varian jumps over Fisher's leg and sits on a red ottoman.

"Yes, I am," Fisher folds his arms across his chest. "I'm *not* too much of a man to admit it."

Varian moves to the other chair. "Boy, you can say that again."

"I thought you kissed and made up?" Becca says as she uncurls the thick scarf from her neck like she's removing a python.

"Nah, we're good." Varian reaches over and punches Fisher in the arm. "Right, Fish?"

"Yeah, sure." Fisher rubs his arm. "But violence is not the answer."

I whisper to Becca. "The bromance is alive and well."

Fisher taps my shoulder and points up to the TV.

I watch as Mitnick steps up to a microphone, flanked by a few other FBI officers. "What's going on?"

Varian yells over the crowd. "Hey, turn that up!"

Some kid increases the volume as Mitnick clears his throat. "A few weeks ago, the FBI went to SocialNet with a warrant to ask questions about some recent suspicious deaths. At the time, we had reason to believe the company had some involvement. As you all know, CEO Gary Host committed suicide at his company headquarters before we could interrogate him."

Becca and I look at each other. She grabs my hand.

"Man, I knew it! The media is just one fat conspiracy."

Varian shakes his head. "They can say whatever they want and everyone believes it."

Mitnick responds to a question. "No. We were not able to capture any data off the flash drive we discovered at the scene." He stares in the camera, and for a second, it's like he's talking directly to me. "But fortunately, we got a break when a hacktivist from the Orwellians sent us files of evidence proving SocialNet's conspiracies and other criminal acts. If anyone knows where the information came from, please let us know. Until then, it's everything we need to proceed with indictments."

The group looks over at me.

I shrug. "That's crazy. You never know what information that group can get. They must have contacts everywhere."

"Hmmm," Varian says. "Somehow you pulled a fast one."

"I don't know what you're talking about."

But he's right. Even though Mitnick's email didn't go through. I gave Taz all the directory information and asked him to send the files along anonymously. Once again, Taz came through for me when I needed him.

A reporter throws out another question.

This time, Mitnick pauses. "Today, we have made additional arrests of employees at SocialNet. They are being charged with five counts of murder in addition to numerous violations. Anthony, or Tony, Carter—a former employee of ReBoot—faces three counts of computer hacking conspiracy, five counts of computer hacking, one count of computer hacking in furtherance of fraud, one count of conspiracy to commit access device fraud, one count of conspiracy to commit bank fraud, and one count of aggravated identity theft. He faces a maximum sentence of 124 years and six months in prison. Mr. Barkley Gavin is still being charged with murder in addition to other felony counts that include kidnapping and assault."

The news station flashes two pictures: one of Mr. Anthony and one of the albino.

Varian mutters, "Those jerks will be in prison until they're nothing but bones."

Becca shakes her head, looking forlorn. "I still can't believe Mr. Anthony was involved in this. He really helped me."

"Goes to show you can never trust anyone," Varian mumbles.

I pat his hand. "I trusted you, and you didn't let me down."

His face turns red.

Then the news show cuts to my dad, decked out in a navy suit. Since he knows everything, I'm curious to see what he says. "I am happy to announce that the Technology Privacy Bill has been voted into law. Our kids will now know what it's like to have private information protected, and we can keep our teens safe online. For now."

Becca cheers. "Your dad is amazing. He's handsome too."

"To celebrate, I'll add a mocha to your cupcake." Fisher hugs me. "But you have to smile."

Reaching up, I kiss Fisher on the cheek. "You spoil me."

"Yeah, I do."

"Get a room already." Varian hits his head on the headrest.

"I'm craving something warm too." Becca jumps up. "I'm freezing."

Varian groans. "We know. We know. It's cold."

Fisher and Becca walk up to the counter and stand in line.

Varian pats my shoulder like I'm his war buddy. "You know, I forgot to mention it before, but in case it's not clear, I win. Two to one."

I push my hair back from my face. "Win what?"

"The contest. You don't think I'd let you beat me in LARP and then not save face, do you?" He raises his eyebrows. "I get one point for tasing and one point for taking a bullet."

"Fine, you win." I grin and throw both my hands up. "I will gladly surrender to my personal hero."

"Yes!" He pretends to punch me playfully in the chin.

I grab his head and kiss his forehead. "Thank you. Again."

He jerks back and wipes his face with his forearm. "Yuk, what's with you guys giving out all the sloppy hugs and kisses lately? You'd think we were friends or something. But how would a gamer like me and a girly hacker like you ever get along?"

I grin. "Very carefully."

Fisher calls out across the whole café. "Andrew, don't make me hurt you. Stay away from my girl."

I laugh as Varian's face turns bright red. "Sometimes I really hate that guy." Then he walks to the counter and stands in line behind Becca, who's bouncing around, checking out the treats.

While I wait for my sugar drip, I stare at the TV, which is still broadcasting about SocialNet's crimes. I can't help but smile. Because I won too. I wish Simone could be here, share the victory. After all, she's the reason we all made it out of there alive. Without her, I'd probably be dead and Gary would be taking people down. One by one.

Becca laughs from the front of the café, jerking me out of my head.

I glance up at my new friends and watch them mess around. Varian and Fisher sword fight with their éclairs, while Becca points happily to the chocolate display, ordering one of everything.

For the first time, I'm a part of something whole. What my friends don't realize is that they saved me from more than Gary. They saved me from myself.

Becca spots me watching and motions for me to join them.

When I shake my head, she holds up a chocolate cupcake as a bribe and smiles, mouthing the word, *please.*

I close my computer and stand. No matter what is going

on in the world, sometimes it's better to unplug. My life feels back on track. I'm no longer the same person as before. Rewired into something new.

At least for now.

Thank you for reading, *ReWired*! Keep reading for a preview of another Shelli R. Johannes book. :)

Prologue

Nature will talk to you if you listen.
Every sound tells you something.

I KNOW THE EXACT MOMENT I WENT WRONG.

Three weeks, two days, twenty-two hours, and thirty-three minutes ago.

I had no clue a few small decisions could puncture the thin bubble of my perfect world.

I zigzag through the forest's brown pillars like I'm barreling in a local rodeo. The internal rhythm keeps me running at a steady speed along the broken path. Left, right, left, right. My muffled breath echoes in my ears, making me feel as if I'm underwater. Sinking. Drowning.

Don't stop, Grace, or you will die.

I veer off the main path and into the arms of the darkening woods. Gnarled branches, shaped like broken fingers, comb my hair and scratch my skin. I fight against a clump of twisted vines grabbing at my ankles. Jerking. Pulling. Ripping. The rhythm of my running becomes choppy and uneven as I sludge my way through the curled tangles of vegetation. My lungs sear from the lack of oxygen. Burning.

Just soon as I round a corner, I slip behind a mammoth oak to catch my breath. A brown rabbit scurries by me and disappears into the safety of a prickly bush, giving me hope that maybe I can escape too.

My eyes dart around, searching the monotonous woods for a way out. I need to calm down. Can't lose it now.

My chest rises and falls as my lungs finally pull in enough oxygen to settle my nerves. Pure air sweeps through my body like the dry wind over a starlit desert. Blowing away the doubt, and erasing any trace of fear. Everything Dad's ever taught me about wilderness survival comes flooding back.

Suddenly, I know exactly what to do.

Examining my GPS watch, I pinpoint my coordinates and map a way out. After assessing the area, I tiptoe out of my hiding place and backtrack down the trail, careful not to disturb anything that will give away my position.

I disguise my tracks all the way back to Dead Man's Cliff. After securing my backpack, I clutch onto the cragged rocks and scale the steep wall, careful to place every toe and finger just right. My palm hits a sharp edge and begins to bleed. Both arms begin to spasm from the strain. My toes cramp underneath my weight as they press against the tiny ledge. I creep up the steep rock like a lizard, careful not to send a shower of rocks or crumbling dirt onto the path several feet below me. My arms quiver, threatening to numb.

At the top, I fight against all the pain and summon every last ounce of strength I have to pull myself over the ledge. Instantly, I roll onto my stomach and flatten against the cool dirt, scanning the horizon. The sun punches through the thick canopy, dotting little amoebas of light along the forest floor. I listen for the slightest sound and search for the tiniest movement.

Nothing.

As a wildlife enforcement officer, Dad believes the woods will talk to those who are still enough to listen. Closing my eyes, I concentrate on the space around me.

Listening. Waiting. Afraid to breathe.

A light breeze slithers through the ghostly forest. The leaves rustle and the trees hiss, whispering secrets to each other. The forest appears to exhale then hold its breath. It's as quiet as a graveyard at midnight. Nothing scurries, burrows, or twitters. The trees stop swaying and freeze, as if they're hiding too. Then I hear it. The distant snap of a random twig.

The hair on my neck bristles.

They're still after me.

End of Sample

To continue reading, be sure to pick up *Untraceable* at your favorite retailer.

ALSO BY SHELLI R. JOHANNES

Nature of Grace Series

YA Thrillers

Untraceable

Uncontrollable

Unstoppable

"A dramatic entanglement of mystery, deception and teen romance."

- Kirkus Reviews

.

On The Bright Side

Tween Paranormal

A tween guardian angel's personal account about the funny side of the afterlife.

"Johannes kicks off...with this fresh novel about an angel's peripatetic path to earning her wings...A humorous addition to the angel story genre."

—Publishers Weekly

.

Children's Books

Penny The Engineering Tail of the Fourth Little Pig

The Vet Visit

Poppy's Pollinators

Poppy's Chicks

Blue-Ribbon Radishes

ABOUT THE AUTHOR

Shelli R. Johannes is the award-winning author of the Nature of Grace novels, including *Untraceable, Uncontrollable,* and *Unstoppable,* as well as *On The Bright Side* and *Rewired.* She is also the author of 25+ children's books. Since leaving Corporate America, she has followed her passion for writing and conservation by working with The Dolphin Project, the Atlanta Zoo, and others. She currently lives in Atlanta with a bird, two doodles, her British husband, and her kids, who she hopes someday will change the world. She also writes children's books.

www.srjohannes.com
shelli@srjohannes.com

facebook.com/srjohannesauthor
x.com/srjohannes
instagram.com/srjohannes
pinterest.com/srjohannes

ACKNOWLEDGMENTS

With this book, I might as well have bled on the pages. Because for some reason, it has been the hardest book for me to write. But after four long years, I finally made it. Alive!

And as always when writing a book, it takes a village. And I could never do it without the support of readers, bloggers, librarians, teachers and friends.

First, I would like to thank Hilarie Cash at reSTART for spending the time to show me around her technology addiction facility in Washington, for answering all my questions, and for giving me insight into the emotional side of the epidemic. And for reminding me to "connect with LIFE not my device." If you know of anyone with a technology addiction (because it is a real thing!), please go to netaddictionrecovery.com. To the Winchester Mansion for the special and spooky tour.

To Ali Cross, Hollie Westring and many others, for making this book look beautiful.

Special thanks to Cynthia (CJ) Omololu, Graeme Stone, Jennifer Jabaley, Megan Miranda, Romily Bernard, Katie Anderson, Kristin Tubb, Courtney Stevens, and Sarah Frances Hardy for brainstorming, ideas, extra reads and critiques, advice, and undying support. Your constant cheering section helped me push through the hard times on this one. And I could not have done this book without your constant support along this crazy, never-ending road.

To Julie Stokes, Tom Stokes, and Joey & Beth Bowers for

opening up your beautiful homes (and hearts) for me to use as my writing sanctuary.

To my friends and volunteer beta readers, Lara and Wendy, for taking the time to do a fast last-minute read, honest feedback, and encouragement when I was questioning everything. I owe you both a martini . . . or two.

To the Country Lane Bookclub and Bar for keeping me reading different genres and for always encouraging me to get out and try new things. You keep me sane.

To Lara Perkins, my agent, partner in crime, advocate, and friend—for believing in this book more than I ever did. She sticks by me (and my writing) no matter what—through all the ups and downs—and she never doubts that I can do anything. Trust me, I've had some crazy ideas and she always encourages me to follow my heart.

To Kimberly Derting—my best friend, co-author, tour guide, critique partner and so much more—she wears so many hats in my life that she looks totally ridiculous and doesn't mind! I don't even know where to start . . . thank you for all the laughs, advice, daily chats, encouragement, blunt honesty, friendship, spare bedroom, tears, and more. But mostly, for asking me "What's the story?" over and over and over until I finally found it. To her hubby Josh, for his patience, awesome ideas and for letting me steal Kim's time when I need her.

To my family, for always supporting my writing and putting up with my moods. To my mom for always reading every single word I write (more than once!) and loving every one of them. You are my favorite reader!

To my sweet babies for never being afraid to voice their amazing opinions (and even when I don't ask for them). You are my favorite people in the whole wide world and I am proud of everything you are—and so excited to see who you will become.

To my husband, Alistair, for the countless things he does

that help me find extra time to write, whether it is helping with the kids and the house or by keeping me fed and hydrated during my long obsessive nights. I would never have followed my writing dream without your undying support or without you by my side every step of the way. Thank you!

And to the real Ada Lovelace, thank you for creating the first computer algorithm and for pathing a way for strong girls and women to make a difference in computer science and technology. I think we would've been great friends.